JERUSALEM'S UNDEAD TRILOGY

VALLEY

OF

BONES

ERIC WILSON

THOMAS NELSON
Since 1798

NASHVILLE   DALLAS   MEXICO CITY   RIO DE JANEIRO

Published in Nashville, Tennessee. Thomas Nelson is a registered trademark of Thomas Nelson, Inc.

Thomas Nelson, Inc., books may be purchased in bulk for educational, business, fund-raising, or sales promotional use. For information, please e-mail SpecialMarkets@ThomasNelson.com.

Publisher's Note: This novel is a work of fiction. Names, characters, places, and incidents are either products of the author's imagination or used fictitiously. All characters are fictional, and any similarity to people living or dead is purely coincidental.

Scripture taken from the *Holy Bible*, New Living Translation, © 1996, 2004. Used by permission of Tyndale House Publishers, Inc., Wheaton, Illinois 60189. All rights reserved.

Scripture taken from the Holy Bible, New International Version®. © 1973, 1978, 1984 Biblica. Used by permission of Zondervan. All rights reserved.

Library of Congress Cataloging-in-Publication Data

Wilson, Eric (Eric P.)
   Valley of Bones / Eric Wilson.
       p. cm. — (Jerusalem's undead trilogy ; bk. 3)
   ISBN 978-1-59554-460-5 (pbk.)
   1. Vampires—Fiction. 2. Jerusalem—Fiction. I. Title.
   PS3623.I583V35 2010
   813'.6—dc22

                          2010002411

Printed in the United States of America

10 11 12 13 14 RRD 6 5 4 3 2 1

A NOTE FROM
THE AUTHOR

My mother was there to cheer me along from my first childhood short story to my recent bestseller. She was a fan of the Jerusalem's Undead Trilogy in particular, with its Romanian and Israeli settings and its themes of life and death.

In December 2008, medical complications took her life even as I completed edits on book two of the trilogy. I still had the third volume to write, but the process was more arduous without her cultural and biblical insights, not to mention the love of one who'd helped foster my creative discipline.

Could I even finish the series? Should I? It felt wrong without her there as part of the process. Felt empty.

And yet this trilogy itself involves rising up from the ashes, conquering our ancient foes of sin and death through the miracle of Nazarene Blood. Such power was the driving force in my mom's life.

Of course none of that changed the emptiness I felt.

In March 2009, I took my second research trip to Israel, a land my mother loved and in which she hoped to be buried. With my wife, daughters, mother-in-law, and an urn of Mom's ashes, I traversed the Holy Land, from the coral beaches of Eilat in the south to Galilee's hilly northern region. We met with some of my mom's friends along the way, those who had been touched by her life—including fourteen Sudanese refugees who called her their "spiritual mother."

After the informal memorial service, we drove to Jerusalem. I parked outside the Old City walls, yards from the Dung Gate that overlooks the Valley of Hinnom and the Field of Blood. We carted our bags to our youth hostel and left Mom's nearly empty urn locked in the rental car's trunk.

The next evening, after visiting the Wailing Wall, Damascus Gate, and Via Dolorosa, I trekked back through cobblestone alleyways to our parking spot. Three Arab boys watched me from a low stone wall while two others eyed me from a bus stop. Were they awaiting their next victim?

I didn't have any cash in my pockets, but I have no qualms about defending myself or the ones I love. If they wanted a fight, they'd get one.

With such thoughts sharpening my vision, I noticed that the rental's side window had been jimmied and yanked off its track. Thieves had reached through and hit the automatic locks, gaining access to the CD player, a pair of sunglasses, the paperwork in the glove box.

And Mom's flower-decorated urn.

I was fuming.

By the time I took stock of the losses, the boys had disappeared and I was left to contemplate the moment's irony. Here within view of the Field of Blood, where Judas hanged himself and where this trilogy began, I had been robbed. The same spirit that drives the Collectors had come to steal away something precious to me, and for a moment I wanted to hurl curses—or even stones.

But didn't the Nazarene tell us to love our enemies?

I took deep breaths and paced beneath the towering ramparts, realizing that Mom would've smiled at such a turn of events and prayed a blessing over the thieves. Just imagine their surprise when they realized what they'd taken. Maybe it would shock them into some other choice of careers.

It was then I decided nothing would stop me from writing this book. What better way to honor my mother than by completing the tale she loved. Yes, it was time to bring this full circle, from betrayal and theft at the Field of Blood to forgiveness and new life . . .

In the nearby Valley of Bones.

—*Eric Wilson, May 2009*

To my father-in-law, Michael Monaghan:

Remember jogging Pre's Trail together in Eugene? You showed me what it took to run with endurance, and I have nothing but respect for you. Oh, and thanks for letting me dash off with your daughter.

And my mother-in-law, Deborah Mart:

Over the years you've given many kids that which was taken from you, and I'm honored to be counted as one of your sons. It was great to have you with us in Israel. Where should we all go next?

WHAT CAME BEFORE

Since days of yore, clusters of Collectors have roamed the earth. They have been called by some Those Who Hunt. Due to their Master's rebellion against the Almighty, they have been Separated from their use of the physical senses, disembodied spirits looking for mortal hosts to both inhabit and infest. They hope to usher in their own brand of Final Vengeance, at which time they will sustain themselves on mankind's torment and blood.

A unique breed of Collectors emerged in 1989 from ancient burial caves beneath the *Akeldama*. This was the very field in which Judas Iscariot took his own life after his betrayal of the Nazarene nearly two thousand years earlier. Filled with enmity, Judas' blood seeped down through the dirt and stained the bones of two households below. Finding unnatural life in their now-polluted corpses, they rose, the Houses of Ariston and Eros, to form the Akeldama Cluster. Undead and immortal, they are able to see things that are dark to mortal eyes, including the letter *Tav* that marks the foreheads of the *Nistarim*.

Cal Nichols is one of the original Nistarim, the Concealed Ones, thirty-six saints raised from their tombs during the Nazarene's death and resurrection (as recorded in the twenty-seventh chapter of the Gospel of Matthew). For eons they have lived and walked among us. Commissioned to neither give nor take in marriage, they bear sorrows and protect humanity. They also seek to recruit Those Who Resist, men and women who find life in the Nazarene Blood while opposing the Master Collector and his legions.

In 1965, in his desire for physical intimacy, Cal lost the distinguishing mark on his forehead by joining himself with a woman named Nikki Lazarescu. Her pregnancy drew the attention of a Collector named Natira, a warrior with a taste for blood. Natira tracked Cal and Nikki, then struck with deadly force, taking the life of their son. What he did not know was that a twin survived, a young girl named Gina.

In recent years, Natira moved alone from continent to continent, tracking the Concealed Ones, hoping to destroy them all in one fell swoop. His mission was delayed, though, by a reunion with Erota, a member of his former cluster. Erota convinced him that he was their "Black King," the fulfillment of an old Rasputin prophecy, and together they returned to Israel. There, at Judas Iscariot's birthplace, the "Haunt of Jackals," the Akeldama Cluster crowned Natira their rightful leader. Megiste, a rival who also sought control of the cluster, was forced to leave. But in one monstrous cave her handiwork remained: a collage of human limbs, skulls, and thorns.

Even as the cluster regrouped, Gina Lazarescu and her adopted Romanian son found refuge in the Pacific Northwest under the names Kate and Kenny Preston. It was during this time that she accepted the consequences of living, loving, and fighting for Yeshua, the Nazarene.

She drank the Nazarene Blood. Became one of Those Who Resist.

With Cal at her side, and with her adopted son guarded by the Unfallen—those entities who did not side with the Collectors' rebellion—Gina defended her home, fighting off a werewolf and a childhood friend. Nevertheless, danger continued to grow, and she faked her own death in a desperate ploy to throw off her pursuers.

Now believed dead and gone, she hopes to pursue matters close to her heart—including the whereabouts of a young man who lived in isolation while she and others mourned his loss.

He is the anonymous journaler, the recorder of these events. And he's been told he still has a role to play.

I was carried away . . . to a valley filled with bones . . .
They all came to life and stood up on their feet—a great army.

—EZEKIEL 37:1, 10

PROLOGUE

April 1911—City of Jerusalem, Israel

The boy was dying, blood thin, body weak, his place among the Russian tsars unable to save him. His parents, Nicholas and Alexandra Romanov, viewed Rasputin as their final hope.

Very well. Who was he to disappoint them?

The shaggy-bearded priest paused in the Garden of Gethsemane's shadows. Here, in this same olive grove, the Nazarene had perspired drops of blood, Judas had planted a kiss of betrayal, and Apostle Peter had raised a sword in meager defense. Here, now, Rasputin sought refuge from the scandals in his motherland while hoping to obtain a cure for young Alexei. Without it, he might never regain his influence among the Romanovs.

"We must hurry, Rasputin. It's nearly dusk."

"To hurry is to invite mistakes."

"Or trouble." His advisor, a bony man with thinning hair, swallowed and peered back over his shoulder into the crowd of gnarled tree trunks. "Am I wrong to think we're being followed?"

Rasputin wanted to shake that scrawny neck. He wanted to say, "You're working for the Russian secret police is what I think."

"Look," the advisor squeaked. "Is someone crouched behind that rock?"

"Stop your quivering, you dunderhead, and come along."

From high above, gilded gold against an indigo sky, seven onion domes beckoned. Built by Tsar Alexander III, the Church of St. Mary Magdalene was already one of Jerusalem's most distinguishable landmarks, and Rasputin's pulse quickened at the sight.

Her beauty hides her secrets, he told himself. A decade earlier he had unlocked those treasures, the same as he'd done with many a Russian mistress. Time to claim what was his.

The advisor said, "You believe you can find it again?"

"Of course."

"Even in the dark?"

"I've not come all this way for nothing." Rasputin combed a hand through his beard, raked the garden path with his eyes. "You've heard of the *Tmu Tarakan,* haven't you? A legendary kingdom, a place of darkness and cockroaches. The name also refers to a chamber hidden here on this slope."

"You have access to this place?"

"'The Black King is key.'" The priest rolled a chess figurine in his palm. Carved from stone, it was one of a kind, with Cyrillic writing around its base and curves tapering toward a six-pointed crown and ornate cross. "Made it with my own two hands."

"You should be careful. What if someone were to steal this from you?"

"Someone such as yourself, perhaps?"

"Me? No, Rasputin. No, I . . . What makes you say such a thing? Why bring me along if you don't trust me?"

"Because I don't trust you."

"I . . . I'm sorry, but I don't understand."

"I'm quite sure you do. By keeping my enemies close, there's less chance I'll be caught off guard." Rasputin patted the bulge in the advisor's jacket. "Not that you would think of using your gun till I've led you to the spot."

The man's expression hardened. "Ha. You think you're crafty, do you?" He waved his standard police-issue revolver into view. "No more use pretending, then. Lead the way."

"Most certainly."

The Tmu Tarakan was a hundred feet farther on. The opening had been first exposed during the church's construction in 1888, then resealed by Tsar Alexander's orders. In the years following, Russian Orthodox monks whispered of religious icons at the site, of Knights Templar relics. It was these rumors that first lured Rasputin here to the Kidron Valley in 1901. Hosting a cluster of Collectors and drawn by the scent of blood, he had moved from white sandstone edifices to the caves and grottos behind the church. When at last he found what he was seeking, he'd knelt and pulled away the rocks, then used a candle to illuminate the cache of reliquaries, dusty icons, gold, and sparkling jewels. It was as he was reaching through the gap that he'd felt the scrape of something sharp.

A thorn.

An entire crown of thorns.

Tips stained reddish-black by the Blood of the Nazarene.

Little wonder the previous tsar had closed off the cavern, fearing the disturbance of so sacred an object. But not Rasputin, no. The village-priest-turned-royal-confidante gloried in his sins, believing salvation was best savored by wandering the paths of transgression.

Here now, ten years later, he spotted that same destination—unremarkable, a place of darkness, disguised as one of the valley's tombs. In a few moments he would snap off one of those Blood-stained thorns and, being careful to avoid pricking his own skin, take back to St. Petersburg this blessed elixir for the sickness plaguing Alexei Romanov's veins.

"Why are you stopping, Rasputin? Move along," said the policeman.

"Tell me, why'd you follow me here?"

"To gather evidence against you. You're a disgrace to our country, a smelly old pervert masquerading as a man of God. Peasants starve while you make fools of our tsar and his wife."

"Oh? But I'm a mere peasant myself."

"You're a demon in disguise."

"Bah. We all have our demons, you dunderhead."

"Move!"

Rasputin moved. His eyes roved the terrain ahead and saw no one to witness the coming violence. This was a holy site, closed to visitors at this hour, and it was only his monastic robes that had granted him access.

The policeman poked the revolver into his ribs. "Take me to this precious treasure of yours, or I'll kill you."

"How would my friends, your beloved tsars, view such an act, I wonder?"

"If you cooperate, we won't need to find out. I'll leave your fate to men much wiser than I."

"And you?" Turning, Rasputin raised an eyebrow. "You are not so wise?"

"I—"

The priest slashed his left hand upward, deflecting the gun, then whipped the cord from his robe with his right. He caught the object as it snaked around the policeman's neck and used it to yank him off balance. In a frantic motion, the man kicked out at Rasputin's legs and tried to bring the gun back around. He was wiry and lean, but the peasant-priest, the insatiable lover, was squat and powerfully built. He was also energized by Collectors within.

Rasputin sidestepped the kick. Drove a knee into an exposed groin. Shoved the groaning man to the dirt and leveraged the revolver from his grip.

In the priest's hands, the rope now became a noose. The policeman coughed. His feet scraped the ground. Hands clawed at the cord about his throat, and the two combatants wrestled in this awkward position for a full minute.

Somewhere during the second minute, Rasputin heard a gurgling gasp that signaled the end.

"I wonder," he said, "will it be eternal rest for you? Or damnation?"

The dead man offered no response.

Rasputin pocketed the revolver, then hefted the body over his shoulder and carried it to the grave guarding the Tmu Tarakan. He dropped his load, pushed aside weeds, sediment, and stones the size of fresh-baked Russian loaves. With his black chess piece's unique design, he unlocked the cavern's small iron door and caught the glimmer of treasures within.

"Go ahead and do what you have come for . . ."

Millennia earlier, the Nazarene had prodded His betrayer with those words, and they now echoed again through this hillside grove, infusing

Rasputin with that same heart-pounding rush he experienced each time he clipped hair from one of his deflowered virgins.

"Go ahead . . ."

Swinging into action, he reached through the cleft in the rock and broke off a thorn from that crude, crusty crown. A balm for Alexei. Blood shed to bring healing. With plans to give it as a gift to the tsars, he wrapped the stained emblem in an olive leaf and shoved it into the folds of his robe.

The secret policeman was still at his feet. Playing host to malevolent entities, Rasputin recognized their desire to indulge in the five senses, and he obliged them by dealing with this final order of business.

His eyes studied the corpse's blank stare, the slack jaw.

His hands grasped hold of those bony shoulders.

Nostrils wrinkled at the stink of defecation, the man's last bodily act.

Ears noted the hiss of the wind in nearby cypresses.

Grunting, Rasputin tossed the traitor and his police-issue gun into the Tmu Tarakan—more relics for his Collection—where they landed together on a mound of coins. The priest pushed sweaty hair from his face, then licked the salty tang from his thick lips. All in a day's work, yes, indeed.

He was struck by a sense of melancholy as he locked away the relics a final time. Who would be next to see this place? Would they play their part on the chessboard of history, as he'd foretold with his prophetic pen?

Before my bones have lain a century in the grave, humanity will be pressed to the brink . . . He will emerge, this Black King, from the holy ground and wage war against Those Who Resist. From the Haunt of Jackals, he will take dominion . . . Yes, the Black King is key. His likeness shall unlock riches to strengthen his campaign, and many shall bow . . . despite the Thirty-Six who oppose him.

Rasputin thrust both hands into his robes, touching the wrapped thorn with one, rolling the regal king with the other.

Holy versus unholy. Sacred versus profane.

That age-old battle was about to turn ugly.

THE FIRST SENSE: SIGHT

"If you are infected," he told her, "I'll do everything I can to cure you."
Her eyes met his. "And if you can't?" she said.

—RICHARD MATHESON, *I AM LEGEND*

Build each other up in your most holy faith.

—JUDE 1:20

Journal Entry

July 12, 2010

I'm still amazed how things have turned around. Only hours after leaving my drafty house on Lummi Island, I met my birth mother. She claims if she had come any sooner it would've caused trouble. She had to keep a low profile because Those Who Hunt are after me. After both of us, actually.

"You have a destiny," Mom said while seated beside me in the diner.

I guess it should feel strange calling her that, but instead it seems like the most natural thing in the world. Self-reliant for so long, I feel like a boy again just being near her.

"You're my own flesh and blood," she said. "We both share Cal Nichols' genes."

"Nickel, you mean."

"How'd you know to call him that?" She touched the lambskin of my denim jacket, and there was a twinkle in her deep brown eyes. Or maybe it was a tear.

"I've been learning a lot. See this map? I think he's the one who sent it to me a few weeks back, and these four droplets have whole lifetimes inside of them. Unsettling stuff. Stories about you, the Collectors, and the Nistarim."

"He must've known you could handle it, Jacob. All part of your training."

"My training? If this has to do with me joining the Concealed Ones, I'm not sure I really belong." At my words, Mom's eyes softened, her own terrible scars a reminder of that link between us. I pushed out my chest and said, "But if I am chosen, I will do my best."

CHAPTER ONE

Her time was not yet over.

Far from it.

Gina settled back to earth through rain-slick tree branches and watched felled Douglas firs slam into the guardrail and cartwheel into space. One impaled her Nissan, carrying it over the cliff toward the river below, while the overturned logging truck responsible for this mess slid another hundred yards down the road and plowed into a bank of roots and mud.

As far as cops and Collectors would know, Kate Preston was dead.

Gone for good.

In reality, Gina Lazarescu was still alive and kicking. It'd worked. Actually worked. She wore a goofy grin, thinking how she and Cal Nichols had ascended through the roof of her car in that moment before impact. She'd put half-immortal lineage to use, bridging seen and unseen, uniting physical and spiritual elements in a dance of molecules that harkened to those first moments of creation.

Beside her, droplets played in and around Cal's form as he too regained substance beneath the concealing foliage, and it made her happy. For this transitory moment he was a mist unfazed by the rain, a soul freed from mortality by the Nazarene Himself.

Plus, he was her father. Nickel, he liked to be called.

"Agggh," he said. "What's that?"

"What's wrong?" Gina scanned the road for signs of more trouble, while her hand reached for the dagger strapped to her shin.

"Arachnids!"

"What?"

Nickel flailed at his shirt collar, where a battalion of tiny spiders had paraglided upon him from the evergreens. Gina was tempted to laugh, but knew his motions might draw attention and threaten this entire charade.

"Just babies," she said. "Keep still. We're trying to stay hidden here."

"Hate 'em."

"Seems kind of wimpy for a man with immortal blood."

"Bears? Werewolves? No problem. Spiders? They're just . . . creepy."

"If you say so, Mr. Scaredy-Pants. So, where am I supposed to go from here? And what about him?" She pointed at the white Dodge pickup on the roadside, at the man climbing into the cab. He looked familiar, although it was hard to tell in this weather. "You think he's noticed us at all?"

"Nah," Nickel said. "He's got his own issues to deal with, but I'll be seeing him again soon."

"You know him?"

"Name Clay Ryker ring any bells?"

"Ryker? Wait, he's one of those you said was keeping watch over Kenny last month, guarding him while I worked at the hardware store."

"You got it," Nickel said. "And he knows your husband's uncle, Sergeant Turney. Clay has a son of his own, and I've asked him to take a personal interest in Kenny's well-being once he's heard that you're dead."

"Dead. That sounds so . . ."

"Freeing?"

"Morbid."

"Least you'll be off the Collectors' radar. That's a good thing."

"You think it's worked this time."

"I'd bet my life on it."

Through sheets of rain, Gina watched Clay back the pickup onto Highway 126 and speed away with someone else beside him in the cab. Cars crawled past the strewn bits of wreckage, and it was only a matter of time before emergency vehicles arrived.

"What now, Dad?"

Down in the chasm, white water had swallowed Gina's Nissan from view, a reminder that her old life was gone.

Nickel's smile shimmered through the rain. "Time to lay low and get ready."

"Ready for what? 'Queen of the Resurrected,' that's what my name means, right? But you're telling me I'm not allowed to watch after Kenny any longer or even know where Dov Amit's hiding. What can I do? What's the point?"

"Your mothering isn't done."

"Sure seems like it to me."

"For now, you'll have to supervise from a distance."

"Supervise? That's not the same thing."

"And remain anonymous."

"What? Please don't mess with my head, not on this subject."

Nearly seven years ago, she'd lost newborn Jacob to a Collector's attack, and minutes ago she'd left behind her role as Kenny Preston's guardian. She was dead to the world now. Also dead to her own desires. By drinking Nazarene Blood, she had chosen to serve with Those Who Resist.

"How," she asked, "am I supposed to resist if I can't show my face?"

"The postcard," Nickel said.

"Say what?"

"In your pocket. The one I told you to bring along."

"This?" She pulled the item from her jacket. The front showed the Campo Santo, a cemetery near the Leaning Tower of Pisa. In the corner, an old smudge of her father's blood pulsed with details of his past—and, by proxy, some of her own.

"You'll find your purpose in there, Gina."

"You're scaring me."

"Trust me."

"The last time you told me to trust you, I lost my—"

"You lost Jacob. I know you blame me for what happened at that clinic, but even then I meant what I said. Go on." He gestured at the post-card. "Find out what really happened."

She dug her feet into good old terra firma. The downpour pasted long chestnut hair to her bronze skin.

Nickel moved closer. "What're you waiting for?"

She touched her tongue to the postcard, felt the bloodstain turn moist. Suddenly, she was careening through her father's recollections, week by week, month by month. What was she looking for? He'd told her earlier she couldn't miss it, yet even now she was missing so much—bits of Romania, of bears and blackbirds, Israeli wastelands and Jerusalem alleyways, and a baby with a knitted cap lying in his incubator.

No!

She gasped. Her eyes snapped open.

"Don't pull back," Nickel said, taking her hand.

"Dad, I can't do this. Please don't make me—"

"Don't look away."

"Why am I watching this?"

"Because you need to know everything."

She knew she had lost her son and also knew her husband, Jed Turney, had split with her a couple of years later as a result of their shared yet inconsolable grief. Was that any big shocker? Statistics showed that many parents separated after the death of a child.

"Keep going, Gina," Nickel insisted.

With heart ready to burst, she pressed on. The scene opened again in her mind, a tableau of broken glass and splintered wood and spattered blood and . . . and little Jacob pierced by the nails of a pipe bomb.

A sob lodged in her throat. She couldn't breathe.

"Jump ahead just a little bit." Nickel squeezed her hand. "Go to the night right after his memorial."

Nearly three days had passed and the news crews had backed off, giving Gina and Jed space to mourn, even as authorities continued sifting through the bomb's aftermath. Above the Chattanooga graveyard, black storm clouds churned. Her baby's tombstone lay humble and undisturbed.

Jacob Lazarescu Turney

Our precious son

Sept. 8, 1997

One day of pain, an eternity of peace

Amid the gravestones, Gina's father appeared with Gina's mother alongside. Nikki Lazarescu in all her middle-aged, raven-haired glory.

Nickel and Nikki . . .

They were shoveling dirt, rubbing sweat from their eyes, wrapping blisters on their hands, shining a hooded flashlight into the ground, pausing to check the graveyard's perimeter, and digging, digging, digging.

And then—

What're they doing? No, no, this can't be possible.

Nickel was cracking open the casket, parting those thin baby lips, dribbling Nazarene Blood from the vial around his neck. Jacob's skin changed from chalky gray to rosy pink. His eyelids fluttered and he let out a life-affirming wail. Alive? Her son was *alive*? Wrapped in a blanket and that light-blue birthing cap, Jacob pawed at the air, tried to suckle at his Grandma Nikki's bosom. Nikki drew him close and wept into his wisps of hair.

"Is this real?" Gina whispered.

"To save his life, he had to lose it," Nickel said.

"You . . . you never told me." Torn between celebration and a long-time deceit, she swiveled her eyes toward him as anger coiled in her chest. "You let me believe the worst."

"It was the only way."

"He's my son."

"And we were thinking of you. If we had told you, it would've endangered both you and Jacob, not to mention the future of mankind."

"Mankind?" Gina threw up her hands. "C'mon."

Her father was resolute. "You've seen what these vampires will do. You've felt their fury firsthand. Don't tell me you still doubt the stakes that we're fighting for. Imagine what would've happened if—"

"Stop!" She shoved at his chest. "Don't go making excuses for this. I deserved to know, and you had no right to keep me in the dark." Tears rolled from her chin. "I'm not a little girl anymore."

"I know that."

"You have any idea what you put me through, Dad?"

"I'm sorry. Believe it or not, I've had my own griefs in all this, starting as far back as my first wife in the days of Ezekiel."

Overwhelmed, Gina could hardly fathom that concept at the moment. "Listen," she said. "Don't you ever deceive me again, you understand?"

He nodded.

"Now . . ." She filled her lungs with oxygen. "Where is he?"

"Jacob's safe."

"He better be."

"He's got some of your immortal genes, and it's only a matter of time till he takes his place among the Concealed Ones. This is part of the reason they gathered in Portland back in '71—an emergency session, strategizing ways to bring about good from my wrong choices."

"I was a result of those choices, you know. Maybe that's why Nikki was always trying to purge my veins, huh? Trying to bleed out my sins and yours."

"Listen to me." Cal Nichols took her shoulders and turned her toward him. His gold-flecked green eyes peered into hers, melting away her doubts. "Sweetheart, don't even begin to believe all that junk your mother lumped on you. She meant well, but she was wrong. Heck, even the Nazarene has murderers and whores in His bloodline. He's all about redeeming the ones who seem most unredeemable."

"Thanks. I think."

He cupped her face in his hands. "You are one beautiful lady."

She set her mouth and looked off through the trees.

"You were not a mistake, Gina. Don't you ever believe otherwise. Say it," he told her. "You were not a mistake."

"I was not a mistake."

"Atta girl."

Though she wanted to stay mad at him, to punish him for the pain he had put her through, she couldn't deny the paternal adoration in his voice. She met his eyes. "Dad?"

"Yeah?"

"Thank you for . . . for everything you did to save Jacob." She brushed a kiss across his cheek. "I love you."

"And I've loved you since the day you were born."

Sirens sounded from down the mountain. He said, "You better get moving. It's gonna be awhile till you see me again, and there can't be any more of our cell phone calls."

"Mine's down there," Gina said. "In the river."

"It's better that way. Don't worry, though—I'll be around."

"Wait. What about Jacob? What's 1971 have to do with him?"

"Oh, the whole D. B. Cooper thing. That was a scheme cooked up at the Concealed Ones' meeting. With Natira closing in, trying to wipe out my bloodline, they decided to act as bait on that plane, hoping to draw him away while Nikki and I escaped with you and your brother."

"Natira wasn't fooled, though."

"No, he . . . well, he killed Reggie. But he never found out about you."

"So now, through me, Jacob's lined up to be a Concealed One."

"Soon as he reaches thirteen."

"Still six years away."

"Plenty of time for you to be a mother to him—from a distance, of course, and without him knowing who you are. That's the way things have to be until we get closer to his *bar mitzvah*. Jewish tradition says that's when he becomes a man, a true 'son of the law.' And that's when he'll be ready for what's ahead."

"Where is he?" Disbelief fell away, and all that mattered now was that she see Jacob for herself. She'd never had the chance to hold him, to feed him, change him, wipe his tears. Who had been there to watch him take his first step? Was he in school? So much to catch up, so much . . .

"Listen, Gina, I can't let you just go running to him. Not yet. I—"

"Where?" she demanded. "You owe me this, Dad. You owe me. I want to see my son."

"You will."

"Please, he needs me." When Nickel stayed silent, she touched her taste buds again to the postcard and tried to dredge up the information. She shot him a bewildered look. "You don't even know where he is?"

"Not exactly, but Nikki does."

"Great. Like she'd tell me anything."

"She's parked at a café just off the Blue River exit, in an Acura NSX with tinted windows."

"Blue River? As in, just down the road?"

"She's waiting for you."

CHAPTER
TWO

Would Gina actually come?

Nikki Lazarescu pressed back against the headrest, catching sight of herself in the Acura's rearview mirror. Her raven locks were fanned around high cheekbones, her eyebrows shaped and waxed above eyes so dark they were almost black. Despite being in her late fifties, she had been told she was a classic beauty, a fact evidenced by the lusty males among her late-night TV show's audiences.

"Hello, Regina," she practiced in the glass.

Much too formal.

"Gina, dear, it's good to see you."

A little better, though there was no need to sound patronizing or glib. That had never been Nikki's style, and she wouldn't kowtow now to the emotions of her only surviving child.

Nearly forty years ago, Nikki had given birth to twins: Reginald and Regina. In 1971, in a desperate maneuver to disappear from the Collectors' crosshairs, she'd lost Reggie.

Lost? The word was grossly inadequate.

No, her son had been murdered. He'd been tapped by Natira's fangs and left for dead in an icy river. Cal Nichols had failed to save him before the end of that third day—a window of immortality allegedly created by Yeshua's victory over the grave. Distraught and nearly penniless, Nikki had run back to her homeland of Romania with young Gina, intent on carving out their own survival.

And I was successful, was I not? Gina's still alive, as am I.

From the mirror, the flat expression in Nikki's eyes argued otherwise. She'd learned to close off the doors of the heart, to lock away the past and keep her focus fixed upon the future. No room for deviation, especially in light of her recent doctor visits.

She clicked painted fingernails on the steering wheel. After making the long drive from her home in Southern California, she was beginning to doubt her daughter would show. Gina, too, had lost a son. Gina had spent nearly seven years believing the worst—and no doubt blaming Nickel and Nikki.

"I'm sorry," Nikki said aloud. "It was all for Jacob's survival."

Tap, tap, tap . . .

She flinched, then turned to see a form at the passenger door. Drawing air through pink-glossed lips, she disengaged the power locks and watched her daughter duck her head.

"Hi, Mom."

"Hello, my angel."

"I'm all wet. I don't know if you want me to—"

"Please." Nikki gestured toward the seat. "Come out of that rain."

Wearing soaked, baggy khakis and a U2 tour shirt, Gina slid in and closed the door. Nikki saw that she was shivering, her thick hair streaked with caramel highlights, her earlobes free of those silly ruby earrings she'd received long ago from her father.

"You look miserable. Let me turn on the heat for you."

"I'm not too bad, but thanks. After walking through the woods, I can't really feel my fingertips."

Nikki started the engine and angled the vent's warmth to the right. She set her jaw, then took her daughter's hands and rubbed them between her own with all the businesslike vigor of a prison nurse.

"*Multumesc,*" Gina thanked her in Romanian.

That simple word thawed something in Nikki's own chest, and she looked away. How much time did she have on this earth? Despite aggressive medical measures, doctors told her she had ten, maybe twelve, months before the cancer in her spine took her life. Was it enough time to undo the damage between her and her daughter?

In the café straight ahead, patrons in wool-plaid shirts and bushy beards sipped their morning coffee from cups that read *Get Oregonized*. Nikki slipped a pain pill into her mouth and washed it down with the mocha in her travel mug.

"Where's Jacob?" Gina said.

"He's alive. Forgive me, if you will, for not telling you sooner."

"Never mind." Gina waved off the apology. "What's done is done, and I get why you and Dad did what you did. I just want to see him, okay?"

"You will."

"After all this time, I better. Can we go already?"

"Is your father also coming? He did explain the parameters, I hope."

"Sorry," Gina said, pulling on her seatbelt. "Looks like you're stuck with just me while he's off making arrangements for Kenny."

"Who? Ah yes, the boy you brought over from the orphanage."

"The one I adopted," Gina clarified. "My other son."

"Well, I'm certain he'll be well taken care of. As for Jacob, there are stipulations by which you must abide." Nikki steered her Acura back to the highway and headed west. "You'll have no direct contact, no phone calls, nothing of that sort. It's crucial that Jacob remain concealed."

"How am I going to see him, then?"

"Binoculars."

"You've got to be kidding."

"It's not been easy for me, either. I am his grandmother, after all."

"He's okay, though? He's healthy?"

"He's fed—fresh seafood on a regular basis, I might add—and clothed. He has a roof over his head, and I'm weighing options for his education, considering it'll require a fair amount of self-discipline and motivation on his part. So far, he shows all the signs of being a precocious child. You have nothing to fear."

"I have every reason to fear."

Hadn't Nikki felt the same after the D. B. Cooper incident, like nothing would be safe again? She said, "Tell me, Gina, did your little charade go as planned? I had a moment's panic when I heard police cars and an ambulance go racing up the mountain."

"Dad told you about our plan, huh?"

"The gist of it, *da*. We must protect the truth that you have survived.

If Collectors tapped my blood"—Nikki pinched the skin at her wrist—"they would learn of yours and Jacob's whereabouts, and that cannot be permitted. The secret must be guarded at all costs."

"If I've been 'erased,' why can't I be with Jacob? Does he even know he has a mother? Is there anyone giving him hugs or good-night kisses?"

"Come now, darling. These are extravagances that cannot be risked in the present scenario. In fact, they would make him more prone to Collector tactics, which so often target the emotions."

"How can you raise a kid without letting him know he's loved?"

"He does know. I've—"

"Hold on. This is *you* we're talking about, Nikki. Guess that answers my question."

Uneasy silence spun a cocoon in the front seat. Gina folded her arms and cracked her neck both ways, staring off at the blur of deciduous trees still heavy and dark with rain. Nikki threaded the car between slopes on one side and the McKenzie River on the other, wondering how her own offspring could let feelings take the place of practicalities. Why hadn't her parenting skills produced a daughter with thicker skin?

Gina's next words found the chink in Nikki's armor.

"Did you ever even love me, Mom?"

Nikki's knuckles turned white on the wheel. "What?"

"Love. You need me to give you a definition?"

"Don't be ridiculous, Regina. I . . . Of course I did."

"I don't mean feeding and dressing me. I mean, you know, all the other stuff. From the moment I laid eyes on Jacob, I couldn't stop thinking about those thin lips of his, the gold specks in his eyes, about that cowlick in his hair, and his long fingers like Jed's—the hands of an artist. I can't even describe that feeling."

Nikki bit back her indignation. She'd given a good portion of her life to raising and protecting this ungrateful child beside her. She'd risked being viewed as the ogre while bleeding out her daughter's memories and impurities, all in an attempt to cleanse the worst bits of their past.

Let bygones be bye, gone . . .

"Did you?" Gina said again, her voice husky and low.

Nikki's eyes burned at the corners.

"I need to know. Please, *Mamica*."

Mom, in Romanian. *Mommy*, in the native tongue.

"For you, Gina, I . . . I left the love of my life to find us safe haven." Nikki felt a droplet run down her cheek. Regret came swishing through her thoughts, rattling doors, shaking loose the rusty locks. "When your brother died, I lost a part of myself, and I didn't know if I could ever get that back. Truth be told, I blamed myself. I lured your father into my bed—an act that's brought about so much anguish—and I've been in survival mode ever since, working to find even a modicum of peace." She lifted her chin and brushed away another tear with her forefinger. "Does that sound selfish? Well, perhaps it is. Perhaps I was hoping to turn you into the woman I always wanted to be."

"You're the woman I wanted to be. Don't you know that?"

Nikki's throat constricted and she tried to watch the road.

"When I was younger, I dreamed someday I would be as pretty as you, as poised. Look at you even now, Mom—every hair in place, the stylish outfit, and your eyelashes . . . I mean, look at those ridiculous lashes. You're so strong and sure of yourself, and all I ever wanted was to be half as put together as you."

Nikki's bottom lip started trembling. "I thought you hated me."

"Never."

"What about the . . . ?"

"The cuttings? You know, I still have your old dagger right here." Gina patted her shin. "Yeah, it was twisted and wrong, but I understand what you were trying to do. I've let it go. There's Nazarene Blood now flowing through these veins, so it doesn't matter anyway. I'm clean."

"Clean? Has your father forced his beliefs on you?"

"My own choice all the way."

"Hmm." Nikki blotted the last of her tears and drove on.

For the next hour, she threaded the car through Springfield and Eugene, catching I-5 North, while Pacific winds cleared the Willamette Valley of its summer storm. Puddled water evaporated in the sunlight and turned things humid. In the passenger seat, Gina dozed off with her head against the window—almost thirty-nine years old, looking barely out of her teens.

That half-immortal blood, Nikki realized. *And without it, I am left to die.*

CHAPTER THREE

Ruins of Kerioth-Hezron, Israel

An hour after the accident, Barabbas conveyed the news. Lord Natira gripped the gothic candelabra to the right of his throne and watched the flames quiver with his excitement. Could this be true? The daughter of Cal Nichols dead at last, no longer capable of producing offspring for the Nistarim?

"You're certain?" he said. "Someone witnessed this firsthand?"

"A Collector named Asgoth."

"Never heard of him."

"He's part of the Consortium in the U.S."

"Come closer, Barabbas. Man of your size, you should show yourself boldly."

"Yes, my lord." The henchman moved into the candlelight, red beard glinting as it brushed the ridges of his chest.

"So this Asgoth fellow, he's convinced the woman is dead? Perhaps he is unaware that she's half immortal, capable of being revived. I discovered that three-day window myself while dealing with my own offspring years ago."

Curiosity flickered in Barabbas' eyes.

"No business of yours," Natira said. "Are you ready to serve your cluster?"

Barabbas had always obeyed without question. Long ago, he'd been imprisoned for murder, then won his release in a swap for the Nazarene's crucifixion. He'd become a servant to Ariston, later to Megiste, and he was familiar with bloodshed, as evidenced by the scars upon his pectoral muscles.

Not that Natira had any fear of him. In hand-to-hand combat, he had ripped the Adam's apple from this man's throat and demanded allegiance. Reinserted, the part had healed, though it lurched now when Barabbas spoke, punching at odd angles from his neck like a rodent trying to burst free.

"You haven't given an answer," Natira said.

"I am ready."

"That's good to hear."

Barabbas lowered his gaze, and the rodent fell still.

Lord Natira grinned. As rightful heir, he basked in his authority over the Akeldama Cluster, over the Houses of Ariston and Eros. He shared his private quarters with Erota, and together they orchestrated the downfall of mankind. Yes, here in honeycombed limestone chambers beneath Judas the Betrayer's birthplace, he and his band of Collectors plied their trade: feeding, breeding, persuading, and possessing.

Scripture listed "six, no seven things" the Lord hated, and for years Megiste had used that blueprint for destruction to gather victims in these caves—young and old, rich and poor, male and female. Despite her current exile, those Six, No Seven Things still throbbed with profane energy. Each of the seven panels around Natira's throne room was a *pièce de résistance*, representing an item from the biblical list; each, to some degree, was a desecration of one of the physical senses.

Hadn't the Separation long ago cut off all Collectors from the use of their senses? What better way, then, to exact revenge?

"I am *hostis humani generis*," Natira declared to all within earshot.

Enemy of mankind.

His words reverberated through the cavern, prompting wails from half-dead victims plastered to the walls. Their anguish should have brought him satisfaction, but instead his temples pounded—a ceaseless hammering, hammering, in his skull—and his thirst was triggered anew.

A wreath of blood-swollen thorns rested atop his head, each tendril linked to the writhing mass of humanity, and he reached up now to partake. His fangs protruded from his gums, ready to drink. With three fingers missing from his massive right hand, he tilted a thorn cup between pinkie and thumb and poured its contents over his tongue.

Ah yes. Unholy communion.

In this act of blasphemy, the symbol of one life surrendered for many became the life of many surrendered for one.

Primed by his desire, the vine connected to this particular thorn began siphoning sustenance from the cave's human collage, oozing it drop by drop down his throat. Natira's eyes brightened, casting forth a pale-green glow. From cavities in the stone, his purrs of pleasure were met—and heightened—by feeble groans. Was anything more satisfying than to tap those created in the Almighty's image?

Natira's thirst, however, remained unquenched.

He took a few more drinks. "What's wrong with this?" he mused aloud.

Tip, gurgle, swallow . . . The droplets squeezing through the vines tasted watery. In his head, the hammers continued pounding. Was it possible the veins of these mortals, like soil tilled in the same spot for too long, had become unproductive? Or maybe the roots were the problem, clogged like arteries and unable to yield their best fruits.

"Barabbas," he barked.

"Yes, Lord Natira?"

"Bring me a thigh."

"My lord?"

"From the wall there. Any one of the panels will do."

Barabbas studied the Six, No Seven Things. For a man with his history, he seemed reluctant to act.

"Do it now, henchman."

Barabbas lugged the requested item to the throne, where he touched his head to a camelskin rug and offered up the limb on hairy arms. Natira took hold of it, latching onto the femoral artery for a drink straight from the source. Though he still found it bland at best, the ache in his temples began to subside.

"How was it you wanted me to serve the cluster?" said Barabbas.

"I must go verify Gina Lazarescu's death."

"You want me to join you?"

"I'll handle this matter myself. I want you to guard our Haunt of Jackals."

"You're sure there is nothing else?"

"And watch over our cluster's women."

"We can watch over ourselves," Erota said, entering through a fissure in the rock, her lithe form silhouetted by stars in the desert sky.

The henchman looked up, desire for her swirling in his eyes.

"Erota, while I'm gone you'll take command," Natira said, "with Barabbas at your beck and call."

That seemed to please the big fellow, if not the former temple prostitute.

"Lord Natira, please, I thought you and I ruled as a pair—the Black King and his queen." She eased up to the throne and stroked his forearm. "What's bothering you?"

"True enough, our recent monstrosities have buckled the knees of the Nistarim, triggering earthquakes and floods. This harvest of humans has turned sour, though. It seems time for us to rotate the crops."

"Fresh victims await in Jerusalem. I'm already training our thorns that way."

"And how long till they provide substantial nourishment? Three years? Four? Such 'wine' cannot be rushed." Despite the glow of beeswax candles, Natira sensed a thickening of the chamber's gloom. "It takes only one Concealed One to bring this world crashing down, and yet the Thirty-Six still have not collapsed. What more do we have to do? These damnable Nistarim!"

"Signs of the end are increasing in frequency."

"As they have for eons, Erota. It means nothing."

She touched soft lips to his cheek. "What're you thinking?"

"I've tracked and targeted these lowly souls and still have eight to identify before we can launch an attack. Megiste's strategies were devious in their way, but much as I've been tempted to banish her, we may need to call on her again. As for me, I am a warrior. Have been since my days fighting off Roman invaders. I'd rather face my enemies than resort to further covert schemes."

Erota's kiss was deeper this time. "Mmm. A man hardened by the rigors of battle." The tickle of her silky hair hinted at untold delights.

Barabbas narrowed his eyes and looked away.

Sensuous as Natira found her gestures—and, oh yes, she was sensuous—he refused to be distracted. He rose and removed the sickly crown from his head. "There's word Kate Preston was killed today on an Oregon mountain pass."

"Kate? Meaning, Gina Lazarescu?"

"One and the same."

"Good news," Erota said. "I wish I'd destroyed her years ago with the bomb that nailed her baby. She's been a thorn in our side—if you'll pardon the expression—since we first tried tracking her in Romania."

"I've been hunting her father longer than that. He was a Concealed One."

"Until he gave in to a woman," Erota noted with a coy grin.

"Not the first man, or the last, to do so, but I've been worried his immortal blood would live on through his children. I singled out and ambushed his son—easy prey at that age. If Gina's also gone, that'll be one less distraction, although I won't be satisfied of it till we pass the seventy-two-hour mark."

"The three-day window."

"Which is why I must view the evidence myself, hear the story firsthand."

"I could go along," Erota said.

"No, let's see what sustenance you can squeeze from Jerusalem's veins. Not to worry. If Gina *has* survived, I'll be more than she alone can handle."

Corvallis, Oregon

A bump in the road caused Gina to mumble and wipe at her mouth. She squinted against the brightness, saw patchwork farmlands hemmed in by peaks to the east and west. Where was she?

An Acura. Her mom's car. Heading into the unknown.

"Hello, dear," said Nikki. "You must've been exhausted."

"Yeah, uh . . ." She sat up. "Dad said that might happen after the bridging."

"The what?"

"Where're we going?"

"Our turn-off's just ahead. Soon, you'll be in your new place in Corvallis."

"Is that where Jacob's hiding, the heart of the Willamette Valley?"

"Heavens, no. It's where you'll be staying from this point forward, though—above a local art gallery, with the two women who run the place."

Gina checked the side-view mirror. "Corvallis isn't far from where I was living in Junction City. Are you sure that's smart?"

"There are hundreds of thousands in the tricounty area. You can change your look, get washed up and rested, and tomorrow we'll continue on to see Jacob. These were arrangements made by your father."

"Okay, then. I mean, if he thinks that's best . . ."

They reached the exit a few minutes later, and Nikki braked to a halt at the side of the off-ramp. "Listen, angel." She pinned Gina with a gaze. "Even though he's your father, Cal's words should be weighed and evaluated. When it comes to Collectors and Concealed Ones, there's no one more knowledgeable, but you do realize, I hope, that he's living his own delusion. This . . ." Her finger hooked the cord around Gina's neck, with its vial of Nazarene Blood. "It's a nice myth that he clings to in order to absolve his wrongs."

"If the Nazarene's a myth, then who exactly did Dad wrong?"

"Oh, I suppose Yeshua's real enough—history bears that out—yet your father insists on adding to the stories. *Se ridica cortina* . . . 'The curtain is going up.' Now is your time, dear. Yours, not anyone else's. I don't believe you find life by letting someone else die for you, but by paying that price yourself."

"I'm not trying to earn anything. That's the whole point."

Nikki edged back onto the road. "I knew your father would get to you."

Gina met her mother's gaze, reining in her frustration.

"In response to your earlier question: yes, Gina, I love you. I can't yet say, though, that I'm proud of the choices you're making. You're an adult now, which means you should take some responsibility."

"If anything, Mom, I'm honoring our Judaic heritage—the Passover lamb and ritual sacrifices." She lifted her vial. "This Blood meets those requirements once and for all. The answer dies within."

"Or so some would have you believe."

Deciding to let it rest, Gina drew comfort from the wings tattooed on her lower back. They reminded her even now that the Unfallen kept watch.

She said, "Who are these people I'll be staying with?"

"Acquaintances of your father. He tells me that one of them could become your relative, considering she's soon to be engaged to Jed's uncle, Sergeant Turney."

"To Sarge? Really?"

"Her name's Josee, I believe. Daughter of the Addisons." On cue, Nikki pointed at a road marker indicating mileage to the local Addison Ridge Vineyards.

"Well, maybe Josee can tell me what Jed's been up to."

"Oh dear. Are you still pining over him?"

"You never did like him, did you?" Gina stared off through the passenger window. "Well, it doesn't matter what you think of him. He's my husband."

"He left you."

"And I plan to get him back."

CHAPTER
FOUR

Cleveland, Ohio

It felt good to be on the prowl again.

Wearing a seam-stretched gray suit with a forged passport in the pocket, Natira shifted in his seat. The airport lobby was only a third full, and he had cleared the space on either side with broad shoulders and a flash of his pincered right hand. He'd already endured the gauntlet of U.S. Customs officials and their inane questions, and now he awaited the flight to Portland, Oregon, that would carry him to his objective.

A day since Gina Lazarescu's death.

Two more till he could be certain she was really gone.

He had other business here as well, starting with the whereabouts of two Concealed Ones: Numbers Twenty-Nine and Thirty. Over the last few decades, he had located five per landmass—in Europe, Africa, Australia, Asia, and South America; after North America, he'd have only the Middle East to dig through. If the pattern held, he would end up with Thirty-Five in his sights, while the Thirty-Sixth remained a mystery.

Was this mystery man the leader of the Nistarim? Where would he be hiding? Did he live on the lam, never settling long enough to be targeted?

There was also one other matter to deal with, if only Natira could—

Keep to the task at hand, he told himself. *I need to know that Gina is dead.*

Corvallis, Oregon

"The Tattered Feather Gallery." Nikki parked beneath a sprawling oak tree on SW Second Street before an aging, yet dignified, home with dream catchers displayed in its large front windows. "My understanding, Gina, is that you'll be sharing a room on the second floor."

"With this Josee chick?"

"Shush. Judging by her picture, she looks only a bit older than you."

Gina grinned. "Looks can be deceiving."

"Ah, how I wish I could compete with your immortality."

"What're you worried about? You're stunning as always."

Nikki wore a weak smile. "Judging by the number of stalkers I encounter each year, I suppose you're right. We've had to issue restraining orders more than once."

"Fans of your show? Scary. Anyway, Mom, it's not a competition."

Gina stepped from the vehicle, her clothes wrinkled and musty. Weariness weighed upon her as she faced this new reality. Starting over. Again. She'd left it all—home, wardrobe, car, friends, work, and her thirteen-year-old son, Kenny.

Don't ever crumble, Kenny. Stay strong and courageous.

Nikki joined her on the sidewalk. "Are you feeling well?"

"I'm fine. Let's just hope Josee's close to my size, since the clothes on my back are now all that I own."

As though summoned by these words, the gallery's front door swung open, and a thin, twentyish girl appeared with the familiar vial of Those Who Resist strung around her neck. Her hair was black and choppy above a silver eyebrow ring. Though shorter than Gina, they seemed to share a lean yet shapely build.

"Well, would ya look at this."

Startled by the deep voice, Gina spotted a man as he joined the girl in the doorway. "Sarge?"

"Heyya. You caught us just in time. Lemme make the introductions." With his left arm over Josee's shoulder, Sergeant Turney led his girlfriend down the wooden steps. Though he was as big boned as she was small, there was no denying the appeal of his chocolate-brown eyes. "This here's Josee." Handshakes were exchanged. "Warning ya right now, she's a fireball, but she's seen enough in her day to be a help to you."

"Sounds like you have a fan," Gina told her counterpart.

"Him? He's a big teddy bear," Josee said. "Got him wrapped around my finger."

Sarge flashed an aw-shucks grin. Dressed in loose black jeans and a striped button-down shirt, he was more formal than earlier in the year when Gina had stopped by his townhouse to visit Jed. In the car, hadn't Nikki mentioned an impending engagement? Gina wondered if Sarge planned to "pop the question" during today's outing—a notion bolstered by his hint of a wink.

Not a word, it seemed to say. *Not one cotton-pickin' word.*

In the lull, Nikki stepped forward and introduced herself.

"Hi," Josee responded. "Aren't you the one on that TV show?"

"*Beyond the Stars*," Nikki said. "Indeed I am, dear."

Josee shifted turquoise eyes to Gina. "And what's your name?"

"Oh, sorry. I'm . . ."

Realizing she'd been given no instructions from Nickel on this matter, she glanced to her mother and received a shrug. She had lived the past few years as Kate Preston, so her actual name shouldn't raise any red flags. There must be hundreds if not thousands named Gina in Oregon alone. She turned back, determined to no longer let fear strip away her identity. She would maintain a low profile, yes—but under her own name, thank you.

"I'm Gina," she said at last. "Just Gina."

"Works for me."

"Jed used to mumble that name in his sleep," Sarge said. "Like I told you before, that boy's still head over heels for you."

"Think so?" Gina said.

"Kiddo, I know so."

With the grief they had shared, she understood her estranged husband's decision to run off and hide. She had to believe there was still something there, though, something salvageable between them.

Josee faced her. "So, you're lying low, right? Needing a place to chill? Nickel tells us you've had some trouble, and Sarge and I know all about that sort of thing. We're here to stand by you, to resist any evil that comes along."

"Thank you."

"Suzette—she's inside, ringing up a customer. She's still dealing with her own past, so don't think that you're the only one."

"We all have our demons to face," Sarge said. "Sorry to butt in, Josee, but we need to skedaddle before I start sweatin' all over my new duds. We're headin' to the Scandinavian Festival over in J.C. Should be a whole lotta fun." Another wink at Gina.

Not one word . . .

"Make yourself comfortable, okay?" Josee urged Gina. "You're up the stairs, last door on the left. See the window there? We'll be sharing that room. Nothing fancy, but there's a towel on your bed in case you want to shower, and the dresser beneath the window's all yours."

"I don't, uh . . . don't really have anything to put in it."

"No biggie. When you're done, just grab some clothes from my closet."

"You don't mind?"

"I'm a U2 fan. Let me borrow that shirt of yours someday and we'll call it even." Josee threw an elbow into Sarge's ribs. "Would you stop gawking?"

"I wasn't even—"

"She's pretty. Yeah, yeah, I get it—the long brown hair, that rich Latin coloring."

Gina felt her cheeks redden.

"Don't worry," Josee said, with a tilt of her head. "He's a sucker for my intellect and pasty, rain-washed skin. Now let's move it, lover boy."

"As you wish," he said. "But today it's me who'll be doin' the driving."

They climbed into a red VW bug with a crooked bumper. Fifteen seconds after they'd disappeared, the rattletrap engine was still audible through the city streets.

"I suppose that's it, then." Nikki rubbed Gina's arm. "Freshen up, darling, and I'll fetch you again in the morning—assuming you still want to see Jacob."

"I'll be ready. Definitely. Guess it'll be BYOB, huh?"

"Pardon me?"

Gina held cupped hands to her eyes. " 'Bring your own binoculars.' "

The gallery was closed, and darkness had settled hours ago over Corvallis. By the light of a Tiffany lamp on the counter, Gina wandered among various Native American artifacts, handmade quilts, framed oil paintings, and consignment sculpture pieces. She paused near a circular jewelry case, then spotted her reflection in the glass.

Yep, the shower had felt great. She'd bleached her hair and trimmed it to shoulder length so that it cupped and softened her features. Hadn't she always despised her unruly, coarse locks anyway? She had also tossed the light-blue contacts that were part of her Kate Preston persona. Kate no more. Just Gina.

"Catch me if you can," she muttered.

A hand tapped at her shoulder and she spun around, reaching for her dagger.

"Caught you," Suzette said.

"Oh. Hey."

"Forgive me if I startled you."

"I . . . I thought I was the only one down here."

Gina left her weapon strapped to her shin and tugged the hood of Josee's sweatshirt over her blonde stylings. Suzette Bishop, the gallery owner, had introduced herself earlier as a former peyote-smoking Nez Perce Indian with a love for the arts—and a love for mischief, too, it seemed. Though her demeanor was demure, sparks played through her wide, dark eyes.

"Do you like it?" Suzette pointed to a jewel-studded object in the case.

"Looks like an egg."

"Not everyone's familiar with Fabergé's creations. Isn't it lovely?"

"Is it real?"

"A real egg?" Suzette winked. "No, it's a remarkable imitation that we call 'Fauxbergé.' The originals were given as annual Easter gifts to the Russian tsars, but many were lost after the October Revolution in 1917."

"Have you ever seen the genuine article?"

"Most have been auctioned off to museums and private collections, so yes, I had the privilege of attending a traveling exhibit." Suzette's eyes twinkled again. "Nothing to compare with Josee's, though."

"As in, your Josee?"

"Sarge's Josee would be more accurate."

"You're kidding. She has her own Fabergé?"

"Not in the gallery, no. If you ask nicely I'm sure she'd arrange for you to have a peek someday. I probably should have let her mention it, but"—Suzette shrugged—"it's my one link to something truly grand. Please don't think because of this that I can't keep your presence here quiet. We'll give you room and board for the hours you work at the counter, and that'll alleviate any need for official forms or paperwork. All off the books, of course. Like you don't even exist."

"If that works for you, Suzette. Don't want to cause any trouble."

From down the street, the sounds of a VW were followed by the dip of its headlights. The engine cut out as the Bug coasted to the curb.

"My, my, look who's home," Suzette said. "Mrs. Turney-to-be."

Gina grinned. "You think Sarge did it?"

"Popped the question? Certainly, most certainly."

Gina detected a hint of melancholy in Suzette's tone, only to forget about it the moment Josee stepped from the car.

Fairy tales and happily-ever-afters took a hit as the passenger door slammed. Josee stomped up the lawn, fumbled with the gallery deadbolt, and blurted, "When will men ever get a clue?" Up the stairs she went, and it was half an hour before Gina ventured after her into the room they now shared.

Portland, Oregon

The Collector gazed down upon the City of Roses, where the Columbia River blushed pink in the sunrise. Runway lights came into view, and the descending plane's tires touched, bounced, touched again, then gripped the tarmac at last. He stopped clicking his pinkie and thumb together, calmed by the ground beneath him. Although he embraced most modern conveniences, he still felt the nerves of his undead host each time one of these iron birds landed.

Natira now disembarked with a single carry-on bag, new vitality pumping through his limbs. He was on the move once again.

For nine months, he'd presided over the ruins at Kerioth-Hezron, reveling in their macabre artistry, even while feeling restrained. On a chessboard, the king played a primarily defensive role, issuing commands from the safety of his castled position, whereas Natira felt most alive while confronting death on the battlefield.

According to Erota, he was the indisputable king.

The Black King.

It was all confirmed by Rasputin's prophecy: *"He will emerge . . . from the holy ground . . ."*

True, Natira had risen from the Campo Santo, the "holy field."

"His likeness shall unlock riches to strengthen his campaign."

Yes, for nearly a century, rumors had circulated of ancient relics discovered and locked away by that lecherous Russian priest, and Natira coveted such a treasure. Most intriguing was the Crown of Thorns, once worn, once stained, by the Nazarene Himself. That sacred Blood was richer, purer, thicker than any the Collectors were permitted to drink. It was anathema to the Akeldama, and yet Natira desired it like no other.

Where was this hallowed Crown? Who held the key to access it? Was there a way to filter its stains for consumption, to tap its nourishment and strength without suffering its wrath?

One day, he pledged to himself, *I shall have that Crown as my own.*

Spurred by this thought, the vampire in the gray suit marched from the Budget Rent-a-Car desk and took control of a silver sedan. On a state map, he'd already circled the site of Gina's mishap on Highway 126.

CHAPTER FIVE

Corvallis

Dawn seeped through the blinds, nudging Gina awake in her new room. Today was the day she would see her son, even if only from a distance. She gazed at her roommate slumbering in the nearby bed, thankful for her generosity. Gina had fallen asleep in Josee's clothes, a bit tight yet functional. She felt safe, expectant, conflicted, and—this part would take some getting used to—blonde.

She flipped onto her stomach and pulled the blanket over her head. At least she might be able to let her hair grow back, thick and chestnut brown, before meeting Jacob face-to-face.

For now, none of it mattered. She was dead, right?

How would her Ace Hardware coworkers react to that news back in J.C.? Maybe her manager would feel guilty for dragging his feet about her raise the past year.

The deception was worth it to protect Kenny's and her own skin; plus, by agreeing to let go, she was getting Jacob back. That was still hard to fathom. Years ago, she'd carried him in the womb, shared those pangs of sorrow that would one day be his permanent cross to bear, then heard the bomb blast.

And yet, he lived. Still seemed hard to believe.

Burrowing deeper under the covers, she recalled the tingling exhilaration of bridging from her car. She'd felt what it was like to stand with a foot in both worlds, abstract and concrete brought together as intended.

Nickel said the Separation was a result of rebellion and sin, both realms affecting each other, with physical illnesses leading to spiritual fatigue and immoral behaviors producing bodily sores and disease. A soul could be worn down by financial pressures, while a meal could be a brush with heaven itself.

Yeshua Himself had shown the way after being raised immortal, walking through walls yet still capable of eating fish and breaking bread.

Could she bridge again? Even without her dad nearby?

Gina closed her eyes and blew out tension and fear—an act of faith, of willful surrender. She imagined herself melting through the mattress and box springs, trickles of subatomic particles drifting between the gaps, drifting . . .

Time's pendulum slowed. As did her beating heart. Minutes and seconds became elastic, flattening like racquetballs driven into a wall, then rebounding, redirecting: *tick-tick-tockity-tickticktick-tockkk!*

She was floating, falling . . .

"Gina?"

From far off, someone called her.

"Hey." It was Josee speaking. "Are you okay down there?"

Down where?

The material realm came into focus once more, and Gina realized she was pressed flat on the floorboards beneath the bed. Yes, she was okay, all in one piece and only slightly embarrassed.

"You can come out," Josee coaxed from her own bed, a pillow bunched beneath her ear. "I used to get night terrors when I was younger, some bad memories burbling up to the surface. Woke up in the closet, on the back porch—wherever seemed safe, I guess."

A dust bunny ran from Gina's exhaled breath, revealing a small spider crouched near the bed leg. She thought of Cal and smashed it with her fist before scrambling out into strips of daylight. "Yuck."

"Old houses and spiders, they seem to go together." Josee pivoted into a sitting position and handed over a Kleenex from the box on the dresser.

"Thanks." Gina perched herself on the mattress edge and wiped off her hand. "Listen, how do you know my dad?"

"Nickel? It's wild how he hardly looks any older than you do."

"Good genes. We're lucky like that."

"No kidding. So I guess Sarge and Nickel met during an investigation this summer—that's what Sarge does, investigative consulting. There were some murders over in J.C., all connected to some artifact tucked away on an old train engine there in Founder's Park."

"Engine 418."

"You've seen it?"

"Came over from Russia or Finland, I think. It was a gift between sister cities, and of course the folks that run the Scandinavian Festival thought it would be fitting for their little town." Gina left out the fact that she had lived in Junction City and visited the train engine herself. Late last year, she'd even played chess with her dad in that same park.

"I'm impressed, Gina. Yeah, some historians believe Lenin was on board that very engine before the Revolution, running for his life after stealing something from Rasputin. Apparently, in all the turmoil, he hid the item and it got left behind."

"What sort of item?"

"Key to a medieval treasure."

"And this led to people getting murdered?"

"Less than a year ago. A pair of Russian mobsters came calling, and also a . . . Well, the point is Sarge and Nickel met during all that fuss."

"Who ended up with the key?"

"Far as most people know, it disappeared again."

"Sounds like you know differently."

"Ah-ah." Josee lifted her hand. "If I told you, I'd have to kill you."

They both chuckled at that.

Gina had no problem embracing Josee's explanation, since she too had found herself ensnared in history's secrets. Wasn't she even now running from Jerusalem's Undead, corpses of the Akeldama that served as hosts to Collectors? And what about the dagger she carried? Nickel had taken it from Judas, who had taken it from Apostle Peter. Its origins went back even further, crafted from the same bronze material as the *Nehushtan*, a serpent wrapped around a pole as an ancient symbol of salvation for the Israelites.

Sure, it was all mind boggling. But hey, it was what it was.

"Anyway," Josee said, "after Nickel and Sarge got to know each other, they discovered the whole family connection between Jed, Sarge, and you. Of course, Jed's moved out of his uncle's place, living over in Silverton now."

"Any chance I could see him? It's been over five years."

"Why not? Listen, if it means anything to you, I don't think Jed's been dating anyone. About all he does is work, work, work, and go fishing with Sarge."

Gina was beginning to understand her dad's reasons for directing her to this house. Would she get to rekindle the flame with her husband? Would she and Jed get to parent their son together at some point, the way it was meant to be?

"You know what time it is?" she asked.

Josee checked her cell phone's display. "Seven forty-eight. I can take you someplace if that's what you need. We don't open the gallery till nine."

"Actually, my mom should be by in a little bit. Thanks, though."

"You ready to head down to the kitchen for breakfast? Telling you now, I make some mean whole-grain muffins, and they go great with blackberries and cream."

Blackberries . . .

Gina could taste them on her lips, spoiled by memories of her child-hood friend, Teo, and the disturbing way in which he had died. The anguish on her face must've been evident, because Josee quickly offered raspberries instead, to which Gina nodded and followed her new room-mate down the stairs.

Enough with her own concerns. Josee had struggles too.

"Not like it's any of my business," Gina said, "but what happened last night between you and Sarge?"

Cascade Mountains

Natira examined the accident scene with a jaundiced eye. Ribbons of yellow police tape still fluttered from tree trunks, and charred red emergency flares marked both ends of the mess. From the gash in the road's muddy bank to mangled guard rails, all the signs of a tragic event were on display.

The Collector parked his rental on the highway's shoulder and climbed out. Chips of paint clung to the metal where a car had gone over. It was still down there, American made, impaled by trees like an animal fallen into a pit of spears.

Where was Kate/Gina's car? A Nissan, according to Asgoth's report.

Nearby, the other railing hung at a precarious angle, held to the cliff by a single pylon. Far below, the raging McKenzie had buried any evidence of a second automobile, but it had to be down there. The authorities wouldn't have left one car in the trees and gone to the trouble of pulling the other from the rapids.

Where was Gina's body? Had she been a good girl and worn her seatbelt, trapping herself in a watery casket?

His eyes roved the steep terrain for signs of a body thrown clear during the fall. Nothing. If he wanted to verify her death, he'd have to locate her Nissan.

By his calculations, his prey still had forty-six hours in which to be revived. The timeframe was one he had discovered during the final days of Hitler's Third Reich. Not only had he served at Kransberg Castle in a Nazi biochemist's lab, but he'd managed to bed the *doktor's* teen daughter—Trudi Ubelhaar, a partner both willing and deeply infested.

Natira knew of no other Akeldama Collectors with progeny of their own, yet with Trudi he had sired twins by the energy flowing from his host's undead loins. The wombs of female vampires were unable to sustain life for the requisite nine months, whereas a male vampire needed only seconds to do his part.

You see, Cal—you aren't the only father of half-immortals.

Clearly, even among his cluster, Natira was a creature of destiny.

Trudi was not convinced, though. In mid-1945, upon giving birth, she had gasped at the sight of her beastly infants and smothered the life from them.

Natira searched nearly three days for his murdered sons, and when he found them buried in the castle yard, he struck out at Trudi in his rage. She clawed back, drew blood. Those droplets sprayed the lips of one twisted corpse, bringing color back to his cheeks and oxygen into his tiny chest.

Shocked by this turn of events, Natira plucked the child from the soil and held Trudi at arm's length. Only later did he comprehend that his own undead blood had revived the boy.

He then tried it with the other twin.

The pale body showed no response.

In this way he deduced the window of time in which half-immortals could be pried from the clutches of the grave, and, on threats of death, he made Trudi swear to keep the survivor alive.

Natira swatted away the recollections the way he'd once fought off the blades of Rome. What did it matter? He had no room for such human trivialities. For the time being, Gina's fate was his sole concern.

The precipice at his feet was steep. In this mortal frame, he might need two or three hours to climb down to the river.

He scanned the morning sky. Maybe he could use a secondary host, a hawk capable of sweeping down the cliff face and diving into the water.

At his back, early rays crested the ridge, and he turned into their embrace. He sneered at the idea that all vampires were vulnerable to sunlight. Perhaps this was the case for Collectors masquerading as Romanian *strigoi* or Russian *uppyr*. Or for Hollywood vamps in high heels and black lipstick. Bah. Aside from occasional sunburns suffered above ground at Kerioth-Hezron, he had more difficulty in cold climates where maintaining core temperature required larger amounts of blood.

Enough, Natira. Enough.

Weekend traffic moved both in directions along Highway 126, and wildlife activity remained sparse.

Even if he were to switch to a hawk, would a feathered creature be sufficient for plumbing the depths of a river? What other host could accomplish such a task? Truly, two-legged humans were the most versatile of all.

With that in mind, Natira made his decision. He inched closer to the twisted rail and gauged the distance to the McKenzie below. Reminded of his otherworldly abilities, he mocked his host's constraints. He was Lord Natira. The most powerful of all Collectors. No reason to let jagged outcroppings impede him.

Risky? Yes. Possible? Absolutely.

He stripped off his clothes and locked them in the rental car before hiding the key behind the rear tire. Later, he would get an eyewitness account from the Collector named Asgoth; for now, he'd do his own up-close investigation.

Deaf to the honks and catcalls of passing drivers, he took a few steps back.

Let them gawk. Let them marvel.

Master, watch me fly.

He filled his massive lungs, then charged ahead on thighs thicker than most men's chests. Behind him, catcalls turned to screams as he leaped into the chasm.

CHAPTER
SIX

Corvallis

August morning warmth was washing over the breakfast nook when the tray of fresh muffins slid onto a pot holder. Gina had already nibbled on raspberries, downed a cup of Stash tea, and now her mouth watered.

"Dig in," Josee said. "Don't be shy."

Gina dug in.

"Soon enough you'll be doing your own share of work around here, but for today—maybe even tomorrow, if you're lucky—Suzette and I'll treat you like a guest. Here, have some butter. Forget margarine, packed full of all that artificial junk."

Gina sliced a muffin in two and slathered both sides.

"Now." Josee flipped aside her oven mitt. "Since my guest is taken care of, I'll give you the lowdown on Sergeant Vincent Turney, the man formerly known as my 'big teddy bear.'"

Taking a bite here seemed like a good idea.

"It all started off fine." Josee twiddled her eyebrow ring as she launched into the story. "The Scandi-Fest was packed, but it was fun holding hands, bumping our way through the crowds, watching the traditional dances. We stood in line forever to get an *aebelskiver*. Ever had one? Oh, you're missing out."

Gina took another bite. Already she liked Josee, and if she hoped for the inside scoop regarding Jed, it was only fair she listen to her roommate's woes.

"Then what does Sarge do? He agrees to meet this guy, Clay Ryker."

"Clay Ryker?"

"You know him, Gina?"

"Uh, not really. Guess my dad does, though."

"Yep, he seems to know everyone, doesn't he?"

Gina had been told that Mr. Ryker would watch over Kenny, but Josee knew nothing of Gina's past or of her children. Best to avoid that subject.

"Well, Clay's one of the good guys," Josee said. "I don't have any problem with him. Point is this is our special night away, and we're now sitting in DQ with my heart racing because Sarge is supposed to propose."

"In a Dairy Queen?"

"He's not *that* dense." Josee popped a raspberry into her mouth. "No, I mean, he's been hinting for weeks that he picked out a ring, so I thought this would be the night, but instead he's digging into a salad—watching the calories, you know—and going yakkity-yak with Clay and company."

"When he should be somewhere romantic with you."

"Hello."

"Men."

"Exactly." If Josee tugged any harder, that ring would tear loose from her brow. A streak of scar tissue implied such a thing might've happened in the past. "So they're talking about Engine 418 and that key that was found there, and just to make sure I'm not forgotten, I toss in a few comments. They bring up some Russian history, which I know a thing or two about, so—"

"Because of the Fabergé egg?"

"What?" Josee's gaze hardened. "Why'd you say that?"

"Well, uh . . . Suzette told me."

"Then you know about my little inheritance gift, huh?"

"Not the details."

"Long story short, my grandfather was in counterintelligence during World War II. Hitler's goons stole a Fabergé egg, Grandpa Addison stole it back and left it tucked away for me in a safe-deposit box."

"Wow. Must be worth a fortune."

"Except it wouldn't seem right to sell the thing, even if the tsars are long gone. For me, it has sentimental value, but Sarge and I now think it's linked to this whole deal with Lenin and the Rasputin treasure."

"I'd love to see it sometime. I mean, if you don't mind."

"It's possible."

"I'll make you a deal: show me the egg, and I'll show you a family heirloom of my own, dating back to the first century AD. Even earlier, actually."

"Deal." With another raspberry clutched between her fingers, Josee gestured. "Hey, by the way, that look really works for you."

"This?" Gina ran a hand over her short blonde hair. "Really?"

"Guess it's your fine features. I hate girls like you."

"And I've always wanted eyes like yours."

"Thanks." Josee gulped down the berry. "Sarge is a sucker for them."

"How long've you two been together?"

"Less than a year, but I guess when you know, you just know."

Gina said nothing. For her, things rarely seemed that definitive.

"Sounds cheesy," Josee admitted. "I've never been the starry-eyed girl, so it's weird to hear this kind of stuff coming out of my own mouth. I've changed a lot since Sarge and I first met. So has he. When he was younger, he lost a fiancée to a drunk driver. He thought he'd never get serious with anyone again, so this relationship has been a big test for him. I mean, what if he lost me too? He'd be crushed big time."

"Maybe that was the problem last night. Nerves got to him."

"About last night . . . Okay, we finally say *adios* to Ryker—nice guy, don't get me wrong, but I'm on a date here. With the man that I love. So he's not the most fit individual, but this culture is so flippin' obsessed with outward beauty that it's nauseating. Before Sarge, I'd never met a guy who could look me in the eye without seeming like he wanted to get me in the sack. Sarge actually *listens.*" When Josee looked up, her eyes were moist. "You know what a turn-on that is?"

Gina knew it well. She thought of Jed and the way things used to be— making meals together, playing chess, listening to old ABBA albums.

"Why am I dumping all this on you? I don't usually ramble like this."

"It's okay, Josee. Really."

"Thing is most people just point fingers at him because of his size."

"Jed always said good stuff about him."

"Jed's from the same mold—quiet and faithful, a big heart. If you have the time, you two really should go grab a bite together and try to reconnect."

"We'll see what happens."

"*Make* it happen."

"I'm hoping to." Gina knew Nikki would be showing up any minute, and her heart ached to see her son. She figured it was time to get to the punch line of Josee's story. "So, did Sarge ever work up the courage to ask you?"

"Sort of."

"And you said yes?"

"What? No way."

"But you just told me—"

"Listen," Josee said. "I'm not giving in just to give in. We're talking a lifelong commitment, and that means he's got to focus and actually go about it the right way if he wants to see *this* girl walking down the aisle."

"Wow. He's, uh, got a tough cookie on his hands."

"Been called worse." Josee shrugged. "So we're leaving DQ, and we see Mylisha, one of the dancers from the festival, and now Sarge is talking to her—blah, blah, blah, blah, blah. Basically, I've had enough. By the time we get in the car, I'm a time bomb. He asks if I'm upset and I think of all the things I want to say, and instead I tell him to just take me home."

"Poor guy was a nervous wreck, don't you think?"

"His hands did start shaking. He reaches into his pocket and pulls out this little box, then he tries getting down on one knee right there in the Bug—yeah, imagine *that*. We're in the DQ parking lot, and he's asking me to marry him. Well, what am I supposed to say?"

"Yes."

"I didn't say anything." Josee began clearing the table. "What if I started screaming at him? Or bawling? No, these lips stayed zipped shut."

Gina heard a car pull up outside and thrilled at the idea of going to see Jacob. She hurried her plate to the sink. "Sounds like my ride's here. Not sure when we'll be back."

"There's a key under the third flower pot to the right."

"Okay." Gina touched her roommate's arm. "Thanks for everything."

Still lost in her own thoughts, Josee said, "Far as this girl's concerned, Sarge knows where to find me when he's ready to try again. One knee? He better get down on both knees next time. Yeah, we'll see if that actually happens."

Gina almost said, "*Make* it happen," then decided not to meddle. She'd been in this house for less than a day and had enough challenges of her own.

With the gallery's business ready to commence, the electric eye chirped as someone came through the front door. One peek down the corridor verified Nikki Lazarescu's arrival.

"Be right there, Mom."

Gina stepped back out of view, sent up a prayer for patience and strength, then marched into the new day.

CHAPTER
SEVEN

Cascade Mountains

Natira came to his senses on a pebbly spit fifty yards downriver. The sun was a yellow-white lance, stabbing unhindered at his vision, by which he guessed a good hour had passed. What had happened? How had he—

Oh yes. The dive from high above . . . the freefall . . .

Bit by bit, it was all coming back.

To his credit, he had vaulted clear of the sloping precipice and hit his frothy white target. What a sight he must've been. Five feet less and he would have been dashed upon the crags. Received instead by the water's more merciful arms, he'd been pummeled by icy fists that broke his ribs and clavicle, tore flesh from his forehead, and ripped one leg from its socket so that it hung leaden in the current.

With the wind prying at his lips during the fall, he had struck the river's surface with mouth open, and the pressure had exploded through his nasal cavities before finding release by blowing his left eyeball from its socket. It remained tethered by the optic nerve, flopping about like a hooked squid.

The agony, thankfully, was short-lived. His human host had gone into shock, a wonderful reprieve from the worst of physical sensations— oh, but the Almighty had thought of everything with His creation—and the cold current turned him blue and numb.

Useless as a rag doll, Natira had dipped, bobbed, plunged, gone under, and careened into a submerged boulder. He'd resurfaced, tried to grasp hold of something, anything.

Gone under again.

Brushed against logs, then smooth metal—*the Nissan?*

Gotten flipped around and rammed headfirst into pitiless granite.

Somehow he'd made it to shallow water.

Now, in the aftermath of his drastic decision, the Collector congratulated himself on a favorable outcome. He was in pain, no doubt about it, yet nothing he hadn't endured before. He was a warrior. He was undead. The main risk had been getting washed far away or dismembered in such a manner that it would take more than a day or two to regroup. Instead, he had only the inconvenience of pulling himself back together, and he'd saved himself some time by making the precarious descent.

He braced one hand on the pebbles and pushed himself into a sitting position. Broken ribs raked at his lungs, provoking a gasp. The intake of air intensified his discomfort, and he switched to short, shallow breaths. With his free hand, he worked the sagging eyeball back into place, then, accompanied by the sounds of grinding cartilage and sinew, repositioned his dislocated leg.

Everything back in place? Ah yes.

"I cannot be vanquished," he shouted at the sky.

Drawn by movement, he spotted a county sheriff at the outcropping high above. The man had both hands on his hips, face hidden by his hat's wide brim. The McKenzie's roar drowned out anything he might be trying to say.

The Collector stood to his feet. "Do you like what you see?" he gibed. "You won't be able to get to me down here, not for a long while."

Upriver, the white water roiled, daring Natira to come hunt for his prey.

"If you're there, Gina, I'll find you."

He clambered over the rocks until he was in line with the compromised railing far above. This, he guessed, was about where the car would've landed. His eyes probed the surface, hoping for a glimpse of the smooth metal he had felt. Down there, somewhere, the Nissan hid from him.

He tore a broken limb from a tangle of logs and stabbed it into the water, trying different angles but striking only liquid. He thrust the branch farther out, letting go with one hand to gain distance, then dragging it back before the current could steal it from him.

Still nothing.

A melee of boulders the size of small houses herded the river over a six-foot drop. Perhaps the car had rolled over the edge and been carried past the falls into the smoother section where water glimmered emerald green.

Up along the highway, the sheriff had been replaced by a pair of state troopers. Natira ignored their gesturing. He gathered ten large rocks from the muddy bank, plucking and piling them at his feet, then waded into the water and began tossing one after the other into the suspected zone.

Ker-plooshhh . . . ker-plooshhh . . .

By the ninth, he was pondering his next course of action.

Ker-thudddd!

He aimed the last rock at the same vicinity and once again heard the metallic thud. Without hesitation, he pushed deeper into the angry current. He had to do this, had to know if Gina was in there.

And if she wasn't?

Well, who better than he to go back on the prowl?

En route to Washington State

Rigid in the Acura's driver's seat, Nikki felt no need to create idle chatter or justify her methods with Jacob. Although her daughter made a few half-hearted attempts at conversation, Nikki rebutted them with silence and Gina finally gave up and stared off at the passing fields.

Nikki stopped once to fill the tank. She thought of buying two coffees while inside the station, then decided against it for fear of spillage in the car.

"How much farther?" Gina asked upon her return.

"We're headed north of Seattle. You still have time for a nap, dear."

"Not tired."

"Will you be hungry for lunch? I know a quiet place in Tacoma."

"I, uh, don't exactly have any cash at the moment."

"How ever did you take care of your adoptee? Kenny, was it?"

"I have a . . . I had a job, Mom. It's not like I was mooching off Dad, thank you very much. Paid my rent, utilities, all that stuff. Now that I'm 'dead,' though, I can't be taking money out at the ATM, can I? And Dad told me not to withdraw any large amounts over the last couple of days. Said it would make the accident seem suspicious."

"That explains his request, then."

Gina cocked an eyebrow.

"Look in the glove compartment, if you will." Nikki patted her leg. "Yes, the envelope. See it there?"

"This has money in it."

"Cal suggested five hundred dollars. He thought that your working at the gallery would serve as a helpful diversion and good use of your time, but that you'd need something to cover this gap between paychecks."

"There's . . ." Gina thumbed through the envelope. "There's a thousand in here."

"Five hundred seemed conservative, don't you agree? Men don't understand the cost of good hygiene and maintenance, and you can't go about in those sort of clothes. You're a woman, no matter how young you look. Faded jeans, studded belts, and hooded sweatshirts are hardly becoming attire."

"They're Josee's. I like them."

"Shush. Take the money and buy yourself something suitable."

"I don't want your money, not with strings attached."

Nikki marveled that God would gift this child with half-immortal genes and still saddle her with a lack of good sense. Where was the justice? If Gina lived on for centuries, would she populate the earth with tribes of the frumpy and forlorn?

As though reading Nikki's mind, Gina said, "I'm not trying to be disrespectful, Mom, but there are more important things, you know?"

"Well, I believe there's something to be said for good first impressions."

"The U.S. of Fake-It-Till-You-Make-It A."

"Pardon me?"

"It'll all come crumbling down, just watch. Aren't you the one who taught me to work my fingers to the bone? What happened to no frills and no extravagances?"

"Dear, don't you think you're overreacting?" Nikki coughed, pausing as agony wrenched through her lower back. "I've gifted you with some money—a generous amount, mind you, which is my pleasure to do—and all I'm asking is that my daughter find something nice to wear. Is that so terrible?"

"Okay, you're right. I'm sorry."

"As you should be."

"But, of all people, you should understand the danger in pretenses. I mean, given the right host, a Collector could come waltzing in in the latest fashions while holding a knife behind her back."

"Honestly, how often does that happen?"

Gina muttered an unintelligible response.

"Speak clearly, please, if you have something to add."

"When I was a kid," Gina said, "it seemed to happen on a regular basis."

"Ahh. That's what you're driving at, is it? Please understand, I was meaning to protect you."

In the passenger seat, Gina tugged at her pant leg and drew the bronze-handled dagger from its sheath. The blade flashed in the daylight, nicked by past encounters yet honed to a lethal tip, which she touched to her neck, to a patch of puckered skin.

"This scar," she said, "was my own fault."

"You cut yourself, Gina?"

"No, it's where my anger against you took root. That's the thing, though—I don't want to pass that on to Jacob. I want him to know forgiveness and love."

"As do I." Nikki shifted in her seat. "Naturally."

"Can we work at this together, then? You and me as a team, Mom, without getting caught up in all the petty issues. Please. For Jacob's sake."

"Certainly, angel. A team. Why would you expect anything less?"

Cascade Mountains

Natira dove upstream with outstretched arms and kicked with all his force. He sliced beneath the surface, lost in a frozen, bubbling cauldron, and then the blast of the falls shoved him toward relative calm where his shoulder struck something curved and polished. He latched onto a metal lip with his fingers and let his head bob up for air.

Do it now, Natira. If you wait, you'll lose your grip.

He went under, feeling along till he touched glass. The rapids dispersed and writhed around his huge back, while the water in front of him met a moment of peace.

He pressed his face to the side window and peered inside. The car, he realized, was turned upside down, with the driver's door torn away during the tumble, the front windscreen reduced to a few fragments, and the seatbelt flapping as though waving farewell.

A normal human could never have survived that fall. Had Gina's corpse been swept downriver?

Then again, she was not normal, was she?

Natira's grip was loosening. He porpoised up for another breath, then clawed down along the undercarriage and curled through the driver's doorway. Spikes of lumber were lodged in the upholstery. All around, the river raged like a concrete mixer, but the cockpit was angled so that a pool of stillness resided there. Using this to his advantage, he ignored his screaming lungs, the sharp pangs in his ribs, and focused on this search for evidence.

A river eel slid past his leg, sparking primal panic in Natira's human host. Eyes wide, he recoiled and kicked at the thing, spinning onto his back as he did so. Overhead, a small purse twisted, hung up on the brake.

Well, well. He yanked it free and exited with his prize.

Once on shore, he shook out house keys, a driver's license, an ATM card, library card, Burt's Bees Beeswax Lip Balm, soggy sticks of gum, a smudged brochure for some women's church retreat, and a cell phone with a cracked display.

Not exactly irrefutable proof of her demise, but it was a start.

With the purse slung over his shoulder, he strode along the bank. He didn't care what any spectators above might think about his fearless river dives or naked strolls. Let them stare.

He moved around the bend, scrutinizing both sides of the McKenzie. Of course, Gina could be anywhere. There were numerous cases where bodies had been trapped beneath overhangs, pinned beneath boulders by an undertow, or ensnared in logs and debris.

That last one brought a crooked smile to his face.

Hadn't he watched Cal Nichols' son die that way?

Yes, he'd drained the boy dry and left him there amongst the tangled branches while he and Cal wrestled in the water.

Perhaps this whole river scenario was a sign, the sort of coincidence the Master Collector gloried in. The more Natira considered it, the more convinced he became. Parallel tragedies for the not-so-immortal-after-all twins.

Good-bye, Reginald. Bye-bye, Regina.

Master, let it be so. And if it's your will, may my own son be found.

To guard against any subterfuge, Natira climbed onto a forested promontory that offered clear views up and down the river. No doubt he would have a ticket at the rental car by the time he climbed out of this canyon, but that was the least of his concerns. With forty hours or so left in this vigil, his goal was to ensure that nobody came to rescue and revive a female corpse.

And if Cal did show up, he'd be greeted with another cold-water tussle.

CHAPTER
EIGHT

Disturbing, that's what it was. Wrong in so many ways.

Outfitted as a county sheriff, Cal Nichols had hazarded a short visit to the cliff's edge, where he was assaulted by the sight of a bare and bloodied Natira. The fiend even had the gall to wave, standing exposed on the river-bank. If Tolkien, by the creative magic of his pen, had planted Gollum's head on the body of an orc, the result might've been something like the goliathan creature in the chasm below. Or maybe if he'd used an orc's head to top off a goblin. Or if—

Nah, don't do this. Don't even go there.

To muddy Tolkien's name in such a manner was a disgrace.

"You're the ugly undead, that's all you are," Nickel said, turning away.

He waved along an SUV, tipped his wide-brimmed hat, then scurried across the highway. Using the forest as cover, he started down the mountain. He'd worn this uniform before—came in handy in these parts—yet out of respect for the badge he tried to keep the deceptions with it to a minimum.

So, as expected, one of the Akeldama Collectors had come to the scene of Kate Preston's/Gina Lazarescu's tragic end.

Why Natira, though?

This über-Collector, this apex killer, had wiped out Reggie, and it seemed he personally wanted to make certain Reggie's sister was also dead.

The good news: Gina was safe. Thirty-plus hours ago, Nickel had sent her from this very spot to meet her mom. By now, she'd be situated in Corvallis, and—if Sarge didn't blow it—Gina and Josee would soon be in-laws.

More good news: Kenny Preston was also safe. Hidden in Nickel's wooded ranch only miles down this same McKenzie River, Kenny now wore the letter Tav on his brow. At thirteen years of age, he'd joined Dov Amit and the other Concealed Ones in shouldering this globe's darkness. That burden was his own to bear, but in the days ahead Kenny would be assisted by Clay Ryker.

Nickel liked Kenny. For the past few years, he'd played the role of an uncle to the kid, instructing him in water survival skills, weaponry, knowledge of the Nazarene Blood, the Holy Scriptures, and the wielding of MTPs—metal tent pegs, those symbolic stakes of old that could banish a Collector for good.

This was what Nickel did. What else was there?

For millennia he had ached for the loss of his wife, and, as he'd explained to Gina, he had later violated his commission to the Nazarene and entered the bed of a mortal woman, Nikki Lazarescu. On his own merits, he could never earn back forgiveness, yet he could set straight the things he had bent and broken. No longer susceptible to the grave, he lived to mentor humble young men for a place among the Nistarim. There were thirty-six of them—in Hebrew, *Lamed Vov*—who girded up weary mankind.

And, at some point, Nickel would gain his release. Even as Enoch and Elijah had been swept up into the heavens, never tasting of the grave, so too he would say good-bye to this spinning earth and find atonement—his "at-one-ment"—with the Nazarene.

He kept walking downhill, slipping between waist-high ferns and dodging sap-sticky branches. He would reach his ranch in less than ninety minutes, and he'd have forty hours or so before Natira concluded his reconnaissance of the river. Without a corpse to latch hold of, the Collector would stay to watch in case someone tried to dredge up and steal away a body.

The bad news: There was no body.

And that meant Natira would come hunting for answers.

Nickel kicked at a toadstool on the forest floor, watched its top spin toward a huckleberry bush. There had to be a way of convincing his enemy of Gina's death, thus diverting attention a few more months, years. How, though?

His next kick found rainwater pooled beneath damp leaves and shot rust-colored droplets into the air.

Droplets . . .

That gave him an idea.

He reached into his shirt pocket, grinning as his fingers found the folded map there. Marked by four separate drops of blood, its most recent stain had come from Gina yesterday morning before they climbed into the Nissan—her small offering for the future preparation of her son.

Nickel veered back toward the highway and the coursing river below.

He was Cal, wasn't he? In Romanian, the "knight."

If this moment were being played upon a chessboard, Adolf Anderssen, that swashbuckling grandmaster of old, would've been first to suggest a stealthy knight maneuver. Yes, this was the time for a bit of misdirection.

Bellingham, Washington

"I typically use private charters," Nikki said as she led Gina along the docks that poked into Bellingham Bay. "Less likelihood of being tracked that way."

Before them, yachts and sailboats filled the waters of Squalicum Harbor, with moorings and ropes creaking, masts swaying in the summer breeze. Nikki sniffed at the salt in the air. She knew this place well. Shifting her day bag from one hand to the other, she pointed out Orcas Island, visible beyond smaller, lesser known islets.

"In the future, dear, we ought to spend a night over on Orcas."

"What for?"

"A bit of team bonding," Nikki suggested with a half grin. "The islands can seem so secluded and quaint."

"Is this where you're hiding Jacob? Somewhere in Puget Sound?"

"Technically, Puget Sound's south of here—a common mistake. As for your question: yes, he's close by, but I'm not the one hiding him."

"Who's watching after him, then? Who feeds him?"

"That, I'll admit, remains somewhat of a mystery to me as well."

"You don't know? Are we even sure this mysterious nanny is on our side?"

"I do know the Unfallen play a part, though your father's coordinated that aspect of things and insisted I maintain my distance." Nikki sympathized with her daughter's worries and decided to dispel some of them with a cheerful addendum. "From what I've observed, Jacob's very resourceful. Some days he goes out on the rocks with the fishing pole I sent him, and I'm told he also barters with the neighbors. Being around adults primarily, he's turned into quite the mature little guy."

"He's all alone in a house, though?"

Nikki sighed. "It'll be best to see with your own eyes. Come, now, let's enjoy the sunshine and these spectacular vistas while we wait."

Gina seemed oblivious to the surrounding beauty—snowcapped Mt. Baker to the east, the sun-dappled bay, and conifers guarding the Indian reservation's shore to the north. "Where's this skipper of ours? Doesn't he want to get paid?"

"It's island time," Nikki said. "Everything's much slower."

"Great."

"Perhaps we should have a light meal before going."

"We ate in Tacoma, Mom. I've been waiting seven years for this."

Nikki held up a restraining hand. She wasn't sure how much longer she would have on this earth, and it was best to prepare her daughter for that eventuality. "When we're visiting this area, it's wise not to draw attention. I like to present myself as simply one more tourist investing in the local economy. I don't complain. I pay up front, in cash. I don't over tip. Don't flirt. As far as anyone else is concerned, I come to view the killer whales, the San Juans, and snap a few pictures along the way."

"Tourists. Okay, I got it. Now when's the tour?"

"Here, maybe this is our man."

A gruff-looking fellow meandered toward them, his legs bowed, shoulders hunched, red hair coiling from beneath a Mariners baseball cap. He squinted, raised an arm dotted with freckles, and said, "You them two ladies that called? Well, whatcha waitin' for? The boat's there, just like you seen in the picture."

Nikki saw no reason to be rude in return. "Good afternoon, sir."

"Skipper. Call me that and we'll get along just fine."

"Listen, Skipper," Gina cut in as Nikki handed the man his money. "We're already an hour late, and we need to get moving before the sun sets."

He counted the bills in a leisurely manner, then swiveled his head on a leathery neck. "Sun's been settin' since it passed high noon, missy. I'll getcha where you're going, and you'll see all you need to see. Hear me and hear me well, though—this is my boat, my time, and I run this operation as I see fit. I don't go falling outta bed just 'cause someone calls for a ride out. Truth be told, I don't fall for much at all."

"You're . . ." Gina stepped toward him. "Are you Unfallen?"

"Ain't sayin' one way or another. You can think what you like."

"You are, aren't you?"

"We gonna stand here all day flappin' our gums, or we gonna go sailing?"

"Sailing."

"Wherever the wind may blow."

"As long as it blows by Lummi Island," Nikki said, "we'll be happy."

CHAPTER
NINE

Cascade Mountains

The *whuppp-whuppp-whuppp* of a police helicopter alerted Natira a full minute before its appearance at the mouth of the canyon.

He hunkered beneath thick foliage as the machine swooped along the river, no doubt alerted by the passing driver who'd watched him vault from the cliff, and by the sheriff who'd first appeared on the scene. Although the response was not as quick as what he had seen from Israeli forces, it was quicker than in many parts of the world.

And all for Natira's sake? He was a silly two-legger, far as they knew.

What was it with these humans and their misguided valuations of life? Didn't they recognize their own filth, their wretched indulgences and endless narcissism? Even their good moments were nothing more than self-promotion in the guise of heroism.

One day, he knew, Final Vengeance would be their just punishment—chaos, destruction, and the Collectors' plundering of bodies and souls.

Of course, the Almighty had a different Final Vengeance in mind, and humans seemed to think they would escape into His arms of undeserved love.

Not likely.

Whuppp . . . whuppp . . .

The helicopter made a return sweep, moving slower this time. In the cockpit, officials surveyed the terrain for an injured man on foot or for a woman's body coughed up by the surly current.

Natira wanted to stand and flash his old battle scars, taunting the helicopter crew with a shake of his hand. It would give them a story to tell their families, a little something to scare the kiddies. He decided against it since it would result in a larger search party, a distraction from his real purpose.

The whirlybird vanished after a fifth pass, leaving heat contrails in its wake. No doubt it would be back, though for the time being he was free to roam again.

Flinging Gina's purse aside, the Collector stretched and stepped out onto the promontory. He'd studied the driver's license belonging to Kate Preston, memorizing the shape of her face and the waves of her thick brown hair. Overall, an attractive specimen. One he would enjoy taking apart.

From below, a smudge of crimson caught his attention.

Blood?

A whiff in the air confirmed his suspicion.

How had he missed that? Faint as the mark was, his trained eyes should've noted it earlier. Perhaps shadows had shifted during the copter's visit, exposing the stained rock slab.

He blinked against the afternoon sun and locked the location in his mind. Cautious, he stayed low as he inched past spruce and fir trees toward the boulders along the bank. The coppery scent tugged at his nostrils as he neared. Thirst rose in his gullet, a coiling serpent that sucked moisture from his esophagus and peeled his lips back in a sneer.

Oh, he was parched.

That cloying smell called out to him from the slab, then turned stale beneath the unforgiving sun. He hesitated.

Don't tease me. Drink, you fool. Drink.

Running his eyes up and down the canyon, he darted into the open and kneeled before the granite slab. His entire being came to attention as the bloodstain melted on the tip of his tongue. It was richer than expected, thick and satisfying. Although a miniscule amount, nothing to slake his thirst, it gave him the proof he had been seeking.

Gina Lazarescu . . . Ah yes, she'd been here, her body probably dashed against this stone as it tumbled along in the current.

Natira siphoned from the sweet droplet an assortment of her memories: marriage and motherhood, a raven-haired older woman, a lifeless child in an incubator, trips in and out of Romania, orphanages, a fight with a werewolf, and—

Nazarene Blood!

She'd ingested the awful stuff? By her own Power of Choice?

Natira's moment of calm passed, and that lonesome red drop raked like a hot coal over his taste buds, boiling with blameless poison.

The helicopter's beating rotors had provided Nickel the opportunity he needed. He knew his foe would stay low to avoid detection, and Nickel used that to his advantage.

With death no concern of his, he'd descended the hillside with economical movements while soaring evergreens formed a concealing curtain. Yes, that had led to a few tense seconds on the riverbank—wiping, smearing—but then he was back among the trees, tucking the map in his pocket and making his way up the slope again.

In the silence of the copter's departure, he crawled belly first up onto the vantage point. He shifted and caught a glimpse of Natira's back and thick neck.

Those Who Hunt had taken the bait.

No, no, nooo, noooo, NOOOOOOOO!

Why hadn't he heeded that warning whiff? This Nazarene Blood was death to Natira. What did it matter if he had confirmed Gina's expiration date? For this scrap of info, he was about to be banished to the Restless

Desert, where blinding sandstorms and blistering heat were only foreshadows of the hell to come.

With pinkie and thumb working like tongs, he yanked the tip of his tongue out over his lips. His left hand searched for something sharp, found a shard of shale, and in one unrelenting motion sliced away the contamination.

"Aaarr*gghhh!*"

He spit the rubbery piece into the McKenzie and watched it bob away. He spit again, expelling the blood and saliva and that ghastly aftertaste. Crouching at the shore, he rinsed his face and winced at the all-too-human throbs of pain.

Never mind any of that. He had survived.

Which was more than could be said for those twins, Reggie and Regina.

It was true that he'd found none of yesterday's memories in Gina's blood, yet it wasn't uncommon for violent head trauma to jar those last few hours loose. Coma victims often experienced it. So did fighters knocked out during boxing matches. As a precaution, he would wait here until the three-day window closed; he would trudge these banks to be sure no female corpses washed up. And, before closing the matter for good, he would speak with the local eyewitness, the Collector named Asgoth.

Was speaking even an option, though?

Natira tested his swollen tongue, heard syllables rumble like chunks of gravel. Saliva and blood misted the air in front of his face. He slipped back into the greenery along the river, determined to retrain his speech patterns during this overnight vigil.

And there was one other loose end.

This Nikki Lazarescu lady . . . If she still lurked there in Gina's memories, she might also lurk once more in Cal Nichols' arms. Imagine the nuisance that could create: another batch of half-immortals.

One good thing was that Nikki had never joined Those Who Resist.

For that I bow in thanks.

Very soon Natira would be ready to flush this seared taste from his mouth with an impure burst from her regular veins. At the thought, thirst rose in his throat. Already he could taste Nikki's blood.

CHAPTER
TEN

San Juan Islands, Washington

The monster gleamed as it broke the surface a hundred feet off their bow. It lifted into the air, water streaming from its fins, then landed on its side, flashing black and white amidst a cascade of silver spray. Gina had never seen such a beast in the wild and was surprised by its natural power and grace.

"Isn't he marvelous?" Nikki gushed.

"Why're they called killer whales?" Gina asked, thinking, *This better not be some kind of bad omen.*

From the yacht's helm, the skipper replied, "Orcas, not killers. Ain't nothing wrong with one o' God's creatures trying to scrounge up a meal. See them reef fishermen up ahead, anchored in Legoe Bay? With them scaring the salmon this direction, you can't blame an Orca for takin' advantage."

The Orca breached again, off their starboard this time. He seemed to wink at Gina before diving with a scaly meal between his teeth.

"That's Lummi Island?" she said.

"What little there is of it. Nine miles long, two miles wide." The skipper pointed. "Some call 'er the forgotten island. From that outcroppin' on down, there's nothing but cliffs and woods, some eagles and deer. Up yonder's where most o' the people live."

Gina saw five cyclists winding along the contours of the bay—three men, a red-headed teenager, and a young boy with tan skin and dark hair.

Jacob?

Heart jolting at the possibility, she stepped past a sealed hatch toward her mother's position at the rail. Nikki was seated, one foot pulled up to her chest, the other toeing the water. Gina said, "You have those binoculars?"

"Sit here." Nikki patted the deck. "Watch that rope above your head."

Gina crouched and accepted the compact field glasses from her mother's purse. Despite their size, the magnification was strong, pulling Gina's eyes to bayside shanties, buoys, and brightly painted homes. She dialed in, dialed out, till she could see the bikes churning along. The smallest rider was standing on the pedals to keep up with the others.

She knew in her gut he was not her son.

"We close yet, Mom?"

"Just around this point the road starts climbing again. That's West Shore Drive, and you'll see a house that appears abandoned."

Gina panned the rocky beach, the grassy slopes, piles of driftwood, and sticker-bush patches. Would she spot Jacob playing in a front yard? If she waved, would he see her? Would he know intuitively, inexplicably, it was her?

"A bald eagle," the skipper noted from behind the wheel, his voice muted by the wind that snapped in the mainsail and raked the strait's blue waters.

Gina paid no attention.

There was the abandoned house, as Nikki had said. With sagging eaves and an overgrown yard, the structure stood in relative privacy behind a wooden fence. It had two floors, though neither looked occupied. In fact, if Gina were to guess, she would have said the place was unsafe for human habitation.

Home to her long-lost son? The idea seemed insulting. It was difficult enough surrendering her adopted son to Nickel and Clay Ryker's care, but thinking of Jacob stuck in this hovel was unfathomable.

"It's not as bad as it looks," Nikki said.

"It looks pretty bad."

"The better for Jacob to remain hidden. That's our paramount concern."

"You sure he's in there? How come none of these islanders have noticed a little kid camped in such a dump?"

"Gina," the skipper called out, "you think I'm the only one o' of my kind in these parts? There's others just like me, watchin' over your boy as if he were the Almighty's very own. Aren't we all, when it comes down to it? Aren't we all?"

"You've been guarding him?"

"A bit here and there."

"Just as I told you," Nikki said.

Gina's mind raced through her knowledge of the Unfallen. They were guardians and messengers, often unobtrusive and unseen. Whereas their counterparts had joined the Master Collector in his mutiny against the heavens, the Unfallen had remained loyal and true. They were immune to the Separation. They did not require hosts for their operations in the physical realm, and they explored the spiritual with even greater liberty.

Back in J.C., Gina had met such a being—a white-haired old woman and her dog. Gina suspected she had unwittingly crossed paths with even more.

Ones such as this freckled, leathery skipper.

She adjusted the lenses, sharpening not only their focus but her half-immortal sight. Had her first bridging experience opened her eyes to another realm? Already, she was able to see the letter Tav when others could not and had identified that mark on her own forehead as she entered womanhood and her role as Jacob's mother. With a little effort, she might spot these heavenly forces marshaled to her son's defense.

"What do you see?" Nikki said. "Is my grandson there?"

Gina grunted, still skeptical of this entire scenario. She pressed her brows against the binoculars' rubber seals to shut out distracting light.

Her doubts crumbled at the sight of the Unfallen on duty.

Three of them.

Cloaked to mortal sight, one was perched atop the house, his stature relaxed yet attentive. The ocean breeze moved around him, blurring his outline while having no effect on his footing.

The second was also cloaked, marching the fence's inner perimeter, bouncing her hand upon the pointed staves but sometimes moving through them—and thus revealing the abstract nature of her form.

The third sported a green T-shirt, knee-length shorts, crew socks, and a pair of green-and-black Nike Airs. His shoulders rolled as he walked, while locks of golden hair swayed on either side of his aquiline nose and high forehead. He lifted a hand at the passing bicyclists and they waved back.

Was he Unfallen *and* uncloaked?

Gina saw Mr. Goldilocks salute the female guard before entering the yard by the narrow gate; she saluted back, two fingers crossed and touched to her forehead.

Okay, well, that answered the question.

Goldilocks loped up the path into the dark interior of the house. Fifteen seconds ticked by. On the roof and in the yard, the cloaked individuals stiffened and surveyed their environs, as though anticipating an enemy salvo.

"What do *you* see?" Gina said, holding the binoculars to her mom's eyes.

"I . . . Well, I see the house, of course, but there's no movement."

"You sure? Nothing in the, uh . . . the front?"

"Nothing yet."

This confirmed Gina's belief that Nikki had no vision for things beyond the tangible. Gina alone had that ability; she'd bridged yesterday with her entire body, and today she was bridging with her vision.

A shadow appeared in the front doorway, joined by a second.

Goldilocks? Yes. In his shorts and green T-shirt.

And . . .

C'mon out, Gina urged. *Let me see you, little man.*

"Is he there? Oh, I hope so," Nikki said.

Jacob!

Twin fists squeezed the air from Gina's lungs. Unable to speak even if she had wanted to, she felt tears stream down her cheeks and off her lips.

"Isn't he lovely?" Nikki said.

Gina nodded. "He's there. He's right there."

Her mother touched the binoculars, hoping for a turn, but Gina wanted to memorize every detail of her son's appearance—each wave of his brown hair; the sparkle of irises blue and wistful as his father's, yet speckled with gold; the puncture scars that dotted his forehead and face and slipped down his neck. He looked thin but healthy. He was wearing a tank top, jeans, and Converse tennis shoes. At nearly seven years old, he already reflected Jed's skinny frame and Gina's fine cheekbones.

Her son. Their son. A precious blend of the two.

The world teetered and she almost tumbled overboard, saved by a strong hand that clamped upon her arm.

"Thank you, Skipper," she managed to say.

"Doin' my job's all."

Two hundred yards out, the yacht was drawing even with the beach and strip of black asphalt that fronted the house.

Nikki grabbed away the binoculars. "Oh," she exclaimed, "I'm so glad. That man in the shorts, he's the one who's been delivering my bundles of clothing, books, and whatnot."

"Goldilocks, you mean?"

The skipper guffawed at that, thumping Gina on the back.

"Does he live there?" she said.

"Don't be foolish. Our kind don't keep homes upon this earth." The skipper made an adjustment to the wheel. "'Goldilocks'? Aye, that fits him. Every fortnight or so, he takes o'er your mom's packages and checks that things're as they oughta be."

"Unfallen or otherwise," Nikki said, "he's been a dear man."

Gina eased the binoculars from her mom and locked on to her son's form.

I'm here for you, little Jacob. Do you feel my presence?

"The islanders," Nikki was explaining, "believe he's Jacob's older sibling—two brothers left on their own by a tragic accident. The story's made that much more credible by the questions it leaves unanswered. Lummi is its own insular environment, and few neighbors meddle. They're curious, certainly, but the more they pry, the more likely their own secrets will be revealed. That's not something most are willing to risk."

"As for them guards?" The skipper leaned into Gina, his words low enough that only she could hear. "They take shifts, coming and going as directed. You got no reason to worry, you hear me? Sunup to sunup, there's always someone watchin'. Always."

"Does anyone else know he's here, besides the locals?"

"My people, you, and your mother . . . That 'bout does it."

Gina watched Goldilocks and Jacob turn toward each other at the wooden gate. The man patted her son on the arm before his departure, and Jacob wore a crestfallen look. His was a face of sorrow that no child should have to endure.

She remembered his suffering even in the womb.

Signs of his future among the Nistarim.

Without saying a word, Nikki Lazarescu slipped a hand into Gina's. They sat, mother and daughter, with the sun flaming out behind Orcas Island at their backs. The gap broadened between them and the shore, but they kept watching, their patience rewarded when Jacob wandered across the road and hopped down a slope to the rock-strewn beach. His fishing pole bounced in his hand.

Gina whispered, "I want to yell his name so bad that it hurts."

"He wouldn't know it anyway."

"Wouldn't know his own name? Oh, right," she huffed. "For his protection."

"A friendly wave might be in order, though."

"Really?"

"It's not unusual when a boat's drifting by. Go on, dear."

Gina wanted to jump to both feet and wave both arms, wanted to scream at the top of her lungs. She wanted to dive into the strait and swim to her little man, yet that would only intensify the danger for both of them. Instead, she lifted one hand in the most casual of greetings. Jacob shaded his eyes against the fiery sunset and waved back to the friendly strangers on the boat, his long fingers paddling at the air.

"I love you," she whispered.

On shore, Jacob returned to the task of rigging his pole.

Nikki patted Gina's leg. "One day you'll get to tell him in person, but until then, no rash actions. That's imperative. To this point, he's remained safe from Collector detection, and the Nistarim believe he will be vital in years to come."

"Assuming he receives the Letter."

"In their minds, that's not up for debate. In '71, when the Thirty-Six came together in Portland—the first joint session in centuries, mind you—their leader made an unprecedented appearance and stated that, despite your father's loss of his own Letter, countless lives would be saved through his offspring."

"Reggie, you mean? And me?"

"Time and circumstance have narrowed that list, haven't they? You remain. As does your biological son, with his share of immortal blood."

Briny spray rose from the bow and spritzed Gina's face. "And this leader"—she licked her lips—"has he been wrong before?"

"Who am I to say, dear? I'm quite certain, however, that you would trust His every word. He's the one you call the Nazarene."

The island was slipping away. Atop the fading house, the Unfallen guard shone like a tongue of fire in the late afternoon sky; from the helm, the skipper claimed he knew a good spot for crab cocktails back at Squalicum Harbor; and on the beach, serene and solitary, her firstborn stood reeling in a meal of his own.

Gina smiled. At least he was healthy and whole.

"Darling, are you ready for what lies ahead?"

"I'd like to think so." She leaned into her mother, resting her head on her shoulder. "How 'bout you?"

"Hmm." As Nikki brooded over the question, her hair flapped in the breeze and brushed like black feathers across her face. "We never really know, do we? Sometimes only after it's too late."

"Well, thank you, Mom. And on that downer note . . ."

"An old woman's thoughts, nothing more. Let's go enjoy some crab cocktails, shall we?"

"You're not old. Please, stop talking that way."

"I'm mortal."

"I don't want to think about that."

"You're right." Nikki pressed her lips to Gina's temple. "It's not fair of me to put a damper on this special day."

CHAPTER
ELEVEN

Late August—Pasadena, California

Natira's vigil along the McKenzie was over. His thigh was still sore, his ribs mending, his tongue a bloated black mess, but he was convinced Cal Nichols' daughter was gone, and that left only Nikki to deal with.

As for Cal? Let the man stew in his grief.

Behind the wheel of a rented black Mustang convertible, Natira wore sunglasses as he coasted through Pasadena's suburbs, admiring rows of palm trees, stucco houses, and the foothills north of the city. He'd culled details from the Consortium, Internet, and cable TV, and wished to meet in person the eye-catching, middle-aged woman who resided within miles of the studio from which her show was televised.

N. K. Lazarescu . . . self-help guru, host of *Beyond the Stars*.

She taught her "life students" to bleed away their failures and visualize dreams becoming reality. Some called it New Age, although as far as Natira was concerned there was nothing new about it.

N. K. was Nikki was Nicoleta. Decades ago, Nicoleta had lived in Romania under the family name Murgoci. In 1989, she and her daughter fled to America, changing the name to Lazarescu—an unoriginal nod at the new life they hoped to lead. It would've worked, if not for Erota's keen eyes and determination.

Gina was tracked down in Chattanooga. Her baby was killed.

Oh, the pain, the pathos.

In the years since, Nikki and Gina had barely spoken, and the local Collectors' observations of the older woman had turned up nothing useful. She was a guilt-tortured windbag with empty slogans to sell.

Natira nosed the Mustang into a cul-de-sac and tilted his sunglasses for a better view of the address on the left. Yes, indeed, this was it.

A red-tiled roof capped the single-story dwelling. Three orange-laden trees lined the driveway, and a small fountain bubbled in the center of a lawn no larger than a Persian rug. Stickers in the windows warned of an alarm system while security cameras eyed the perimeters.

Fakes? There was no reason to take a chance just yet.

Without slowing, he continued his sweep and exited the cul-de-sac. He parked a half block away, his rearview mirror angled for a view, and settled in for another wait.

Two hours passed. He reclined in the driver's seat, made an adjustment to the mirror, and pressed his tongue stump to the roof of his mouth. He had learned patience for this sort of thing since his rise from a bomb-gutted Pisan cemetery in 1944. He'd hunted down the majority of the Concealed Ones, shadowed them across countries and continents, marked their locations, and anticipated their grisly ends. One day he would strike, but until then he tried to limit his aggressive nature.

Which made this afternoon a special treat. A bone to gnaw on.

The thought caused his stomach to grumble, a reminder that his undead host still labored under human tendencies. The flight crew from PDX to LAX had provided a light lunch, hardly satisfactory for a child's belly, not to mention a beast of his size.

Come to me, sweet Nikki. Let me bleed away your failures.

She was one of history's biggest failures. With only thirty-six Concealed Ones on a planet of billions, she had managed single-handedly to find and tear down one of them, threatening the safety of mankind. She just couldn't keep her legs together, could she? Couldn't keep her lovely hands to herself.

Once Natira was done exploiting her desire for love, he would put her out of her misery once and for all.

Patience, though. Patience. This could take—

There she was.

In the mirror, the Collector watched a woman with pink-glossed lips and black hair come straight at him in an Acura NSX. She had a cell phone pressed to her ear. The moment she turned into the cul-de-sac, the tinted windows blocked her from view and her car slipped out of sight.

He gave himself a self-congratulatory grin, pushed his shades up his nose, and stepped out onto hot pavement. This would be fun.

Corvallis

Gina's worldview had shifted on its axis. She felt shallow because of this, so easily swayed, yet her cynical mind couldn't deny the effects of the past few days. She and Jacob had waved at each other across the waters; she and Nikki had sat side by side on a yacht, shoulders touching, feet splashing in the Pacific; and in the nearby mountains, she and Nickel had explored realms beyond the Separation, bridging an escape from her undead foes.

Collectors . . . Tainted by the Betrayer's enmity, they had emerged from the Field of Blood and even now gathered strength at the Haunt of Jackals.

None of that mattered to her. Jacob was alive.

She spent the next week gathering a care package—clothes, home-made goodies, books—that Goldilocks could deliver to him. She'd make another trip on Monday. Sure, she would exercise restraint, but if it weren't for her father's stipulations she'd be camping out there every hour of every day.

Pasadena

Nikki Lazarescu was a survivor.

She had endured her son's murder, an oppressive regime under Romanian Nicolae Ceausescu, the burden of her own mistakes, and the resulting

Collector threats. She'd lived with beauty as a curse. Superstition and religious tangents were chains she had never managed to shake off.

And now she endured tumors that had metastasized around her spine.

Nevertheless, she pressed forward.

One component of her long-term survival was the watchful attitude by which she navigated even mundane activities. Three years earlier, she had moved from Chattanooga, Tennessee, to smoggy Southern California. It was a practical decision. TV career and all. As a stranger on L.A.'s fringes, she was quick to install topnotch security measures in her new home.

The cameras were the most trusted feature. Not only did they deter the amateur thieves and psychos—being in the public eye, she'd run into her share of them—they also fed live-action clips to an off-site location. With her cell, she could access mpegs of the latest activity around her home, and she had made a habit of doing so at the stoplights leading into her neighborhood.

Oh, naturally, she had spotted some odd behaviors in her time here, though there had never been much trouble. Nothing of consequence.

This trip, Nikki had been gone for nearly a week, choosing to make the drive to Oregon and Washington state. It'd given her time to weigh the life she led, the decisions that had brought her to this point, and had also given her a chance for more intimate dialogue with her daughter.

The healing process had begun, had it not? Gina had even gone so far as to lay her head on Nikki's shoulder.

So why the glum outlook on this long journey home? It seemed the closer she got to Gina, the more Nikki was confronted by her own shortcomings and infirmities.

She had compromised a righteous man.

She'd scarred her own child with the edges of a knife.

I don't deserve them. I truly never have.

Her self-chastisement was interrupted by an image of a Mustang convertible in today's video feed. She would've believed it was someone lost in these quiet lanes, except that she spotted it again as she neared the cul-de-sac.

Without shifting her head, she lifted the cell to her ear to shield her peripheral glance. There, in the Mustang's rearview, a pair of sunglasses seemed to be staring back at her. The top was down and the driver's seat reclined, providing a peek at gargantuan shoulders. The same convertible, according to the security's digital clock, had passed her place more than two hours ago.

Two hours? Top down? In this late-afternoon heat?

Nikki flipped the passenger side visor and hit the garage-door opener. She coasted into cover and was about to close the door when she decided being trapped in her own home was not the ideal scenario. She had a registered handgun by her bed, but she'd never even fired the thing. She barely knew how to load it.

For that matter, was it loaded? She couldn't remember.

Change of plans.

She backed into the cul-de-sac—forgot something, just running down to Vons for a gallon of milk—and checked her mirrors and windows for the Mustang. No sign of it. Perhaps there was nothing to this after all. She powered down the garage door.

Then she stopped again. Why was she letting fear run her off her own property? Did she want to play hostage to paranoia?

Logic told her that she had no reason to worry. She'd existed in relative calm here, making bimonthly visits to Seattle and the San Juan Islands under the guise of TV work, and had never come home to any trouble. Well, yes, there'd been the rash of neighborhood burglaries blamed on a gang of delinquents, and the random gifts at the doorstep from obsessed fans.

But in three years, no threats from her Akeldama foes.

She tapped the remote one more time and edged into the driveway. She'd spent much of her life on the run, had she not? No more. Her oncologist had told her not to drink while on this medication, but tonight she would savor a glass of red wine in the comfort of her air-conditioned home.

A blur of movement from her left.

Oh my. Who was—

An orange exploded against the driver's window.

Nikki stared through the pulpy mess and saw a sneer curl the Collector's lips, revealing crooked fangs as he came at her from the cover of the citrus trees. Toying with her, he took a bite from a second orange, rind and all, then hurled it in the same trajectory as the first.

She ignored the spray of juice and hit the power door locks.

He sped forward, slammed into the side panel, and rocked the entire vehicle on its struts. As he did so, his shades fell away, revealing eyes like chunks of obsidian that glittered soulless and black. His face was chiseled stone, a crude yet complete bust of some ancient god.

Natira?

With his left hand, he clamped onto the frame around the windshield; with his right hand—or, to be more accurate, two clawlike fingers—he pried at the edge of her window.

Yes, Nikki realized, it was Reggie's killer. Just as Cal had described him.

CHAPTER
TWELVE

Corvallis

"Shalom, shalom . . ."

That was the refrain in Jerusalem, the famed City of Peace. If Gina remembered correctly, Scripture said people would claim there was peace, peace, but there would be no peace. Until recently there'd been little of it in her own life, but now was the time to turn a new page. To flip the script.

Standing at the gallery counter, she decided she would spend her next few years making an honest wage here at Tattered Feather, getting to know Josee and Suzette better, paying discreet visits to the waters off Lummi Island, rekindling love with Jed Turney, and savoring her moments with Nikki and Nickel.

With her family coming back together, Gina was losing her urge to fight or place herself in harm's way again. Being one of Those Who Resist didn't mean she had to go looking for trouble, did it? In fact, she'd noticed that some who drank Nazarene Blood bunkered down to avoid it.

Was that the best reaction, though, ducking the battle?

Gina subscribed to the idea of protecting and preparing—a more proactive, less fatalistic, approach. But how could she blame them? Who didn't want a little peace?

Of course, *shalom* meant something else to Gina as well.

Shalom, daughter of Lord Ariston, had held her captive in Zalmoxis Cave and later pursued her through Romania's Busteni Mountains. If it weren't for a drop of Nazarene Blood shoved down the Collector's throat, Gina would have died upon those slopes.

"Yeshua, I owe you my life," she whispered. "I'll fight, if that's what you want, but until I hear otherwise I'm sticking to my plan."

The chirp of the electric eye snapped her from her thoughts, and she spent the next twenty minutes helping two men pick out a chest-high myrtlewood clock. She rang them up, and one dropped a business card—SNL Photography—into the pottery contest bowl next to the register.

"You can't win if you don't try," he said.

"The free dinner? Yeah, we do the drawings every Saturday."

"Must we be present to win?" asked the second man.

"No, Lyndon, you *mustn't*," the first responded with a hint of mockery. "Read the fine print."

"I *never* read the fine print."

"He never reads the fine print," the first told Gina.

"Sam, be sure to get a receipt."

Lyndon walked the clock toward the door and Sam followed. Gina hid her amusement and bid them farewell, then moved to the Fauxbergé display. There was something enamoring about the intricate designs of the jeweled eggs.

"You feeling hungry?"

"Josee." Gina turned. "I thought you were at the library."

"Came in the back way. Sorry if I caught you off guard."

"It's these eggs. I get so mesmerized."

"Not once you've seen mine." Josee flipped the sign at the front door to *Closed* and turned the deadbolt. "We'll make a day of it sometime soon."

"You think maybe you could ease Jed into coming along?"

"You're still hitched, right?"

"Technically."

"Then there's nothing easy about it. You just make it work."

"This, coming from Miss No-to-Sarge."

"Ouch." Josee acted as though she'd been slapped. "You play dirty. Hey, while I toss together a salad, you can count down your drawer and take it to Suzette in the back office."

"Sure thing."

"You like chanterelles?"

"What?"

"Mushrooms."

"Yeah, I—"

"Gorgonzola? Please tell me you know what gorgonzola is."

"I know *where* it is. A small town in Italy."

"Double ouch." Josee slung her chin the other direction. "You should take a few swings at Sarge. He used to be a prizefighter, you know."

"Didn't know that. But I guess I could just ask him about it myself."

"Huh?"

Gina pointed at the locked door, where Sergeant Turney stood only partially visible behind the narrow glass panel. "Looks like we have a late customer."

He tapped once, then held up a finger—*wait just a sec.*

"What's that boy doing now?" Josee folded her arms, tufts of black hair bristling above her eyebrow ring. "I hope he knows I'm not falling for this."

The big man moved his entire girth into view at the picture window and lofted something thin and square above his crew-cut hair. Even with shirt buttons straining and belted pants sagging, he didn't budge. His eyes locked on to Josee's, unblinking and full of affection.

"Looks like that's a record he's holding," Gina said.

"A record?"

"You know, some classy old-school vinyl."

"The good stuff."

"Go see what it is."

"That's just playing into his hand."

"Is there something wrong with that?"

"Forget it. He's not suckering me in that easy."

"Josee, you are—"

"What?" With a hand on her hip, Josee rotated.

"In love."

Turquoise whorled like ocean tide pools in Josee's eyes.

"Go look," Gina urged.

Josee snorted. "He is so confusing." She stomped along an aisle of Nez Perce artifacts and faced the man locked outside on the front porch.

Sarge hadn't moved. Between his thick fingers, the cardboard sleeve appeared nicked at the edges and dog-eared on one corner. Gina could see now that it was a single, nearly twenty years old, and worth every penny he must've paid for it.

U2 . . . "With or Without You."

Knowing Josee was a fan, Gina had to congratulate Sarge on his choice—so long as he didn't break into song.

He was opening his mouth.

No, Gina thought. *Don't do it.*

"Don't," Josee muttered at the glass. "Please, don't sing it."

Sgt. Vince Turney sang anyway. The man was in his early thirties, his military-style buzz cut at odds with the extra weight around his middle. And yet he stood there singing his lungs out about life without his beloved.

"Don't," Josee said again, shaking her head.

Sarge wrinkled his brow and warbled another line. "Oh, oh, oh, ohh-hhh . . . oh, oh, oh, ohhh . . ." A button popped loose from his overstretched shirt, twanged against the window, and still he soldiered on through the musical bridge. "Oh, oh, oh, ohhhhh . . . oh, oh, oh, ohhh . . ." He buckled beneath the strain of falsetto, landing on both knees, and a second button bounced off the glass.

"I love you," Josee breathed.

Sarge squeezed the cardboard sleeve and shook an object into his hand.

A ring? Gina felt like an intruder on this special event.

He held the diamond ring to the window and gasped, "I don't . . . don't wanna live without you, Josee. You hearin' me in there? I know I ain't whatcha call the pick of the litter, but I love you. I do. Please, will you marry me?"

Josee lifted her chin. "Just this once."

He nodded. "Once is all it takes."

They kissed through the window, then met at the door and kissed again—much longer this time—under the eaves and in full view of the world.

Once upon a time, Gina thought, *that was me and Jed.*

Not wanting to disturb the lovebirds, she removed the gallery till and inched off down the hall.

Pasadena

With Natira glaring at her through the glass, Nikki leaned away and hit the accelerator. Panicked, she left the car in Drive and the Acura shot toward the open garage. She cranked the wheel to the right to avoid trapping herself. Foot still on the gas, she spun the car onto the lawn.

The Collector's mammoth body careened into the near corner of the garage, then peeled away in a collision of bones and anchored framework. Wood splinters carved the air, and a hooded lantern burst. Grass spewed from tire treads as Nikki steered to avoid the fountain, but the vehicle was sliding, skidding, out of control.

She gritted her teeth against the flares of pain in her back. The car's front panel scraped the fountain base, slowing her, then broke loose. It clipped the mailbox, bounded over the curb, and aimed for the mouth of the cul-de-sac.

She'd been targeted. Surely Collectors had located her years ago, so why attack now? Did they suspect the truth? They must be after the information in her blood.

My daughter . . . my grandson . . .

Nikki would never risk revealing the livelihood and locations of Gina and Jacob. She could never come back to this address. She couldn't even call from her cell to give warning, for fear of having the recipient's number traced.

Where could she run? Was any place safe?

From the passenger side, Natira caromed into view again. His teeth shone between bloody lips, fangs long and razor sharp. He was keeping pace with the car, angling across neighbors' lawns to catch her at the stop sign.

CHAPTER
THIRTEEN

"You murdered my son!" Nikki screamed at the foul thing.

Though it was doubtful Natira could hear her, he could not misread her rage. He snarled back, and she yanked the car toward him, taking him out at the knees. She heard the satisfying crack of metal and flesh, noted his look of astonishment. He was catapulted over the hood and windshield before reacting to this unexpected aggression. His fingers screeched along the roof like steel hooks, wedging in at the windows on either side. The panel sagged beneath his weight so that it almost touched Nikki's head.

He was so close, right there. A serrated fingernail pierced the metal.

She weaved from curb to curb, ran the stop sign, and raced along the next block with the Collector still there.

He was almost . . . touching her.

Clawing, scraping at her scalp.

"You demon!" She punched at the roof. "Get off my car!"

Her foot mashed down the brake pedal, and the Acura's antilock system did its best to compensate and keep the vehicle from fishtailing. The front end nosedived, and the mound of rock-hard Collector shot forward, flopping, rolling, skidding across the pavement, leaving bright-red streaks and strips of dark skin.

Nikki thought of running over the abomination, then imagined the Acura's low chassis becoming tangled with his bulk. Natira was undead anyway. A revenant from burial caves in Jerusalem's Valley of Hinnom.

Now that he'd pinned her in his sights, would he ever stop hunting her? He was more than some robotic terminator from the future; he was an Akeldama Collector, enervated by his Master's hatred and pervaded by counterfeit life.

This would never stop, never end. It never really had, had it?

And, pulsing through these veins of hers, volatile secrets still threatened those she loved dearest.

She felt along her scalp. Parallel grooves burned where the monster's fingernails had peeled back skin and hair, yet she found no traces of blood. Thank goodness for that. She twisted the car through a quick U-turn on this final departure from her palm-tree paradise, while in her mind a plan took shape.

Corvallis

With till in hand, Gina met Suzette in the back office, a converted bedroom dominated by an old maple desk at which Suzette now prepared a bank deposit bag. A door led into the backyard. Two bikes leaned against the wall, evidence of this household's commitment to gas conservation and fitness.

"You missed all the excitement," Gina said.

"Referring to that howling I heard?" Suzette winked. "I knew he was coming. Sarge called to make certain she'd be here."

"Little matchmaker, huh?"

"I could've lied and said she wasn't here."

"Aren't you happy for them?"

Suzette took the till. "Did everything balance?"

"Three pennies short."

"Please understand, Gina, as a habit I keep out of others' business. I do. What Sarge and Josee decide is between them, don't you agree? Affairs of the heart are difficult enough to maneuver on one's own, without the interference of well-meaning friends."

"Is that the voice of experience I hear?"

"Love is a fickle thing." Suzette broke eye contact and took a sip of ginger lemonade from a bottle on her desk. "Sit and tell me what's on your mind. If you like, there's more Genesis Juice in the fridge."

"What about the deposit?"

"I'll use the night drop box. Is there something worrying you?"

Gina shifted weight from one leg to the other, glanced back along the hall. She felt as though her heart had dislodged in her chest, as though some awful thing had just happened. Had her mom made it home safely?

"It's probably nothing," she said. "Guess I'll go on up to the room."

"Nickel tells us you've had some turbulent times."

Shrugging, Gina covered her scarred arm with her hand.

"Evil's out there," Suzette said. "A fact I know better than most. I'm still learning how to resist, and since you and I'll soon be the single ladies of the house, we mustn't let anything come between us. Agreed?"

"Actually, I'm a married woman."

"Oh?"

"To Jed. Sarge's nephew."

"I know Jed. I heard you'd been split for a number of years."

"We've both had issues to deal with."

"Why is it, Gina, that so many women let their men wander off?"

"Excuse me? You have no right assuming—"

"Please, please. I don't mean to implicate you in any way." The gallery owner pulled long black hair over her shoulder, combing fingernails through the tangled ends until they splayed over the buttons of her blouse. "It's simply that some of us desire relationships, while others seem to treat theirs with disdain."

"I love my husband."

"I'm sure you do. Yes, I'm sure you do."

With worries now joined by indignation, Gina pushed back from the desk. She was determined to make this living situation work, even if it meant biting her tongue. "I'll talk to you later, Suzette. Think it's time for me to call it a night."

Cascade Mountains

The place was hard to find, set off the mountain pass, surrounded by an alarm-wired fence. Nickel tapped in the code at the gate, watched it roll aside. The driveway carried his GMC pickup between ferns and rhododendron bushes to a huge log cabin that overlooked the McKenzie River. Dense stands of evergreens stood as sentinels on the ten-acre property.

This was his refuge, a former summer camp donated by an unflagging member of Those Who Resist. It was also his training site.

Here, he tried to right his wrongs by investing in the potential Concealed Ones. Here, he put them through obstacle courses, taught them how to start campfires without matches, how to navigate icy currents without flotation devices, and how to hammer tent pegs. Here, he provided concealment from the Master Collector and his minions, and even now a dozen Unfallen patrolled the ranch's perimeter.

Nickel set the pickup's brake, his headlights illuminating the river's opposite bank. Clay Ryker helped carry groceries inside.

"Thanks for being here, Clay."

"Better than living at my parents' house."

"That's tough on any grown man. How's Kenny been?"

Though the kid believed his mother was dead, he'd been prepped for his role among the Nistarim and accepted it without hesitation.

"He's coming around," Clay said. "Getting back to his usual self. I think it helps that my son's here to hang out with him. Kids are resilient, you know? Shoot, we could learn a thing or two from them."

Nickel had befriended this man in J.C. and found him to be a dependable sort, one of Those Who Resist. He had offered Clay the chance to stay here while working through marital issues and in exchange assigned him to watch over Kenny Preston. There were other young men disbursed throughout the nations, ready to step in should one of the Nistarim collapse; for the time being, though, Kenny was Nickel's favorite. His adopted grandson.

"You're here," Kenny said, coming down the stairs. "Finally."

"Hey. Like the hoodie."

"Oregon Ducks."

Nickel wrapped an arm over the kid's shoulders.

Kenny bounced on his toes. "Wanna see what I put together this week?"

"Should I guess?"

"A bigger doghouse for Gussy. Has windows and everything."

"Sounds fancy."

"Come 'n look. It's around back."

Nickel had a hard time keeping up with Kenny as they glided through the sliding doors to the patch of lawn that faced the river. The last of the daylight brushed the frothing waters.

"You like it?" Kenny said. He picked up a hammer, knocked it on the doghouse roof. "Made it all by myself."

A tan-colored mutt emerged, tail wagging, head cocked as though following their conversation.

"Man." Nickel peeked inside. "Makes me wish I was a dog."

"No, it doesn't."

"Almost. I'd say Gussy's got it made."

The boy's eyes moistened. "I won't let anything happen to her."

"You, that hammer, and your MTPs—there's a combo even I wouldn't mess with." Nickel yanked the hood over Kenny's head and planted a quick kiss on the green fabric. "You're one tough kid."

CHAPTER
FOURTEEN

Early September—Big Bear Lake, California

Nikki huddled in the darkness, scratched at the wound on her scalp—it was oozing pale green pus now—and wondered how much longer she could remain hidden.

Knowing the tenacity of her hunters, not long.

This cabin she had holed up in belonged to one of her show's coproducers, Greg Simone. He wouldn't mind her being here. If this ended as she suspected, though, he and the other producer would soon be forced to scrounge up fresh ideas.

Hemmed in by white firs and lodgepole pines, the cabin looked out over the lake. Though used infrequently, the place was kept ready for guests, with clean linens set out each Monday by an Hispanic maid who left the key in a lock box hanging from a peg beneath the back steps.

Nikki had visited a number of times in the past and knew the box's code. She'd let herself in through the back, kept the curtains closed, lights off. In the days since, she'd spent hours reading classics from Greg's shelves—from Dumas' *The Three Musketeers* to Steinbeck's *East of Eden*—doing her best to tame taut nerves.

Not that it was working. With senses attuned to every sound and shifting shadow along the curtains, she could barely eat or rest.

She felt trapped indoors, yet too vulnerable to venture outside.

The waters looked inviting. Then foreboding.

The sun lifted her spirits. Then left her feeling exposed.

This double mindedness had grown worse each day, and she knew it had something to do with the scratch. What had started as an itch now festered in her hair, with the infection from the Collector's curved nails seeming to take root in her very brain. Gina would say it could be cleansed with "just one drop"—always that talk of Nazarene Blood—but Nikki knew it had to be cut away.

None of that mattered at this moment. She was safe now, wasn't she?

Most definitely not. She was most definitely cornered.

Stop it, Nikki. Stop! Don't take leave of your senses.

To the best of her knowledge, she had escaped Pasadena earlier in the week without leaving much of a trail for Natira to follow. She'd withdrawn money at the drive-thru teller, then ditched her car at a small church in Monrovia and tucked into their mailbox an envelope containing the keys and the signed title. She'd removed the battery from her cell phone and tossed the separate pieces in a Dumpster behind a grocery store, then called a taxi from a pay phone, ridden to Echo Park, and switched to another cab. That one took her to Santa Monica, where she bought a gutless old Subaru wagon from a sixty-eight-year-old man wearing parachute pants and a muscle T-shirt. She had then backtracked along I-10 and chugged up the winding road to Big Bear, arriving just before midnight.

She hoped now that the troubles she'd gone through to disguise her movements had worked. Self-preservation was only secondary; if the vampires of the Akeldama found her, if they siphoned her blood, everything she had fought for over the past four decades would come to a premature end.

And Cal's hard work? Useless.

Gina's tenuous existence? Over.

Jacob's survival? Futile.

Hell's Canyon, Oregon

That Nikki woman had proved feistier than Natira expected. Not only had she eluded his clutches, she'd left him balled up and broken in the middle of Pasadena. Nothing irreversible, of course. Did she think it would be that easy? Bah. He possessed recuperative powers beyond her puny comprehension. Even his tongue had healed over enough to roll out semicoherent syllables.

For the time being, however, he'd give Nikki a little space, let her settle back into the complacency so endemic to these shortsighted beings, and then he would strike again.

No warning next time. No mercy.

Now in a rented Buick, Natira moved his hunt from Southern California to the deepest canyon in North America. He threaded along the Snake River on Oregon's eastern fringe, between stark peaks and timbered draws that harbored rattlers and free-ranging elk. While the sun baked the land to a red-brown crisp, Ponderosa pines stood defiant in armored bark.

He'd been told by Consortium leaders he would find Asgoth here, reduced to a mere vapor and haunting the waters above the Hell's Canyon dam.

Asgoth. Lone witness to Gina's demise.

Maybe this creature could cough up a helpful crumb.

Natira saw the dam now in the twilight. He parked, waited. Best to let the discarded Collector come begging for a little notice. He rolled down the window, took a slap across the face from the heat. What a godforsaken place.

Before ten minutes had passed, a zephyr stirred, then sashayed up the bank toward the road. It swayed in front of the car's grill, as though vying for attention, and Natira marveled at Asgoth's disproportionate sense of importance. Did he not realize he was formless, powerless?

"Are you the one they sent?" Asgoth wheezed.

Natira smirked. "I am the one."

"What do you want?"

"Don't you have a host you can occupy, something more substantial?"

"Stop gargling rocks and speak clearly."

Natira pulled on his seatbelt. "I'm leaving, if you don't wish to talk."

"No, no. Stay. I'm Asgoth—a ghost, and nothing more nowadays. But I've had my share of hosts over the ages. Some names that might impress you."

"I've heard only of your recent failure."

"The Consortium, did they tell you?" Barely visible, Asgoth slithered about the Buick's radio antenna. "It was no fault of my own. My target was a two-legger named Clay Ryker, and I was on Highway 126, aiming for him with a logging truck, when another vehicle came along and confused things."

"None of that matters to me." Natira wiped sweat from his chin. "Who are you? Why'd they tell you to come here?"

"I need to know about Gina."

"Who? Really, you sound like you have a mouthful of cotton."

"Kate Preston," Natira amended. "She was in the Nissan that was cru—"

"Oh, ha-ha. The Nissan. Well, she paid the price for getting in my way."

"You saw her die?"

"Her car got rammed over the cliff."

"Was she the only one in it?"

"I'm told she was headed to some women's church retreat. Lot of good it did her. Ha. To answer the question—yes, her spirit went wafting into the air, and that's how I knew she had gone bye-bye. For a fleeting second, I thought there was another spirit beside her, but I'm sure it was only her shadow playing against the trees."

"Or maybe the Nazarene scooping her into His arms."

"Does He do that? I don't think so."

"I think," Natira said, "that He's a blind fool for loving any of these humans."

"Love is a sign of weakness. Hate is our fuel, don't you agree? And pride."

"You seem to have your share of it."

The ethereal form danced across the window. "What am I without it?"

"Nothing either way."

"What?"

"Enjoy your exile here in the canyon."

"No. You can't go."

Natira started the engine. "You've told me all I need to know."

"I know more, much more. Try me. As a Collector, I've traipsed the far reaches of the globe, inhabited men of position and power, gathered facts and secrets galore."

"Another task awaits me. So long, Asgoth."

"What is this task? I can help."

"Is that so?" Natira scoffed. He'd seen women on the battlefield beg with more dignity than this piddly creature. "What do you know about the Crown of Thorns or the Black King? Are you privy to Rasputin's prophecies?"

"What don't I know? It's not often you inhabit someone of that caliber."

Natira eyed the wisp in disbelief. "You mean to tell me you inhabited Rasputin?"

"Along with a legion of others."

"You don't say."

"By allowing us entry, he made us partners with him. I don't think he knew how deeply we'd persuaded and possessed him. He mouthed his prayers, poked about in the Holy Book, but he was driven by his more earthy passions."

Natira rested an arm out the window, convinced Asgoth was lying. Nevertheless, he decided to play along. "What went wrong, then? How'd you end up bodiless?"

"That was nearly a century ago," Asgoth said. "Rasputin was poisoned, shot, and then—for good measure—rolled up in a carpet by political rivals and drowned in the Neva River."

"Convincing details."

"What happened next, though? Did my cluster leaders recognize my persuasive powers, the debaucheries I'd carried out through our grimy priest?" There was acid in Asgoth's laugh. "No, I was left to roam."

"Right. And that's how you ended up in Oregon."

"Only because of the black king Lenin stole from my host."

"The black king?"

"A chess piece handcarved by Rasputin. Lenin was forced to flee

Russia, and he did so aboard a Finnish locomotive. Check the history books, if you don't believe me. He stashed the item on the engine, but never managed to come back for it. Decades later, that same engine was sent to Junction City, Oregon, and put on display in honor of the town's Scandinavian immigrants."

"So that's why you came to Oregon?"

"One of the reasons."

"An interesting fabrication, Asgoth, though a bit farfetched. Why would Lenin steal a simple chess piece in the first place? Talk sense or I'm leaving."

"Don't go. Please."

"I have other prey to hunt."

"It's the key," Asgoth yammered. "Key to the priest's cache of relics."

Ah, now that caught his attention. Natira pondered Asgoth's words a moment, then lowered the passenger-side window, believing he might indeed find some use for this pathetic vapor, lies or no. "Here, come inside. We don't want a hot gust along the canyon blowing you loose."

Asgoth drifted from the antenna into the Buick, the setting sun showing him to be motes of inconsequential dust at best.

Natira tried to disguise his interest as he weighed this Collector's claims beside the words of Rasputin's prophecy. Perhaps Asgoth was stretching the truth or gluing together tidbits he'd collected from various experiences, yet he was making sense—a convoluted, delightfully twisted sort of sense.

Once again, Master, I feel your hand leading me.

"If," Asgoth added, "it's the Crown of Thorns you're after, you'll find it in the Tmu Tarakan."

"A legend. It doesn't exist."

"It does, and it's hidden in Jerusalem."

"Under our noses all along," Natira whispered.

"Rasputin made reference to it after two pilgrimages to the Holy Land, but we never knew its exact location. Our cluster entered the picture following that second trip, and he sealed off the secret from friends, lovers, even his wife. Later, Lenin tried to pry it from him, in hopes of desecrating the sacred icons."

"'The Black King is key . . . His likeness shall unlock riches . . .'"

"Oh, so you know that prophecy."

"How are you familiar with it? It's been hidden away for many years."

"In Bran Castle, with Queen Marie of Romania. Yes, I know these things." If dust could be said to display arrogance, Asgoth's head cocked at a jaunty angle. "Or are you forgetting Rasputin was once my host?"

"Right." Natira swatted at a gnat. "Tell me, how do I access this place?"

"Once you know its location, all you need is the key."

"You seem more than willing to hand out information."

"What do I care now that Rasputin is gone? I'm trapped in this canyon in the middle of nowhere with my memories and little else."

"Take me to this key, then."

Asgoth sighed. "Can't be done. It was found, then disappeared again."

"From the locomotive in Junction City?"

"Engine 418. The Unfallen are now guarding the site."

"Out," Natira said. "Get away. What use are you to me?"

"But I . . . I've heard rumors of a duplicate, and I think I know where it is."

"Anything to keep me talking, is that it?"

"It's not far from here. And you should know that Rasputin also spoke of a Knights Templar signet ring, inscribed long ago with a map to the relics. Fearful that someone might use the thing to locate his treasure, he tried tracking it down himself. Never did find it, though."

"You're quite the tale spinner."

"He did learn that the ring was entrusted to Mary Queen of Scots—a sympathizer with the Templars—and later passed on to the Masons."

"Hmmph." Natira's temples were throbbing, his back drenched with sweat. It was always this way with other Collectors, trying to discern between truths, half truths, and untruths.

Asgoth wavered in his seat. "All I ask for is my release. I'm much too valuable to be left on the sidelines."

"Clearly you find yourself indispensable."

"I beg of you. You've heard it said a Collector can come back from exile, if only joined by seven others even stronger. It's in the Holy Book—

yes, yes, never mind the source. The point is with your cluster's sponsorship, I would be free to help you search for the key, the ring, the map . . . whatever it takes to find that Crown of Thorns."

"I could talk to the local Consortium, I suppose."

"Oh, thank you, my king. I'm ever here to advise you."

"Does that make you my court jester?"

"Please. I'm much more valuable than—"

"Jester it is."

CHAPTER
FIFTEEN

Corvallis

"What did you think?" Josee asked over the rattle of the VW engine. "Was that what you expected when I said we'd be getting prepared and equipped?"

Gina shook her head. "Hardly."

"What you just experienced, that's what I call 'church.'"

"Uh. Okay."

"Not quite your mother's version, is it?"

Another shake of the head. For years, Gina's mother had foisted religious rules upon her, turning spirituality into a weapon of self-justification and fear.

I forgive you, Mom. But that's a version I can do without.

Along the city streets, lights flickered on in store fronts and lamp stands, warding off the coming darkness. Earlier, Gina, Josee, and Suzette had joined Sarge and a dozen others at a park on the Willamette River, sipping smoothies and espresso drinks from a nearby café, discussing Yeshua's interaction in life, morality, and love—including Sarge and Josee's recent engagement.

They'd ended their time by breaking off chunks of fresh-baked bread, partaking simultaneously, and then washing it down with red droplets from the vials around their necks and in their pockets, or with gel capsules such as those once contained in Gina's earrings.

The elements of communion.

Of community found through the One who gave His life.

"Originally," Suzette said from the back of the car, "'church' was people gathering in unity, equipping each other for the work ahead. Josee's been teaching me that we all have different gifts and tasks."

"That's right. We're not supposed to be Those Who Hide, Those Who Cower, Those Who Live in Perpetual Fear, or Those Who—"

"Think I get the point," Gina broke in.

Downshifting, Josee chuckled in apology and turned on her blinker.

"I believe what she's getting at," said Suzette, "is that it has little to do with all the paraphernalia you see nowadays. Should we be spending millions on new buildings when people are trying to keep on the lights and feed their kids?"

Gina had weighed similar questions.

"Sure," Josee said, "some of those buildings are put to good use—don't mean to imply otherwise—but if it's all about staying safe and sanitized, it misses the point. Not to mention, it often leads to spiritual, even emotional, scars."

Gina rubbed her hand over the scar tissue on her left arm. She thought about the contagion present in the hearts of mankind, lingering in the blood, passing through the genes. Each person had the ability to make a stand, to exercise free will, but once Power of Choice was surrendered, a Collector's bite could trigger a full-blown infestation of thorns.

She closed her eyes, pressed her head against the Bug's plastic headrest. Her Jewish heritage had taught her to avoid blood because it contained life—which was true. Drinking the Nazarene Blood did mean ingesting Life.

No wonder rabbis and Mosaic Law forbade anything else, anticipating that very day when death and iniquity would be conquered upon a Roman cross by the Author of Life Himself.

Yet, even now, He was a Concealed One to so many.

Josee parked outside the Tattered Feather Gallery, and the three women headed indoors. Gina plopped down on her bed to read a book, only to be interrupted by her name being called from the foot of the stairs.

"Yeah?" She poked her head over the rail.

Josee waggled an envelope in the air.

"What is it?"

"A letter."

"Okay, Ms. Smarty Pants, so who's it from?"

"Hmm." Josee studied the sender's address with feigned ignorance. "You know some dude named Jed Turney?"

Gina's pulse quickened as she jogged down and carried the envelope back up the stairs. Though she'd left Jed a few phone messages, she had heard nothing back. Now, via old-school snail mail, her husband was making a move.

By the time she landed facedown on her bed, she had peeled back the flap and withdrawn the single sheet of paper. With hope twittering in her ears, she read the letter.

"What?" She snapped up on the edge of the mattress. "That's the best you can do, after all this time?"

Josee peeked around the door. "Safe to enter?"

"He says he's supposed to lay low, let me get situated."

"Jed said that? That's so flippin' lame."

"I don't know. Maybe my dad told him to do that."

"Least it's not an outright rejection."

"What's the difference? He either wants to see me or he doesn't." Gina ran her finger over the sentences. "And all this stuff about finishing up a big project at his job . . . C'mon."

"I bet he's scared, just like Sarge was."

"Forget it. You were right, Josee: men don't have a clue."

Her roommate smiled. "He'll come around. Don't give up on him yet."

"Give up? He's the . . ." She almost said he was the father of her son, then remembered that Jacob's existence was unknown to those in this household—as a safeguard for all concerned. "Jed's the only man I'll ever love. 'Till death do us part,' right?"

"Right."

Even as she verbalized her commitment, Gina was struck by the consequences of her genetic disposition. 'Till death do us part' took on a whole new meaning with her. Assuming they ever got back together, she would level off at forty as Jed wilted into old age. He'd find himself hobbling along on brittle legs with a healthy, bronze-skinned woman hanging from his arm.

Well, lucky him.

Not that any of it changed her feelings for him.

Big Bear Lake

At the cabin curtains, Nikki watched another sun go down behind the San Bernardino Mountains. She could do with a good mocha. She'd seen a shop in Big Bear called Brewed Awakening, but decided the risks of leaving this hideaway were too great. Instead, she vacillated between ways of handling the maid's arrival tomorrow morning.

She could leave tonight.

Or maybe she could step out before dawn and hide in the woods.

If she did stay, she was sure her producer wouldn't mind.

Stop this . . . this . . . double-mindedness!

Her head hurt. It felt as though thumbtacks were chugging through her veins, pricking, prodding, poking. And stabbing into her temples. She backed into the bedroom and tucked herself under the covers—still clothed, shoes on, primed for a mad dash to safety. She gulped down a double dose of her medication, a prescribed narcotic, needing rest from the pain and the questions.

Was any of this worth it? They'd find her soon enough anyway.

No, that couldn't be allowed. By all means, no.

CHAPTER
SIXTEEN

Goldendale, Washington

Queens and kings guarded glass display cases, marshalling their armies, while rows of mahogany pawns hinted at hard-fought battles and sandalwood rooks, prancing knights, and ivory bishops stood upon checkered boards, ready for the tourists who would wander these hallways tomorrow. For the time being, though, the chess sets were quiet.

And soon to come under attack.

Natira had read online about the Maryhill Museum, and now, from the cover of the trees, he studied the imposing chateau on this bluff above the Columbia River. Lights stabbed up from the lawn, bathing thick granite walls.

Inside, the night watchman wasn't doing much watching; he was flipping through a glossy magazine, entranced by its female images.

"Tell me," Asgoth said, "are we going to do this or not?"

Grunting, Natira rubbed his thumb and pinkie together in anticipation. After months of Kerioth-Hezron's dreary routine, he was ready to search this chess collection for something tangible that could lead him to the Crown of Thorns. Let Erota watch over their cluster. Let her amuse herself with simple-minded Barabbas.

"Bet I can get that guard to open the door," Asgoth said. "Yep, yep."

"I'm sure you can."

"I'll go over and tap, tap, tap." Asgoth fidgeted as he outlined his idea. "He'll wonder what a bird of my sort is doing outside."

"Of your sort? A grouchy old parrot's all you are."

"Not by my own choosing."

Natira guffawed. "Consider it a lesson in humility."

With the Consortium's permission, he had taken this menial Collector into custody and subjected him to a host both feathered and verbose. Perched on Natira's shoulder, Asgoth seemed less a conniving spirit and more a colorful prop for a pirate's costume. All Natira needed now was a peg leg and an eye patch—which, come to think of it, would match some of the wounds he'd received along the McKenzie.

"You think the risk here is justified?" Natira said.

"What risk? You're undead."

"And what happens each time Those Who Resist read about our activities in the papers, huh? They chant their little chants, calling on the Nazarene like lost children who can't do anything for themselves. Pathetic, but that's the way of it."

"It's worth the risk." Asgoth ducked, weaved. "You want the contents of the Tmu Tarakan, and there's a good chance we'll find the key in there. Remember, this museum was dedicated by Queen Marie of Romania herself. In 1926, she came all the way from Bran Castle to—"

"She was friends with the builder. Yes, I've read all about it."

"And since she's the one entrusted with Rasputin's prophecy, she must've known about the black king. Maybe she formed a replica and hid that likeness on one of the sets she brought here? Could explain her coming halfway around the world, donating crates of her relics and jewels."

"You believe the key to the Tmu Tarakan is here?"

A wing lifted toward the museum. "I vote we go in to find out."

"This isn't a democracy. I'm the king and you're my jester."

"Ha, ha," Asgoth said.

Although Natira relished the idea of an explosive entry, there was something to be said for exploiting a two-legger's curiosity. "Go on," he said. "Go knock or whatever it is you birds do."

At the door's glass panel, Asgoth pecked.

True to their assumptions, the watchman was roused from his desk by this unlikely guest and moseyed across the foyer with keys swinging from his belt.

Peck-a-peck-peck . . .

The watchman tapped back, repeating this three times before the bird angled a nervous glance at Natira's hiding place behind the stonework. Asgoth fluttered his wings and tried once more, rapping his beak against the glass until his persistence was rewarded.

"Whatcha doing out here, pretty bird?"

The parrot hovered out of reach.

The man planted a foot against the door and stretched forward. "Polly wanna cracker?"

"Polly wanna cracker?" Asgoth mimicked.

The watchman pushed farther out, creating enough space for Asgoth to zip through. With the winged Collector leading his pursuer down a corridor, Natira vaulted a low stone wall and dashed toward the closing door, wedging his left wrist into the gap, then squeezing inside. His research told him the chess sets were on the lower level. He waved away feathers, floating like blue-and-green confetti, and padded down the stairs.

Wall sconces lit a long hall where the handiwork of international artisans was featured. Rajasthan chess sets boasted elephants in place of rooks. Modern styles obscured the pieces' individuality. An English set stood regal and tall.

Natira knew his progress would be marked by cameras. Upstairs, he heard screeches, profanities, and pounding footsteps, suggesting that the birdbrain was making himself useful after all.

Not much time to do this, though. The watchman would soon tire of the chase and return to his panel of monitors.

Natira focused on one wall of display cases, passing ten, twenty, thirty, forty. He eliminated possibilities with grandmaster-like logic, narrowing in on the best options. Finally, he stopped at a Romanian set. A description plate claimed it was from the early 1900s, a gift from Queen Marie. Ornate, yet solid in appearance, the white king wore a crown of seven points topped by a cross.

The Collector compared it to the black crown. One, two, three . . .

Six points.

This anomaly in the black king's design convinced him he had found the desired object. With anticipation sweeping away any concern of being found out, he placed both hands on the corners of the glass and yanked it from padded grooves. A silent alarm may have sounded, but with prize in hand he didn't care. The piece gleamed, charging him with excitement.

Then he spotted the damaged point. This figurine was no different than its white counterpart, simply marred by a breakage.

Had Asgoth intentionally led him astray?

The parrot fluttered into view at the foot of the staircase. What was he doing? The plan was for Asgoth to keep the guard distracted while Natira slipped back outside. Natira took long strides, cuffed the bird, and mounted the steps three at a time.

In the foyer, the guard was gathering feathers. He was bent at the waist, pale flesh peeking from the back of his pants, belly hanging over his belt. His jingling keys provided background noise as Natira approached.

"Collector wanna cracker?" Asgoth screeched.

The big white watchman failed to catch the pun. "Where are you?" he said, rotating his head. "You're a hard one to—"

Natira backhanded him into the nearest wall. The clash of skull and stone echoed through the high-ceilinged space as the man slumped to the floor. In Natira's other hand, Asgoth tried to wriggle free.

"You deceived me, didn't you?"

"It was all true," Asgoth said. "I thought maybe you'd find—"

"Bah. This has been nothing but a wild goose chase."

"Wait, my king. I have another idea."

"You manipulated me to avoid the Restless Desert, didn't you?"

"No, I—"

"You're done, birdbrain."

Not only had Natira let a mortal woman elude him, he'd allowed Asgoth to divert him from his goals for another week or two. It seemed the Collectors' self-seeking, self-preserving ways were always at odds with their larger objectives.

Before the parrot could respond, Natira crumpled the thing in his huge hands. He felt the twitch of talons against his palms, heard the crack of small bones. Furious with this one who called himself Asgoth, he squeezed until the bird was reduced to a gelatinous mass. Thus released from its earthly host, a smear of black curled through Natira's fingers and dissipated in the draft of the museum's AC.

"A ghost indeed."

He tossed the feathered remains at the watchman's face, prompting a weak groan. The man struggled to one knee while fingers tugged at his holster. The vampire drew air through large nostrils and detected the fellow's fear, his slothfulness, his lust. Mmm. Were there thorns here to be savored?

He reached over the guard desk and scooped up the magazine with its images of soft curves. No doubt this watchman had forgotten the wedding band on his left hand and told himself he was immune to the adulteries that lurked in male minds. Or perhaps he wallowed in them, excusing them with such banal phrases as, "You can look, you just can't touch."

Yes, that was a favorite of clusters everywhere.

With pinkie and thumb, Natira hooked into his victim's fleshy neck; with his left hand, he fanned the magazine before the man's face.

"Why're you doing this?" the watchman puffed. "Who-hoo-oo are you?"

Natira kicked at his groin. "You can't hide your infection from me. I've seen your type countless times."

Thorns responded to the Collector's authority, twining into view over the guard's corpulent belly, writhing from roots in his midsection. Crusty vines glowed red. They clawed up his uniform, blotted his nametag, and encircled his chest.

Ka-boom!

The gunshot tore a chunk from Natira's undead thigh, and he threw back his head in a chuckle of pain. Did this flabby fellow think he could prevail against the alpha Collector of the Akeldama?

Natira knocked away the weapon, shoved the magazine into the man's mouth, and cinched briars into his skin. As the victim wrestled against these restraints, Natira broke off a pair of thorn cups and slurped blood from both. The liquid was pallid, almost tasteless, but enough to warm him for another day.

Finished, he drove the pair of empty thorns like stakes into the captive's eyes. The watchman screamed through the rolled pages, sounds of insincere repentance. To shut him up, Natira slashed his throat with incisors as large as any Native American arrowhead, then latched onto the carotid artery, slurping down hot juice, gnawing on bits of gristle and bone.

"The wages of sin is death . . ."

Ha. The Holy Scriptures did get that part right.

Once he was done, he lapped up any spillover, fetched the security camera footage, and carried the body out into the trees.

Redlands, California

This was no way to live.

For nearly a week now, each animal sound in the woods had set Nikki on edge. Each passing car posed a potential threat to her family's survival. She had cowered behind the tree line while the maid worked in the house, then crept back indoors to her self-imposed exile. Was she supposed to cower in eternal fear? Supposed to wait for the Collectors to hunt her down, rip into her throat, and suck the secrets from her blood?

She felt their animosity even now, a poison seeping through her torn scalp. She'd done what she could to hide this long, but she was tired, so very tired. Dying and alone. The Collector's infection had shredded her resolve.

It was time, she told herself.

Time to accept the inevitable and stop fighting.

As another day slipped beyond the horizon, she pulled into a Redlands electronics store and purchased a cell phone—something untraceable, with prepaid minutes. She used it once, then disposed of the thing in a trash bin behind a Chinese buffet. Inside the restaurant, she savored each bite of Peking duck, each scoop of fried rice, and washed them down with oolong. Breaking years of routine, she left the fortune cookie untouched.

As night descended, she fueled up the car and headed east.

Tonight, Nikki Lazarescu was choosing her own fortune.

Corvallis

Once the gallery's midday crowd dispersed, Gina was released from her duties and spent the afternoon browsing the impressive city library and watching families in the park. She missed Jacob. Soon, she'd make another trip to Lummi Island. Her years of mourning had given way to the bitter-sweet reality of a son she couldn't hold or kiss, couldn't make cookies for, couldn't help with his math.

At sundown, she cycled home and brought the bike inside. Suzette caught her as she was tromping up the stairs.

"Not to frighten you, Gina, but you might want to check the messages on the business phone. There's one from your mother, and she seemed to have a degree of urgency in her voice. Probably nothing, of course. Nothing at all."

CHAPTER
SEVENTEEN

Western Arizona

Nikki drove into the night, heading across hot sands that connected California and Arizona. Earlier in Redlands, she had dialed the gallery in Corvallis and said her piece: "Regina, this is the last time you'll hear my voice. You may never understand this choice I am making, but please know it's done to protect you. I cannot let them find me, not ever. With cancer eating at me, I'm ending this on my own terms. I love you, my angel. Good night."

Under fifteen seconds. No need to be maudlin about it.

Ahead, stars shimmered in a sky tinged purplish-black by the day's residual heat, and a quarter moon rested atop a distant mesa. Nikki cut south from I-10 toward the desert town where the solution to her troubles lay.

She coasted the Subaru to the only traffic signal, held up there for a half minute despite the absence of movement along the main street. Her head was pounding. Her veins burned beneath her skin. She tapped her water bottle against her thigh and inched forward, then realized a cop could be hiding behind the gas station.

Best to play it safe. Best that her whereabouts never be discovered.

Still red.

"Darling," she whispered into the car's lonely cockpit, "it was my mistakes that brought you and your son into this world. All of this has been my fault."

Green: time to go.

"This," she said, "is for you and Jacob."

Although pain writhed beneath her scalp, answered by the torture in her spine, she kept both hands on the steering wheel. Eyeing the GPS coordinates on her phone, she made three turns and found a rutted road that wound through an arroyo to a lonely trailer home. The ruts smoothed out, reaching flat dirt raked in precise diagonal lines and bordered by white quartz. The trailer itself sat primly on scrubbed cinder blocks.

She rolled down her window and left the engine running, with headlights aimed at the front door where an Airedale dog barked at her intrusion—though only as a formality, the way a butler might inform his master that a desired guest had arrived.

Potted plants graced the porch rail, green and healthy. A garden hose hung off to the side in tight, even coils, and a ceramic sign above the doorbell read, "There's no place like HOME."

If you're looking for Kansas, Dorothy, you're a few states off.

Was this the right place? It looked so tidy, so . . . domestic.

The first hint of something off kilter came from a crimson glow pulsing against drawn lace curtains. The trailer was one huge heart, beating, beating, trying to sustain life despite unknown injuries sustained.

The second hint came from closer inspection of the sign at the door. The word HOME was in caps, bleached white, and fashioned from slivers of bone.

Welcome to wonderful Oz.

She took a swig from the water bottle, tasting vodka. Took another.

A male figure appeared in the entryway. He nudged the dog against his leg, then directed it indoors without a sound. His right arm was folded behind his back, his left angled across his groin. "There's no outlet here," the man said.

Nikki figured she had one last chance to swing the car around.

"You made a wrong turn," he said.

She recognized his face, those gaunt cheekbones and that large frontal lobe. She knew that Collector's infected nails had disrupted her thinking processes, yet still she could tell this picture was askew. Perhaps it was the lace apron tied about the man's waist, as though she had caught him doing the dishes.

At 1:14 a.m.?

"A wrong turn," he repeated, fingers fiddling with the lace. A turtleneck covered his neck and arms. "It's understandable, of course. Humans are flawed organisms, every one of them."

"We must bleed out our imperfections," Nikki agreed.

The fiddling stopped.

"Yes, Erwin, you heard me."

He bobbed back and forth, plucking at the apron, pinching, tearing. Behind him, the glow swelled and shrank and lent him the appearance of some post-apocalyptic survivor standing on the brink of a brutal new reality. His eyes glinted in the headlamps, revealing melancholic gray that swirled into bottomless pits of black. The same color she'd seen in Natira's eyes. Was this man hosting a Collector of his own?

Regardless, this man's documented antisocial tendencies made it unlikely he would communicate with the Akeldama Cluster.

"You are N. K.," he said.

She gulped from her bottle and turned off the car. "Hello."

"You came to me."

Erwin J. Marstens sounded lucid and soft spoken, in contrast to the tone of the demented letters he had sent her. He was an intelligent man, holding multiple correspondence degrees—including one from Stanford University—and by all accounts this only intensified his torturous instability. Nikki's attorney had filed charges sixteen months earlier, after Erwin's stalking efforts turned bizarre.

A large doll sent to her studio . . . face painted to match her own.

Carnations in a vase . . . and a note that read: *"Dear Mother."*

"I want to see you," he called from the porch.

"You will, Erwin."

Nikki reached into her purse and popped the childproof lid from her bottle of pills. Of late, the medication had helped her face studio audiences and the world at large; it would help her now. She palmed all thirty

of the remaining capsules into her mouth and washed them down with
quick draughts of alcohol.

This desert heat was making her dizzy. Her pus-filled wound seeped
into her hair, and she felt as though thorns were creeping through her
limbs. She needed air. She climbed from the car.

"You're skinnier than you look on TV."

"Camera adds weight. That's . . . that's what they say."

In a closed courtroom, psychologists had outlined Mr. Marstens' history of emotional trauma, starting with his single mother's death and his
belief as a young boy that she'd intentionally set her bed ablaze. He'd
brought home his report card that day and endured the angry stabs of her
cigarette. He was sleeping beside her when the fire occurred. He escaped
with a severely burned neck, back, and arms, convinced that she had meant
to take him with her into the flames of eternal hell.

Nikki remembered the clinical descriptions of this man aching for
maternal bonds while simmering with disdain for all who represented
them. Although indicted for violent crimes in the past, he had never been
convicted because the lack of any bodies left room for reasonable doubt.

In such extreme cases, rehabilitation was unlikely, and tonight Nikki
Lazarescu was counting on it.

"Why is it you've come, N. K.?" he said, suddenly wary.

"Call me Nikki."

He fidgeted. Bobbed.

"There's no place like home," she said, feeling like Dorothy in this
nightmare scenario. She moved forward, gritting her teeth against the pain
in her temples. "And I want to make certain I don't lose my family."

The house still pulsed with its heart-red glow.

"Just as you lost yours, Erwin."

"This," he snapped, "is my home."

"But you're all alone, aren't you? That's why I came."

"Did you like the flowers I sent? I grew them myself."

"That was long ago. I'm here now, though. Soon I'll be feeling very
drowsy, and it'll be time to bleed away my sins. Do you understand what
I'm saying? If you know a way to alter VIN numbers on a car, you're welcome to use mine, but please dispose of the plates." Her stomach lurched.

She took another step toward the trailer, fearing the horror to come while hoping for escape from her ills. "I have one more request. Are you listening, dear?"

"I've been listening to you for years."

"I . . ." She felt her mouth go dry. "I need you to . . . to make sure I'm never seen again. They mustn't ever find my body, is that clear?"

A glint in his eyes. A tweak of his apron. At his back, a flat-screen TV became visible, filling half a wall with images of artificial coals glowing in a rustic hearth. His longing for home? Or a longing to join dear Mother in her fiery grave?

"Can you do that for me, Erwin?"

He bobbed faster. Gave emphatic nods.

This was the only way, she'd decided, to guarantee Gina's and Jacob's permanent protection. She had once bled out her daughter's sins, trying to make Gina forget, trying to purge her soul. Now Nikki was purging her own.

"I should be out soon," she said, voice beginning to slur.

"You sound sleepy."

"Truth be told, I'm dying. All I ask is that you speed it along. Can you . . . can you do that for me, please? Can you promise me?"

"I promise you, Nikki."

Mr. Marstens worked until dawn fulfilling his word.

THE SECOND SENSE: TOUCH

It could make them lonely, soul-lost slaves of the night,
often seeking solace in the soil of their native land.

—RICHARD MATHESON, *I AM LEGEND*

They are like wandering stars, doomed forever to blackest darkness.

—*JUDE 1:13*

Journal Entry

July 18

We spread my topographical map on the table, and Mom explained that it's an overview of Kerioth-Hezron. To me, the Hebraic writing is nothing but scribbles. Hard to believe Judas was a little boy running around in this village. Is it possible to know what's in the heart of a child at that age? Why do some become heroes, while others grow into figures of infamy? Mom tells me it's the Power of Choice.

"So how come Nikki chose to die?" I asked. "You think it was a good decision?"

"In her own mind," Mom said, "I'm sure your grandma felt she was doing the right thing to help pay for other choices she'd made."

"I wish we could choose just once, good or bad, and that'd be it."

Mom drew me close. "Each day we come to a crossroad, sweetheart, and that's what we get to do . . . Day by day by day, we choose."

Staring at the map, I had the sense that my choices would someday lead to this small slice of Israeli desert. My grandpa, Cal Nichols, must've picked out this specific map for a reason before it was sent to me. As for the blood, these drops have given me peeks into everything leading up to now—Natira, the Collectors, the Akeldama, and the Nistarim. The future, though, seems vague.

Uncertain I could live up to my own words, I said, "I want to be the good guy."

"I'd expect nothing else, Jacob. Your birthday's coming soon, and you'll get your chance." A tired smile crossed Mom's face. "You know, this is the part I was afraid of. I finally have you safe by my side, and already you're being called to put it all on the line."

CHAPTER
EIGHTEEN

Lord Natira was in a foul mood. Standing beside him at his throne, Erota could see it in his glowering eyes, feel it in his tensed muscles. Was he displeased with the work she'd done while he was gone?

"What're you thinking this morning?" she said.

He said nothing. His pincers tore at the briars on his armrest.

"Talk to me, please."

"Barabbas." Natira gestured at the henchman. "Leave us."

"My lord?"

The revenant tore away his crusty crown and marched from his seat. He hooked fingers around that same Adam's apple Erota had seen ripped from Barabbas' throat sixteen months earlier and pulled the man close. "Don't you hesitate when I give a command. You think you have the Power of Choice? You think I'm running a democracy here?"

Barabbas shook his head, breaths escaping in gasps.

"Now go."

Released, the bearded man slunk across the cave into darkness.

"You are upset, Natira," Erota said. "What's bothering you?"

He gave a bitter laugh and settled back in his seat. "Are you going to pester me now with your questions?"

"Why'd you return if you're so unhappy here?"

He slammed down his fist. "Because I am lord of this cluster."

"Yes," she said. "You are."

Last October, Natira had flown back from the Pacific Northwest with news of Nikki Lazarescu's disappearance and of her daughter's death. This meant, of course, that Gina had not died years ago in Bucharest as reported by the *Cronica Romana* newspaper. As for Nikki, there were indications she'd hidden at her producer's cabin before scuttling off once more—a pest, afraid of the light.

Erota recalled her own encounter with N. K. Lazarescu, near Atlanta in 1997. Playing the role of an autograph-seeking fan, she'd pricked the woman's hand with a pen and pretended to kiss the blood-dotted wound.

A treacherous kiss.

Like that of the Betrayer who'd been born at this spot.

Erota resorted now to another kiss, pressing full lips to Natira's earlobe and simulating moans of pleasure. Though he pulled away, a second and third attempt brought forth the expected male response, and she led him by the hand to their private chamber, where black candles crackled above soft fur pelts and strings of victims' jewelry.

When Natira was done, he pulled a robe about his chiseled frame and paced the floor. He'd shown no affection in his touch. He'd treated her no differently than those customers in her days as a temple prostitute.

This was her Black King? What girlish fantasies had blinded her to his self-absorbed ways?

Sitting up, she said, "What have I done wrong?"

He kept pacing.

"Lord Natira, do you hear me?"

"Nothing," he grumbled. "You did well while I was gone."

Indeed, she had. Under Erota's guidance, Shelamzion had sold off Totorcea Vineyards in Romania and brought along the youngest Collectors, Kyria and Matrona, thus uniting the households. Together, they had increased productivity, weaving new limbs into the panels' fabric of flesh, splicing more veins into the root system that supplied their quarters with sustenance.

Erota, always attentive to detail, had kept attendance in times past, and she now ran down that original list in her mind, tabulating the cluster's present strengths and weaknesses.

House of Ariston:

Ariston—Former cluster leader, husband, and father (deceased)

Shelamzion—Ariston's first wife (at Kerioth-Hezron, widowed)

Sol—Ariston and Shelamzion's son (deceased)

Natira—cluster leader, Ariston and Helene's son (at Kerioth-Hezron)

Shalom—Ariston and Shelamzion's daughter (deceased)

Salome—Ariston and Shelamzion's daughter (deceased)

Helene—Ariston's second wife, mother of Natira, sister of Dorotheus (at Kerioth-Hezron, widowed)

Auge—Sol's wife, Kyria's mother, daughter of Dorotheus (deceased)

Kyria—Sol and Auge's young daughter (at Kerioth-Hezron, orphaned)

Nehemiah—Ariston's brother, Shabtai's father (deceased)

Shabtai—Nehemiah's teen son (deceased)

Matrona—Nehemiah's young daughter (at Kerioth-Hezron, orphaned)

House of Eros:

Eros—household leader, father of Erota and Domna (deceased)

Hermione—Eros' sister (at Kerioth-Hezron)

Dorotheus—mother of Eros, Hermione, and Auge (at Kerioth-Hezron)

Megiste—Eros' former mistress, former household priestess (in exile, location unknown)

Domna—Eros' teen daughter (at Kerioth-Hezron)

Erota—Eros' teen daughter, interim cluster leader (at Kerioth-Hezron)

Barabbas—household attendant (at Kerioth-Hezron)

"We may be fewer," she told Natira, "but I believe we're stronger."

He grunted.

"And, don't forget, we're working on a new vineyard to be harvested. New wine to be drunk. You've seen the vines I've trained through the passageways, one from each of the Six, No Seven panels, now winding toward Jerusalem."

He nodded. "Even that Holy City has unholiness to be tapped."

"That's right. And what better way to break the backs of the Concealed Ones, to tear the heart from the Almighty's chest. Final Vengeance is only a matter of time."

"Time," Natira said, "is our enemy."

It was true these human hosts seemed to amplify its headlong rush. It rotted flesh from the camel skulls in this valley and carved wrinkles in the faces of Bedouin goat herders. It also brought this planet closer to the Nazarene's return. If the vast Collection of Souls was not soon completed, the Almighty would put an end to this charade and swoop down for His beloved knuckle-draggers.

"We'll focus on our work," Erota said to Natira. "Whatever's been gnawing at you, it'll fall away as we get closer to our goals."

"No!" He raked the candles from a natural shelf in the sandstone. "That's just it. The prophecy stipulates that I need a key to 'unlock riches' for the advancement of our cause, and that's a goal I have not met."

"The key's been lost, you told me. And the duplicate was a fake."

"I let that Asgoth play on my hopes."

"Maybe there's something we've missed. Is there another 'likeness' of the Black King? A carving? A statue?"

"I want that Crown of Thorns."

She frowned. "You're sure it's part of Rasputin's treasure?"

"How do you think he healed Alexei Romanov's blood disorder? He was no magician, no miracle worker. He used that Nazarene Blood."

"And such Blood can only bring us trouble."

At Natira's feet, a candle ignited the hem of a purple tapestry. He ignored the growing flames. "You think I'm not aware of the danger? That's why I want the thing. If I can't wear it, I'll crush it down upon the head of another."

She pointed. "The fire."

He ripped the tapestry from its wall hooks and wadded it till the conflagration had been smothered. When he'd finished, his face was darkened by soot, but for the first time in months he was smiling.

"What?" Erota frowned. "Was it something I said?"

The hammers in Lord Natira's head had stopped. He knew—oh yes, he knew—this reprieve was only temporary, yet he couldn't suppress a surge of excitement. With silky brown hair draping her olive skin, Erota still awaited an explanation.

"I'm flying back," he said.

"Where?"

"To the Pacific Northwest. And while I'm in the area, I can ferret out more of the Concealed Ones."

"What're you saying, Natira? What's this all about?"

Squealing kids dashed through the curtain at the entryway, Matrona and Hermione chasing Kyria, who waved a severed appendage. Another addition for the panels, no doubt—a "hand that killed the innocent." Had this particular piece come from a suicide bomber? Perhaps a drunk driver? It was good to see these younger Collectors harvesting from nearby townships, even if their child hosts turned the task into playtime.

Helene peeked in. "Forgive the intrusion. Come, children—not in here."

"Thank you, Mother," Natira said.

"Go on out," Erota shouted. "Go, Kyria. Take the others with you."

The trio disappeared as quickly as they'd entered. Erota closed the curtain and turned to face him. "Why this sudden change of moods? You mean to tell me you're leaving again, abandoning me here on these desert fringes?"

"You're doing good work."

"Why, my lord? Tell me why."

"It *was* something you said." He rubbed charcoal smudges from his angular face. "Yes, there *is* another 'likeness' of me."

"In America?"

"That I don't know. But his mother should."

"You . . . you're saying you sired a son?"

"With one Trudi Ubelhaar. She's an old woman now, a Nazi war criminal, and the latest I've heard is that she's locked up in an Oregon prison."

CHAPTER
NINETEEN

Early March—Florence, Oregon

Her mother was dead. Even now, in Josee's VW on the way to the Oregon coast, Gina felt an emptiness in her chest. After Nikki's phone message last September, Nickel had poked around, found security footage of a huge Collector attacking Nikki's car as she arrived home one evening, and theorized that her disappearance was meant to protect her family. A final closing of the curtain.

"You mean, suicide?"

"Basically."

"But why not just go underground?" Gina had demanded. "You know, lay low like she did before? Nope, you're wrong, Dad."

"You heard the message. She was already dying."

"Who knows? Maybe that was a ruse of some sort."

"Doctors backed up her story."

Gina closed her eyes. "They could've been in on it."

"Then why haven't we heard from her in months? Why hasn't she been back to her place in Pasadena or paid the mortgage? What about her producers? You know as well as I do it's not like her to dump her responsibilities. Greg Simone hasn't seen head nor hair of her."

"*Hide* nor hair, Dad."

"Hide? Ah, okay. Still working on my slang."

"Not bad for a guy who's been around for a couple millennia. If you can't even keep that straight, though, how can you be so sure of what happened to Mom? She kissed me, while we were on our trip up north. Did you know that? Right on my temple, as if that was the way things had always been between us."

"It's a memory to hold on to," he said.

"Forget that. I'm not buying she's gone."

"Here's the deal, Gina. She already blamed herself—and me—for your brother's death. She couldn't let the Collectors get to you too. A sip from her veins, and they would've had all they needed to know, causing her more guilt she didn't need."

"I think I'd feel it in my gut, at least some clue that she was gone."

"Gina . . ." Nickel paused for a full ten seconds. "I know."

Confronted by his certainty, she knew it too—and broke down. She had known from the night she listened to Nikki's message over and over, hoping for a suggestion otherwise. With her father confirming the worst of her fears, she could no longer skip along in denial.

She sniffled now in the VW. Over six months had passed, but the loss caused a breath-catching ache that felt terminal. Would it ever go away?

"You okay?" Josee said from the driver's seat.

"Yeah."

Sarge filled the small space in back, his snoring punctuated by snorts and garbled sentences. When he'd offered earlier to drive, Josee said she could better fend off car sickness by navigating the roads herself.

Trees and ribbons of fog welcomed them on their winding descent through the coastal range. Josee turned off the wipers. "Thinking about your mom again?"

Gina nodded.

"I can't even imagine what's going through your head, but you're not alone, Gina. Need to unload? I'm right here."

"Okay."

"Right here," Josee said again. "Look, we've got a straight shot into Newport, and then we'll cut south through Yachats to Florence. Supposed to be dry along the coast. Not that it really matters. My Fabergé's in a bank vault."

"You come over here a lot?"

"Not too often." Josee checked her mirrors, touched fingertips to the silver ring above her eye. "Sarge and I, we met while dealing with stuff similar to what you've been facing, and it all culminated at Heceta Head Lighthouse just down the road from here. Wanna know the truth? I get a little spooked being back in this area."

"Least you're still alive and kicking."

"You too. I bet your mom would want you to keep kicking."

"And hard."

"As for him?" Josee jerked a thumb toward her fiancé. "Try waking that sleeping bear, and you'll see kicking like never before. He's mellow most of the time, but he can fight when necessary. Stand back and watch out."

"Jed told me the same thing about him."

"Speaking of . . . Did Jed ever return your calls?"

Gina shook her head. "He's moved on. Whatever works for him, I guess."

"He's not as far away as you might think," Josee said, then shifted the conversation to the Pacific Ocean now stretched out before them. "There's an amazing sight. Kind of puts things in perspective, huh?"

The Bank of the Dunes security guard had Josee sign in at a leather-bound register before ushering the three of them into the vault. "Got your key on ya, miss?"

Josee wiggled it in the air.

"Just holler when you're done," he said.

Although Sarge was still rubbing sleep from his eyes, Gina felt hers widening as she looked around the room. Here, behind reinforced bars, their voices bounced off marble flooring and rows of safe-deposit boxes. In the upper corner, a camera watched the proceedings.

Josee unlocked Number 89 and carried the metal box to a viewing table. She withdrew a felt bag, loosened the drawstring, and revealed a jeweled Fabergé egg.

"Wow. You got this from your grandpa?" Gina said.

"Grandpa Addison. Shhhh. He stole it fair and square from the Nazis."

"Who stole it from some Russian museum or whatnot," Sarge said. "Far as anyone knows, it's been lost forever."

"Here. Hold it if you want."

"You serious?" Gina cupped the glittering object in her hand. "It's smaller than I expected, but definitely not light."

"Real gold. Real diamonds."

The imitations back at the gallery were beautiful, yet nothing comparable to this. Standing on cabriole legs and a garnet stem, the oval egg was no more than four inches tall. Translucent turquoise enamel gave it an ethereal sheen and provided a backdrop for its band of resplendent rose diamonds. Classy, even magnificent, it remained small enough not to appear gaudy.

"Those initials on the base," Josee said, "they're from Henrik Wigstrom, one of Fabergé's master workmen. We've pieced together that Rasputin commissioned this as a gift for the tsars. The color of those diamonds? At the time, red wasn't allowed because it reminded the Romanovs of their son's blood disorder. Alexei had hemophilia."

"So, what changed?"

"You tell her," Josee said, bumping Sarge with her hip.

"'Kay." He dwarfed Josee's hand in his own and turned to Gina. "Well, it's plain historical fact that Rasputin helped out Alexei for a coupla years, keepin' him mostly healthy. Way we figure, Rasputin decided to reveal his cure to the tsars, maybe even tucked it inside the egg. Most of 'em held hidden things, symbolizing Easter and new life. You look at the pics online and you can't help shake your head at all the stuff this Fabergé guy came up with. A real ar-teest."

"Is the treasure still in here?"

"Not unless Josee's got some secret she ain't telling."

"Nope. Nada. The day I opened this deposit box for the first time, the bag and the egg were all I found, along with a personal note from Grandpa Addison. The egg opens up, though. You wanna see?"

"If you don't mind."

"Hold it up. Yeah, like that. See there?"

"Gotta get it just right," Sarge said. "Tilt it under the light."

"I still don't . . . Okay," Gina said. "I see letters, real faint, like they're floating under the turquoise. Looks Russian—which would make sense, I guess."

"Says, 'Tmu Tarakan.'" Josee gripped the upper half with her free hand, pressing down and twisting. "An old phrase referring to darkness and cockroaches, and it's where Rasputin hoarded away his relics."

"Allegedly," Sarge noted.

"Oooh, good word."

"There's more where that came from." He thunked knuckles against his skull. "You're not marrying no slouch, I'll have you know."

"Well, that's a relief—for me and for any kids we might have together."

Even as Gina chuckled at their repartee, she wondered about the egg's concealed space and the mechanism locking it from view. Josee guided the top of the egg through another turn, squeezed together the cabriole legs, and was rewarded with a soft click. As the legs flattened, the upper portion lifted and released four golden tabs. Each bore a word in that odd Cyrillic lettering.

"'Black King Is Key.'" Josee translated.

"Or," Sarge said with a grin, "it could be 'Is Key Black King?'"

Josee elbowed him. "They're cockroaches," she said, turning to Gina. Indeed, the tabs were fashioned into insect shapes with diamond-chip eyes.

"A cockroach compass," Gina said. "See the four points."

Josee nodded her head. "A flippin' compass."

"Sorry. I'm not trying to demean your Fabergé or anything. I'm just—"

"No, you're right. You're right."

"Indubitably," Sarge said.

"Don't you realize?" Josee gave Gina a jab. "This could lead us to the Tmu Tarakan. No one's ever been able to find it—not that we even know where to start—but we have a compass for the task."

"What if it's locked?" Gina said, playing along.

"I've got the black king," Sarge said. "A chess piece, that's all it is.

Quite the hot item last summer, during my investigation in Junction City."

"Okay, hold on. I bet my dad knows about this, doesn't he? It's probably why he connected us in the first place. Does this mean we're all going on a treasure hunt?"

"Are you mocking us?"

"No, I'm not mocking. Don't forget," Gina said, "I have a little goodie of my own to show you, a few thousand years old."

"You have it with you?"

"A deal's a deal." She pulled the bronze dagger from the sheath on her shin. "Long, long ago, this belonged to Apostle Peter, before he cut off some dude's ear and left it—the dagger—in the Garden of Gethsemane."

"In Jerusalem? That garden?"

Even as Gina nodded, her weapon flashed in the overhead lights and triggered immediate action from the security guard. He must have been monitoring the camera, because he appeared with his hand on his holster.

"Put the knife down, ma'am. Nice and easy."

"It's, uh . . . ornamental."

"Set the ornament on the floor, please."

She sighed, rolled her eyes, and complied. This wasn't downtown L.A., but if he was so worried, maybe the bank should follow the example of airport security and invest in a metal detector.

"You need me to take off my shoes also?" she kidded.

The guard studied the dagger, even tested its blade with his thumb, then shot her a reproving look and said she could retrieve it on her way out.

After his exit, Josee took one last glance at the Fabergé before stowing it once more in Number 89. Sarge commented that the guard was only doing his job, and Josee said Gina would forget it had even happened once they got back outside. At the register, Gina strapped the dagger back into place, thinking of the experiences it had taken her through so far—from the caves in Romania to a showdown with a werewolf.

Yep, she'd killed with this thing before, and she would do it again.

"You coming or not?" Josee said.

"We in a hurry?" Gina shot back, feeling testy.

"Got someone waiting out by the car, that's all."

As they exited the Bank of the Dunes, sand gusted across the parking lot, stinging their exposed skin. Gina squinted and covered her face with an arm. Beside her, Josee and Sergeant Turney jogged toward the Bug, calling to mind the unlikely escape of an antelope and pachyderm from the zoo.

Shame on me for even thinking such a thing, but there it is.

Why, Gina wondered, did some relationships work and others fail? For certain people, chemistry could flair and sizzle in a matter of hours, while others bumbled their way through a lifetime of steadfast devotion. She'd seen couples who fought each other also fight to keep their marriages together, and others who interacted with meek nods and glances before deciding to call it quits.

She had her hand on the car door when she remembered what Josee had mentioned inside. "Wait, where's the surprise you were telling me about?"

"Who."

"What?"

"No, who."

"I'm confused. You told me—"

"He's right behind you," Josee said. "Hey there, Jed."

CHAPTER
TWENTY

Gina turned. The form before her was manlier than she remembered, more muscular. Beneath the pall of a winter sky, he appeared in Technicolor, his jeans black, his Levi jacket lined with soft lambskin, and his stark blue T-shirt matching his round, bright eyes. The last time she'd peered into them, they'd been ensconced behind black-rimmed glasses, but he seemed to have switched to contacts—which wasn't a bad thing, not at all.

No more Weezer lead singer. Hello, Mr. Patrick Dempsey. Except mussed hair and slumped shoulders revealed him as her loveable Jed.

"What're you doing here?"

"Came to see you, Gina."

"If Josee put you up to this, let's stop now."

"No, I'm the one who asked where I could find you. I'm ready to talk."

"Ready to talk? You make it sound like you're giving in to torture."

"The only torture's been being away from you."

"Cheesy, Jed."

Gina swiveled back toward the VW, finding that her theatrics lost some of their flair without a long chestnut mane to toss. Did she think she was proving something with this juvenile behavior? Sure, she appeared nineteen or twenty, but she was twice that age. Shouldn't she be the one setting the mature tone?

"You think I'm kidding?" he said. "For five years I've lived in a daze, trying to figure out what went wrong. It wasn't my fault, what happened to our son. I get that now. Just one of those horrible things that happens, no rhyme or reason, but I wasn't prepared for it. I lost Jacob—we lost Jacob—and then I lost you too. My head was a mess for a long time. Is that so hard to understand? Don't you still have some rough days?"

Gina saw an image of Jacob casting a line from Lummi Island's shores and was struck by the grief she knew Jed must still be carrying.

"A lot's happened," she said.

Jed moved closer. "When Josee said you'd be here today, I hoped maybe we could . . . I dunno, work things through."

"Really."

"Or I can go," he said, hands shoved into the pockets of his jacket.

"No. I mean, you don't have to do that."

"Does that mean we can talk about us?"

"Does 'us' still exist?"

"That's what I want to talk about."

"Well, there's no use talking about it if it doesn't."

"Anything you want to sling at me, Gina, go ahead. Just tell me when you're done, because I have a few things to get off my chest too."

"You? Like you've put any effort into this. When we agreed to meet at your uncle's house last year in Corvallis, all you left me was a note. A stinkin' scrap of paper. And then, instead of returning my calls, you send a letter and tell me you need more *time*?"

"Call me an idiot."

"A stupid idiot."

"Just thinking about seeing you brought back all the other stuff, all the memories of . . . the hospital, the bombing. I wasn't ready for that." He hitched his shoulders. "Now I am. If it means giving us another shot."

Though he was saying all the right things, she too had barricaded herself against pain. The blows had come in devastating succession—Jacob, Petre Podran, Teodor, and most recently her own mother. This fortress was built of buttressed rock, held together by mortar; yet where spears, arrows, and swords failed to force their way through, a secret passageway remained. She'd let her husband through before, and, despite encroaching vines and creaking hinges, she believed she could let him through again.

"Another shot?" she said. "Maybe."

Sergeant Turney slapped the roof of the VW twice. "'Kay, boys and girls, why don't Josee and I let you two have some privacy."

"Thanks, Sarge," said Jed.

"Gina?" Josee gazed over the top of the car. "You okay with that?"

She pursed her lips and nodded.

"I've got wheels, so I can take her home," Jed said. "I'll swing by on my way back to Silverton."

Biting her lip, Gina nodded again. She'd waited for this opportunity, and now that it was here she felt clumsy, hopeful, and full of stories that should and should not be shared. She wanted to tell Jed that Jacob was alive. Wanted to run off with them and live in the middle of nowhere.

Just the three of them. A family.

Sarge and Josee said their good-byes, and a minute later they pulled from the bank onto Highway 101, with gray and pink clouds marking the way over the mountains. Josee had mentioned a surprise. Well, here it was in front of Gina.

"Let's go someplace private," her surprise said.

"You mean, other than a parking lot?"

Jed smiled. "I built a driftwood fort for us just down the beach. Thought maybe we could go sit and watch the tide roll in."

"Just like that. As if the past few years never happened."

"I can't go another day, not after seeing you in person again."

"Is that a compliment?"

"Definitely."

"Even with my hair like this?"

"Like what?"

"Short and blotchy blonde."

"I wasn't in love with your hair, Gina."

"Me either, actually."

"I'm still wearing my ring, if that means anything to you."

She snatched his hand from his pocket. Yep, there was the wedding band she'd placed on his finger during a civil ceremony in Chattanooga. In the same way it had sealed their commitment then, it sealed her decision now.

"Okay, Mr. Driftwood, show me your handiwork."

Ruins of Kerioth-Hezron

Erota ran her eyes over rock-strewn ground. The thistles that grew at the feet of these ruins wedged up through the cracks and provided refuge for serpents, spiders, and lizards. How had mothers handled life in those forgotten days of Kerioth? Had they huddled with their children in tents and cave dwellings, hoping to guard them from dangers without? Had Judas, the only one of the Nazarene's disciples not from Galilee, viewed things through harsher eyes because of it?

Feeling maternal urges for her cluster members, Erota wanted to see them nourished. The slow growth of her vines toward Jerusalem made her impatient, and Lord Natira's prolonged absences from this cluster felt like the abandonment of a father.

A new opportunity had presented itself, though.

Last night a message had come from Megiste, offering a partnership of sorts while the lead Collector was away—all for their collective good, of course.

"Is there something I can get for you?" Barabbas said, jolting Erota from her thoughts.

She shook her head.

He squeezed through a fissure, leaving behind the cavern of thorns and arriving on the rocky slope beside her. "By Sodom's salt, it's cold out here."

"Leave me alone."

"Maybe some jackal pelts to cover your shoulders?"

His husky voice laid bare his desire, and she felt his eyes pawing at her smooth skin. Poor boy. His hormones seemed on constant high alert, and he missed the ministrations of their exiled priestess, Megiste. Erota had also lured quite a few over the years with promises of pleasure—or pain, if that was their particular interest—yet always to advance her own goals. Now she felt nothing but goose bumps rising along her arms.

"Sure, Barabbas," she said. "Bring one that's thick."

"I'll be back."

She watched him duck through the opening. The animal skins were piled deeper in the hillside, in the chambers that housed the cluster's members. She would have a few moments of reflection while he crossed their cathedral, with its engorged vines, arched bowers, and hideously grandiose Six, No Seven panels:

Haughty eyes . . . a slew of eyeballs and the skulls that held them.

Lying tongues . . . a wagging collection of rumors and dissent.

Hands that killed the innocent . . . angry fists and prying fingers.

Hearts that plotted evil . . . black hearts in brittle ribcages.

Feet that raced to do wrong . . . a stampede of violence and greed.

False witnesses who poured out lies . . . curved fangs pumping out venomous deceptions.

And those who sowed discord among brothers . . . words turned into scimitars, swinging this way and that, cutting down families, churches, cities.

Despite her frustrations, Erota had to admire Lord Natira's commitment to a task. He, too, wanted to bring down the Nistarim, and they both knew this collage was not accomplishing that as quickly as hoped. They needed something more.

Such as a vineyard of souls in Jerusalem.

Such as the Crown of Thorns—though Natira's macabre plans for that honored relic were anyone's guess.

Or she could respond to Megiste's summons. No harm, was there, in finding out what the former priestess was up to?

"Here you are, my queen," Barabbas said from behind her.

"Oh. You again." She wanted to tear at his beard, put her nails to good use. She would never let him bed her. What could be gained from such a dalliance?

"The thick one, like you requested."

"Thank you."

She snugged the pelt around her neck, drawing warmth from tan and black bristles once belonging to creatures for which these ruins were named. To this day, jackals haunted the landscape, scavenging for easy meals and carrion, staying mostly out of sight, yelping in witchy, high-pitched tones.

Erota wanted to yelp. She felt extra witchy herself.

"You're shaking," said Barabbas.

"What?" Erota spun around. "Why're you still here, you oaf?"

"The pelt is not enough. Maybe I should help warm you."

"I'm angry, not cold."

His Adam's apple lurched. "At me?"

"At Natira," she blurted out. "Why isn't he here with us?"

"You've always cared for him, haven't you?"

"I don't care for him, no. Don't care for anyone. We're Collectors, not emotion-ridden fools. We can't let the proclivities of our human hosts distract us."

"I feel more human when I'm near you, Erota. Do you ever tire of the maiming, the killing?"

"Get away."

"Are they the only reason we exist?"

"What is this you're babbling on about?"

"I wonder if . . ." He tugged at his beard. "If there's something more."

She backhanded his chest and he stepped back, seemingly perplexed that his servitude had earned displeasure. Well, it was time he realized he was nothing to her but a slobbering hound, panting at her feet, licking at her hands.

"Please," she said, weary of it all. "Just go away."

Alone again, she looked across this desolate landscape. Near these borders of the Judean and Negev Deserts, Hebrew armies had once fought the giants of Anak. Here, too, the one called Yeshua had tangled with the Master Collector. There was little doubt this was cursed soil, and yet the Almighty seemed ever busy with His schemes of redemption, ever alert to ways of working things together for good.

It was unfair, really. How could Collectors fight such illogical love?

Love . . .

Even Barabbas seemed tainted with that divine weakness. Of course, testosterone played a major role in his pandering, but there was something else, something very near to sincerity, to humility, in him. It was disgusting.

A beetle scrabbled through the dirt at Erota's feet, and she crushed it with her toes before returning to the warmth of her own rug-draped cavern.

CHAPTER TWENTY-ONE

Florence

Gina and Jed strode to the sand dunes, removed shoes and socks, then continued along a path that fed onto the beach. Overcast skies mirrored a moody surf. An elderly couple was strolling along the waterline while a man with thick beard and eyebrows coaxed a kite into the air, running and tugging to keep tension in the string. He veered toward them, watching the kite over his back, and nearly bumbled into Gina.

"Hey," Jed said.

The man frowned. "Sorry 'bout that." The wind plucked the spool from his hand, and he dove after it, planting his face beside strands of washed-up kelp.

Gina pinned down the string with a stomp of her foot. "Here you go. That wind's really picking up."

"Blows where it wants, that's a fact."

Bushy beard. Bushy red beard.

"Skipper?" Gina gasped.

He pushed himself up onto his knees and muttered, "Not a word 'bout Lummi Island to this fellow o'er here."

"But he's—"

"Not a word, missy. He'd never believe it anyway."

"You coming, Gina?" Jed was ten feet away. "You all right?"

She cleared her throat and straightened to full height, then followed her husband, her son's father, past hollowed crab shells and scattered wood, through dune grass that pricked at their ankles as they cut over a mound. A driftwood structure awaited, with four walls, a crooked doorway, and a ramshackle roof.

Jed waved his arms and bowed. "Your castle, milady."

She folded her arms. "And a right dingy dump it is."

"Get inside."

"Ohhh, he thinks he's Mr. Tough Guy now."

"He thinks he wants to talk to his wife. Call him sentimental that way."

"I've called you a few other things."

"Probably deserved most of them. Come on."

He took her hand and they ducked inside. Despite gaps between the logs, the walls muted the breakers' roar. Sand was already between their toes, salty air in their hair and on their lips—and Gina loved it. Loved being here with Jed. Loved the sea's visceral power and its ability to bring life into focus.

"Tell me up front," she said. "Have you been seeing anyone else?"

"I've been working too many hours."

"Not even a date."

"Thought that girl in *Spider-Man* was kinda cute. Does that count?"

"She's a blonde."

"So?"

"So that makes me feel a little better."

"Yeah, but you're just a bottle blonde. That doesn't count."

Gina aimed a punch at his shoulder, which he caught and used to spin her into his embrace. Her back was to him as they plopped onto the sand, leaned against the driftwood. His arms stayed folded around her, and it felt like slipping into her own bed after years of life in strange places.

The scar from her old thorns knotted like a muscle in her neck, but when she refused to give it a foothold, the discomfort subsided. She was done holding grudges. Although explanations might come in handy—and the sooner the better—she wouldn't be robbed of her openness to this man.

"Don't you love the smell of the ocean?" he said.

"Why'd you run off every time I came to meet you at Sarge's place?"

"Why'd you close me out after what happened to Jacob?"

"I didn't."

"You did, Gina. Even when I tried to work it through with you, you locked me out. You'd sit in the bathtub and tell me you needed time alone. Maybe I could've done something different that day, somehow saved him. I play it over and over in my mind, thinking how it might've gone differently if I hadn't gone to call my boss, if I had just stayed there next to you."

"There's no use beating yourself up over it."

"I know. It's just that you want to believe you're big enough to save your own child. Isn't that what every dad imagines? That he'd take a bullet to the chest, if he had to? Instead, I was as helpless as anyone else. Not a thing I could do." His jaw muscles worked beneath tapered sideburns. "When you showed up here in Oregon and tried getting ahold of me, it just . . . I didn't know if I could face that baggage again, while I was getting things straightened in my own head."

"Baggage?" Gina said.

"I'm not saying that you—"

"You're right, sweetheart. It was my baggage too. Every time I saw you, I'd think of Jacob and how he would've looked just like his daddy one day, and how I . . . how we would never get to see that. I didn't blame you. Never. But being with you stirred all that up in me, and I wasn't ready for that either."

"So it wasn't all on me?"

She rested her head on his shoulder. "No."

"Because it sure felt like it when you started cutting me off, barely even letting me kiss you after a while."

"I closed down," she conceded. "Didn't know what else to do."

"And I left. Sorry, Gina, I should've stayed by you."

"So what're we doing here now?"

"I don't know."

She nudged back, tilting her chin to place a peck on his cheek. He turned, brushing her lips with his own and sending a shock wave through her that ended in warm tingles. It had been years since she'd exchanged anything other than a motherly kiss. She pulled away, searching his eyes with hers.

"Bad move?" he said.

"I'm not sure." Her heart was racing. "Good move, maybe."

He kissed her a second time, longer, deeper, until making the decision himself to pull away. "Still okay?"

"Mmm," she said. "I think this queen's in trouble."

Corvallis

The day had gone better than imagined, and Gina floated up the steps to her bedroom. She felt at home, felt safe.

"Am I good to take a shower?" she called down the hall.

Josee peeked up from the stairwell. "You got first dibs, but I doubt you'll be able to wash that smile off your face."

"Not that she'd want to," Suzette said.

Hot water rinsed the ocean salt from Gina's skin, flowing from her short hair over her mouth. She traced fingertips across her lips and grinned. After she toweled off, she changed into white shorts, a soft cotton sweatshirt, and flip-flops and padded down to the kitchen, where the aroma of cinnamon, syrup, and egg batter greeted her.

"Feeling better?" Josee said from the stove.

"Yum. French toast for dinner? Sounds dee-licious."

"Spill it, Gina. Did he give you a kiss when he dropped you off?"

"Josee." Suzette's fork rattled onto her plate. "Leave her be."

"Hey, no reason for her to be shy. It's just between us girls, right? And don't even pretend you don't want to know. Just because love hasn't come your way yet doesn't mean you have to punish us for it." Josee soaked another slice of toast in egg and flipped it into the pan. "Ignore her, Gina. Underneath, she's the biggest romantic of the bunch."

"That's still no cause for being nosy," Suzette said.

"It's all good," Gina said. "Ask away."

"So?" Josee asked. "Did he?"

Although Suzette's fork was back in hand, laden with a thick buttered morsel, she paused to hear the reply.

Gina shrugged and grabbed a plate. "I'll never tell."

"What? Oh no, you don't. You can't stop there."

"I said you could ask, Josee, but that doesn't mean I have to answer."

"Now, now." Suzette clicked her tongue. "There's no reason to tease us. Josee asked politely, and—"

"A minute ago you said she was being nosy."

"No, I—"

"Yeah, you did," Josee said.

Sulking, Suzette found solace in another bite. Gina helped herself to two pieces of French toast from the stack in the table's center and wondered about Suzette's past. She knew the woman had experimented with tribal customs and herbs before choosing to follow Josee's example as one of Those Who Resist. Had she never even had a boyfriend? Never been married? No wonder she spent hours holed up with office ledgers or out seeking new acquisitions.

Gina took a sip of apple juice. "Listen, thanks for dinner. I should tell you both how much I appreciate you letting me live here."

"We're pleased to help," Suzette said.

"I've been in your shoes," Josee said. "No place to stay, on the run, trying to deal with family issues. Pass it on, right?"

Gina nodded.

"Don't think this means you're in the clear. We can talk later in our room, but you're not out of sharing the details about you and Jed."

The skin at Gina's throat flushed. This morning she would've guessed it would take months to work back into a relationship with her husband, would've scoffed at the idea that flames could come roaring back from those long-abandoned embers. Now she felt like a schoolgirl. Which made her feel like a grown woman. Giving love away always seemed to enlarge her like that.

With the sweetness of Jed's mouth still on hers, she drizzled syrup over toast and took her first blissful bite.

CHAPTER
TWENTY-TWO

April—Walla Walla, Washington

Sometimes, he decided, a king didn't wish for a triumphal entry. Sometimes he had other stratagems at work.

Lord Natira, former insurgent against the Romans and current leader of the Houses of Ariston and Eros, warrior at heart and scarred giant of a human, had lumbered into downtown Walla Walla five weeks earlier with odiferous rags hanging from his limbs. He was one of spring's early arrivals. A bum. He had found this region somewhat lenient toward the homeless, and was there any better disguise for observing passersby?

Natira's season of the thorn was not yet here—soon enough, soon enough. To strike down his prey, he first needed to locate them.

Which, he had to admit, was a specialty of his.

As an Akeldama Collector, he had risen from an Italian cemetery in 1944, and in the six decades since had assisted Nazis, bedded women, killed men and children, and tracked twenty-eight of the Nistarim—quite an accomplishment considering the billions of humans upon this spinning sphere.

He needed only eight more Nistarim.

And, when that was done, the Crown of Thorns to bring them down.

"Where are you, Number Twenty-Nine?" The Collector was seated at the mouth of an alleyway, a vagrant muttering to himself. "Why the Almighty would bring you here, I do not know, but I'm sure you're nearby."

By experience, Natira had learned that Those Who Resist strengthened and multiplied around a Concealed One's location. He had Twenty-Nine and Thirty left to pinpoint in North America, and this college town was a recent nesting place for the Nazarene's fledglings. Not only had certain crime statistics plummeted, but coeds expressed new joy and commitment to serving others.

What a waste of good meat.

Walla Walla was not far from last year's activities at Maryhill Museum. How serendipitous that his activities kept centering here in the Northwest, as though the Master Collector himself had a hand in Natira's fortunes.

Ever at your beck and call, my Lord of the Flies.

Hunkered in the alley, the vampire considered the repercussions should he and his cluster fail. As punishment, the Restless Desert's scorching terrain awaited all Collectors who botched assignments or lost their permanent hosts.

Natira's head pounded. He needed to drink soon, and this breeze was cutting through his layered rags. Where was this town's Concealed One? When would his undead eyes spot that distinguishing Hebrew letter upon a forehead?

He cupped his hand, stretching it forth the way he'd seen beggars do around the world. No matter the culture, there were those in need of alms.

"Here ya go." Two quarters dropped into Natira's palm.

He mumbled a thanks.

Ten minutes later, a dollar bill floated into his hand with the instructions: "Don't spend it on booze, okay? Buy yourself something to eat." The next donation came with different rules: "Life's too short, buddy. Go get yourself a drink and enjoy every drop."

Bah. These two-leggers were endlessly entertaining.

With midday crowds dispersing and donations falling off, he thought of heading back to the seedy motel on the outskirts of town. Perhaps he could come back to this later, after paying a visit to Trudi Ubelhaar. Not that she'd be going anywhere soon, locked away in a prison cell.

Speaking of elderly women . . .

One hobbled by now, her walker squeaking over the concrete. She was followed by a family out for a brisk stroll.

The husband and wife held hands, chatting, grinning, despite the two teen boys who circled them in a game of tag and the pretty girl who shuffled along with her nose tucked into a book. The smaller of the boys stopped, his gaze fixed upon the hulking vagrant. He whispered something to his parents.

"Go on, Elijah," the dad said. "Why don't you take your brother with you?"

The young men disappeared into a convenience store, and Natira was about to lose interest in their actions when they reappeared with a plastic bag that hugged the shapes of a peanut butter jar, a loaf of bread, and a honey bear.

What was this all about?

The boys advanced. Still hunched against the corner, Natira kept his arm outstretched, his chin down.

"Sir," the taller one said, "here's some food for ya, if you want it."

He accepted the bag with a grunt.

"My dad," the other added, "used to work with homeless guys over in Amsterdam, and he says everyone needs help now and then. Each time you take a bite, remember that the Nazarene loves you."

The Nazarene? They were blaming this kindness on Him?

Natira's attention snapped up, finding two sets of dark eyes that locked onto his without an ounce of judgment. Startling as that was, he was more stunned by the glowing blue marks upon not one, but both, of the boys' brows.

Numbers Twenty-Nine and Thirty? Together?

Well, imagine that. These teenaged brothers, these Concealed Ones with their giving attitudes, had stumbled upon their worst nightmare.

"I, uh . . . don't know what to say," he stammered.

"See ya later," they said in unison.

You can count on it, he vowed. *Thanks for stopping by.*

Once they were gone, he wadded the plastic bag into a doughy ball and dumped it in the nearest trash can.

Ramon Crater, Israel

Erota scooted along on her lean belly, navigating serpentine channels and caverns, funnels and sinkholes. This subterranean maze was home to various wildlife and venomous snakes, explored by only the most intrepid of spelunkers. She was headed for a rendezvous in hopes of expanding her cluster's sphere of destructive influence.

Who, though, would believe she was stooping to this? By meeting with Megiste, was she about to violate the Principles of Cluster Survival?

On the contrary, she was shifting to the end game, refusing to play along with petty rivalries that plagued clusters around the planet. She and the priestess had their differences, but who was she to deny Megiste's request?

Erota had left Barabbas posted at their thorn-infested haunt. For over a day now, she had crawled belowground, following flood-carved tunnels to a crater that marked the Negev Desert like an unwashed belly button. Huge plates of collapsing earth had pocked this wilderness, corroded by time and water, leaving a massive *makhtesh*—erosion crater. It was a natural phenomenon found few places in the world, and Makhtesh Ramon was one of the largest of all, spanning forty kilometers lengthwise.

Megiste couldn't have picked a more remote point in Israel.

And Erota was almost there.

The message from the cluster's former priestess had come to Erota last week, delivered by a boy with handsome features and a swagger in his step. Megiste had promised him he would receive sensual pleasure as a reward for the task, and Erota honored that vow—before taking him on a detour to hell.

Oh, those haughty eyes of his. They were not so haughty once added to the great cavern's collage.

Barabbas had seethed throughout. From jealousy? Or perhaps he had lost his stomach for their sort of work, sickened by the use of torture.

She was so tired of his fawning, tired of these human hosts, undead though they might be. To live each day with thoughts of food and water, sex and companionship . . . It was exhausting in the extreme. No wonder the wretched knuckle-draggers clamored for medications and illegal drugs; no wonder they tossed down alcohol like water and pursued carnal pleasures that led to bodily harm and disease.

Light winked at her now from the tunnel's end, and she forced herself through the gap, punishing her host by leaving curls of skin on ragged rock.

Yes, she could've taken a local Egged bus and skipped this lacerating journey through the earth's bowels, but to do so would've risked Barabbas or one of the other Collectors tailing her. No, she was done with all that.

She climbed to her feet on the crater's north rim. To her surprise, willowy Megiste waited only a few steps away, her ringlets of auburn hair draped over bare, slender shoulders.

"Why, *there* you are, Erota. You're bleeding."

"I'm thirsty." Erota sucked at her raw forearm. "That was hard work."

"Thank you for answering my summons."

They stood side by side on a slope that dropped hundreds of feet into the makhtesh. The midday blaze simmered, and weather-beaten walls encompassed the sandy cauldron as far as the eye could see.

Each year, ill-prepared hikers died here of heat exhaustion.

And thousands of years previous, hadn't the Almighty used barren soil such as this to swallow up entire clans of disobedient Israelites?

The Oh-So-Angry Deity . . .

It was an image the Collectors worked hard to magnify, although Erota knew the full story. Those piddly Hebrews had received a stay of mercy, hadn't they? A second chance. By His crucifixion, the Nazarene had carried out a clever scheme to enter hell's gates, where He offered His Blood and New Wine to thirsty prisoners. Then by conquering death, He led the willing ones free from that infernal Collection of Souls.

Was the Master Collector's fury any surprise?

I'll do all within my power, Erota thought, *to take back souls, even if it means collaborating—for now—with this reprobate priestess.*

"I realize we've had our differences," Megiste said, her voice treacly and soft. "Who doesn't? Yet we both seek Final Vengeance, do we not? Of course we do." She fanned her neck with an alabaster hand. "So let us find a way to usher in that day."

"I agree. Why don't you come work with us again? Submit yourself to Lord Natira's rule."

"Submitting? Is that what you're doing by meeting with me now?"

"I'm hoping to unite our causes."

"Rumors are that he's gallivanting about the States, neglecting his cluster."

"He left me in charge. We've done fine on our own, even increasing production in his absence. The caves are more glorious than ever, and we have tendrils growing toward Jerusalem."

"I'm hardly surprised, my dear. If you'll allow me to say it, warriors really make the most *awful* kings. History's rife with the messes such men have made."

"Natira's not just any king. He's the Black King."

"So it would seem. He's the cluster's rightful heir—oh, I'm not disputing *that*—and I do understand your feelings for him."

"I don't have feelings for him."

"Your feelings of loyalty, shall I say? Yes, well, the problem has always been our fellow Collectors, so often thwarted by their hosts' needs and desires."

"You don't have to convince me."

"Oh, Barabbas has been annoying you, hasn't he?" With bracelets tinkling, Megiste brushed a hand over Erota's. "I'm sure he's missed my touch. Delectable as he can be, he's such a brute and, like most men, so easily derailed from the more urgent matters. It's almost as though he's . . . he's human." She giggled at her own joke. "Which is the beauty of my latest scheme—no Collectors, no two-leggers, and not one animal harmed in the process."

"You find this funny?" Erota thrust a finger at the cliff and its jagged fissures. "I burrowed through all that dirt and sand to come entertain your latest flights of fancy? If you're so wise, o priestess, tell me what you've created now."

"Created? You know better than that, Erota."

"What, then?"

Megiste's thin lips curved upward. "We've never been able to *create*, but that's not to say we cannot manipulate, distort, and deform. Give me a bit of flesh and blood, a few pinches of dirt, and I'll counterfeit the Almighty's ingredients."

"I'm still not sure I understand."

"Although the job will be painstaking, perhaps years to complete, I can give a crude demonstration a few hours from now. If that fails to pique your interest . . . Why, then, we'll part ways, and you'll keep my whereabouts secret."

"Is this where you've been living? In this crater?"

"My, oh my, no. Have you ever known me to forgo material comforts?"

"It's not your style."

"Not my style. Precisely. I *do* enjoy my womanly pampering, after all." She rattled the bracelets on her wrist. "No, in a few short weeks, this'll be my *work*shop."

"I've seen this makhtesh before. Did you call me here simply to brag?"

"To be frank, I'm seeking your permission as the interim leader." Megiste's eyes twinkled with mischief. "You see, Barabbas would be a splendid helpmeet for this project, but he's hamstrung by obligations to the cluster. Principles of Cluster Survival being what they are, I'm begging your leniency."

"To take the big lunk off my hands?"

"If you could spare him."

Despite the appeal, Erota was reticent. "You're already in exile, but this could be mistaken as rebellion on my part."

"Rebellion? Oh no, dear, not at all. With Barabbas' help—and yours, I do hope—I plan to raise up an army. Although I've fallen from Natira's favor, perhaps I can work my way back by offering him these troops to command. For the good of us all, of course."

"Why don't you approach Natira yourself?"

"He could banish me in a moment. It would be *sooo* much easier if I could show him the rewards of my labor. Only then, if he is pleased, will your name be mentioned."

Erota still believed Lord Natira was the Black King, yet questioned his judgment on certain matters. Yes, there might be advantages to playing along with this priestess.

"Why not?" she said, a counterplot brewing in her mind. "Barabbas is all yours."

"Oh, I can't tell you how this pleases me." Megiste took her by the hand, just as she'd done centuries ago while parading her nineteen-year-old prostitute outside the temple. "Come, Erota—let me show you what we'll be working on."

CHAPTER
TWENTY-THREE

Early May—Corvallis

Gina didn't see the man until his hand was resting upon hers.

Seated at one of the library's public computers, dressed in black shorts and an orange, long-sleeved shirt to cover her scars, she was helping coordinate Josee and Sarge's upcoming wedding. It was no easy task finding a cake for the Fourth of July. Traditionally a jam-packed date, it fell on a Monday this year, but Josee swore it had sentimental value beyond the fact it was her birthday.

More power to them if they wanted to compete with parades, cotton candy, and fireworks displays. Shoot, maybe they'd create fireworks of their own.

Hopefully, Jed and I won't be far behind.

Between Jed's work schedule in Silverton and Gina's trips to the San Juans, they had managed to fit in some recent outings together, including a hike of nearby Mary's Peak. They were comfortable in each other's presence, natural as always. Yet there remained things unsaid, secrets roiling beneath the surface, and one day they would have to address some serious issues—the truth about their son, the Collectors, Those Who Resist, as well as the discrepancies in their aging processes.

How would Jed react to it all?

Gina's right hand was guiding the mouse toward a baker's price list when a man came from behind and touched her wrist, his fingers cool upon her skin. She flinched.

"Don't worry," he said. "You're not dying anytime soon."

She glared back at the tall, sandy-haired man. "Take your hands off me."

"Technically, it's only one hand. Singular."

"Take your ugly mitt off me."

He did so.

"Who are you?" she demanded. "Why do you look familiar?"

"I'm a friend of your dad's."

"What do you mean, 'not dying anytime soon'? What kind of thing is that to say to someone?"

"Take it as a good sign." He shrugged. "Nickel told me to pass on the message that he'll be seeing you within the next few weeks. Also said to stay cautious because the trouble's not over yet."

"And why should I be listening to you? How do you even know him?"

"Nickel and I are buds. You remember me now, don't you?"

"You're . . ." She raised an eyebrow. "You're Clay, right?"

"Ryker, not Right."

"What?"

"Otherwise I'd be Mr. Right, and that would be absolutely wrong. I mean, you're attractive and all, but my wife and I are still making a go at it. She's got strawberry-blonde hair and freckles, which—let's face it—are just about the cutest thing in the world."

"Hurray for freckles. You're too tall for me anyway."

"Six-three."

"No wonder I'm staring at your belt. So Nickel sent you?"

Clay nodded and took a knee beside her, one arm resting on the desk.

"Seems risky, you meeting me here in public." Gina panned the computer area. "You're sure no one else knows I'm here?"

"If you signed in for this computer, someone knows."

"I used Josee's card number."

"Josee? Sarge tells me the two of them're tying the knot."

"Why'd you come?" Another swift pan of the area.

"Nickel thought you'd want to know that Kenny's doing great these days. He's training, staying in shape, keeping up on his school work. My own son's getting to be good friends with him, and I've made sure they stay away from anything canine and furry—after that little scare last year."

Kenny had faced dog attacks during his paper route, but nothing like the confrontation with a *vircolac*, a Collector in the form of a Romanian werewolf. Kenny rose to that challenge, stabbing at the creature with one of his MTPs, nailing its foot to the hardwood floor of their old home. Clay apparently knew about the battle.

Gina said, "Thanks for helping him, Clay."

"Sure thing. I better get moving, but wanted to pass on the message."

"Hold on." Now that she knew this man was linked to her father, she wanted him to stay. She lowered her voice. "Can you tell me, does Kenny know what really happened to me in the Nissan?"

"Your dad says it's best that he doesn't."

"So he thinks that I'm . . . Ohh, Kenny."

Clay rested an arm on her shoulder. "Case you're interested, you had a nice funeral. Got your own gravestone in the cemetery west of J.C., nice little hillside plot, paid for by Nickel. Your old Ace Hardware buddies helped arrange things, and Kenny tried to be brave throughout the ceremony. He knows you loved him with your whole heart. Says you're just like Susan."

"Susan?"

"From The Chronicles of Narnia. Steadfast, pretty, and unflappable. That's the word he used, if you can believe that. Unflappable."

"I was helping him with his vocabulary."

"No kidding."

"I feel very flappable, but I can imagine him saying that."

"Remember," Clay said. "Not long and you'll be bumping into Nickel."

"Good to know. Thanks."

Her skin still cool from his touch, she watched the tall man stroll from the library. Though she longed to see her dad, her anticipation was tempered by longing for her adopted son. She and Kenny had shared some good moments together, both growing past their fears and doubts. She'd helped him work through the horror of watching a Collector impale his brother.

Regina Lazarescu . . . In Romanian: "Queen of the Resurrected."

First she had revived Kenny from his despair, and now she had her biological son back from the dead. With the gallery closed on Mondays, she'd be leaving to see him again early tomorrow.

At the moment, however, she had a wedding to plan.

Gina printed out a price list from the bakery Web site, committed to finding the right cake for her roommate. Sad to think that in two months Josee would be moving out and leaving Gina alone in the gallery bedroom, but it was fun thinking they would be in-laws. Now there was something to look forward to.

The Almighty kept finding ways to put a smile back on her face, and a smile still meant something—didn't it?—even when shaded with grief.

En Route to the San Juan Islands

Gina's first hint of trouble came ten days later. She'd been varying her modes of transportation to Jacob's location—this was her ninth visit—so as not to establish any compromising patterns, and today she was on the northbound Amtrak when a passenger left his newspaper while disembarking in Olympia.

"Hey." She tried to flag him through the window. "You forgot something."

The man turned on the platform, touched two crossed fingers to his head in salute, and shrank from view as the train continued toward Seattle.

Well, that was weird. Was he one of the Unfallen? A messenger?

She spread the *Seattle Post-Intelligencer* on her lap. It was dated from September of last year, folded over to a section of statewide news that included a museum robbery. The watchman on duty had disappeared, leaving behind a mangled bird and a discharged cartridge; security tapes had been removed; and, despite pricey Rodin sculptures on exhibit, the sole item tampered with had been the black king from a chess set donated years ago by Queen Marie of Romania.

Gina had been to Bran Castle, home of the former queen, and recalled tossing coins into the courtyard well with Teo. Strange to think this honorable woman had visited the Northwest, carrying out duties both public and private.

Honor . . . duty . . . sacrifice . . .

The principles were ones Gina had learned from Nickel on the chessboard. He'd schooled her in theories of connected rooks, bishop pairs, passed pawns, and centrally posted knights. She'd learned to subdue foes with skewers, forks, and pins, then transferred that knowledge to the real-life board where she fought off her vampiric foes with metal tent pegs, a bronze dagger, and sacred blood.

She had also honed her sense of danger.

Alert to subtleties that could spring a sudden counterattack, she now felt uneasy in this Amtrak compartment. Spiked thorns flashed through her mind, gnarled roots. She touched the cord around her neck and glanced back along the aisle.

Nothing to worry about, Gina. The Nazarene Blood will prevail.

Once more she read through the article. She had no excuse for letting her imagination run wild, yet she could not shake the image of four golden cockroaches bearing the words: "Black King Is Key."

Was someone after Josee's and Sarge's objects?

She rubbed a hand over her head and expelled air. Already, J.C. had experienced a rash of murders related to Rasputin's legacy. If an old train engine could travel from one continent to another with a decades-old secret onboard, was it any less likely Josee's Fabergé egg could end up in an Oregon safe-deposit box? Or that Sarge's chess piece could access ancient riches?

Maybe the surprising thing was that the dots hadn't been connected sooner, all pointing to the tsars and their motherland.

Sarge knew it. Josee knew.

Did someone else? Were they zeroing in even now?

Gina watched the landscape slide by, with snowy Mt. Rainier looming to the east. She longed to be at rest with her husband and son, hiking or skiing these mountains, perhaps exploring Orcas Island. Would that day ever come?

The second hint of trouble came as the train neared the Seattle station.

Gina was standing, stretching, reaching for her duffel bag, when a familiar face zipped past.

"Suzette?" She waved. "Hey, Suzette, what're you—"

The figure had already gone through the door at the compartment's far end. Gina followed after her, thinking it would be nice to have some company, then realized it was a risk she could not take. Not with Jacob's safety on the line. Already, though, the issue was moot, because the woman had vanished.

Scanning the station crowds, Gina saw no sign of Suzette Bishop. Why would the gallery owner be here anyway? Plus, if that was her, why hadn't she acknowledged her own name? Obviously, a case of mistaken identity.

Lynden, Washington

Feeling all the lonelier without her mom along for the trip, Gina walked the streets of quaint Lynden. Banners still heralded the town's recent Holland Days, and she thought of the equally festive Scandinavian Festival in J.C. Of course, none of it interested her now. This was a diversion from her true destination of Lummi Island, a means of testing whether she'd been followed.

She ran her fingers over a pair of painted wooden shoes, pretending to check the price tag. She sampled saltwater taffy. She skirted the decorative windmill on the street corner, and—

Is that Suzette again?

A woman with her build and coloring slipped around the building before Gina could see her face. Though it wasn't uncommon to see Native Americans in this part of the country, the coincidence was too much to ignore.

Gina jogged after her, yet once again the figure disappeared before she could get a good look. Determined to know what was going on, she hurried up the tree-lined avenue, scanning storefronts. At the third one, she saw flowers, souvenirs, and a female customer stepping to the counter inside.

Gina pushed through the door. "Suzette?"

The woman turned. "Gina? Why, hello."

"What're you doing here?" She tried to eliminate any accusatory tones. "Small world, huh?"

"Indeed, it is. Indeed. You sound out of breath."

"I . . . Yeah, I thought I saw you, and I . . . Well, I ran over here to find out if it was really you."

"It's really me." Suzette turned back to the store employee. "Please pardon the interruption. Would you tell me the price for the quilt there on the wall? Yes, that one. Just look at the coloring, Gina. It's like nothing we offer, is it?"

"It's nice."

"Are these all made by the same person?" Suzette asked the employee. "I run a gallery out of state, and perhaps we could arrange terms of consignment."

As the two discussed that possibility, Gina found herself disarmed by her friend's casual manner. This town was known for its shops and crafts. How could she suspect her of anything? Was she becoming paranoid? While never shy about confrontation, Gina had no desire to offend this woman who had provided a place to live, a refuge. Plus, wasn't Suzette one of Those Who Resist?

The employee was spreading more hand-woven quilts on the counter for perusal, and Suzette cooed in appreciation.

Think about it, Gina. What're the odds of you both being here today?

"Suzette?"

"Yes?" Her eyes remained on the quilts.

"I need to know if you followed me here."

"Followed you?" Suzette tilted her head. "Why, if you came on the Amtrak and then took a taxi this direction, I suppose I did. You realize there aren't many options for public transportation between Oregon and Washington."

"Did you hear me calling out to you?"

"When?"

"Never mind. Why today, Suzette?"

"Why'd we both wait until Monday to leave town? The gallery's closed, of course. You can ask Josee, but it's long been my habit to seek out the work of other craftspeople on my days off."

Nonplussed, Gina moved along a shelf of colorful ceramics. She almost believed—*wanted* to believe—the explanation. She had put her faith in the few who knew she was still alive, and her father had directed her to the Tattered Feather with clear trust in the ones involved. Surely, he wouldn't have sent her into the jaws of a trap.

The real question . . .

Could Those Who Resist be contaminated?

Gina was still growing in her own knowledge, and such a thing had never crossed her mind. Although she had seen religious extremists who operated in fear and aggression, trusting their own methods to fight the Collectors, she'd always recognized they were operating outside the bounds of true faith. She'd also encountered those who lived quiet, moral lives, erroneously thinking this would hide them from the Collectors' attention.

What about those infused with Nazarene Blood, though? Did the Power of Choice leave them room for fresh betrayals and selfish diversions?

According to Nickel, serving the Nazarene was a daily decision.

Day by day by day.

Come to think of it, Gina couldn't recall Suzette partaking of the Blood at their most recent get-together in the park. Was the woman's will to resist weakening? Perhaps an old thorn was creeping back in, trying to take root.

"Suzette?" Gina strode to the counter. "Need to ask you one more thing."

"Yes? Please tell me you're all right, Gina."

"I'm fine."

"You do look a bit pale. Are you feeling well?"

"I'm confused is what I am. If we both came all this way and just happened to run into each other, why haven't you asked me what I'm doing here?"

Suzette smiled and guided Gina out of earshot of the shop employee. "Your father was very specific about your privacy," she said. "Have I probed into your family history? Have I demanded details about what precipitated your arrival on Josee's and my doorstep? No, these are answers I've gone without because I trust Nickel and his plan for you. If we happen to be in Lynden on the same day, I'm going to assume the best and leave it at that."

"You're right. Maybe I'm not feeling good." Gina fingered the cord at her neck. "Do you think we could, uh . . . you know, take a drink together?"

"Of the Blood? This very moment? Let's save it for a later date, shall we?"

"Your choice, Suzette. Listen, I better be going."

CHAPTER
TWENTY-FOUR

Wilsonville, Oregon

From his rental car, Natira considered the night beacons and rolled razor-wire of Coffee Creek Correctional Facility. Not far off the main interstate, it held many of the state's worst female felons, and a part of him wanted to rampage through the facility, testing his battle skills against theirs.

Certainly they were nothing compared to Roman warriors of two thousand years ago. These inmates hadn't grown up in a country where hands could be amputated for stealing fruit from a neighbor's tree. Here the toughness was mostly an act—pierced, inked, muscled bodies, but the majority weak of mind.

There was one, however, that Natira knew was tougher than she appeared. She'd been with him during the final days of Hitler's madness.

Trudi Ubelhaar . . .

A remarkable achievement for a female in her late seventies to end up in a place such as this. From his own experience, Natira knew it hadn't been enough for Trudi to assist her father in experiments on Jews; she had unleashed his own snakes upon him in his lab, then plotted to spread that death even further. News archives told of last year's anarchist plot in which she had played Pied Piper to dozens of local Oregonian youth, arming them with canisters of toxin to use against government facilities.

Quite a woman. What wasn't there for a Collector to adore?

Young Trudi Ubelhaar had bedded a number of lovers—SS men in Hitler's breeding program—but when Natira alone managed to impregnate her, he felt remnants of human, fatherly pride swell in his cavernous chest.

Trudi was less enchanted. Even tried to kill their unnamed sons. Once Natira had revived the one boy, he made her promise on her life to spare the beast. She agreed. Soon after, she turned to oncoming Allied troops, deceived a counterintelligence officer, and arranged passage to the U.S. with her son tucked out of sight.

What had happened to Natira's "likeness" in the span since?

Surely somewhere his child's counterfeit heart still beat, and Trudi should be able to provide answers. Natira had trekked here to Coffee Creek, believing his offspring might help unlock Rasputin's treasures. In fact, maybe he had been granted a son for this very reason.

A personal key to success.

Ever grateful, my Master. And ever here to serve you.

Driving along SW Grahams Ferry Road, he pictured Trudi's cell location within the facility. A formal prison visit would require paperwork and background checks—complications he wished to bypass.

His alternative rested in a perforated box on the passenger seat. From within, a tongue flickered at one of the holes.

"Are you ready to go hunting?" Natira said.

Boomslangs—tree snakes—were not common pets in the U.S., but there were always buyers willing to dance with danger. The seller of this particular green and black male had gone on about their resurging popularity due to mentions in a recent Harry Potter book and a Stephen King short story. They were mild mannered, he said, yet pointed out that the venom was some of the most toxic in the world, causing victims to bleed out through every orifice on the way to painful deaths. This same hemotoxin had provided the base ingredient for Doktor Ubelhaar's poison gas—an irony that would not elude Trudi.

Natira parked in a copse of trees two miles from the penitentiary, then emptied a flask of Jim Beam out the window and set it between his legs. If his permanent host was discovered, he would appear to be in a drunken stupor on the roadside.

He turned off the dome light, left the door ajar.

Time to carry out his plan.

With a surge of adrenaline, he removed the box lid and found the sleek boomslang coiled in a bed of straw, eyes large and alert. The Collector gained access by meeting that fearsome gaze, then leaving his human shell slumped at the wheel, he slithered from the box and out the door.

The snake's temperament made it an ideal temporary host, submissive and pliable. Being an arboreal creature more accustomed to stalking through leaves and branches, its emerald form, slipping through underbrush en route to the prison. There was an odd comfort in the vibration of scales over coarse ground, in the silent glide of this five-foot-long vessel.

Boomslang and Collector moved as one, thought as one. Through stereoscopic eyes, they processed the approaching lights. A forked tongue tested the night, gathering and deciphering details by instinct.

They were at the perimeter fence. They glided under.

Pushing onward, they skimmed over pebbles and weeds toward a door in the prison yard made evident by refracted lights.

In the shadows of a wall they waited. Time was less pressing within this reptilian host, and the entire world shrank down to basic survival. A loud croak came from nearby and the snake's head lifted. Though North America was not his native environment, he knew a frog when he heard one, knew that throaty vibration as it carried through the air.

No. We're not eating yet, the Collector insisted. *We're going inside.*

A hard plastic pipe sent a new set of vibrations along the wall. Voices? Together, they tracked the sounds and writhed into an opening that vented the septic system. A circuitous journey fed them into the latrine.

Swampy liquid. Putrescence. Floating objects.

They emerged through a wet porcelain tunnel and splashed down onto a cement floor. They were inside. Carefully, now, carefully.

Utilizing Natira's recollections as a map, they searched the darkened cells one by one, sliding through plumbing, under beds, between pairs of shoes. Spurred by predatory hunger, the boomslang never slowed. Hours passed—or only minutes?—until they happened into a room where the smell of the skin, the heat of the prey, tripped a switch.

More likely, it was the prisoner who first recognized them.

"Why, look at you," Trudi said. She closed the book in her hands and swung her feet over the edge of the utilitarian bed. "You're beautiful, indeed you are, and a welcome sight to this old woman."

Eyeing her, the boomslang puffed its neck and rose back into a striking position. The Collector wondered if this hag knew he was onboard.

"I've used your sort before," she was saying. "Yes, you and I are fast friends."

Flick of the tongue. Ambient heat. Veins beneath that papery skin.

"Perhaps," Trudi said, "we can be partners again, hmm?"

Her penetrating gaze. An invitation.

Sorry, woman. You had your chance and you bumbled it.

The snake snapped forward, a green and black whip. With jaws coming unhinged, rear fangs dropped, locked, and stabbed into her foot, a direct envenomation into the bloodstream. Nothing made a boomslang's bite more deadly than a hit on a vein, and it would be only a matter of time till her body shut down and bled out.

Trudi screamed in rage. Tried to tear free.

The twin fangs curved deeper, injecting more venom.

As the ex-lover/former Nazi/anarchist ringleader flopped back on her mattress, the Collector dredged her blood for encoded memories. He found her mind still spry, her life-flow filled with a hatred that worked like formaldehyde, preserving her most vile thoughts and schemes: abusive SS men . . . a detached father . . . an adulterous relationship ending in yet one more heartbreak . . . plots to maim and kill, to inflict widespread damage . . . the roar of an ocean, spears of light, and . . .

Where, though, was the son fathered by Natira?

He rummaged deeper until an answer swam up from the morass, a remote location accompanied by a repugnant face. The moment segued into another, years later, with Trudi paying a maternal visit . . . wandering between trees . . . holding a cinched pouch . . . searching for her deformed offspring . . .

She knew more. More secrets.

The Collector pried further into her mind and found images of a Russian man called Oleg, a member of the Brotherhood of Tobolsk . . . of Oleg coming here to speak with Trudi . . . sharing information he'd gathered while exploring Engine 418 . . .

What did this man know? What had he told her?

Focused on these questions, the snake remained attached to the elderly woman's foot and failed to notice the descent of her hardcover book. The desperate blow flattened and stunned the creature. To remain here was to risk permanent damage.

With the sought after knowledge already stowed away, the Collector gave the order to release the woman. Fangs unhooked from Trudi's muscle and tissue, and she pulled up her legs, whimpering as bright red droplets leaked onto the sheets.

"You dreadful thing. Why, look what you've done."

Move back, the Collector directed his host. *We have what we came for.*

"Ohh," Trudi gasped. "We were so good together, and you've gone and ruined it, haven't you? Destroyed it once and for all."

Move. Do it now!

Even as serpent and Collector squeezed beneath the steel door into the walkway, the victim came unglued. Wracked with terror and pain, she cursed and flung herself from the bed, stamping at the floor, at the retreating serpentine form.

"You wretched creature, what've you done?"

She was only accelerating the venom's effects, which, the Collector realized, may have been her express intent. The same insidious hemotoxin used against her father, against local government institutions, now pumped from her extremity to her core and outward again. In this part of the world, few medical facilities had boomslang antivenom on hand, meaning before the night was out she would be a wrinkled, leaking mess.

Trudi Ubelhaar cried out, "I knew you would come."

The boomslang elongated itself in the shadows at the base of the wall, letting guards rush by to investigate the warbling screams.

"You filthy beast! Don't think I was fooled, not in the slightest." Defiant cackles reverberated down the corridor. "I knew one day you would come for me! Oh yes, I always knew."

CHAPTER
TWENTY-FIVE

Jerusalem

Although Jerusalem was a different world from the one Cal Nichols had left in Oregon, the same battle lines were drawn. The Unfallen moved to and fro, Concealed Ones bore sorrows and woe, while ultimately it was Those Who Resist who would have to confront the Collectors and their desire for blood.

A personal battle, yes.

And a global one, with long-ranging consequences.

Nickel stood on the Mount of Olives, overlooking the Old City walls tinged pink by the morning sun. In the valley's shadows below, tour buses plied the narrow road to the Garden of Gethsemane and the Church of St. Mary Magdalene, while Jewish and Muslim tombs clung to the hillsides.

These slopes of the Kidron Valley merged with the nearby Valley of Hinnom, and when flooding occurred, they funneled dust, bones, and refuse through arid wastelands to the Dead Sea about fifteen kilometers away. For ages, the good and bad had washed by here—saints and sinners, icons and idols, flowers and thorns.

Prophets of old called this the Valley of Jehosophat, and it was said the Messiah would come here to judge the nations. In a few months, Jews would celebrate *Rosh Hashanah*, the Day of Reckoning, in recognition of that time to come.

Final Vengeance . . .

Ushered in on the Almighty's terms? Or the Master Collector's?

Nickel perched himself on stone steps and pondered the waking city with its Christian steeples, Jewish synagogues, and Muslim minarets. Church bells sounded, blue domes and gold glistened amongst rooftop laundry lines and power cables, and the King David Hotel stood guard off in the distance. So much had changed since his first lifetime here, two-plus millennia ago. Who would believe the things he had seen?

Born in Cyprus in 617 BC, he had moved to this land with his Jewish parents while still a babe. His birth name had been Lev. He'd grown up and married. In years following, many of his countrymen endured Babylonian exile, and the Holy City was polluted by Asherah poles and Tammuz fertility gods. As a result, the Almighty meted out purifying judgment, yet spared thirty-five men and their families as they lamented their people's iniquity.

He could still feel the touch of paint bristles, the wet smear of ink.

The letter Tav on his brow.

Regardless, nature had taken its course and laid him to rest years later in his grave in this very vicinity, next to his beloved Dinah.

His second lifetime, the one bridging him into immortality, had started in the first century AD. Yeshua's victory over death triggered an earthquake that not only tore temple curtains and rattled the home of Pontius Pilate, but also broke open tombs from which thirty-five men came forth.

Led by a Thirty-Sixth: Yeshua Himself, the Nazarene.

So much had changed since then—politics, religion, culture—and yet there was really nothing new under the sun, was there? Although Asherah and Tammuz reappeared under new guises, the Master Collector's basic strategies remained the same. If he and his kind were to suffer eternal damnation, he aimed to take along as many of God's children as possible.

"It's beautiful, no?"

Nickel turned toward a stout Jewish merchant. "Shalom, Isaac."

"Shalom. After these many years, I never do tire of this sight. Even this day, though, she is under siege, yes? The Akeldama Collectors, they come with more of their thorns. They breed infection."

"Sometimes I get tired of this fight," he said.

Isaac joined him on the steps. One of the original Thirty-Six, he owned a spice shop on cobblestoned David Street, and his loose trousers wafted hints of cumin and turmeric. Remembrance tassels, *tzitziyot*, hung from the bottom of his shirt in honor of Mosaic Law. Isaac said they kept him mindful of his heritage.

"What is it you ponder this morning, my old friend?"

Nickel frowned. "I miss her, Isaac."

"You speak of Dinah? But it is long ago, no?"

"Do our hearts ever forget? Sometimes I wish mine would."

"You were one flesh, man and wife. It is normal, I think, to feel this way, and she was a rare woman. I can say this now, yes? When I was your neighbor, I dared not dwell upon, much less speak, such a thing."

"You were a good neighbor. Still are."

"*Todah*," the merchant thanked him in Hebrew.

These thoughts of Nickel's had been stirred anew by the coming nuptials between Sarge and Josee. He had tried not to think of his wife, Dinah, tried to stay busy, but the longing for intimacy that had driven him into Nikki Lazarescu's arms still taunted him at times. He'd turned to Nikki as much for her willingness as her outward similarities to Dinah—raven hair, intense eyes, dark skin. Both women were gone now, and yet he was still here, committed to setting things right.

He said, "Why us, Isaac?"

"Why did we get the Letter? We are who we are. This we cannot deny."

But Nickel had denied, hadn't he?

"We are weak, each one," Isaac said, anticipating his thoughts. "You were foolish, but you stood back to your feet and continued resisting. It's a good thing, I think. An example for others to follow, no?"

In a burst of morning radiance, sunrays fanned over the city's walls and rooftops, and both Cal Nichols and Isaac were struck dumb by this momentary glimpse of majesty to come. Through the nearby Golden Gate, the Messiah would make His prophesied entry, and both men believed Yeshua to be that Messiah. Until then, there was work to be done.

"One day soon," Isaac said, "you will see your Dinah again."

"You think so? It's been over twenty-five hundred years."

"It will not be the same, of course. Yes, you will recognize her, but you'll be married to the Almighty's wishes. Earthly love will have less weight, I think."

"Will she remember me?"

"You're a hard one to forget," Isaac said, wearing his permanent grin. "What shall be shall be."

"So you don't know for sure."

"Ahh, I do know that the Akeldama Collectors are up to no good—the thorns gathering here, and also some secretive busywork in the makhtesh at Ramon."

"Do we know what they're doing?"

"Secretive, as I said."

"What's in Ramon?"

"Surely your travels to Eilat have taken you by there. Not much to speak of, my friend, except dirt and clay, vipers and scorpions."

"As long as there are no spiders, I'm good."

"Arachnids? Yes, these also. I know you have good reason for despising them."

Nickel grimaced. "Considering you called me here, I assume you know more than you're telling me."

"These bloodsuckers from the Akeldama, they want our kind to crumble, no? If they are busy, they're busy making trouble. You are the man to look into this because you're not bound by the Separation, your senses are not dulled, and"—Isaac shrugged—"you're no longer Nistarim. It is safer for all, I think."

"Meaning if I bite the dust, the world'll keep spinning."

"We must use it to our advantage."

Cal Nichols thought of all that he'd lost and found during his earthly sojourn. How could he begrudge these Nistarim who continued to stand beneath unimaginable burdens? Of course he would respond to their summons. He would fight as he must. He would spy out the land. He would mentor. And, despite his mistakes, he would take comfort in his part-immortal grandson Jacob, who was being raised for such a time as this.

As for Nickel, when his own time came, he would welcome it with open arms and be swept up into glory. Until then, there was much to be done.

Even so, he prayed, *come quickly.*

CHAPTER
TWENTY-SIX

Silverton, Oregon

Was her cover blown? What had possessed Suzette to trail her to Washington? In reaction, Gina had skipped the last leg of her trip to Lummi Island.

In the driver's seat of the borrowed VW Bug, she now checked her mirrors and eyed each passing vehicle. She was going to see Jed, one person she still trusted despite their years apart. Though he knew little of her past with the Collectors, he knew her. Cared for her. Sometimes that was all a girl needed.

Gina's gaze darted to the mirror again.

Stop, you schizoid. Enough.

Signs for Oregon Gardens appeared ahead, and she considered pulling off, waiting for pursuers to reveal themselves by following after her. Or she could turn on South Water Street and head toward the nearby state park. Another test.

It would prove nothing, of course. On a mild spring day such as this, cars heading for either destination would be no shocker.

Silverton was less a destination than a gateway to one. From here, campers and day hikers headed into the misty, waterfall-rich chasms of Silver Falls State Park, while young families and elderly couples chose the more serene beauty of the botanical gardens. During her stint as Kate Preston,

Gina had walked the state park's trails on a field trip with Kenny's class. She thought it one of the most magical places she had ever seen, and that did lend this area some appeal should she ever happen to live here with . . .

Oh, say with Jed. Just for example.

Now that she thought about it, was she threatening Jed's safety by coming into town? What if the Collectors meant to wipe out everyone linked to her?

Enough, Gina.

She didn't want to do this, didn't want to slip back into hyper-vigilance. She told herself that the Collectors couldn't know where she was. Impossible. Her faked death in the Cascades had been a success. Brown-haired, blue-eyed Kate Preston was no more than another tragic statistic. She'd been mourned, buried, eulogized.

Even Kenny thought she was a goner.

Now all that remained in her place was a blonde, tattooed girl, with deep-brown eyes and a will to live. Her name was Gina. Just Gina.

As far as the Collectors knew, Nikki, Gina, and Jacob were nonfactors in an ongoing battle. The Lazarescus had been wiped from the map. Meanwhile, Gina worked for Suzette at the counter of an art gallery, helped Josee plan a wedding, and shared rent and utilities with the two.

So why had Suzette tried tracking her movements?

Ruins of Kerioth-Hezron

The glow of swollen scarlet vines and golden candelabra bathed the main cavern in soft hues that faded upward into blackness. Moans laid a foundation of sound, with screams building upon it as the days progressed.

In these predawn hours, Barabbas appreciated the relative quiet. He dragged his kill across the cave floor into the central corridor. From here, tunnels ran to the cluster's various quarters, and he chose the one leading to Erota. She had a taste for fresh game, and he hoped to impress her with this horned ibex.

"How did it die?" she inquired from her bed.

"Wrestled it down by its horns, snapped its neck."

"Did he feel any pain?"

"It was quick."

"You're to show them no mercy, you oaf. I keep telling you, I want *terafiya*—meat flavored by those final agonies. There's a reason such food's considered unkosher. The Jews and their God forbid it, and for that reason I desire it."

"Next time, Erota. Take it now, please. It's for you."

"My breakfast, I suppose." She flung aside her bedspread woven from jackal hides and fox pelts. Long tan legs snared the henchman's attention and drew a smirk from Erota's face. "Stare all you want," she said. "After today, you're no longer my problem. You can go help your beloved Megiste and see if she's more attracted to that ruddy beard of yours."

Barabbas had served the former priestess years ago and met with her favor, even shared her chamber and bed. He was glad to know she had requested him for this mysterious assignment, and yet he still coveted Erota. She was his forbidden meat, and with his size he was accustomed to getting what he wanted. Her disdain for him only increased his desire to please—and be pleased.

"I can cut this off," he said, grabbing his wiry facial hair.

"Let Megiste decide. I'm done with you."

"The ibex?"

"Leave it."

"Where's Lord Natira? Has he granted me permission to go?"

"He's left us here on our own, so what does he care?"

Barabbas had been steadfast since days of yore, serving the House of Ariston after his stay of execution, then standing beside his leaders in this present age. He knew the Principles of Cluster Survival were clear: *"When a challenge arises from within the cluster, the leader will determine its validity and, if necessary, banish any Collector that displays mutinous intentions."*

"Does he know I'm following orders?"

"Stop, Barabbas. As usual, you're thinking too much. If he chose not to banish Megiste when she fled, I'm sure you'll be quite safe."

"But you'll tell Natira for me?"

Erota strode toward him and gave his beard a sharp tug. "As your interim leader, *I'm* tempted to banish you for these nonstop questions."

He stiffened at her nearness. He could smell her skin, her flowing hair. Years ago, with Megiste's permission, he'd tried taking Erota by force, only to find her a cunning foe who left him keeled over and bloodied.

"I'm willingly giving you over to Megiste," she said. "Just do as you're told."

"What'll I be doing?"

"Men's work." Erota scowled. "And whatever the priestess wants. Now clean up, pull on some regular clothes, and get walking."

"Where to? I've been given no instructions."

"There's a bus that passes on the main road south of here. You'll transfer in Beersheva and head for Ramon Crater."

"And Megiste will be waiting?"

"She's excited to put you to work. Don't worry, Barabbas—I'm sure she'll be there, ready to take her big puppet by the hand."

Silverton

Jed Turney arrived twenty minutes after Gina did. She was leaning against the VW's curved red wheel well, and he hopped down beside her from a paneled van with Gelfand Garden Supplies painted in yellow and green on the side.

"What're you doing here, Gina?"

"Well," she said, folding her arms. "Good to see you too, buddy boy. I figured it was time I found where you holed up after leaving Sarge's place."

During her wait, she'd studied the trimmed shrubs, mowed lawn, and a sprinkle of dandelions along the cracked sidewalk. The house itself was circa 1960s—flat and low, a whitewashed brick entryway, and faded yellow siding with white trim. Not much of a bachelor pad. A glimpse of fishing poles and a snowboard in the garage were the only indications that Jed had a life away from his work, which both gladdened and saddened her.

"This is it," Jed said. "It's not much, but it's mine."

"You're buying?"

"Two bedrooms, one and a half bath. It's all I really need."

She wondered what it would be like to live here together, Mr. and Mrs. Turney. Considering their recent dates, she almost believed it was possible. She said, "I was hoping we could talk. Josee let me borrow her car while she and Sarge went out to dinner with her parents."

"Should've called first. What if you'd shown up and I wasn't here?"

"You are here. What's the problem, Jed?"

"Nothing."

"I would've, okay? But I don't have a cell—too easy to trace—and I didn't want Suzette listening in on the gallery line."

"Are you hiding something from her?"

"What kind of question is that?"

Jed's blue eyes had lost their sparkle, and he shifted them to the stained knees of his work pants. "Here," he said, "let's go inside. I need to clean up, and then we can talk. You hungry?"

"Not really, but I can make you something while you're in the shower."

"You don't have to do that."

"I want to. Just like the old days."

Jed tensed at her words, then skirted her questioning look. He opened the door and led her into a sunken living room with a tan brushed-leather couch, matching armchair, and dark cherry end tables. A flip of a switch brought the soft glow of box lamps.

"No TV?" she said.

"It's in the bedroom."

"Is that what you do all weekend, play games and watch DVDs?" She realized she was nagging, when all she really wanted to know was if he had room for her in his life. Maybe she should just ask him that, show some maturity in accordance with her age. "Not that it's any of my beeswax," she added with a light laugh.

"Most nights I sleep right there."

"The couch?"

He shrugged off his shirt. Though he'd never been built like an athlete—more like a musician with lean arms and a thin waist—his landscaping work had added definition to his abs and deltoids. She took in the small patch of hair in the center of his chest, the single dark mole below his rib cage.

Yep, he's the man I once shared my bed with.

"What's that look for?" he said.

She chuckled. "Nice farmer's tan."

"Gimme ten minutes and we can talk."

"You want dinner or not?"

"If you're offering. Kitchen's all yours, whatever you can find."

"Fifteen minutes," she said. "And make sure to shave."

He lifted one shoulder and trudged off down the hall. Where, she wondered, was the playful banter they'd shared in their last get-together? Was he still shaking off a hard day at work, or was there something more to it?

In the kitchen, Gina found matching pots and pans, matching dinnerware and utensils, even matching place mats and candles. Jed's high school aspirations had revolved around graphic design, and some of that sensibility was on display here, but she read more into it than that. This place was equipped for a married couple, for a small family.

The poor guy's in love with me again. I bet that's it. No wonder he's nervous.

Seemed obvious now that she thought about it. Her husband wanted to make this reunion between them official, and he was simply scared that she would say no. Hadn't his uncle also acted out of character while getting ready to propose to Josee—fumbling, bumbling, resorting to U2 poses and a falsetto never meant for human ears?

The more Gina considered it, the more convinced she became.

Had he bought a new rock for her finger?

Was he in there cleaning up so he could come take a knee?

Though she knew she might be reading too much into this, the idea was intoxicating. She told herself to stay calm. Put her man at ease. If he hadn't purchased a ring yet, she'd let him know it was unnecessary. She still had hers tucked away and he was wearing his old one. They'd done without pomp or ceremony the first time around, so why go to great expense now? The goal was a lifetime together, not one extravagant day leading to years of financial gloom.

C'mon, Gina. Dinnertime!

A nice meal would help soothe Jed's nerves. She remembered that much from their days in the Chattanooga apartment.

She flung open the fridge door, the freezer, the pantry, and cupboards. She gathered supplies on the counter, rummaged up a polished cutting board—had he ever used the thing?—and selected a knife from the matching block next to the range. She considered her options, from sweet Walla Walla onions to bow-tie noodles to cans of Progresso soup, tenderloin cutlets, and stalks of celery.

The way to a man's heart was through his stomach?

Okay, then. Time to get cracking.

CHAPTER
TWENTY-SEVEN

"You can forget dinner," Gina said as Jed entered the dining area. "I ruined it."

"I doubt that."

"Can't you smell that?"

"Uh . . ." His brow furrowed. "What?"

"Great." She smacked her spatula on the counter. "Now I've permanently singed his nasal membranes."

"I just got out of the shower, so I smell like shampoo and aftershave, okay? Help me out here. What am I supposed to be smelling?"

"Burnt steak. Scorched vegetables. A full-on charcoal smorgasbord."

"No problem. I like my meat well done."

"Please."

"Roll it in ash and I'm happy."

"Hardy-har-har," she said with all the sarcasm she could muster.

She braced her arms on either side of the range, eyes blurring as she examined overcooked tenderloin medallions in the pan. In her hurry to get everything ready, she'd cranked the burner too high and even managed to blacken the sliced onions. She'd added noodles and chopped celery to the soup that now bubbled in a pot, but it too would be a disappointment since it was store bought—and out of a stinkin' can. Nikki would've slapped her hand for that.

Thoughts of her mother further stoked Gina's emotion, and she dropped her chin to her chest. She had to get a grip here. How was she supposed to respond to her husband's love if she was falling apart? He was in his late twenties now and didn't need some adolescent basket case on his hands.

Especially when that woman was nearing forty.

Oh, the things he had yet to find out.

She took stabilizing breaths and was preparing to turn around and offer soup with a smile when Jed approached from behind. A whiff of his aftershave brushed past, conjuring memories. She envisioned his arms slipping around her waist, pulling her close as his lips nuzzled her neck, and she closed her eyes. She missed the intimacy of their early marriage, his ability to lose graciously at the chessboard, then win her over in the bedroom.

He was her king. She, his queen. That's the way it was meant to be, and she rued the years robbed from them. They'd let the Collectors gain more ground by deciding to go separate ways, hadn't they?

Tonight that would all be reversed. If the cooking could be overlooked.

Turning, Gina opened her eyes. "Jed, are you . . . ?"

He was no longer there. He'd taken the pan from the stove and was sliding a few of the black tenderloin disks onto his plate. Against the bright white surface, they were puckered polka dots.

"They don't look half bad," he said.

"You're a brave man."

He took a bite. "Don't taste half bad either."

"Seriously?"

"Mm-hmm." His throat constricted as he worked down a second bite.

She snagged a medallion from the pan and took a nibble. "Uggh. I'm not sure which is worse—the dry meat or the bald-faced lies."

"Lies," he said, "are always worse."

"Hit me with the truth. I can handle it."

"These taste like cardboard, nicely roasted, with a hint of onion."

"And a dash of fresh-ground pepper," she added.

"Now it's your turn."

"For what?"

"The truth, Gina. I need to know what's going on here."

Heart catching behind her ribs, she turned off the burners. "You're the man here," she said. "Why don't you take the initiative?"

"Okay." Blue eyes drilled into hers, smoldering with uncertainty and concern. "You ready for me to lay it all out?" He fielded her nod and continued. "I'm still in love with you, have been since the day I first saw you in second-period art at Lookout Valley High. I thought maybe I could do this on my own, live life, forget about all that's happened, about . . . our son. Sarge has helped me work through a lot."

"I like your uncle. He and Josee'll be such cute newlyweds."

There's your opening, buddy boy.

"He's shown me how to pay attention," Jed said, "if that makes any sense—how to take in the trees, the mountains, the waterfalls."

"Yeah, I love Silver Falls. We should go sometime."

He tilted his chin as though weighing her words against some other voice in his ear.

Hello, she thought. *That was another hint. Anyone awake in there?*

Jed stumbled on. "Might sound strange, but something changed up here"—he tapped his head—"when I was skiing at Mt. Bachelor a few weeks back. It was a weekday. I was all by myself, and I went skidding off one of the runs into a snow bank. I'm shaking powder out of my hair and trying to find my poles, and I see this little blue flower poking up. I realize I may be the only one in history to ever see that flower, and it's just doing its thing, growing, lifting its petals toward the sun, not worried one bit whether it gets noticed or not. That made me think about how there's a Creator out there going to all this trouble simply because He's an artist."

"Pretty cool."

"I got back and talked it over with Sarge." Jed pulled a vial from his jeans pocket. "And that's when I decided to drink the Nazarene Blood. What I'm saying is that even with all the ugliness that goes on, there's something better and beautiful, something worth living for. Am I wrong?"

"I don't think so," Gina said in a hush.

"So even if you don't love me, I'll survive."

"What?"

"I'll admit I was hoping we could make another go at it. Humble little Silverton doesn't have much to speak of, but it's a nice town. Did you know Billy Bob Thornton and Bruce Willis shot a scene for a movie here?"

"Is that a selling point or a bad omen?"

"Hmm. Good question."

"Go on."

"All that to say, I just want you to be straight with me. Yes, I came apart after Jacob died, but I've done some growing up. I'm not the college kid I was then, so I can handle hearing it from your own lips."

"My own lips?" She saw his eyes fall to her mouth, the way they used to before he kissed her.

This time he moved back with arms folded. "The truth, Gina."

"Fine. I can do that."

"I'm all ears."

"The truth: yes, I want to be Mrs. Turney again. We're both human, both wounded, but that doesn't mean we can't make a life together, does it? You know, I pulled up this afternoon and saw your mailbox and thought about our names being on there. I thought about us growing old in this house together, and—"

Jed slammed his hand onto the table. "Don't! I need to know *all* of it."

"That . . . that's the truth."

"*Everything*, Gina."

What had set him off? Had Nickel come along and unveiled the secrets of the Lazarescu past? Did Jed have some knowledge of the Collectors . . . or Jacob . . . or . . . ? Maybe that was it. Maybe he was the one who'd had her tailed to Washington State in hopes of discovering his son's where-abouts.

"Did you tell Suzette to follow me?" Gina said.

"Oh. So you're admitting it, huh?"

Still uncertain how much he knew, she said, "Admitting what?"

"She told me about *him*."

"Who? You have no reason to be yelling at me."

"Your boyfriend. How am I supposed to know his name?"

"Are you serious?"

"Suzette gave me the whole scoop. Listen, I can't tell you who to love and who not to. I left. I deserve this. But be honest with me, at least. Don't string me along."

"Is this why you've been acting so distant tonight? Why'd you have her follow me instead of just asking me to my face?"

"Suzette did it on her own, trying to spare me some heartache. Least she can see what's going on here. She knows how crazy I am about you, and how hard I'd take it if I found out you were seeing someone else while dating me."

"Dating? That's what we've been doing?"

"Is there something wrong with me wanting to date my wife?"

"I'm not seeing anyone else, Jed. C'mon, that's not my style. I don't know what Suzette's talking about, except she must've misread things and made some very wrong assumptions."

"Then who's this man you snuck off to visit?"

"This *man*," Gina blurted, "is named Jacob."

Jed bumped into the dining table.

"As in, your son. Yeah, you heard me. Our son."

"Jacob?"

"He's alive. For a long time, I didn't even know it myself."

"You're . . . You're using our dead son to cover an affair?"

"I know it's hard to believe, but that's the truth, just the way you wanted it. I'm not even supposed to have said anything, and you can't say a word to anyone, you hear me? Not Suzette, Josee, Sarge. No one."

"Jacob Lazarescu Turney."

"Yes."

Jed's voice turned cold. "Okay then, let's go. Take me to him."

"I can't. I mean, not right now."

"Of course you can. I want to talk to him."

"See, the problem is I'm not even allowed to do that. It's too risky. I have to look through binoculars."

"Binoculars? Mm-hmm."

"It's better than nothing. He's gorgeous, Jed. He has your eyes and—I don't know, maybe it's genetic—he's really into fishing, same as you. He's taking some correspondence courses I ordered online, and he—"

"Stop, okay? Just stop, Gina. This hole keeps getting deeper."

His skepticism was understandable. Even though the story sounded preposterous, she was relieved to share this secret with her husband. He had a right to know, and perhaps they could protect their child together. Team Turney to the rescue.

"Jed, listen—"

"Don't. Please, just stay back." He fixed his eyes on the ceiling, blew out air in a long gust, then rolled words off his tongue in soft syllables. "Suzette says she saw you arm in arm with this man, this boyfriend of yours. Saw you kissing. Whatever. Watched you get into his car and drive away."

"That's ridiculous."

"Instead I'm supposed to buy this alibi of yours?"

Tears welled in Gina's eyes. "I don't even know why she'd say that."

"He's been dead seven years and eight months. And you dare use him to protect yourself."

"That's not at all what I was—"

"Please get out."

"Wait, Jed. You have to let me—"

"I don't have to do anything. This is my house, not yours. Not ours."

"You wanted the truth. I told you the truth."

He dumped the pan into the sink. "If Jacob's alive, why would you hide him from me?"

"No, not from you, sweetheart. From the Collectors."

"Who?"

"If they find him, they'll kill him."

"Are they coming in black helicopters?" Jed stomped to the window and parted the curtains. "Are these mysterious killers out there now?"

"I hope not."

"Don't force me into making a scene. Please." He guided her to the front door and held it open, waving off her protests. "Good-bye."

CHAPTER
TWENTY-EIGHT

Eilat, Israel

Dov Amit was feeding dolphins in the Gulf of Aqaba. Here at the Red Sea's northernmost tip, choppy saltwater rocked the wooden platform on which he sat, yet he seemed impervious as he dropped fish into upturned beaks.

He was wearing a black wetsuit ribbed with blue, his nearly twenty-one-year-old body stocky and toned. On one foot, a nub remained where his big toe had been chewed off years ago by a wolf, and he moved with a slight hitch in his step but not an ounce of pity. As a trainer, he'd established a rapport with the sleek gray mammals that populated Dolphin Reef, and his joy in that was obvious.

Cal Nichols watched from among the small group of tourists gathered on a viewing dock. He gripped the railing, feeling the sea breeze ruffle his hair and tug at his khaki shorts and shirt.

Crikey, mate. I must look like the Crocodile Hunter.

No sooner had Dov finished with the morning feeding then he was surrounded by young ladies asking if he just loved his job, if he thought dolphins were the most *gorgeous* animals ever, would he mind posing for a picture, and, *oh*, did he know of any good places to get a drink once the sun went down?

There were a few such places, but to his credit, Dov grabbed his bucket and angled back toward the Employees Only area.

All business. Nary a glance at the well-oiled bodies.

Nickel loved this city. Despite being an international destination, Eilat was still small and untainted by kitschy tourism. This reef was a good example, offering scuba and snorkeling opportunities with dolphins while maintaining a pristine beach cradled by palms and flowering fauna. Visible across the gulf, Jordan and Saudi Arabia boasted a row of low mountains stripped of vegetation and shaded in pastel hues. The clash of colors and landscapes was spectacular.

What a reward, he thought, for all who braved the journey through the Negev. Hadn't Moses and his Israelites wandered very near to this spot?

"Nickel?" Dov appeared beside him on the deck. "Why're you here?"

"Bottle blond all the way." A way of reminding him of his daughter. "Good to see you, Dov."

"You too. I'm working, so I can't talk long."

They spoke in Hebrew, the first language for both of them. Nickel, however, had learned his during the days of Ezekiel and old Jerusalem.

"You like my new look?" Nickel said. "Bottle Blond."

"Are you supposed to be Australian?"

"G'day, mate."

Dov groaned. "I've heard Americans do it better than that."

"Owww, that's rough." He shifted to more serious tones. "I'm just checking up on you. You still over at the Shelter? You staying strong?"

The Shelter Guest Hostel was a long-time resting spot for many a weary traveler, and Dov had come here after his time with Gina in the Romanian orphanage. The couple who operated the Shelter were among Those Who Resist and provided parental examples. With only vague awareness of Dov's special role, they instructed him in scriptural methods of warring against the Collectors.

"Strong?" Dov flexed his biceps. "You tell me."

"Do I detect a bit of pride?"

"Confidence, Nickel. You're the one who taught me the difference."

"Which is?"

"You never stop teaching, do you?"

"You don't remember the answer, I take it."

"'Pride,'" Dov quoted, "'is lifting yourself and your desires above all others. Confidence is a healthy self-awareness that empowers you to help others.'"

He slapped the damp arm of Dov's wetsuit. "Proud of you, kid. And in this case, it's justified. Pride mixed with joy can be a good thing, and I think God takes pride in the way you interact with those dolphins."

"Thank you."

"And," Nickel noted, "in the way you interacted with those girls."

"They were after only one thing."

"You think so? Most guys would be glad of that."

Dov's face darkened. "I'm not most guys."

"Listen, I know you're carrying a lot on your shoulders. I've been there, don't forget. But you're not under the same stipulations as the original Nistarim, since you stepped in as a mortal. God made men and women to complement each other, and while you're in this temporal frame of yours, you have freedom to find some comfort in that—under the right circumstances, of course."

"I want to be like you, though."

"Single till the end of time? No, you don't."

"I want to serve the Nazarene."

"Then do it. Follow Him."

"I want to be strong where you were . . ."

"Weak?"

Dov nodded and looked off over the bay, where sailboats and cargo vessels cut through the waves. The weight of the world showed in his eyes.

Nickel thought about Nikki, now dead and gone. He'd wronged her by giving in to his own loneliness; and she, in her guilt, had tried bleeding those wrongs from herself and from her daughter. He said, "You don't have to carry my sins, I hope you know. If you do what you're called to do, and that happens to bring you and some young lady onto the same path side by side, join your hearts and serve Yeshua together."

"You think that'll happen?"

"It can. I once had a wife of my own, a beautiful lady named Dinah. Thing is, Dov—doesn't matter what I think. What matters is that you go where the Nazarene goes and let the rest work itself out. In the meantime, those dolphins are going to keep loving you."

"If I give them food, sure."

"Nah. You've got a pretty obvious connection with them."

"Really?" The young man's lips turned up in a shy grin. "I should go. We're supposed to spray out all the buckets and clean off our wetsuits."

Nickel stepped closer to the railing. Lapping at the wooden structure, crystalline waters offered views of the coral below and of dolphins bulleting by. One lifted its shiny head above the surface, hoping for more fish from its trainer's hand.

"Not now," Dov said. "You just ate."

"He's beautiful," Nickel remarked.

"She."

"I'll take your word for it."

As the kid turned, the gulf wind pushed aside his curly black hair. "Was there anything else you needed to tell me, Nickel?"

Freed from mortal bonds, Cal Nichols spotted the luminous blue Letter that identified Dov as one of the Nistarim. In the future, the foreheads of all Those Who Resist would be sealed by the Almighty's own hand, Jews and Gentiles alike. For now, however, the Concealed Ones alone bore that symbol of life and death and salvation.

Doubly alive or doubly dead?

Those were mankind's options for what was to come.

"I know you can't see it," he told Dov, "but do your best to keep that mark hidden from the Akeldama Cluster."

Dov combed his hair down over his brow.

"Believe me," Nickel said, "they've already targeted many of the Concealed Ones, keeping them under observation, waiting till the day they can take out all of you with one blow."

"Do they know I'm here?"

"Not yet. They're getting fidgety, though, closing in on this region."

"What do I do?"

"Stay close to the Nazarene. Stay alert."

"Okay."

"Don't crumble."

Dov squared his shoulders. "Never."

"I need to check on some of the others, talk to Gina—she's got some troubles of her own—and make sure things are in order. You've got it covered here, so I may not be coming back around for a while. Could be months, even years, but when I show up, you'll need to be prepared to act quickly. If Natira and his horde want to blast you out of the water, we're gonna give them that chance."

"What?"

"A trap needs bait, doesn't it?"

"I don't like the sound of this."

"Hey, we're coming up on *Yom Ha'atzmaut*, right? Israel's Independence Day. You think freedom comes without a price? 'Course not. So what're you going to do, wait for Those Who Hunt to track you down? Always wondering, always checking your back? Nah, you can't let evil get the best of you. You get the best of evil by doing good."

"And doing good means setting a trap?"

"In this case, yes."

"That's all you're going to say?"

"Pretty much."

Dov mulled that over before clamping a hand on Nickel's arm and staring him in the eye. Though he'd gone through his bar mitzvah years earlier, ceremonially becoming a man, Dov seemed to complete that process now in the voicing of his decision. " 'All for one, and one for all,' " he said. "I'll be ready."

Corvallis

Gina's first instinct was to do what she'd done most of her life—go on the run, go into hiding, and never come back.

She considering driving east over the Cascades and the Rockies, past the Mississippi River, to some New England lighthouse where she could hole up as the haunted widow that locals said was a little batty but harmless enough.

Three things kept her from doing so.

First, she could not leave Jacob behind. Second, she had promised to have Josee's Bug back to her tonight. Third, even if she couldn't earn back Jed's trust, she'd coughed up secrets under pressure and now owed him an explanation. Perhaps in a week or two—or a year—he'd be willing to give her that chance.

She splayed her hands over the steering wheel as she headed back along Silverton Highway. Hours earlier she'd dreamed of a romantic outcome to this evening, and now all she felt in her fingertips was Jed's final stiff reaction. If body language could be converted into words, he'd told her that it was over.

Why had Suzette lied? That was the infuriating part.

Gina pounded the wheel. "You're supposed to be my sister," she yelled. "One of Those Who Resist."

She could understand if the gallery owner had formed wild assumptions based on Gina's occasional trips up north, but to claim she'd seen Gina involved with some guy? What crazy jealousy would prompt her to make such a statement about her own employee, her housemate? There was no excuse.

Or . . . could it be that Suzette liked Jed?

Awhile back, Josee had said something at the dinner table: *Just because love hasn't come your way yet doesn't mean you have to punish us for it.*

As Gina pulled up outside the Tattered Feather, she knew there was no disguising the VW's arrival. She parked beneath the big oak tree and hoped the light in the upstairs window meant Josee was back from her date. Of all people, she might offer some insight into Suzette Bishop's behavior.

However, Josee was not yet home, and the moment Gina entered their room, she realized someone had gone through the drawers, nightstands, closet, and bedding. Was anything missing? What could anyone possibly want of hers? With her roommate away with fiancé and parents, this left only one suspect.

Gina barged through Suzette's door. "What is wrong with you? What were you doing in my room?"

The gallery owner looked up from a stool at the vanity, the globe lights reflecting in her wet eyes. "Your room?"

"Don't play dumb with me."

"It's my house, is it not? Only out of courtesy have Josee and I agreed to offer you safe haven, and—"

"Safe haven? This coming from a woman who spies on me, goes through my things, and spreads rumors not even close to the truth."

"The truth is I'm sparing you the heartache."

"Sparing me? Right."

"Both of you, actually. Only of late has Jed come out of his shell, and he can't handle another letdown. As for you, Gina? You have men falling over themselves to speak with you, yet their intentions are shallow at best."

"Most men, sure." Gina put her hands on her hips. "Jed's different."

"Don't be naïve."

"He's my husband."

"Those Who Resist should not be unequally yoked."

"Who are you to make such judgments? You're jealous, Suzette, plain and simple. I'm sorry things've never worked out between you and a guy, but you can't punish me for that." She retreated to the doorway. "And, in case you missed the latest newsflash, Jed's now one of us."

"You're quite sure of this?"

"Quite."

Suzette swiveled back to the vanity, brushing her long dark hair. In the mirror, this picture of serenity was distorted by the skin writhing above the V-neck of her blouse, and it called to Gina's mind the root that once throbbed at her own throat. She diverted her eyes from this discovery and saw something nearly as shocking.

Her wedding ring lay on the vanity.

Gina marched over, snatched up the ring, and said, "This is mine. Why that's a problem for you, I don't know, but if you can't accept it . . . too bad. I love my husband and I'll fight to get him back, you hear me?"

"He'll leave you again, you know? That's what men do." Suzette covered her neck and glanced away. "Please believe my motive was to protect you."

"Thanks, but no thanks. I'm done using lies as protection."

Back in her own room, Gina straightened the ruffled clothing and blankets before Josee could return and have her own anger stirred toward Suzette. Obviously, the woman had some issues, yet harboring bitterness toward her would only reawaken thorns Gina herself had rooted out.

None of that excused Suzette's actions, of course. Why had she sabotaged Jed and Gina's reunion? What past hurts had activated this venom in her? Did she have her own infestation of thorns writhing beneath her skin? It certainly seemed so.

Gina fell facedown on the bed. She recalled that first morning when she'd bridged through the mattress onto the floorboards and wished now that she could bridge somewhere far from here—to Lummi Island or her childhood home in Romania. If there were specific distance restrictions or dangers to overextending oneself, her father had not told her.

Where was Nickel anyway? Hadn't Clay said he would show up soon? With her mother gone, Gina could sure use a visit every now and then.

You listening, Dad? I'm waiting.

Her face was burrowed deep in the pillow when she heard the deadbolt disengaging downstairs. She rolled over and leaned on an elbow. Maybe she and Josee could confront Suzette, as was the proper procedure among Those Who Resist.

Those plans went out the window when the giddy bride-to-be walked in.

"Mmm, what a night," Josee purred.

"You look beautiful. Bet you knocked Sarge right off his feet."

"And that's no easy task," Josee said with a laugh. Her spiky hair was in cute disarray, her turquoise eyes highlighted by tasteful eye shadow and liner. "But, okay—yes, he was duly swept away, if I don't mind saying so myself."

"Everything go good with your parents?"

"Good? Get this: they're giving us a share in their winery, Addison Ridge Vineyards. Know what that means? Sarge and I won't have to save up first to have kids. With him being thirty-two now, it's like a dream come true for us."

"Uh, wow." Gina decided her own problems could wait. "Tell me more."

CHAPTER
TWENTY-NINE

Late May—Mt. Hood National Forest, Oregon

Up there among the ridges and trees, a fanged creature roamed. His legs were bowed, his knees knobby, and his arms fell far past his waist. Unkempt hair shrouded much of his deformed frame, and obsidian eyes glared from beneath thick hooded brows.

Pilfered from Ms. Ubelhaar's memory, this image guided Natira.

The Akeldama Collector parked his latest rental car in the Multnomah Falls visitor lot and strode toward the trailhead, scanning the cliffs ahead.

If he had this right, Trudi had smuggled the monster into the country in late 1945, then released him into the wild somewhere nearby. By doing so, she'd washed her hands of responsibility while keeping her word not to kill him.

Why here, though?

By studying a tourist brochure, Natira believed he knew the answer. Over a million acres of forest were bordered on the north by the Columbia River Gorge and on the south by imposing Mt. Hood. In between stood the Angel's Rest outcropping, as well as a wooded knob called Devil's Rest—an appropriate hideout for a hellish child.

Natira realized that in his hunt for the Nistarim he had seen few sites that could surpass this beauty. Joined at the base of the fall by tourists from around the world, he was bathed in silver mist as waters plummeted over five hundred feet into a mossy grotto.

Bah, he thought. *You want beauty, I'll show you beauty.*

Did anything compare to the Master Collector's radiance? Sure, the Almighty had set into motion the marvels of evaporation, clouds, precipitation, rivers, and waterfalls. It was all self seeking, though. He seemed to think His putrid little humanoids would notice His handiwork, would actually revel in the evidence of His adoration. Did He believe things would be that easy?

"Wow," said the woman next to Natira. "Oregon really *is* God's country."

He wanted to tear her hair from its roots and shove it down her throat, but such an act would compromise his goal of finding his son. Instead, as he turned to leave, he mashed his heel down onto her toes.

She yelped. Grabbed her foot.

"Hey, pal." Her male companion stepped into the revenant's path. "I think you owe her an apolo—"

Natira's pinkie and thumb stabbed upward into the man's solar plexus and left him gasping beside his girlfriend. The roar of the water covered most of the exchange, and a handful of witnesses chose to stay uninvolved.

"If this is God's country," Natira spat at the couple, "then ask Him why He lets rapists and killers run free. Or don't you read the news?"

It was a common tactic, steering minds back toward domestic abuses, rampant crime, Third World poverty, and corporate corruption, all of it perpetrated under the Power of Choice. Freewill: that'd been the Almighty's big mistake.

Sometimes, though, that freedom backfired on the Collectors.

Sometimes these humans made astute decisions that caused ripples throughout clusters globally.

Sometimes, but only sometimes . . .

The Collector left the summer crowds and headed up the trail, encountering fewer people the higher he climbed. At the top, he risked a peek over the edge of the falls. Guide books claimed a bus-sized slab of stone had broken away in 1996 and caused a disastrous wave upon impact far below. He pictured himself plunging from here and doubted he could pull himself back together with the same efficiency as last year's dive into the McKenzie.

Across the Columbia River Gorge, the Lewis and Clark Highway carved through the countryside. Not far from this point on the river, an old branding iron had been discovered belonging to Capt. Meriwether Lewis himself.

Natira returned to the task at hand.

The climb to Devil's Rest. The search for his son.

Cal Nichols had produced hybrid offspring as well and tried to parlay their unique abilities into a weapon against Collectors. Thanks to Natira's persistence, Cal's little experiment had failed, yet Natira saw no reason he couldn't attempt one of his own.

May it be according to your plan.

Formed in Natira's likeness, this creature might be just the thing to unlock the Tmu Tarakan. In addition, his half-immortal vision would be alert to the letter Tav. Together, father and son would hunt down the last of the Concealed Ones—those sprinkled through the Middle East—then work with the cluster at Kerioth-Hezron to set a thorny trap.

Well, well. Final Vengeance might be even closer than imagined.

Ruins of Kerioth-Hezron

Was it okay for Collectors to feel tranquility, to experience—dare she even say it—peace? No, Erota told herself, this could not be allowed. She'd enjoyed a period of time without Barabbas gawking at her, or Natira questioning her cluster leadership, and in so doing had let herself become lackadaisical.

"Don't you think it has some benefits?" said her seventeen-year-old sister.

"Peace is a drug, Domna."

"We've used all sorts of drugs to further our purposes. I don't understand why this has you so upset this morning. Relax, would you?"

"Relax? That's the problem." Erota rose from the spiked briar throne and paced the cavern floor, her anklets jangling above painted toenails. "Don't you see what I'm saying? Over the past few months we've grown too relaxed now that our old foe Gina Lazarescu is gone. Lazy, even. I've given this a lot of thought, and here's what I have decided: peace, when it has no active purpose, ferments into complacency. We can use that complacency to lure others, but we cannot become victims to it."

"You're overreacting, sis. We add to the Six, No Seven panels every day—adulterers and murderers, thieves, the most deadly of rumormongers. The Collection is outgrowing our walls, clawing out into the tunnels and along the passageways."

"Oh yes, that's intentional. Come, let me show you something."

Erota grabbed a candlestick, swept silky hair over her shoulder, and headed for an exit on the far side of the cave. With her younger sibling in tow, she passed by the montage of "things the Lord detests" and breathed in the rank odor.

On the way to the hall, she paused at the panel of lying tongues and studied them.

"What're you doing?" Domna said.

"Hmm. I want a piece."

"But you said—"

"I want a piece of this." Erota pinched one of the tongues between her long fingers, twisted the pink meat, and tore it from the gaping mouth. A fresh volley of screams erupted throughout the panel and spread, forming a discordant symphony. "I want back my hunger for Final Vengeance."

Domna caught the chunk that was tossed her way.

"That is what I'll do to you," Erota said, "if you keep trying to talk me back into complacency. Do you understand? We are Collectors first and foremost. Don't let these human shells or relationships corrode your resolve."

"Okay, I get your point."

"Call the others. Tell them to join us in the main corridor now."

Two minutes later, the cluster was gathered for an impromptu meeting. Flames danced in evenly spaced sconces. Stone walls arched overhead and curved out of sight, evidence of flash floods that had burrowed through the Negev.

"Dorotheus."

"Here."

"Shelamzion."

"Here."

Though the group was small without Barabbas, Megiste, and Natira on hand, Erota called role to reinstitute formality and discipline. By these same principles she would strike at the priestess and her henchman, but that could hold till later—part of Erota's own little scheme.

She went on: "Helene . . . Kyria . . . Matrona . . . Hermione . . . Domna . . ."

Domna smirked.

Erota lashed out and snagged the tip of her sister's tongue, using it to pull the smaller Collector toward her. "Domna . . ."

"Here," she mumbled. "I'm here."

Erota studied the fine, seventeen-year-old face as though it was unfamiliar to her, a pimpled chicken leg to purchase or an urn to fill with flour. By shoving aside her host's vestigial memories, she saw in this countenance only a means to an end.

She released the extended tongue, dried her fingers against her hip, and led the cluster up the corridor.

Thorns and foliage crept at waist level along the walls, pulsing red as they branched out from the central cavern; they bypassed certain passages, moved into others, and formed a vast network of veins and arteries as though sustaining a giant who slumbered in these ancient hills. Down through the ages, thousands had been slaughtered here, from Israelites and Canaanites to Saracens and Crusaders to modern Arabs and Jews. Kings had been brought low, idols forged and lifted high.

Erota said nothing, her candlestick illuminating chalky limestone as they pressed onward. The cluster had now traveled five or six kilometers in a northerly direction. Surely they'd crossed from the Negev into the Judean Desert and would soon reach Hebron, one of the cities of refuge designated by Mosaic Law as a sanctuary from the Avenger of Blood. The nearby Cave of the Patriarchs was said to hold the bones of Abraham, Isaac, and Jacob.

As though reading Erota's thoughts, the vines detoured sharply from this sacred ground and continued their circuitous push toward Jerusalem.

Sacred? The Collector knew some might scoff at the premise, yet there was no denying the creative power locked within bones and blood. The Ever-So-Tedious One's fingerprints were all over human DNA. She knew the Scriptures even told of a dead man thrown into the grave of Elisha who came bounding back to life the moment he touched that prophet's old bones.

"Look here," Erota said, coming to a stop.

The cluster formed a half circle and waited.

"These thorns are those we've been training toward Jerusalem, but their slow growth reflects our complacency, as they have yet to breach the city."

"*Yerushalayim*, the City of Peace," Dorotheus said. Being the most senior of the group, she seemed to feel an obligation to dispense such tidbits of knowledge.

"Peace? Oh, I know these corporeal hosts of ours have a desire for peace programmed into their very bones—a lingering residue from the Almighty—but don't let it muddle your thoughts. We are Those Who Hunt. This thing called *peace* is like an inoculation in the humans, slowing their blood flow so that our infestations cannot spread as quickly. It makes it more difficult for us to sup."

A few in the group murmured in agreement.

"It's no wonder," Helene said, "that some call the Nazarene the Prince of Peace. His elixir is something we want no part of."

"No more peace," Kyria squeaked.

"No more peace," the others joined in.

Erota smoothed long fingers over a tendril on the wall. "I say, let these precious thorns crawl on into Jerusalem. Let them turn it into a city of the walking dead." She lifted the candlestick, bathing upturned faces in golden hues. "Reports from other clusters show Lord Natira has been busy in America. He's pinned down more of the Concealed Ones and even tapped clues to his son's whereabouts. My guess is he'll be heading this way soon, and we want him to see that we've been aggressive in his absence."

No need, she decided, for him to know about Ramon Crater. Not yet.

Mt. Hood National Forest

Evergreens and ferns led the Akeldama Collector upward from the thundering waterfall, until he passed the trail signs to Angel's Rest and reached the junction with Devil's Rest instead. Switchbacks carried him higher into stands of cedar and old-growth Douglas firs. Temperatures dropped at this elevation and a fog rolled in that blanketed the slope in an eerie calm. Moss-draped branches poked through the gray and looked like skeletal fingers still bearing strips of tissue and skin.

Though Natira had surveyed his environs the entire time for a glimpse of his little beast, he'd seen only backpackers, two deer, plenty of mosquitoes, and a long black millipede. Once or twice he thought he heard heavy breathing, but it faded when he stopped to listen.

Probably his own laboring lungs.

This entire scenario seemed unreal. For decades the creature must have wandered these ridges and forests, aging half as fast as mere mortals, surviving on vegetation and wildlife. Surely he'd been sighted a time or two, leading to speculation, yet mentions of Sasquatch and such only amused the more rational minds.

Did the boy have any cognizance of his lineage?

Though his mother had refused him a proper name, could he sniff out his own undead flesh and blood?

Natira continued his climb, shaking off the sense that he was being watched. This was common in the woods, due to the presence of stealthy animals. He passed the time mulling over names for his child.

Tracker? Hunter? Beast?

A low growl jolted him from his thoughts, and a figure appeared from the fog. The thing's height was blunted by its twisted limbs and spine. A layer of nut-brown hair covered much of its body, combed back from the high forehead to bare a contorted countenance. It was nothing typical of these woods, nothing found in the science books. What else could this be but his forsaken mongrel?

They eyed each other. Neither made a sound.

Natira kept his arms down, his posture relaxed, and took note of wide nostrils above bared teeth. He surmised that this beast had tracked him through the mist and hemlocks, locking on to his scent, identifying him as kin the way mammals were known to do. After decades of scrounging, surviving, he must've thrilled at the nearness of a parental figure.

"I am here for you, son."

The figure's black eyes widened, his nose flared. He stepped closer, blood dripping deep red from his fangs. Suspended from a cord about his waist, a drawstring pouch contained tools with crudely carved handles—a gift from his mother, apparently. He offered a roan-colored stag on outstretched arms.

"For me?" Natira said.

He marveled at this monster—neither man nor bear, neither dead nor alive. Had the hemotoxin in that Nazi lab seeped into Trudi Ubelhaar's skin, rendering her offspring something horrible and fantastic?

"His likeness shall unlock riches to strengthen his campaign . . ."

With a glance at those grotesquely crooked fingers, he imagined one of them prying at a keyhole, working the tumblers within. Could it be as simple as that? Could these knuckles' bony protrusions match the knobby crown of a chess king? When it came to the Rasputin prophecy, Lord Natira was willing to believe even the most surreal of possibilities.

He felt, however, little paternal response to this being in front of him, only a sense of pride that his loins had loosed such a creature long ago in the cellars of a German castle. That castle's name now seemed a fitting moniker.

"Kransberg," he said. "It's good to see you, my son."

THE THIRD SENSE: SMELL

He straightened . . . heart beating senselessly . . .
bones and muscles and tissue all alive and functioning without purpose.

—RICHARD MATHESON, *I AM LEGEND*

Like unthinking animals, they do whatever their instincts tell them.

—JUDE 1:10

Journal Entry

July 27

We've spent the past week on a yacht, slipping through the San Juan Islands down into Puget Sound. Mom says we're laying low. We heard from the Unfallen that Those Who Hunt ransacked my old house on Lummi and went through the stuff I left. Not that it matters. I've got my bag, my map, and that's about all I need. The only other thing I care about is hidden in the cemetery by the church—and they won't be looking there.

Mom also says my dad will be coming to join us on the boat. I've seen him through the memories in the droplets, but I'm still trying to wrap my head around it. A flood of questions poured out: "When will he be here? Do I look like him? Why wasn't he with you at the diner when you met me?"

"He should be coming aboard later tonight," Mom said. "As for your questions, I'll let him answer those himself. Believe me, little man, he is so excited to see you."

Honestly, I don't know how to react. I've spent all these years on my own—fishing, combing the beach, reading, doing my studies—and now I'm going to have a full-fledged family. Is this the way it normally happens? Is there such a thing as normal? There's still so much I'm learning about life off the island, but I sense things have irreversibly changed for me. Mom calls it a destiny.

My Unfallen buddies on Lummi won't be forgotten, of course. Even though they have other things to do now, I hope to still see them from time to time.

Skipper just poked his head into my cabin. He's the gruff big-bearded guy who owns this boat. "You hungry, boy?" he asked. "Got Dungeness crab in the galley, but ya won't be getting much if you stay planted on that backside."

CHAPTER
THIRTY

Florence

"Really? Jed made this for you?"

"Our own driftwood fort," Gina said. "That day we came here with Sarge."

"I'm surprised it's still standing." Josee's knuckles elicited a hollow thunk from a limb stripped of bark. A brisk wind carried the sound away, and she knocked again. *"Casa de Turney."*

"Not now that Jed's ignoring my calls. But, hey, once you're officially Mrs. Vince Turney, it's all yours. You can raise your adorable mini-Sarges in there."

"Mini-Sarges?"

"If you have boys, I mean."

"You know, Gina, I never even wanted children till just recently. It's like something stirred in me the moment Sarge proposed, like I want to keep our bloodline going. Does that sound strange? And now my parents're itching for a grandbaby—if their early wedding gift's any indication."

"They make good wine?"

"Their Pinot Noir has won all kinds of awards. My father's been invited to other countries to share his secrets with their winemakers."

"So much for being secrets, huh?"

Both of them chuckled. Gina dropped onto the crest of a small dune and peered over the empty beach and rolling surf. Josee plopped down at her side.

For a week now, Gina had worked and eaten meals in the awkward tension at the gallery. Suzette was avoiding all contact, focused on business matters in the back office and on privacy in her own room.

On edge, Gina had expressed some of her frustrations to Josee and asked for advice. It was Josee's suggestion they come spend this Monday at the coast, work in some girl talk, maybe peek at the Fabergé again.

"How flippin' cool is that?" Josee said, digging her toes into the sand. "A few more weeks and we'll be related."

"Not that Jed wants any part of it."

"He'll swing around."

"Why'd you pair us up in the wedding party? You know he won't escort me down that aisle."

"He's a grownup. He'll do it."

Gina uprooted a piece of dune grass and speared it through the air.

"Has he returned any of your calls?" Josee said. "No? Well, there you go. He's still got a soft spot for you or he'd have no reason to worry about letting you back in. Take Sarge. Being the teddy bear he is, he used to keep up his guard, afraid of disappointing others or getting hurt." She bumped Gina's arm with her fist. "Let's face it . . . we women are just better at bouncing back."

"I love him."

"He's your husband. Duh."

"It's been years since . . . Listen, I'm just tired of trying to hold it together."

"Yourself? Or the relationship?"

"Right now, they feel like the same thing."

Even as the confession spilled out, Gina knew she was touching a deeper nerve. Was this the same weariness to which her mother had surrendered? If pushed, would Gina also succumb to some misguided martyrdom? Nikki had always gone to extremes to cleanse and safeguard her family, trusting in her own methods and strength; and later, when presented with the cure of Nazarene Blood, she'd balked. In her mind, to accept the sacrifice of another would have meant her own sacrifices were made in vain.

"I'm not ready to give up," Gina decided.

"'Course not. You're one of Those Who Resist."

"I don't think I can get through this on my own, though."

"None of us are meant to."

"Okay, but you're moving out soon, which leaves me alone with Suzette. And I'm not sure what her deal is."

"She's jealous. We both know that now."

"Thanks to her," Gina said, "there's nothing to be jealous of."

"Think of it from her perspective. I'm getting married, and you're always the center of attention in the gallery. She's the artsy introvert, intelligent and nice, but—let's be honest—not exactly a love magnet. The one man she actually did like moved away."

"Who?"

"It was after everything went haywire during a local anarchist plot. ICV? You remember them?"

"Saw something about them in the news a year or two ago."

"Yeah, Sarge and I got mixed up in that whole deal. My parents too." Josee ran sand between her fingers. "It was a mess, all of it instigated by this psycho ex-Nazi woman named Trudi Ubelhaar. She used local art classes to draw in the counterculture types, then turned them into pawns in a scheme to spread poison gas."

"Sounds like something out of a suspense novel."

"They tried recruiting Suzette. She only went to one meeting, and while she was there met this Portland dude with tattooed forearms—the bad-boy type, intriguing for all the wrong reasons. 'Course, she thought it was love at first sight. Right after the whole ICV thing went down, he moved out of state."

"Were they together at the time?"

"Nah. Honestly, I think the attraction was more on Suzette's end. She's just never been able to find a good match."

"So she has to ruin it for everyone else."

"Childish, sure. Aren't we all, in our own little ways?"

"She's one of Those Who Resist, though. That's what confuses me."

"What, that she's normal? Has emotions?"

"The thorns—I saw them moving under her skin."

"First, Gina, I'll admit I've never personally seen infection shown through thorns." Josee rested both elbows on her knee and touched her eyebrow ring. "During my little run-in with ICV, I saw the sickness in the form of snakes."

"Snakes?"

"Hissing, fiery-eyed ones. Think Medusa on steroids."

"Hmm. Thorns or snakes? Not sure which is worse."

"No matter the shape or form, it all starts in the blood, ends in the blood. Yes, Nazarene Blood purifies, but if it's not renewed daily, it gets diluted and infection sneaks back in. You, me, Sarge, Suzette—we're all susceptible."

"But she purposefully tried to tear me down."

"Listen, I'm no fount of wisdom here. Even Apostle Paul said he dealt with a thorn in his flesh. He talked about how we don't do the things we want to do, and end up doing the things we hate. It's a struggle. Always has been."

"Fine. But I don't see how any of that excuses Suzette."

"She's still our sister. 'All for one, and one for all,' right? If she'll let us, maybe we can help cleanse the wound and then watch so the infection doesn't come back."

Gina plucked another blade of grass.

"Would you be willing to help?" Josee said.

"If she'll admit to Jed that she lied."

"Of course. Confession's part of the cleansing."

Gina drew a letter Tav in the sand, then brushed over it.

"There's one part I don't get." Josee swiveled her gaze to her roommate. "Why would Jed believe Suzette over you in the first place? You're his wife."

"Because I . . ."

"Yeah? Is there something you haven't told me?"

"It's complicated."

"Please tell me there isn't another guy."

"There isn't another guy."

"Then what?"

"Well . . ." Gina ran a hand through her hair. "There is another guy, though not the way you might think. Like I said, it's complicated. I can't go into the details—you have to trust me on that—but it has nothing to do with romance, okay? Jed has no competition."

"But Suzette might've seen something that made her *think* you were—"

"No," Gina stated. "She flat-out made it up."

Josee cocked her head.

"Hey, just calling it like it is."

"Okay, Gina, so you love your husband and he loves you, our friend Suzette's green with envy and starts spitting out rumors, and meanwhile you're hiding deep dark secrets in order to protect someone. Does that about sum it up?"

"I guess."

"Then get over it."

"Say what?"

"Don't let this beat you down. Sarge is always telling me how this old world'll never stop trying to suck the air from your lungs, and the best thing you can do is stand in the wind and yell back. Show some resilience."

Gina wanted to point out that she was nearly fifteen years older than Josee, a tad more tired and jaded, but that would lead to more questions and circular explanations. She kept her mouth shut.

"Here," Josee said, taking her hand. "Stand up."

"What're you doing?"

"Look out at that huge ocean and let the breeze blow through your hair."

"Okay."

"Now yell," Josee said.

"Right now?"

Her roommate squeezed her hand. "Tell the world you're not done yet."

"I'm not done yet."

"That's a yell? Come on and let it out."

"I'm not *done* yet."

"Louder. Like you mean it."

"I am *not* done fighting!"

"Together. Top of our lungs."

"I am not done fighting!"

"We are *Those Who Resist!*"

"We are *Those Who Resist!*" Gina echoed.

Sands shifted behind them and footsteps rustled through the grass. Gina turned, realizing as she did that she was not so much embarrassed by their outburst as alert to potential danger. She was startled to find herself staring into green eyes that glittered with flecks of gold.

"Dad?"

"Not too shabby for a coupla girls," he said.

"Hey, Nickel," Josee said. "We didn't know you'd be out here."

"And miss out on some high-pitched screams? Fat chance."

Gina said, "Clay told me you'd be coming by, but that was a number of weeks ago. Where've you been?"

"Here and there. What about we go down to Mo's for a bowl of clam chowder, and I'll fill you in on the details over a game of chess."

"Oh, now you're asking for trouble."

"I'll show you another classic game from—"

"Don't say it." Gina pretended to be stumped. "Adolf Anderssen?"

"You know his Immortal and Evergreen Games, some of the most famous in chess circles, but this one's between him and Joseph Blackburne. I call it the Sovereign Game because the white king's under siege from the beginning and still pulls off a surprising counterattack."

"I take it black lost?"

"Black*burne*, to be exact."

"Funny."

"Does this have anything to do with the black king?" Josee said.

That got Nickel's attention. "What?"

"You know, the figurine Sarge recovered from Engine 418."

"We'll talk about that later. It all fits, all has its place." His tone became solemn. "The question now is, what're we going to risk for an opportunity to win? The battle's not over yet. You think you'll be able to lay it all on the line when that time comes?"

"Of course she will," Josee cut in. "What about you, Nickel?"

"Let's do this," he said.

In response to the girls' questioning looks, Cal Nichols whipped a ram's horn from his JanSport daypack. No longer than his forearm, the curled, polished *shofar* was used traditionally for a call to war, to arms, or to repentance. It was the same instrument blown by the Hebrew priests as they marched around Jericho's mighty walls once a day for six days, followed by seven full circuits on the seventh. Thirteen total. An unlucky number for those buried in the rubble.

"I'll blow," Nickel said, "and you shout."

Gina and Josee looked at each other. "We're ready."

Even straining their vocal chords to the point of turning hoarse, they could barely hear themselves the moment Nickel's shofar blasted. That primal sound called up fears and sent them running, churned up courage in their place; it rolled in raw, rumbling waves to meet the rising sea, where nature amplified the roar and sent it rolling back toward them on the wind.

Side by side, Gina and Josee stood with hands clasped, salty mist dampening their eyes, and yelled: *"We are Those Who Resist!"*

CHAPTER
THIRTY-ONE

Columbia River Gorge, Oregon

Kransberg was a mangy mess.

Hidden by trees along the moonlit Columbia River, Natira considered the brute and the best ways to manage his appearance. He was as tall as his father, though bent by deformities at his knees and spine, and his fingernails and teeth were formidable weapons, curved and razored for easy disembowelment. Between fleas and clumps of mud-caked hair, he was no better than a dog. Or a werewolf, for that matter.

"You make Shabtai look like a puppy," Natira said.

A few years back, a teen male from their cluster had explored the possibilities of lupine hosts. Shabtai had prowled Romania's Carpathian foothills and assumed increasingly wolfish traits until there was little distinction between him and the legendary vircolac. In the end, though, he'd been vanquished.

Natira's mouth turned dry. Once they were finished here, he would see that his thirst was met.

First, he wanted to be certain this was his progeny. If Kransberg was his own, with undead roots in his veins, he should be nearly indestructible, able to be revitalized by a sip of his father's blood. Natira stepped forward. He stared into the monster's eyes, and it was like staring into his own black soul.

He said: "You are Kransberg."

"I . . . Kransberg."

"Yes, very good."

"I . . . good."

"Not too good, let's hope."

He moved another step closer and still Kransberg showed no fear, accustomed to his role as apex predator in this forested terrain. Natira was pleased, both as warrior and father, but that didn't stop him from ripping a branch from the tree trunk on his right and swinging it into his son's hairy thorax.

Small twigs snapped away on impact, while the wood's blunt force drove a roar from Kransberg's mouth. Betrayal welled in his eyes. Confusion.

"I assume you are my son, yes," Natira said. "But what're you made of?"

Kransberg hunched lower, his expression that of a child wanting to please, his eyes searching yet chilled by a void. Chances were he'd picked up some words, even sentences, from hikers passing through the woods over the decades, but his comprehension level was still up for debate.

"Our human connection means nothing." Natira slapped a hand across the stubbled face. "Is that clear?"

This time, anger erupted in a howl.

Slap!

A low snarl.

Slap-slappp!

The creature absorbed the blows in silence now, his bent spine stiff, his feet planted, head jerking and tool pouch swaying from the force of his father's gargantuan palm, while his eyes turned sharp as flint.

"That's better, my son. If I think you need toughening, you will take it like a man—or whatever it is you are."

"I . . . Kransberg."

"Come, now," Natira said. "Come here." He stretched out both arms, clasped them behind the boy's neck as though drawing him into an embrace, then jerked that large head down into a pistoning knee.

Blood sprayed from Kransberg's nose. He wobbled back, blinked twice, and narrowed his gaze onto his abuser.

"Are you a warrior, I wonder?"

Kransberg gave no reply.

Natira coiled his body to the left, then whipped back around with a jagged elbow aimed at his son's temple. The creature ducked underneath, bellowed, and hammered his skull up into Natira's jaw. The impact rattled teeth in their sockets, and Natira grinned despite the burst of pain. He nodded in respect, then reacted with a left jab, followed by a right hook that crunched against bone and tore at his son's tangled fur.

Probing inside his own mouth, Kransberg produced a broken fang.

Natira snatched and lifted it. "I am hostis humani generis," he growled.

Kransberg locked on to his voice. "I . . . hostis . . . humani . . ."

"Generis."

"Gen . . . eris."

"That's right. We are the enemies of mankind."

"We are . . . enemas."

Cackling at the mistake, Natira nodded his head.

Corvallis

With bellies full of chowder and the sun setting at their backs, Gina, Josee, and Nickel returned to Corvallis. Earlier, they'd paid another visit to the Bank of the Dunes in Florence—the Fabergé egg hadn't lost any of its luster—then to the local seafood joint, where Nickel won two out of three chess games while Gina complained she couldn't concentrate amid the clinking bowls and spoons.

"Mental toughness," was her dad's response. "Gotta stay focused."

Between moves, he shared stories of Kenny's development and Dov's diving with dolphins. Although he wouldn't let on where either was stationed, Gina thanked him for these vignettes of boys whom she had helped raise.

Suzette was gone when they arrived at the gallery. No shocker, since it was her day off also. Praying this wasn't all a mistake, Gina shifted from foot to foot while Josee opened the front door and switched on lights.

"Something to drink, anyone?" Josee called from the kitchen.

"Water's good for me." Her dad must've noticed Gina's expression. "Don't worry. I'm not going anywhere till we get this resolved."

She gave him a weak smile.

"Remember, these are thorns Suzette's dealing with. Not Collectors."

"I've had my own thorns," Gina said, "so I know they won't just go away."

"You were fighting them alone. Big mistake. Here we'll be joining together, two or three of us, to help a friend."

"Hope it works."

They took seats in the gallery's dining area, and Gina touched the tip of her tongue to her bottom teeth. This was an old habit of hers, a means of cooling anger and animosity. She counted them individually, stopping at each tooth to think of someone to bless.

One: give Josee some gas money to cover the trip to the coast.

Two: thank Nickel for being here to confront Suzette.

Three: show Suzette some appreciation for supplying me a job and a—

The technique's intended goodwill dissipated the moment the gallery owner came through the back door with her bike. Suzette shook out her hair, tucked her feet into a pair of moccasins she wore around the house, and stepped into the dining room.

Well, lookie here—the liar, the rumormonger, dared to show her face.

"Good evening. I do hope I'm not interrupting anything."

She even dared open her mouth.

"Suzette," Josee said, "we were getting worried about you."

"Oh?"

"Out there on your bike in the dark."

"I didn't go far, not far at all. Plus, I had both lamps on, and in that reflective jacket of mine I'm more noticeable than E.T."

Though Gina wanted to sneer, she couldn't help feeling a tinge of mercy. Suzette was unpretentious, unassuming, and she'd opened her home and workplace to a complete stranger—all at Cal Nichols' request. In addition, she wore a vial around her neck, marking her as one of Those Who Resist.

There. See, right there. That was the part that stumped Gina.

In her own mind, she'd been freed from her thorns the moment she drank that Blood, the root of her bitterness expelled, whereas Suzette still seemed to be carrying sickness within. Weren't Those Who Resist inoculated, immune? Wasn't the Blood enough? If not, then what was the point of going through the motions, meeting in the park, jabbering about the Nazarene's instructions, and partaking together as though sharing some miracle cure?

From its leather sheath, Gina's dagger begged to be of use. She imagined touching that blade to Suzette's skin, making the first slice, spilling her blood while exorcising her rottenness.

No.

Nickel said, "We're glad to have you home, Suzette."

"Thank you, but isn't that an odd thing to say, considering we're in my house?" Suzette refreshed herself with a splash of water at the kitchen sink and fetched a bottle of Genesis Juice from the fridge. "Naturally, you're a welcome guest, Nickel. Are you in need of a place for the night?"

"Appreciate the thought, but I'll be leaving soon."

Gina shot her dad a look. Had he forgotten their plan?

"You'll stay for supper at least?" Suzette said.

"Ahhh." Nickel rubbed his tummy. "Had Mo's chowder already. I'm good."

"I'm not good."

At this statement, three pairs of eyes turned toward Gina and she rolled back her shoulders. She refused to take the passive-aggressive approach and in fact thought it would only turn up the tension in the house—or in her own head, anyway. Nope. The thing to do was deal with dishonesty straight up.

"Suzette, you and I need to talk."

"Is this about the other night?"

"For the most part you're a wonderful person—don't get me wrong, okay?—but you poisoned Jed against me with your lies. And why you would go around spying, making up stories about my personal activities, I have no idea."

Her father scooted his chair back from the table. "Gina, let me—"

"Let you what? Is this like all the other things in our lives: cover it up and pretend it'll get better? I thought we were done with that approach."

"We're gonna speak the truth here, but we'll speak it in love."

"It's not love to let someone slide by."

"Slide by?" Josee said. "You really think that's what's going on here?"

"It's not love to let the thorns keep growing."

"Thorns? Is this me you're discussing?" Suzette resigned herself to the lone empty chair at the table, screwed the cap back onto her juice. "It's true I've said some hurtful things."

"We all says things we regret," Nickel pointed out.

Suzette lowered her eyes and covered her throat with her hand.

"Right now," Gina said, "we're not dealing with everyone. This is concerning the rumors Suzette has spread about me. Where'd you even come up with this stuff, huh? Me kissing some guy, getting into his car. It's so stinkin' ridiculous, and now Jed won't even to talk to me. My own husband told me to get out of his house."

"You've not lived with him for years, as I understand it."

"Excuse me? Our relationship's none of your business. This is about you."

"Is it?" Nickel said to Gina.

She fixed her gaze on Suzette. "There's a cure for your problem, you know? Back in my day, my mom knew how to bleed out impurities and she wasn't afraid to do what had to be done."

"Whoa." Josee raised both hands. "What're you suggesting, Gina?"

"If you guys won't call her out on this, I'll do it myself." Even as she spoke the words, she felt tendons knotting on the left side of her own neck. "Which is fine. I mean, I'm the one who's been slandered here."

"She's already admitted she said hurtful things."

"Too little, too late. The damage is already done."

"Let her undo it," Nickel said.

"Okay." Gina massaged her neck, felt a knot beneath the skin. "How?"

"First, we don't go back to your mom's way of dealing with things."

"Hey, if it works . . ."

"Nikki's gone for good, Gina. Think about what you're saying."

She blinked, not wanting to think. Not wanting to feel.

"Sure, you cut away the bitterness," her father said, "but it was always rooted in Nikki's self-righteousness. Don't let that start growing in you now."

She pressed her tongue against another tooth, another diversion.

Four: make cookies for Jacob and try to hold it together.

"You ready to do this, Suzette?" Nickel unclipped a cell phone from his belt, slid it across the table.

Suzette sat back as though the object would scald her.

He said, "You know we love you. As one of Those Who Resist, there's no way you can leave false accusations floating around out there. That's been a favorite tactic of the Master Collector's from the beginning, trying to drive wedges between us. If there is a shred of truth in anything the Collectors say, it's only there so they can breed more lies with it. Divide and conquer."

"Love?" Suzette whispered.

"What?"

"You said you love me."

"Of course we do." Josee covered Suzette's hand with her own.

"Not you. Him." Hope flickered like fireflies in the woman's eyes, and she combed her free hand through her hair. "Nickel, did you mean that?"

His confusion would have been comical if Gina hadn't spotted the earnest expression on Suzette's face. With Nickel's comings and goings, the gallery owner had clearly found a soft spot for him and read more into his visits than was warranted. How those feelings had led to manufactured untruths about Gina was a mystery. Perhaps Suzette had taken on a motherly role in her own mind, an unspoken partnership with Gina's father, and started spying in hopes of keeping Gina out of trouble. Who knew how these things worked?

Regardless of the reasons, Gina knew what it meant to live as an outsider, feeling as though few understood or loved you, warts and all. She saw Suzette as a little girl, caught between tribal traditions and a white man's world, struggling to fit in, to find her niche.

For the first time, she saw a friend.

"Listen, Suzette . . ." Gina swallowed against the tightness in her neck as she left her chair and went to Suzette's side. Josee was still touching the woman's hand, and now Gina rested her arm across her shoulders. She wanted to come up with something wise or poignant, but all she could think to say was: "He's my dad, and that would be more than a little weird."

The room paused for a reaction.

"Not to mention," Gina added, "he's a lot older than he looks."

Nickel nodded. "This hair's been dyed more times than I can count."

Suzette gave a rueful chuckle.

"As for the other part," he said, "I do love ya, Suzette—we all do— but it's like one of those plutonic kind of things."

She chuckled again. "Platonic, I'm sure you mean."

"Platonic? Uh, yeah. Okay, got it."

"Hey, now," Josee said. "Even people on Pluto need love."

"Don't we all?" Nickel said. "And that includes my daughter. She's gone through a lot, lost a lot, and if there's one thing Gina probably wants more than anything right now, it's to be back together with the man she married."

Suzette looked off to the side.

Nickel wasn't done. "Tough, I know, but you've gotta see what's at stake here. Sarge and Josee'll be getting hitched in a coupla weeks—Independence Day, am I right?—and you can invest in your own future by supporting theirs."

"I am," Suzette said, sniffling. "I'm trying to be happy for them."

"You're just tired of being alone."

"Is that a bad thing?"

"No, it's . . ." Nickel's jaw stiffened. "It's a very normal thing."

Suzette closed her eyes as a tremor shook her, disrupting the vines that lay in her chest. Filled with tender resolve, Nickel's gaze turned to Gina, to Josee, then back to Suzette. On the table, the cell phone awaited its part in the matter.

"Suzette," he said, "you do know that you're infected?"

"Yes." Eyes still closed. Tears brimming on lashes. "Yes, I know."

"Then whaddya say we do something about it?"

CHAPTER
THIRTY-TWO

Columbia River Gorge

Lord Natira threw his son's busted fang into the mighty Columbia, while Kransberg watched with unreadable eyes. Far down the river, an electric storm blossomed in the night sky, followed by a thunderous concussion, and Kransberg's head swiveled in concern. No doubt he'd seen tree trunks split by lightning before.

"You, my son, will need to shave, and clothes will be required in public."

Kransberg mopped the blood from his mouth.

"And if you want to look less the caveman and more the modern gentleman, you'll need to do away with that tool pouch."

Kransberg grunted, clutching the object to his side.

"Very well," Natira said. "I'm sure you derive some sentimental pleasure from it, but it'll need to remain hidden beneath a shirt or jacket. There's much to teach you. That much is clear. Nevertheless, I smell in you a sense of destiny."

Kransberg moved to the pebbled bank and thumped his chest. "Destiny," he said. "Des . . . ti . . . ny."

"Good for you. You know how to parrot my words."

Another flash brightened the sky, and Natira thought of his own first-century AD assignment, fighting invaders at Jotapata. Some portion of his host's memory churned with sounds of blades and armaments and the stink of Roman candles scorching the ozone. As a Collector, he had used various vessels over the ages, though none as effective as this present specimen from the Field of Blood.

And it was from these undead loins he had sired a son.

Half Collector. Half human.

All blasphemy.

In the days of Noah, similar abominations had roamed the earth—the Nephilim, the Anakim, and giants such as Sisera. Sisera had raged against the children of God, only to be lulled to sleep by a warm tent and warm goat's milk, then vanquished by a metal tent peg through his temple.

Crude symbolism, at best.

True enough, Hebrew Scriptures spoke of the Messiah being the "tent peg," the stake that held things fast and secure. But hadn't Collectors succeeded in turning that symbol on its head? Yes, indeed. At Golgotha, they'd stirred the soldiers to drive metal spikes into the wrists and feet of that Messiah.

The Almighty's Son crucified on an accursed tree.

Mocked with that Crown of Thorns.

Yet here, two thousand years later, Cal Nichols and his tagalongs still put such weapons to use. Over a third of the Akeldama Cluster had been banished with MTPs, a dagger, and Nazarene Blood, while Those Who Resist seemed to be growing in boldness—growing, growing, growing.

Corvallis

"It starts with confession," Nickel told Suzette.

"I've tried. I've truly tried."

He nudged his cell phone toward her hand and she opened her eyes. "All you have to do is hit Send and it'll redial Jed's house. He's expecting a call."

"If you told him already, then I—"

"I've told him squat. He needs to hear this from you."

Although Suzette's blouse covered most of her skin, there was no missing the twitch of vines along the gentle scoop of her collarbone. The movement paralleled the bone at first, then anchored around it, serpentlike.

Empathy welled up in Gina as Suzette trembled at the dining table. She remembered her own helplessness and trepidation as thorns spiraled from their place of hiding in her neck. Before that, at almost twelve years old—or so she'd believed at the time—she had gone under her mother's blade for the sake of a simple mosquito bite. *"That's the only way to avoid the disorder . . . Get me the knife."*

The sad part was that in attempting to cleanse her daughter, Nikki Lazarescu had opened a wound and left it vulnerable to infection.

Bitterness. Unforgiveness. Self-righteousness . . . They'd sprouted from that one incision and later entangled Gina in a Romanian mountain cave, nearly resulting in her death. Even after her escape, those thorns had persisted.

She'd hacked at them.

They had grown back again, weaker yet still there.

Nearly two years ago, she'd bitten into her ruby-orb earring, ingesting the Nazarene Blood and letting it cleanse away that infestation at last, but she now realized that the washing was a continual process. Daily communion. New life through the remembrance of death.

"Is this necessary?" Suzette asked.

"It is," Gina said. "For your sake and mine. Take it from someone who's been there, you need to get this out."

"Either way, it's your call." Nickel tapped at the phone. "Literally."

Suzette flipped it open, stabbed at the Send button. With eyes closed, she held the cell to her ear and waited. "Hello? No, it's . . . This is Suzette Bishop."

The serpent coiled. Vines cinched tighter.

"Jed, I'm here at the gallery with Josee, Nickel, and . . . and your wife. If you'll give me a moment, I need to clarify some things I told you earlier."

She spent two minutes listing and tearing down each of her own fabrications. To her credit, she plowed ahead without stopping. She signed off in a voice that sounded exhausted yet relieved, then closed the phone on the table and rested her face in her hands.

"You did good," Nickel said.

"What'd he say to all that?" Gina wanted to know.

"He said he would need to process it."

The bulged skin at Suzette's throat showed no sign of activity.

"Nothing else?"

"He seemed stunned. Now that my own credibility's been called into question, what's he supposed to believe?"

"The truth," Gina said, trying to corral her frustration.

"You'll get your chance to touch base with him later," her father said. "The important thing is that Suzette cleared the air. That's step one."

"And step two?"

"That part should be obvious," Josee interjected. "We partake as a group."

Thorns twisted, tugged.

Short of breath, Suzette said, "I don't know that I'm ready."

"Who says we're ever ready?" Josee raised her vial on its braided cord, unscrewed the lid. "Suzette, you've done what you were supposed to, but it's less about us and more about the sacrifice made for us. Am I the only one who needs to do this, or is anyone else going to drink the Blood?"

Suzette's fingers hooked the cord around her neck and pulled it up past the vines that throbbed in her chest. She set her jaw and opened her vial, averting her eyes from the swelling, the blotchiness, the sharp angles that trolled along her skin. There was no reward in acting like the thorns didn't exist, only in addressing them without fear.

"Never mind those old things," Nickel said. "You've got the confession off your chest, and the rest you do by faith in the Nazarene."

Around the table, all four lifted the elements as one.

"The Nazarene Blood will prevail," Nickel said.

"The Nazarene Blood will prevail," the others responded.

They drank.

Gina felt the rich red wine slide over her tongue and down her throat, felt its warmth spread through her limbs and melt away obstructions. Modern science told her DNA was contained within a double helix of spiraling codes that outlined hereditary disease, alcoholism, heart trouble, and so on—things referred to in the Scriptures as generational sins and sicknesses passed through the bloodline.

No one was immune. No, not one.

And yet there was One who'd bypassed the male channel into the womb, thereby born of spirit and flesh.

Yes, Yeshua had bridged the Separation and brought about healing through His own unblemished Blood.

"Ohhh!" A short gasp burst from Suzette's lips.

At her throat, the thorns squiggled from their original entry point, fleeing the hot rush of liquid. They spooled onto the tile floor, withering, crackling, until nothing remained except a husk like shed snakeskin. Without fanfare, Josee swept up the refuse into a dust pan and strode down the hall.

The flush of a toilet put an exclamation point on the evening's events.

"Now that," Nickel said, "is what I call a good day."

Columbia River Gorge

Natira turned back toward shadowed spruce and hemlock, contemplating his next step. He believed Kransberg to be his key to the Tmu Tarakan, and yet the treasure's coordinates in Jerusalem remained a mystery.

Should he trust Asgoth's words about the rumored duplicate key and the inscribed Templar ring? An ancient map to sacred relics?

And what other secrets had Trudi harbored in her blood?

She'd had a prison visitor . . .

Oleg. Part of the Brotherhood of Tobolsk.

Natira knew the Brotherhood hoped to restore Mother Russia to her former greatness, and Erota had once shared Rasputin's prophecy with them in hopes of furthering her own schemes. Had Oleg descended upon the old Finnish train engine in Junction City? Had he discovered the items there, then consorted with Natira's former lover in hopes of beating the Black King to the hidden cache of riches?

Shaking free of this conundrum for now, Natira thought of the six Concealed Ones left to root out. It was a task that would be accelerated with Kransberg's half-immortal eyes, and as a father-son team, they would pillage the Middle East for the remaining Oh-So-Humble Ones.

"I need to acquaint you with better language skills," Natira said.

Kransberg grunted.

"If I could retrain my speech despite this stump of a tongue, you'll be able to do so."

"I . . . talk."

"Like a caged gorilla." Natira shook his head. "Never mind. Before we worry about any of that, you need to pass a simple test."

"Test," Kransberg mouthed.

Taking advantage of the pause, Natira filled his lungs, hooked his pinkie and thumb, and with all his strength and momentum lunged forward on rock-solid quadriceps. He had used these pincers before to pop out eyeballs and crack craniums like crab shells; this time, however, he slammed them between hair-covered ribs, ripped through the layer of flesh, and raked the counterfeit heart from Kransberg's chest.

Birds screeched in the branches and took flight, distancing themselves from this killer on the riverbank, while electricity crackled once more overhead.

Wide eyed, Kransberg dropped to both knees.

Collapsed into the dirt.

In Natira's hand, the charcoal-colored heart shriveled. It twitched, squirmed, pumped out fluids that smelled no better than maggot-covered corpses. This was not the rich, savory aroma of Nazarene Blood—oh, that was a tantalizing poison, one he knew firsthand—or even the diluted scent released while tapping a two-legger.

No, this was unnatural, unholy life.

He squeezed out the last of the juices, pushed the deflated organ into his pocket, and headed for the rental car parked out of sight beneath the trees. He would come back in a day or two to complete the test, but all this work had left him parched.

CHAPTER THIRTY-THREE

June—Ramon Crater

By the sails of Sicily, it was hot today. Was there no shade, no refuge? Barabbas drew a weathered arm across his forehead, mopping at rivulets of sweat. His beard hung like sodden rags against his bare chest, and in his grip the chisel's handle was damp.

This was hard work, tedious and mind numbing. At his feet, however, the first of his projects was taking shape.

First of thousands, if Megiste had her way—and she usually did with him.

The henchman rested one leg upon a rock, examining the scorched terrain that stretched for kilometers in every direction. The makhtesh was breathtaking in its cruel beauty, walled in by dun-colored cliffs, heated by desert sun. Ibex climbed the ridges, while lizards and scorpions waggled under rocks and vultures circled on hot thermals.

Of course, a small number of humans came to gawk at this spectacle of erosion. Most took their photos and jumped back into air-conditioned vehicles, while a few braved the trails, and fewer still made it out alive.

Eons ago, deep seas had drained through a narrow outlet here, slowly eroding this basin in the middle of nowhere.

And it was now home to Barabbas.

More important, it was his and Megiste's workplace.

He kicked at the clay form he'd been fashioning with hammer and chisel. Today's progress was slow. This unforgiving soil refused to cooperate, and the water necessary for mixing, softening, and shaping was found in subterranean crawlspaces accessed through nearby cliff openings. To creep in, fill a bucket, and scrape his large body back into daylight could take an hour, even two. On the hottest of days—and today was one of them—he might need three or four buckets just to keep the clay moldable.

Would Megiste's idea work? Would it be worth his sunburned skin?

"Dear Barabbas."

He dropped his foot from the rock and turned to see cinnamon robes clinging to Megiste's lithe body. Behind her rose a hill of black basalt.

"You don't seem as enthused as you were a few days ago. Is it the heat? It is simply *terrible*, isn't it?"

"Work is work," he said.

"You were daydreaming, perhaps? Forgive me if I startled you."

"Resting for a moment, Megiste."

"Indeed, we do all need our rest."

"These human hosts of ours—always hungry, thirsty. I'll get back to what I was doing." He bent to one knee, positioned the chisel beneath his hammer, then struck a blow that rang sharp and metallic before the sound was swallowed by the crater's vastness. "I won't let these weaknesses stop me from my work."

"Admirable, but don't be a *bore*. I come not as your taskmaster, rather as your adoring priestess. Let me minister to your needs, hmm?"

His next blow clanged sideways, nearly crushing his thumb.

"Careful there."

"I'm okay."

"Distracted, were you?" Her fingernails ran across his shoulder blades. "Let me give you satisfaction, so that when you come back you can give it your best effort. That's where Erota *miserably* misunderstood you—and to think, after all my years of training her. Never mind. You're here with me now."

Did he care that he was being manipulated?

Last month, the bus had brought him from the Betrayer's birthplace at

Kerioth-Hezron to the town of Mitzpe Ramon. A handful of tourists had gathered at the observation center perched high upon the northwestern rim, cameras clicking, while an Israeli flag snapped in the wind. He'd headed down into the crater where Megiste in all her auburn-haired splendor had greeted him.

He now touched a crude form on the ground, tracing long lumps that would soon look like legs. "You really think we'll succeed?" he said.

"At finding satisfaction?" She grinned. "Dear me, need you ask?"

"At bringing these things to life."

"To life? No."

"Then why—"

"Tell me, Barabbas, have you seen those children's books where one flips the corner of the pages and watches a character jump over a rock, or wave a hand? Yes, well, it's not live-action film, is it? The animated form is not *truly* alive, and yet it gives every indication of being so. The magic is in the artist's skill as well as the viewer's imagination."

He'd seen such stories, yet failed to understand her point.

"When we're done here," Megiste explained, "I will employ some of my skills as a priestess—a dab of water to each sculpture, a dab of blood, a few carefully spoken words, and a rolled scroll."

"A scroll?"

"All part of the magic, my love. Surely, you've heard of the *golem*? They are giant, human-like creatures culled from Jewish tradition, and we'll simply give them a tweak of our own. When we're finished, we will have an entire army of the mindless monsters, each and every one ready to obey my whims—and yours."

"Mine?"

"Certainly. Sculpted by your hand, they'll be enslaved to your will."

Barabbas gazed with new awe upon the lifeless simpleton at his feet and envisioned it rising from the basin floor, an ogre of sand, water, and clay. How could he doubt Megiste with her centuries of experience in such endeavors? A golem of his very own. Thousands of them.

Something she had said, though . . .

"Lord Natira? Does he approve of this?"

"No, I suppose not. He's a warrior—not an ounce of imagination, those boys—so he'll need a hands-on evaluation of the finished product. He'll be suitably impressed, and no doubt give you high praise for your work. Until then," she said, brushing closer, "this is between you and me. Not a word."

He wished some days that he was free of her seduction, of Natira's tyranny. He was an underling, though. A minion. What choice did he have?

Megiste's practiced sensuality blurred his discontent.

Belly down on an outcropping hundreds of feet high, Cal Nichols dialed in his field glasses for a look at Barabbas and Megiste's busywork in the crater's red-hot skillet. Although a shelf of rock provided him some reprieve from the sun, sweat stung at his eyes like tiny insect bites, and he swiped his face with a long cotton sleeve.

"What're they up to?" he grumbled. "And why here?"

This was his second reconnaissance of the site, and still his field glasses provided few answers. At this distance, the Collectors' actions were hard to discern, and they seemed to be doing the bulk of their work in an old streambed that cut them off from the prying eyes of adventurers or archaeologists. Nickel had been instructed by Isaac to only observe for now. No interference. Well, if he was going to see anything, he'd have to move closer.

Were there risks involved? Yes, they were always in his thoughts.

He could be immobilized if caught, and even with immortal genes he would need the rejuvenating Nazarene Blood. Which could be hard to come by if he were six feet under in this godforsaken crater.

The other danger was that the Collectors might simply relocate and complete their work before he could find them.

This was all part of his job as an intel broker. He took great risks to gather and interpret facts, then to issue corresponding warnings to Those Who Resist and the Nistarim.

How to get down there without being seen?

He tucked the glasses into his shirt, pulled himself to a crouch on the precipice. A scorpion scurried past his hiking boots, claws raised, tail curled and translucent yellow-orange. Not his favorite creature, but he knew the thing would leave him alone so long as he presented no threat.

Still, it was one more reason to seek a better vantage point.

He took a slow deep breath. Closed his eyes.

Leaned forward.

Bridging was an activity Nickel did not take lightly, due to the energy it sapped as he hovered between seen and unseen. One day, the Almighty's loved ones would cross this divide without trouble, enjoying the interplay between physical and spiritual; for the time being, however, the Separation still imposed itself on mortal souls. Even that über-Collector, Natira, had suffered from his reckless cliff dive last year—torn limbs, broken bones, bloodshot eyes.

No fear, Nickel. Trust and let go.

His feet left the outcropping, and the hot wind curling through the basin caught his prostrate form. In this gap between the two realities, the wind was as strong as bands of steel, an invisible conveyor belt catching and carrying him.

He was

     l i g h t a s a i r . . .

His molecules were gyrating, rotating,

         neurons

           and electrons

       spinning, spinning, spinning

    his entire being s p r e a d i n g

e   l   o   n   g   a   t   i   n   g

in the same way water would have come apart if tossed from these heights.

Even while unleashed from physical bonds, his body maintained a unity in spirit tighter than any in the natural realm. He felt safe. Felt liberated. Wanted to stay in this place forever, to dance in this freedom, in this weightlessness and warmth.

But to do so would drain the remainder of his strength.

Sliding down the air current, toes beginning to drag as his tangible form reappeared, he swirled toward a boulder near the Collectors' streambed, and the crater's pocked floor came into focus.

Earth. Dirt.

Scrub brush and reptiles.

Blazing, mind-frying heat.

Back on terra firma, he gathered his energy and scooted behind the rock. A sand rat stared at him in shock, whiskers twitching, then darted off.

Nickel peeked into the wadi. Not twenty yards away, Megiste stood by Barabbas, who was on his knees scraping at a mound of clay that looked like . . . well, like a man spread-eagled on the ground. It was one of a dozen laid out in an even row.

Good ol'-fashioned idols? Attempts at creative expression?

There was a laughable thought. The Akeldama Collectors weren't your typical arts-and-crafts crowd—unless, of course, they were adding to their collage at Kerioth-Hezron. Just being near that place gave Nickel the heebie-jeebies.

For the next hour, he watched Barabbas chip away at the form's crude face. Megiste poured water from an earthen pitcher, murmured instructions, and cajoled her helpmate with sultry kisses. Next, Barabbas drilled two nostrils into a large nose, as though this rudimentary creature might one day need them to breathe.

It was then Cal Nichols realized what he was looking at.

He'd heard tales of the Prague Golem, and to this day stories persisted of a Jewish rabbi who needed a strongman to guard his synagogue from persecutors. He'd shaped a beast from the clay, calling upon elements of earth, wind, fire, and air to give it life.

Golem . . .

The Hebrew origin was *gelem*: raw material or unshaped form. The same word was used in the hundred and thirty-ninth psalm, referring to a child being formed in the womb.

Nickel, being the oldest of all Tolkien fans, couldn't help but wonder if that master linguist had thought of this when naming his corrupted creature Gollum.

In Jewish tradition, the golem was a crude variation of God-given life, possessing no sense of right and wrong. He existed only to serve the will of his master or masters. In the right hands, he proved a valuable asset. In the hands of less scrupulous souls, he became a living terror.

CHAPTER
THIRTY-FOUR

En route to San Juan Islands

In the past, Gina's rides out to Lummi Island had been skippered by her bushy-bearded friend, and he'd always seemed to know when she was coming. Today, however, he was nowhere to be seen.

Should she and Jed move forward with their plan?

Would it endanger her son?

Gina called around to boat charters, private charters, nearby marinas, and found no evidence of an old-timer named Skipper. Most everyone she spoke to considered themselves skippers of their vessels, but none used that tag as a forename. "Makes you think of *Gilligan's Island*," one man told her, "and we all know how that turned out."

Was it really any shocker Skipper had gone unnoticed, being one of the Unfallen? His type never seemed to appear on demand, and in fact showed up at the least expected of moments. Unlike Collectors, they made no obvious plays for attention, instead going about their business as messengers and guardians.

"We're doing this," Gina decided.

"You sure it's safe?"

"C'mon, Jed, I've been out there a bunch of times."

"Your dad didn't seem too enthusiastic about us making the trip."

"He's not thrilled that I told you, but he agreed that you should see

Jacob yourself now that you know." She ran her gaze along Squalicum Harbor, hoping Skipper would come walking their direction as he had that first day with her and her mom. "Anyway, I say we do this together. I mean, he's your son too."

"I still have this feeling it's all gonna be a mean prank."

"You think I made these for a figment of my imagination?" She wiggled her Ziploc bag of peanut-butter cookies. "Of course, without Skipper to help, I have no way to deliver them."

"See, there. How do I even know this Skipper dude's real?"

Gina scanned the boardwalk. "Seriously, he'll show up."

"You realize Jacob would be coming up on eight years old."

"Not past tense. He *is*."

"I want to believe. It's just . . . it goes against everything I've spent the last few years trying to reconcile in my head."

"For nearly seven years I didn't know either."

"We watched him get buried. Explain that, Gina."

"There's lots to tell. Can it wait till we get out on the water?"

Jed shoved his hands into the pockets of his Levi's denim jacket. Despite clear skies, a brisk wind rippled the sails of berthed boats close by.

Gina slipped an arm through his. She knew it was no easy thing to build up the castle defenses, then lower the drawbridge to let some unsubstantiated rumor come clomping across with enough explosive energy to blow it all to smithereens. She'd accepted her son's survival much easier, trusting Nickel's memories as seen through the droplet on the postcard, watching the events unfold as Jacob Turney Lazarescu was retrieved and revived. Her husband hadn't had that luxury.

"We're doing this," she said again. "You already drove me all this way."

Jed nodded his assent.

She veered along the boardwalk toward the nearest storefront charter. After nearly a year at the gallery, Gina had earned her second raise and she used some of that money now to rent a small pilothouse boat with a Cummins engine that spewed diesel fumes and rattled its discolored brass railings.

"We'll get used to the fishy smell," she told Jed. "Had to take what we could get or leave it for another day. And that, buddy boy, was not an option."

"Agreed. Either way, I want to settle this."

She guided the boat into Bellingham Bay. No more waiting around for skippers, signs, or visions. At a chessboard you could calculate forever, yet at some point you had to commit and see your plan through.

Another belch of fumes curled up from the stern.

"So much for the romance of sailing the San Juans," she said.

Jed smiled, seeming to warm up to this adventure now that they were en route. He said, "Here comes the cheese. You ready, sweetheart?"

"Hit me with it."

"What makes this so romantic is being alone with you."

"Ohh, that's cheese in big slices."

"Warned you."

"There's Lummi Island straight ahead," she said.

They chugged past Portage Island toward Lummi's southern tip. Late June sun warmed things into the high sixties, which was much better than the drizzly dreariness of a Northwest winter and spring. Standing at the wheel, she waved at a passing sailboat but received a less cheerful response than she had when aboard sleek yachts.

"Snobs," she mumbled.

Jed came alongside, kissed her cheek. "Who cares what they think?"

"Not like I'm thrilled to be on this noisy old thing, but I'd use a battleship if that's what it took to see my boy."

He tilted her chin with his hand, this time aiming for her lips.

When he pulled away, she said, "There's more to tell you."

"About these Collectors you mentioned?"

"Chattanooga. The bombing. All of it's tied back to them and their desire to destroy our family. Should I wait till you've seen him, or are you up for this?"

"Collectors. They're the reason for your scars, aren't they?" He traced a finger over her left arm. "It wasn't a grease burn, was it?"

She shook her head.

"Did you ever even work at a Krispy Kreme?"

"Love their donuts," she said. "Does that count?"

"Nickel told me this would flip my world upside down and even gave me a teaser about the Concealed Ones. What's their Jewish name?"

"Nistarim."

"Krispy Kreme."

"Nista . . . Okay, hardy-har."

"They were the Thirty-Six," Jed recited. "The Lamed Vov in Hebrew. According to Nickel, some collapsed beneath the weight and had to be replaced."

"It's an ongoing struggle."

"Here," Jed said. "I'll take the helm while you give me the rundown."

"Just like that? You seem pretty nonchalant about it all."

"What do you want me to do, Gina? I've lived all this time thinking my son was dead and that I'd lost you too. While I was living with Sarge, he told me some of his stories, showed me the scars on his own arm. You ever seen 'em? They oozed with pus till he stopped ignoring them."

"Ignoring them doesn't work. That much I know firsthand."

He pointed north. "We going that way, along the west side of the island?"

"Beautiful shoreline, huh? It's so serene."

"You ever been on the island itself?"

"Dad made me promise not to go, not till he gives the okay. He thinks I'll break the rules and ruin it for all of us, running up to Jacob and throwing my arms around him, causing a scene. He's probably right."

"And you're sure it's Jacob? You have some kinda proof?"

"Just wait till you see him."

"Listen." Jed's voice took on a conspiratorial tone. "If it's really him, I say we grab him and run this boat up the coast into Canada. I'll empty my bank account and we'll sneak away as a family, just the three of us. Never come back."

"What about your job? Your house?"

"I'm not losing you again, Gina. First time was a huge mistake."

"This . . ." Her throat constricted. "This is going to be the hardest thing you've ever done, Jed—it's hard for me too—but after you see him, you cannot take things into your own hands. No matter how much you want to. This cannot go beyond these regular checkups from a distance. Jacob's not alone, not totally, and we have to trust that. He has the Unfallen watching after him."

"Right. Like this Skipper who, uh, skipped out on us?"

"Will you let me explain?"

Gina's lecture lasted nearly ninety minutes with brief interruptions from her husband. His experiences with Nickel and Sarge had been preparing him for this, and he seemed to weigh her words fairly, circumspectly. Much of the time was spent patrolling the waters along the upper end of the island. She panned the coastline with binoculars and pointed out the decrepit house that was their son's hideaway.

Where was Jacob, though? Where were his Unfallen guards? Had Suzette's spying somehow compromised this place?

No. Impossible. Gina hadn't come to the island that day.

Had some tenacious Collector discovered Nikki's body and tapped her blood, ascertaining Jacob's and Gina's existence?

That was a possibility they could never discount.

Across the waters, the house looked empty. Long grass waved along the picket fence and thorns twined up either side of the gate. A sign of something more pernicious? Or simply poor groundskeeping?

A few cars meandered past, cyclists, a lone jogger. None of them gave any indication of being Unfallen. No crossed-finger salutes. No knowing glances at the woman in the pilothouse boat.

"Gina, am I missing something?"

She turned, saw that Jed too was scouring the shoreline for signs of a young boy. She hugged him from behind. "He's here. I know he is."

"Maybe Nickel arranged for him to be moved after you spilled the beans."

"No. I mean—yeah, that could be, but he would've told us not to waste our time coming up today. Remember, he gave me permission to bring you along."

"Wait. Who's that?"

Gina followed Jed's outstretched finger and saw a man in the distance puttering along on a red Vespa. He was angled toward them, climbing a small hill, golden hair flowing about his ears.

"Goldilocks," Gina cried. She patted Jed's arm. "Cut the engine."

He powered down. "What?"

"He's one of them, the Unfallen."

"I thought they were into being invisible and all."

"When they want to be, sure, but they also move among us in human form."

"And ride mopeds?"

The man was coming closer, the sound of the laboring motor just audible over the waves that lapped against the hull.

"Apparently so," Gina said. "They're not like the Collectors. They function freely both in this realm and the next."

"The next?"

"The spiritual. Abstract. Whatever you want to call it."

"*The Fifth Element*."

"I don't know what it's called, but—"

"Love."

"Huh?"

"It's from that movie with Bruce Willis," Jed said.

"You seem to be a big fan of his."

"Sweetheart, you're a whole lot cuter. No, what I was getting at was that in the movie, love was the fifth element."

"Really? You might be on to something there. What's that verse? 'There is no greater love than to lay down one's life for one's friends.' In the Nazarene's case, He even did it for those who hated Him."

Goldilocks was cresting the hill now, his moped gleaming in the sunlight as it turned toward home. Visible at this angle was a smaller rider gripping the back of the seat with both hands, face aimed into the wind, mouth grinning beneath the visor of his white helmet.

Neither Jed nor Gina said a word.

Enthralled.

The Vespa came to a halt at the gate, where Goldilocks climbed gingerly from the vehicle. Was he hurt? Why was he limping? He scanned the road in both directions as he helped remove the boy's safety gear. Jacob's brown hair was unruly, his face and brow pockmarked by scars, his eyes bright blue and sparkling with gold in the radiant sun. He peered out at the boat offshore, then skipped down the path in the guardian's shadow.

CHAPTER
THIRTY-FIVE

Walla Walla

Kransberg had passed his first test, back in the Columbia River Gorge. Thanks to sips of his father's aberrant blood and the reinsertion of that puckered wad that masqueraded as a human heart, he was alive again.

Or, as the Akeldama Cluster preferred, *doubly dead*.

Here in this eastern Washington town, Natira would give him a second test. It would require Kransberg to be communicative and presentable in public.

This transformation began in a rundown motel. Under Natira's tutelage, the beast worked on his language skills while dealing with his outward appearance. He scrubbed, trimmed his crown of hair, and shaved. The lack of dexterity in his crippled fingers resulted in nicks and cuts, and Natira backhanded him each time he flinched.

Clothes came next. He donned huge canvas work pants from a thrift store, as well as a Seattle Mariners baseball jersey and matching cap. For his feet, only the largest sandals would do. It mattered not that his toes dangled over the edges, so long as the nails and tufts of hair were trimmed.

Today was his first day out.

"Stay close, Kransberg, and don't speak unless spoken to."

"Yes. I stay close."

Natira found a parking place, then repeated the instructions in Hebrew and Arabic to ready his son for their trek to Israel and the Middle East. There, he believed, this likeness of his would open the way to the Crown of Thorns. That relic, that red-stained nest of briars, would bring the Nistarim to their knees.

A map was all that was missing.

And the locations of six more Concealed Ones.

"You do know what you're looking for, don't you, my son?"

Kransberg nodded. "Letter Tav. On two males."

"That's correct." Natira led the way up the street.

"How old?"

"Ah. No assistance from me. You'll need to spot them yourself."

"I . . . we . . . are Those Who Hunt."

"Pass today's test, my son, and you and I will be hunting partners."

That seemed to please Kransberg. With baggy clothes covering his bent spine and limbs, he looked like a bottom-rung thug as he lurched beside his father, except he was a head taller and a hundred pounds heavier than most of those gathered in front of the gas station.

"Stop slouching."

The creature tried to straighten.

"You can't hide your size," Natira said, "so it's better to hold your head up."

Striding beside his son on this sidewalk, the Collector felt his emotions seesaw between pride and annoyance. Enough of that. What were emotions, if not genetic backwash from the Almighty's ever-bleeding heart?

They neared the alley where Natira had found the Lettered boys.

Did they live on this street? Go to school in this neighborhood? Attend one of the wretched youth meetings that seemed to appeal to Those Who Resist?

"Pay attention," he said. "They could be close."

It seemed love was in the air.

Nickel, upon hearing Clay and his wife were back together, had agreed to let the Ryker family rent the entire second floor of his expansive log cabin. Despite his occasional loneliness, he kept his focus on the Nazarene. One day, he assured himself, he would see his Dinah again. One day, there would be a wedding feast like no other, as Those Who Resist were united and drank the New Wine.

Speaking of weddings, a very special one was taking place eight days from now. That was one he could not miss.

Yesterday, Cal Nichols had wrapped up work in Israel and flown back to Seattle. During the flight over the Atlantic, images of golem armies and vampire clusters had plagued him, and he longed to be back on his wooded property, to spend a day on the McKenzie with Kenny.

Duty first, though.

A house visit to two beleaguered Nistarim boys.

He made the journey to Walla Walla by car and was now camped out in the living room at the pastor's home. It was a rare stopover for him, but he liked this family, and they'd had some heavy burdens to bear.

Last night the two sons had detailed the paralyzing stiffness in their bones and wrenching stomach pangs. They were strong. They carried the burdens of others. But this was worse than usual, a reaction to some specific grief. Nickel listened, comforted, and drank Nazarene Blood with them; then, as one, they filed a request for increased Unfallen support.

"How're the boys today?" he said to the pastor. "Better, I take it."

"Seem to be. They both begged to go to Saturday afternoon youth group, when two days ago they could barely get out of their beds. In the summer time? That's not like them."

"Maybe we could all go fishing tomorrow."

"Tomorrow? I'll be giving my sermon, fishing for men."

"Oh. My bad. Well, the more of Those Who Resist the better."

"Listen, Cal—thanks for coming all the way out to our humble abode."

"Any time. You know, most of my favorite people live in out-of-the-way places. Don't ever believe for a moment that you are forgotten."

Bellingham

Gina leaned into Jed's chest, clasping his hand that was slung over her shoulder. Her ears were still ringing from the diesel engine, her legs still wobbly from the last hour of choppy waves, yet none of that mattered. Arm in arm, she and her husband together had seen their son for the first time since Jacob's memorial in Chattanooga.

"I don't want to leave this place," Jed said.

"I know the feeling."

"We really can't go onto the island?" He turned with her on the walkway that overlooked the piers and they stared back over the bay. "Maybe we should make him a scrapbook of pictures, write him some notes."

"Nickel says no. It might draw him out into danger."

Jed shook his head, still coming to terms with this new paradigm. At last he said, "What about the cookies you made?"

She shrugged. "Guess I'll make more on our next visit."

"This really sucks."

"Big time."

She nuzzled against his neck, her bleached hair flattened beneath his chin. Across the water, the hazy shapes of islands were layered like colored strips on a child's collage, with boats in the foreground and trees spiking the cerulean sky.

"I can't stand this," Jed whispered. "I want to go to him."

"I wish that every single day."

Gina felt warm drops splash down upon her head, then bead along her temples and onto her cheeks—as though his tears were her own, as though years of anguish apart had been rolled into one shared longing.

"Jed," she said, "don't you see? There will be a next time and another time after that. We have Jacob back, and that's something we can hold on to."

"How long're we supposed to wait?"

"My dad believes Jacob will be one of the Concealed Ones. Somewhere, sometime, someone will crumble and our son will take his place. Until then, we have to keep our distance."

"Because of the Collectors?"

"The Akeldama Collectors, to be specific. They're the ones who'll be able to see the Letter on his forehead."

"Right. Because they inhabit undead hosts."

"You're catching on quickly."

"No." Jed shook his head. "No, listen. I can protect him."

"You don't know the enemy we're dealing with."

Cold determination filled his voice. "Well, they don't know how far this father'll go to save his child."

"They do know. They watched the Almighty give up His Son for the rest of mankind. You think they haven't seen the extremes of a father's love? I mean, it's one thing to give your own life, right? But to give your only son's life? Think of Jacob. Would we be willing to—"

"Don't!" Jed pulled away from her. "Don't even say it."

"It may come to that."

"Then I'm going over there now. I'm taking him away from this craziness that you and Nickel keep rattling on about."

"You can't."

"Watch me." Oblivious to passersby, Jed paced the walkway, eyes fixed on the dim outline of Lummi Island. "Let someone else step up instead of Jacob. I lost him once and I'm not gonna let it happen again. If you had any sense, you'd understand what I'm saying. The three of us, Gina. I love you. I don't want to lose either of you. Let's go. Let's go now and never show our faces again."

She ached to go along with his plan. She reached for him.

"I'm serious." He pulled her close, his blue eyes magnified by their moisture. "I've been working, saving money. We can do this. We need to do this."

"You know I want that more than anything."

"Then let's go. Who's stopping us?"

A large hand clapped onto Jed's arm and he swiveled toward the intruder, only to find himself face-to-face with a burly, red-bearded man.

"Skipper?" Gina said. "Where've you been?"

Jed scoffed. "Oh, so this is the guy who bailed on us."

"Had myself a li'l trouble this morning, me and the rest o' the gang."

"The other Unfallen?" Gina said.

"We scrapped with a coupla them Collectors, nothing too serious."

Skipper tugged up his sleeves for Gina and Jed to see the slashes on his freckled forearms. "Seems that friend o' yours—Suzette, is it?—she drew some attention this way when she followed you. These filthy creatures started sniffing about, utilizin' their local hosts and hoodlums. They don't got a clue what they're after, but they got closer than we could permit."

"Closer to Jacob, you mean?"

"No need to worry, missy. They have no idea he's on that island, and they're not the top of the food chain anyhow. Thing is, they could stir up enough activity to get them Akeldama boys 'n girls interested."

"Hold on." Suspicion flared in Gina's mind. "Suzette hasn't followed me here again, has she?"

"No, only that first time. Josee's keepin' an eye out just to be sure, but the gal seems to be cured of her thorns. Still, Nickel says this is the end."

"End of what? What do you mean?"

"No more Lummi visits. Done risked too much already."

"Forget it," Jed said. "No way. That's our son you're talking about."

"Wanna see him survive into his teens, dontcha? Hate that it's got to be this way, but there ya go. Nickel's direct orders. If you come back, make a scene, any of that, he's directed us to move the kid far, far away. 'Course you can still pass stuff along through us. I'll come around time to time, see whatcha got."

"Homemade cookies." Gina shoved the bag forward. "Let's start there."

"Give him this for me." Jed slipped out of his Levi's jacket. "Don't want him catching cold on the oceanside of that island."

"We'll back off for now," Gina said, taking her place beside her husband. "But you better believe we're going to talk to my dad about this ourselves. You know where he is?"

"The man just got back into the country, and he's already dealin' with something else. Don't ya worry, though. Says he'll be here for Sarge and Josee's wedding, figurin' as you two'll be renewing your vows that same day."

"Say what?" Gina exclaimed.

Cheeks reddening, Jed gave her a bashful grin.

"Oh really? So, Mr. Turney, do I get any say in this matter?"

Skipper chortled. "Best be going. I'll leave you lovebirds to work this out."

Walla Walla

A group of teenagers crossed the intersection a half block ahead of Natira and Kransberg, chatting, elbowing, laughing. Two of the boys looked familiar, though it was hard to be certain amidst the energetic motions and flurry of color.

"Stay alert," Natira told his son.

The teens were turning this way, coming nearer.

"I . . ." Kransberg paused. "Letter Tav is blue?"

"Yes. Yes, it is. What do you see?"

Along the sidewalk, a sudden, dry wind swept up dust. Familiar with arid climates, Natira was unfazed, whereas Kransberg teared up, rubbed at his eyes, and snarled as the particles ground deeper into his corneas. Sand was not something he'd encountered in the national forest.

"Burns like fire," Kransberg said, still rubbing. "Eyes burn."

Natira questioned the value of this creature. Maybe it would have been better to eat his grimy heart and leave the corpse on the riverbank.

During the brief commotion, the teens moved around the corner and out of view. Natira stiffened with suspicion. Much as he hated to dwell on it, the Unfallen were capable of interacting with time and space. They enjoyed using their five senses. And, unlike Collectors, they needed no hosts to do so.

Something very odd about that dry wind . . .

"Stop your whining, Kransberg. Tell me, did you see the Letter?"

"I saw, yes."

"On which one of the kids?"

"Brown hair. Yellow shirt. But . . . wind and sand came."

"Hmmph. Well, you've passed your test, but I think there's someone guarding those measly boys."

CHAPTER
THIRTY-SIX

Early July—Corvallis

"Can you believe it?" Josee said. "The big day's finally here."

Gina fluffed the train of the bride's gown. "What I can't believe is how gorgeous you look. Never thought I'd see you in a full-on dress."

"With lace, even. Think it'll be worth the expression on Sarge's face?"

"That boy's going to pop every last one of his buttons."

Josee winked. "That's the plan, as long as he can wait till later tonight."

Folding chairs lined the lawn, each row marked by a big satin bow. White carpet ran up the center aisle to a pillared archway draped in English ivy and sprigs of baby's breath. Candelabras stood tall on either side. The backdrop for the entire affair was a vista of hillside wine trellises laden with grapes that glowed in the late-day sun. Although there would be Syrah, Chardonnay, and Pinot Gris to come, the coveted wine was a velvety Pinot Noir.

Addison Ridge Vineyards, home to Marsh and Kara Addison, Josee's parents, had been planted by First Lieutenant Chance Addison in the aftermath of World War II. Marsh had inherited the venture and turned it into one of the region's most lucrative, most decorated wineries, a mandatory stop on any of the Willamette Valley wine tours. Success had taken Marsh far and wide, and vintners from Germany to Argentina to Romania called upon him for advice.

"You should see Sarge," Gina said. "He's practically radioactive."

"Glowing already, huh? Lemme have a look."

From behind her veil, Josee peeked between the vineyard's wooden warehouse doors. Surrounding her, groomsmen and bridesmaids were gathered for the wedding processional.

"Ahhh," Josee sighed. "There's my big teddy bear."

Gina smoothed her own dress—fitted, knee-length, and turquoise, with a scooped neck, tapered sleeves, and matching footwear. She felt slightly ridiculous, and the color was one better suited to Josee's eyes than her own bronze complexion. She had to confess, though, that the fabric hugged her hips and accentuated her curves without seeming trashy. Even in her days of black skirts and boots, she'd adhered to her mother's standards of modesty.

Gina's tattoo, on the other hand, had never been a hit with Nikki. Those angel wings were still spread across her lower back, and after recent warnings up north she wondered if there would be any Unfallen in today's congregation.

"To your places, everyone," said Suzette. "To your places."

Suzette Bishop was the wedding coordinator, a role she'd stepped into with enthusiasm. Now, as music filtered across the grass, she gave final instructions to the ladies and gentlemen in her charge.

Gina came alongside Jed. "You look good in a tux, Mr. Turney."

"Does 'debonair' even scratch the surface?"

"More like 'insanely hot.'"

"That goes both ways." He tilted his chin toward her. "You ready?"

"You sure you still want a woman with scars and blonde hair?"

"Sweetheart, there's no doubt in my mind."

"You believe in this, in what we're about to do?"

"I believe in us," he said. "I believe in a God who creates art even when nobody's watching."

Deep inside, Gina knew this was the right move for them, a chance to start over with a proper foundation. She squeezed Jed's hand as the doors creaked on large hinges and ushered them onto the narrow white walkway.

By design, each couple omitted the stilted march and took casual, even strides toward the front. Soon, three women and three men were fanned out on either side of the arch with a young minister in the center, his hands clasped around a leather-bound book. Gina knew he had come down from Bothell, Washington, for the event, a former Oregon boy and friend of the Addisons.

The music softened as he greeted all present and led them in a short prayer. He explained that the bride would be coming up the aisle momentarily, but first a different couple would be renewing their vows.

"A Fourth of July sale," he said. "Two for the price of one."

Everyone laughed, which set Gina to shaking.

What? I can't start falling apart now.

No, she'd been fine all day, and this was not on her agenda. Trembling like a school girl? Like a kitten in a hurricane? She'd made it through breakfast, helped Josee with makeup, even picked up the cake with Suzette. Now she was about to pledge herself again to the man she loved. So what was her problem?

"It'll be quick," she and Jed had agreed at rehearsal. "No big fanfare."

Josee told them to take as long as they needed.

"We don't want to mess up your special day," Gina said.

"It's just one of thousands to come," Josee countered. "Plus, you and I are going to be in-laws, so for heaven's sake let's have some fun with it."

Still trembling.

Heart galloping, palms and forehead perspiring.

Gina's lips felt numb, her tongue swollen, as she followed along with the minister and repeated her handwritten vows. Next, he read a passage from his open Bible, upon which sat Jed's original wedding band and her simple solitaire. Both objects glittered as though they had been washed by the pages' hallowed words.

Her pulse was racing: *thu-thumpa-thump, thu-thumpa-thump* . . .

The minister said, "Jed and Gina stand before us this day as proof that no union is beyond repair, that the Lord still works in all those who seek Him . . ."

Gina had been keeping a low profile for the past months, avoiding conversations that might segue into questions about her past, and so she recognized only a few faces in the crowd—the Addisons, Clay Ryker, a customer or two from her work behind the gallery counter.

She wished her mother was alive to witness this. Wished her sons could be here for the event.

Thu-thump, thu-thump, thu-thump . . .

From the front row her dad flashed a supportive smile and that settled her pulse back into its normal gait as she and Jed exchanged rings.

"They've already been legally married," the minister continued, "in the state of Tennessee, but we're here to acknowledge before God and those present their desire to be of one heart, one mind, one soul, and one body. It's my privilege to present to you, Mr. and Mrs. Jedediah Turney . . ."

Polite clapping. Jed's caring blue eyes. Rays of sun through the trees.

"You may now kiss the bride."

Familiar hands cupped Gina's face and lifted her chin. Soft lips pressed into hers. And then she was letting go, spirit and flesh coming together in a moment that paused the clock and found two bodies, two souls, dancing in unison on eternity's stage, urged along by a still, small voice: *Long ago, I bridged the Separation. What I now join together, let no one separate.*

At last they ended the kiss. Had it been minutes, hours, mere seconds? Together they faced the crowd, then moved back to their places on either side of the archway.

Gina grinned as strains of the wedding march sounded.

Yep, now it was Josee's turn.

Cal Nichols was still cheering as his daughter returned to her position among the bridesmaids. What was he supposed to do? Yawn and twiddle his thumbs? He'd recently been summoned back to Jerusalem and gone through the rigmarole of renewing his U.S. and Israeli passports, but there was no way he would miss this date. He was even tempted to sound his shofar—boy, that'd rouse this crowd. Of course, weddings weren't on the horn's list of specific uses.

Well, in that case . . .

Demonstrating what he considered admirable restraint, he turned instead to raucous hoots and pumps of his fist. Both Gina and Jed laughed aloud.

Those assembled loosened up after that, rising to their feet as the traditional music signaled Josee's approach. She, too, looked amazing, bedecked in a strapless wedding gown, and it took only one glance at Sgt. Vince Turney's dropped jaw to know he was a goner.

What was it about weddings, Nickel wondered, that made "women glow and men thunder"?

Get a grip, man. We don't have time here for eighties pop songs.

He must be venting the pressure of the past few days—or centuries.

The minister said those words again: "You may now kiss the bride."

Sarge bellied up to Josee, his tux stretched to its limits, his cummerbund threatening to revolt. Josee melted into his arms and peered into his chocolate-brown eyes, her lips parting as he—

Can't do this. Nickel looked down, suppressing his own desires. *Can't watch another smoocharoo. My allegiance is to Yeshua and the task He's given me.*

When the applause started up, he knew it was safe. He lifted his chin, smiled wide, and started hooting again.

As the sun died out and citronella candles gave off their lemony scent, as chairs were cleared and replaced by a makeshift dance floor, Nickel washed down raspberry-filled cake with a cup of Sprite. This wasn't the traditional Jewish wedding, yet the joy was the same, a foreshadowing of that day when New Wine would be served to all Those Who Resist.

He waited through the bouquet toss and the launching of garters, then joined the onlookers as Sarge led Josee onto the parquet floor.

The DJ eased into things by spinning a U2 single on his retro turntable. The newlyweds slow danced into the second verse, then invited Jed and Gina to take the floor. By the third verse, elbows and feet were vying for room—Marsh and Kara Addison, bridesmaids and groomsmen, flower girl and ring bearer.

"I can't live . . . with or without you . . ."

Yeah, that about said it all.

Nickel moved from the crowd, figuring a walk between the grape trellises might help him iron out his melancholy.

Gina's voice stopped him. "Where you going, Dad? You okay?"

"I'm . . . Yeah, just thinking."

"About Nikki?"

"About lots of things, I guess." He embraced her. "You know how proud of you I am? I've watched you grow from a tough little girl just trying to survive into a mature young woman who's assertive and strong."

"Like you taught me at the chessboard." She checked for eavesdroppers. "I'm not so young anymore, actually. Turning forty in a couple of weeks."

"And twenty by the looks of it. Does Jed know?"

"He knows. I'm not sure he completely buys it, though."

"Buys what?" Jed said, popping loose from the swirl of revelers.

"My age. The whole immortality thing."

"Well, if you have to die to prove it, I'd rather just take your word."

Nickel slapped his arm. "With smarts like that, you can be my son-in-law. Of course, as time passes, Gina'll be the one getting the raw end of the stick."

Jed raised an eyebrow. "The what?"

"C'mon, Dad. Raw deal. Short end of the stick. You can't mix the two or it sounds wrong. Anyway," she added, turning to Jed, "you don't even want to know the truth about *his* age."

"We're not going there," Nickel said. "I'd have to pull out my abacus."

As a Pat Benatar tune blasted through the speakers, his daughter linked arms with him and begged him for a dance. Her persistence won him over, he put one hand around her waist, then led her through a simple box step. Okay, so he was a little behind on the latest dance crazes.

She fixed him in her sights. "Dad, there's something we need to discuss."

"About the new restrictions, I bet."

"So it's true? You're asking us not to see our son?"

"Hey, you got one joint visit, right? Sorry to be the bearer of bad news. You move anywhere near him, though, and it could be the end. *Kaput. Sayonara. Finis.*"

She blinked, dark brown eyes pleading. "There must be some way. How long do you expect us to wait?"

"Till he's ready."

"Meaning?"

"When he reaches manhood."

"Thirteen? That's five years away."

"I'm serious, Gina. The Nistarim believe he has a unique purpose, and even now, if you remember, there's an über-Collector, Lord Natira, who's been hunting in this area."

"You think he knows? How could he?"

"Not yet." Nickel spun his daughter away from the other dancers, kept his voice low. Firecrackers exploded nearby as the fourth of July celebrations got under way. "But he's here in the Northwest, and he's found his very own halfling."

"Halfling?"

"Seems I'm not the only one with half-immortal offspring, which means this *thing* can probably spot the Concealed Ones just like his father."

Gina ran a hand through her hair.

"That's why you and Jed have to keep a low profile. Settle in Silverton, go about business like a regular couple—mow your yard, pay your bills, help your neighbors, go fishing and hiking. Nothing out of the ordinary."

"Like any of this is ordinary. What mother is refused the chance to—"

"Shhh, let's keep it down."

"So it's all decided. We just roll over and play dead."

"I'm not asking you to be complacent. Be vigilant. Stay in touch with Those Who Resist, sharpen your dagger skills, and teach Jed how to handle MTPs. Few more years, that's all I ask, and then it'll be hands-on, no-holds-barred. Until that time, you can't let on to anyone—not Josee, Sarge, or Suzette." He scanned the crowd. "Do any of them know about Jacob?"

"Only Jed and me."

"Good. Not a word. Don't go anywhere near him, and make sure to keep your dear ol' hubby in check."

"Or what?"

"Or," Nickel said, "it'll be checkmate for the Nistarim."

THE FOURTH SENSE: TASTE

*He let the words soak into his mind
and displace all else. A man had a choice, after all.*

—RICHARD MATHESON, *I AM LEGEND*

Show mercy to still others.

—*JUDE 1:23*

Tonight, we talked about the dangers ahead. Dad is with us, and he looks the way I'd look if my face wasn't criss-crossed with scars. We've been at sea for weeks, still hunted. We are Those Who Resist, and Mom's been teaching me that you can only hide so long before it's considered a form of surrender.

"Which is something we'll never do, Jacob." She spread out a black-and-white board, situated the carved stone pieces, then slid her king's pawn forward. "That's why we're going on the attack. In chess, it's called seizing the initiative."

I mirrored her move with a black pawn. Mom offered a gambit, and I—caught up in the moment—went in for an ambush of her king, allowing her to develop aggressively while I scrambled to coordinate my queen and the forces I'd left behind. Mom talked about players such as Alekhine, Anderssen, Fischer, and Kasparov—the way they would gaze into the heart of a battle and seize advantages through sacrifice and strategic boldness.

"They didn't play not to lose. They played to win."

"No fear," I said.

"But with calculated patience. Anticipate the risks and plan accordingly, then"—she pinned my bishop with her queen—"go in for the kill."

The consequences of her move left me dumbstruck. "There's nowhere to go without you getting an easy checkmate." I toppled my black king.

"Careful with that," she said, eyes twinkling. "That king is key to our plans."

CHAPTER
THIRTY-SEVEN

March 2006—Arad, Israel

On Arad's outskirts, an apathetic moon stared down through acacia branches as Erota suckled at the eyes of her prey. Though she most often craved the blood of her victims, there was something to be said for optical juices and the way they coated her taste buds.

Mmm. Tangy and tart.

Arad was a convenient hunting ground, the town overlooking a number of wadis that carved through wastelands to the Dead Sea. Bedouins roved the area, often blamed for the thievery of cars, goats, even laundry hung out to dry. This provided a convenient alibi for Erota and the Akeldama Cluster as they daily collected souls from throughout the Negev.

She drew up the last drops now, siphoning gummy liquid over her tongue. She plucked the wrinkled white raisins from their sockets and severed their bloody tendrils with long nails.

Haughty eyes.

One of the Six, No Seven Things.

Ah yes. These specimens were infected, indeed.

Arrogance was on regular display in this township. Arad was home to a large group of ultra-Orthodox Jews who antagonized those cleansed by Nazarene Blood. Most religious Jews lived humbly before the Almighty, whereas these men earned points—or so they seemed to believe—by adhering to laborious rules and regulations. Supported by donations, they spent much of their time mocking Those Who Resist, trying to subjugate, intimidate.

It was an old tactic, really. Two thousand years earlier, men known as Pharisees had behaved in a similar manner. Acting in cahoots with Roman oppressors, they'd incited a mob to call for the Nazarene's crucifixion while the rabble-rouser Barabbas walked free.

Barabbas . . .

She bristled at the thought of the henchman's wiry beard and sweaty skin. Let the priestess have the oaf all to herself.

Erota pocketed the collapsed eyeballs, then hefted the male corpse into a wadi where vultures would dispose of the evidence.

Ruins of Kerioth-Hezron

In the hour before dawn, the high-pitched shrieks of the jackals awakened her. Erota sat up in her underground chamber, felt cool air push beneath the camel skin that draped the opening to outside. Three black candles fluttered, and shadow wraiths clawed the limestone walls.

Another set of screams pierced the gloom.

Witches cackling?

Erota grimaced at her overactive imagination and rose from the bed, tuning out the scavengers. Sheer material clung to her olive skin, while fingernails showed stains from her recent catch. She licked them clean and recalled last night's celebration in the central cavern.

"More earthquakes were reported today," Helene had said to the cluster's amusement. "We stack iniquity upon iniquity, causing the Nistarim to stumble—and the ground itself quivers as a result."

"Doom is inexorable," Kyria chipped in.

"Indeed it is, darling," said Helene. "Tsunamis become increasingly common, and coastlines are ravaged by hurricanes. Final Vengeance is a matter of time, for the Thirty-Six cannot stand forever."

With the others watching, Erota had inserted the absconded eyeballs into the cave's appropriate panel and let the vines coil outward in response, inching a bit closer toward Jerusalem. Rarely did the thorns reject such an offering.

The jackals shrieked again, snapping her back to the moment.

What was going on?

She poked her head outside, letting her vision adjust to the darkness that hovered in the valley. Two figures approached from the northeast, legs hurdling ruin walls the way average men might step over bricks. One walked with stiff arms and a tilted gait; the other she recognized by his warrior's demeanor.

"Lord Natira," she said as he drew near. Here was the man she had long desired, a far better option than crude Barabbas. "It's been awhile."

"Over a year."

"But who's counting?" Her snide laugh betrayed disillusion.

So, then, their rightful cluster leader was back and her reign as queen was over. She knew better than to expect any verbalized thanks, yet that didn't quell her host's desire for appreciation.

If Natira noticed, he paid no mind. "A lot has happened, and I've been preparing my son. Erota, meet Kransberg."

There was no denying their similarities in size and facial structure. Despite Kransberg's awkwardness, he exuded a sense of menace. Perhaps it was his hooded eyes, his flared nostrils. Or the tufts of hair curling up from the shirt collar along his neck. Or the huge feet tucked into makeshift tire-rubber sandals.

"Hello," she said. "Come inside if you like."

"Where's Barabbas?" Natira asked. "He wasn't at his post."

"Oh, he's . . . I sent him on an errand to the south."

For now, Erota chose to keep silent about the golems in Ramon Crater. Megiste and Barabbas would pay for their mutinous ways, but not till their army was complete.

Musky from their journey, Natira and son shouldered through the gap into her chamber. They gazed at her as she smoothed her gown over curved hips, and she felt glad to be noticed—for her womanly wiles, if not for her leadership. She still felt a pull toward Natira's chiseled physique, and it had been some time since she indulged her libidinous nature. Even as she lured them into her bed, her mind boiled against their craven appetites.

She bit into Natira's arm, drawing blood that tasted of his most recent meal—a sickly lamb and a fellow steeped in stale tobacco.

She raked Kransberg's back with her nails, eliciting a grunt of pain.

Men . . . How she loved to hate them.

By late morning, Natira had gathered his cluster in the main cavern. He twined together a cape of briars and tied it about his neck, then settled onto his throne. He had forgotten the satisfaction found here amid the howls and whimpers. What better art than that made up of half-dead subjects?

He smiled out over his ragtag group. "It seems you've stayed active."

Erota's eyes met his, then darkened.

"We have indeed," Helene said. "All for you, my lord."

"Thank you, Mother. I see the evidence all around."

Awash in a crimson glow, vines borne from mortal agony grew from the Six, No Seven panels, writhed about the stone chamber, out into the tunnels, and up the cave's high ceiling. Their aroma clung to each oxygen molecule, teasing the senses of the vampires present. Overhead, the mesh of tendrils pulsed, providing enough light to make the hundreds of candles superfluous.

"You've all met Kransberg." Natira clasped his son's deformed arm. "He's my undead flesh and blood. As a baby in Nazi Germany, he proved himself nearly indestructible, and his mother carried him to the United States along with other objects from the war. She despised him, though. Abandoned him."

The towering beast showed no reaction.

"He survived in the Oregon woods, bigger than any Sasquatch—or perhaps, the basis for such a legend—and I tracked him down."

"I am hostis humanis generis," Kransberg said.

"He is in my likeness, and together we'll accelerate the hunt for the Concealed Ones. There are six of them left, five here in this region."

Erota said, "And the sixth, Lord Natira?"

"I suspect the discovery of the others will flush him into the open. Once we have all of them, we will crown one of them—or perhaps all of them—with the Crown of Thorns. It rests even now in Jerusalem, in Rasputin's cache. With your collective assistance, we will find it."

"We will hunt?" Domna's fangs dropped down at the idea.

"For information. For a map of sorts."

"And you will lead this hunt?"

"No, Kransberg and I will track the Concealed Ones, while—"

"You're leaving us?" Erota cut in. "Yet again?"

"While you and our cluster follow the trail of a Crusader-era signet ring. It's our guide to the Crown, and that Crown bears the Blood, with history's iniquities captured therein. The Nazarene bore it all—every sickness and sin and sadistic act. If He could not survive such a weight, then certainly His adherents cannot. Let those spikes pierce their skulls. Let them feel that same dismal blackness."

Spellbound, the cluster listened.

"It will crush them," he said.

Overhead, the web throbbed.

"And our Collection of Souls will be complete, producing at last our Final Vengeance."

"Final Vengeance," they echoed.

From the panels, the victims moaned louder while Akeldama bloodsuckers cheered. Natira took note of Erota's downcast eyes, though he had no time for her petty grievances. He was the king, the Black King. And the board was being set for ambush and annihilation.

He shot a glance at Kransberg, who stood twisted and tall at the throne's right hand, fangs gnawing at the air, lips lined with speckles of foam. His knobby fingers fumbled at the pouch hidden under his shirt, as though seeking the tools by which to hammer out his father's designs.

Erota kept her eyes down, worried her cluster leader would find disloyalty in them. She wasn't disloyal, not really. She wanted only to please and impress, according to her own plans. Indeed, she did yet have a task to carry out, one that would take time, caution, and a good deal of blood.

Always more blood.

So what if she, Megiste, and Barabbas were fashioning an army like no other? Would the warrior-king complain when he saw what they had accomplished, saw clay-red soldiers ready to march upon command?

CHAPTER
THIRTY-EIGHT

August 2007—Silverton

Seven years ago, Regina Lazarescu had died. Corroborated by police reports, the Bucharest papers had carried the story, and a body was cremated the next day. Her beloved kids were returned to Tomorrow's Hope Orphanage in Arad, and although the source of the '89 HIV outbreak was no longer a mystery, many of the infected still faced dim futures.

Three years ago, Kate Preston had died. Junction City locals had mourned her, buried her, and by now mostly forgotten her. Her son had gone to live on a wooded ranch with Nickel—aka Uncle Terry—and, unbeknownst to most, the mystery of D. B. Cooper had been solved. As for Kate's Nissan, it still lay rusting beneath the McKenzie.

So much lost . . . Nikki, Petre, and Teo.

So much gained . . . Nickel, Kenny, and Jacob.

And, for over two years now, Jed and Gina Turney had lived a quiet existence in Silverton, restoring the marriage they'd started in Chattanooga. He landscaped. She worked three days a week at the gallery in Corvallis. They were doing as Nickel had instructed—living, loving, laying low. Not that it was trouble free. Half immortal though she be, Gina was still human, after all.

"Jed," she called from the brushed-leather couch in their living room.

He was humming in the bathroom. Did he not realize they were running late? Although they often met for meals with Sgt. Vince and Josee Turney, there had been hints on the phone from Josee that tonight might include a surprise.

"C'mon." Gina clicked off the box lamps. "You 'bout done in there?"

"Be out in a sec."

"That's what you said a hundred and twenty seconds ago."

"I cut myself shaving."

"Don't forget to wash the blood down the drain."

"I know, sweetheart. I know."

She chided herself for being schizoid about such a trivial matter. The truth was that if the Collectors ever traced them to this small Oregon town, to this nondescript house, they would go straight for Gina's and Jed's jugulars instead of sneaking around in hopes of lapping up stale spillage. By that time, their secrets would be secrets no longer, and the future of the Concealed Ones and the world they upheld would be in the hands of someone else.

"Sorry," she said. "I didn't mean to nag."

"S'okay."

According to Nickel, only ten Akeldama Collectors remained from the original nineteen, only ten able to visually identify her or the Nistarim. He told her they were busy little bees, going about their work at the Betrayer's birthplace and elsewhere, showing no signs of knowing Gina or Jacob still existed. If so desired, they would be able to keep tabs on Jed Turney, but he'd become persona non grata to them after leaving Gina in the summer of '99. Nickel said the best strategy for the time being was to avoid disturbing the hive.

"I thought we were done living in fear," she had challenged him.

"It's not fear, Gina."

"We want to see Jacob. We could protect him under our own roof."

"Remember," Nickel said, "we're preparing, not just protecting. We're not hiding out. We're not cowering in the corner. But we are measuring our opponent while getting ready to counterattack."

"Let's attack now."

"There're still a few things I'm piecing together back in Israel. Not to mention we want to find the Tmu Tarakan before the Collectors can plunder it and use its contents against us. Thankfully, Sarge has the key, and Josee has a compass. We just need to be pointed in the right direction."

"Any ideas?"

"Moscow. St. Petersburg." He shrugged. "Not really sure."

"What's so stinkin' dangerous about it anyway? You telling me Rasputin discovered sarin gas or the atomic bomb?"

"He hoarded icons and riches. Think of how we use the symbolic power of the MTPs and the Nehushtan against the Collectors. Well, Natira, Erota, Megiste—all of them will try to twist these relics for their own purposes, as validation for their warped little schemes."

"There's been enough of that down through the ages."

"You're telling me."

"You know, none of it changes the way I feel. Jacob's my *son*, and I want the chance to take care of him. You're a father, so you should understand."

"I do." Nickel touched her cheek. "I had to let you go—one of the hardest decisions I ever made. But look where we are now. You've gotten back some of the things you thought you'd lost. Your son's safe. Trust me on this, please."

"Trust me . . ."

It was the same enjoinder he had given in Chattanooga just before the bombing at Erlanger East Medical Clinic. For years she'd been convinced he had failed her, and he had absorbed those frustrations for the sake of her son.

"Okay, Dad," she told him. "I will. I do. I trust you."

Now on the couch, Gina still waited for Jed. She heard him singing, heard the toilet flush, and wondered why she was the punctual one in this relationship. Not that she minded these familiar patterns. She felt as though she'd pulled on a favorite pair of jeans, the ones that fit just right, that moved with her instead of against her, and—

Oh yeah, but they also had that itchy tag in the back.

Creative, adorable, sometimes irritating Jed.

Ramon Crater

Sixty-six clay men, sixty-six lifeless shapes . . .

Last night Barabbas had left them side by side in long rows, golems spanning the narrow gulch in the crater's northwest sector. Each bore a clump for a nose, two holes for eyes, ears to receive orders, a gaping mouth. Each would function as a male, though by anatomical design they were sexless. If the next months went as planned, these stout creatures would arise, prototypes of more to come, all of them ready to do their masters' bidding.

"We are their masters," Megiste told Barabbas as they trod rain-softened soil toward the gulch. The milder temperature was a reprieve from the usual summer heat. "They'll respond to you and me only."

"You're sure Lord Natira won't be upset about this?"

"Oh, *him*? He's been wandering the globe for years now, so honestly, my dear, the state of his emotions is immaterial to me. We are Collectors from the Akeldama. Though we have our differences, we're all working toward the goal of triggering Final Vengeance, and if the cluster leader has any wish to benefit from our army's services he will need *us* to command them. Don't you see how *delicious* it all is? Natira's a warrior, and I'm sure he'll understand the practicalities of such an alliance."

Barabbas frowned, realizing he might be overthinking this. He was a glorified servant, after all, called upon for his brawn, not his brains. He said, "You've thought everything out, haven't you, Megiste?"

"Why, of course." She patted his freckled cheek. "These are matters more suited to my female mind. Your role is as a craftsman, a laborer—oh, and yes, a nighttime companion besides."

"I do what I can."

"Indeed you do, dear. Now come along. We need only one more thing to bring our friends to life and for that we require Erota's help. Once again, Natira's left her for his own activities—a male trait, to be sure—and she's understandably motivated to be moving along with our work."

Salem, Oregon

Forty-five minutes after leaving Silverton, they were in south Salem on a waiting list at an Italian restaurant. Table candles flickered, and the scent of parmesan and oregano hinted at pasta yumminess to come.

"Hey," Gina said as they joined Sarge and Josee on a padded bench in the lobby. "It's the Turneys."

Josee played along. "Well, look who we bumped into: the Turneys."

"Let the family insanity begin," Jed said to Sarge.

"Wouldn't have it any other way, kiddo."

Josee nudged Sarge. "I thought I was 'kiddo.'"

"I'm thirty-four, practically the old man 'round here. Look at you skinny-as-a-rail twentysomethings, nothing but kids to me."

Gina and Jed exchanged a glance. Her genetic anomalies had been kept hidden even from these relatives, which meant Sarge had no clue she was nearly eight years his senior. Not like any woman in her right mind would try arguing that.

"Sarge," she said, "you care if I call you Gramps?"

"Woo-boy. Now there's a low blow. Wait for me to be a daddy at least."

Josee socked him in the arm. "You said I could be the one to tell them."

"Ain't said a word."

"Ah-ah-ah." Jed toggled his eyebrows. "You just did."

Gina grabbed Josee's hand. "You're prego?"

"Been trying since the wedding, so I guess all our kisses paid off."

"Uh, hello," Gina said. "Takes more than that."

Sarge beamed.

"When is it due? You know if it's a boy or girl?"

"Whoa," Josee said. "We only found out yesterday."

Sarge crossed his arms over his belly. "If my math's any better than my English—and I ain't sayin' it is—should be sometime next April."

On the bench, Gina felt Jed stiffen beside her. Jacob's existence also had been protected from Sarge and Josee, so they meant no harm by their words. For Gina and Jed, though, it was difficult to imagine the joy of a newborn without recalling their own son pierced by the nails of a homemade bomb.

Of course, those same scars had confirmed his identity and resurrection life.

Gina kissed and pressed her fingertips to her husband's cheek, then turned back to her in-law. "Josee, you're going to be the cutest thing."

"And with a belly just like mine," Sarge said.

Josee socked him a second time.

"I used to be a fighter," he told Gina. "So she thinks she can beat on me."

A third time.

"Ooooff."

Gina laughed. "She's a tough cookie, but I'm telling you she's going to be an amazing mother. Lots of love, with no room for sass."

"Agreed," Sarge and Jed said in unison.

It was Josee's turn to beam.

CHAPTER
THIRTY-NINE

Mid-September—Amman, Jordan

The search for the Nistarim was narrowing.

On a crowded street corner in Amman, Natira flagged down a taxicab and gave the driver directions. He was headed for a falafel shop near the city's Third Circle where, according to local clusters, a man had worked for over a decade, serving meals to beggars and businessmen alike. Those Who Resist had grown in strength during the same period, lifting their tongue-wagging chants to the Almighty.

Could this fellow be Number Thirty-Three? Natira and Kransberg had pinpointed two others in the last nineteen months, a welder in Dubai and a Syrian school teacher.

The cab veered back into traffic while the loudspeakers of a nearby minaret disseminated a *muezzin*'s cries, calling Muslims to midday prayer. The warbling grated on the Collector's ears.

"Music, please," he said to the driver in English.

"You from America?"

"Most recently, yes."

"Yes? Okay, I give bounteous song."

"Bounteous?" Natira shrugged.

Whether an atheist or one of the city's purported Christians, the man seemed just as eager to drown out the muezzin. He cranked the volume on a station of American pop tunes—a song by Billy Joel.

With the Hashemite Kingdom of Jordan being one of the more lenient Muslim countries, it came as no surprise to Natira when the next song on the playlist featured the ubiquitous Neil Diamond. Was there anywhere the guy wasn't heard?

The cab zipped between two cars, rode the curb beneath eucalyptus branches, and took a side street to avoid the crush of honking traffic.

Natira clicked pinkie and thumb to the rhythm of the song as he pondered his son's concurrent search in the Negev. Mounting evidence pointed to Number Thirty-Four's presence there, and why not? Where better to hide than beneath the cluster's very noses?

Once all of these men had been located, Natira hoped the enigmatic Thirty-Sixth would show his face. Even now, across this spinning planet, clusters kept tabs on the Nistarim already identified. From a Papau New Guinea jungle to a Beijing bicycle shop, from Germany to Brazil to Mexico, men marked with the Letter went about daily routines, their movements monitored by local Collectors.

Such Collectors, however, could not be counted on for the final act. Lord Natira trusted solely in the Houses of Eros and Ariston. They, the Akeldama Cluster, could withstand the sting of death, could spot things visible to few others.

But where, oh where, is the Crown of Thorns? Master, I beg of thee.

Cluster members had spent hours on the Internet, in museums, seeking a clue to the vaunted trove's whereabouts. Where the Six, No Seven panels had failed to tear down their foes, Natira counted on this Crown for the *coup de grâce*.

"Here." The cab squealed to a halt. "Here you find falafel."

"*Shukran,*" Natira thanked the driver in Arabic, paid him with *dinars*.

"Very bounteous welcome."

The revenant watched the car speed away, then turned his attention to a storefront with bright, hand-painted letters. Customers lined the glass counter inside, where a short Jordanian man with glistening blue-black eyes slapped meal after meal onto paper plates. He spoke with each customer as a friend, his dark cheeks split by winsome dimples.

A Concealed One?

Unlikely. He showed no signs of the backbreaking load such men carried. Probably a false lead, like so many others through the years.

The line shuffled forward, and Natira angled for a glimpse of the man's forehead beneath curls of black hair.

"Welcome, welcome," the shop owner said in cheerful Arabic. "How may I serve you this fine day?"

Natira coughed out his order, in no mood for pleasantries. He spotted a young boy in the back kitchen, stuffing pita bread with vegetables and meat. He worked quickly, silently. Was he Number Thirty-Three? Surely the shop had been here since before the child could walk.

"You are enjoying this warm afternoon?" the owner said.

"Too warm for me." Natira pointed at the oscillating fan perched on the counter. "Maybe you should turn it on."

"Of course."

The fan whirred into action, sweeping along Natira's chest. He put out his hand to accept the plate of food, and as the owner leaned closer his hair fluttered to the side in the airflow.

On his dark brow: Tav, in radiant blue.

The shop owner combed down his hair and said to Natira, "I gave you extra, no charge. A big man needs more to fill his belly, I think."

This kindness stirred a bilious taste in Natira's throat. He stammered his thanks and shuffled out the door. Before him, that Hebraic symbol still hovered, an irrefutable sign.

Impossible. Why was Number Thirty-Three so ever loving, ever smiling? He ought to be stooped and crabby. What about the hundreds, thousands, millions, infested by thorns? What about those mutilated in the Haunt of Jackals? Natira ignored the stares of passersby and dumped his falafel on the sidewalk.

So he had found his man. He'd succeeded. All well and good. How, though, was a Collector to enjoy a meal from such a happy, humble soul?

Without even one bite consumed, he ducked into an alley and vomited.

Early November—Silverton

"Jed, you think this place will work?" Gina said.

"Hey, you're the expert."

Silver Falls was the largest state park in Oregon, with over twenty miles of trails and plenty of places to relax beside plunging cataracts and dizzying trees. They had followed the Trail of Ten Falls toward the highest of them all, the South Falls, and passed only two other people on this cold Tuesday morning.

Jed said, "Mind if we eat our lunch first? Hiking makes me hungry."

"Lunch'll be our reward."

"Is that a no?"

"With a capital N."

"You're no fun."

Beneath dark hair that poked from his hoodie, Jed's face dropped. He slipped a sports bag from his shoulder and let it drop to the forest floor, where it clinked like pots and pans.

"Oh, stop your whining, buddy boy, or you won't get any lessons today."

As she said it, Gina took a step forward, dipped down, and drew her dagger in one fluid motion. The blade sang through the air, threaded between tall Douglas firs and cedars, and *thwunked* into the bole of a fallen maple.

Red and gold leaves fluttered on the branches, tongues of fire in the mist, and she thought about that invisible yet tangible energy that hummed between earth and sky. Most Westerners discounted it altogether, while many Eastern cultures approached it with superstition and dread. She'd walked the tightrope between the two realms, knew it was real and to be respected, yet also knew the Nazarene had bridged the divide. His perfect love cast out all fear.

"Nice throw." Jed tugged the dagger from the wood.

"Your turn."

He examined the object. "You say this is from the days of Moses?"

"The metal, yep. Wasn't made into a weapon till much later."

"That's what Nickel told you?"

"When Judas killed himself, he dropped the dagger there on the Field of Blood's slopes, and my dad picked it up before anyone else could misuse it. He knew the power in its origins."

"The Nehushtan."

"You remembered."

"I'm trying to take it all in."

"So let's see how far you've come with your MTPs," Gina said.

He hefted a metal spike. "Hmm, look at this. Says, 'Made in China.'"

"Very funny. More like, 'Made on Nickel's Ranch.'"

His fist closed around the MTP's shaft. He took ten steps back, then launched it toward the maple trunk, where the blunt end bounced off into the ferns. He dug around and retrieved it.

"When you're holding it," she said, "point your index finger down along the metal in the direction of your target."

"Sorta like throwing a football, huh?"

"Uh, sure. If that helps you narrow your aim."

Jed tried a second time.

Thuddd.

And a third.

Thuu-wunkkk.

"Touchdown," he said. "And Turney spikes it in the end zone."

She nodded at the bag of MTPs. "Keep practicing till you've gone through all of those. Don't stop till each one's pierced the wood."

"What? Not even a cheer from the crowd?"

"Not yet. You miss once in a real battle and it could be all over. Anyway, we're not talking Tennessee Vols football here."

"Sweetheart, you know I'm a Ducks fan now."

"And I still think you're a traitor for it."

"Once I'm done, can we eat lunch?"

"Traitors don't get to eat."

"Hey, I've lived here six years. Blame it on the Quack Attack. All the rain we get, I guess I grew me some webbed feet."

Gina rolled her eyes. "Once you've landed every one of the stakes, use your hammer to pound them deeper. Those spikes might seem clunky now, but believe me, you'll be glad the first time you see what they can do to the Akeldama Collectors. Put a bullet in one of their heads and you might stop him or her for a few moments. An MTP through the skull? End of story. My goal is to eliminate every last one of them. How 'bout you?"

"If that's what it takes to get our son back. All of us safe under one roof."

"The time's getting closer. Keep practicing."

Raindrops pattered on the forest canopy. Jed's eyes took on a steely glint. He nodded, selected the next weapon from his pack, spun, and torpedoed it through the forest gloom.

Thuu-wunkkk.

"First down," she said. "And eighty-nine yards to go."

An hour later, he had hammered his full set of stakes into the fallen tree and was working them free again. From the corner of her eye, she saw him wipe his brow and glance in her direction. She'd been exploring various ways of throwing, different angles, and she was on one knee now by a boulder, dagger aimed at a hemlock stump split and blackened by lightning.

"We about done?" he asked her.

"My last throw."

"Show me what you've got."

She'd been perfecting a side-arm technique for such situations, and she used it to whip her weapon around the boulder toward the target. The downpour compromised her grip at the last second and she had to accentuate her wrist's follow-through to correct the dagger's trajectory. Sharp metal careened into wood, creating an explosion of charcoal and splinters.

"Okay," Jed said. "That means it's lunch time, right?"

"Don't I get *my* cheer from the crowd?"

"The crowds are fickle, my queen." When she laughed, he added, "Come with me. In this weather, we practically have the whole place to ourselves, and I know a great spot to eat out of the rain."

Gina shadowed her husband to the South Falls that roared down from an overhang. She remembered her days working at Ruby Falls in Chattanooga. Now she was in Jed's territory, on moss-hemmed trails.

He led her behind the falls and helped her onto a hidden ledge, then joined her with his bag of munitions, as well as sandwiches, jerky, fruit, and sports drinks they'd picked up at Silver Crest Store. They ate without talk-ing. The crystalline scent of water engulfed them. Feeling cold, Gina gulped down the last of her sandwich and leaned into Jed. This time of year, the Oregon dampness worked its way into her bones, but she told herself it would do her good. Make her strong. Less complacent.

She had acquired a small blister on her thumb during weapons prac-tice, which she picked at with her fingernails, knowing that such testing produced endurance. She sensed the time for battle was drawing nearer, and it filled her with determination.

She took a sip of the Blood from her vial. Jed, too, had committed himself to the Nazarene's purposes, and he sipped alongside her.

"You looked pretty good slinging those spikes," she said.

"Thanks. You're a regular vampire huntress with your dagger."

"No, that's where I draw the line, mister. We'll never be Those Who Hunt. We are Those Who Resist."

"A vampire resistress," he amended.

"With one mean little duckling by her side."

"Quack, quack."

CHAPTER
FORTY

Ramon Crater

Even at a distance of fifty steps, the golem army—over a hundred strong now, with hundreds more to come—was indistinguishable from dips and mounds in the terrain. Barabbas hurried forward, panicked that last night's rain had washed away his work. Hadn't this makhtesh itself been formed from water erosion?

"They're still here," Megiste assured him. "Awaiting our summons."

He halted at the edge of the wadi, able from this vantage point to pick out the clay men on their sandy beds. He tugged at his beard and emitted a sigh of relief. "But how will you call them to . . . to life?"

"You're right to hesitate. It's not *truly* life, rather a shadow cast by those who once had it. You did bring the scrolls, I hope? Please, if I could see one."

The henchman relinquished one of the rolled papers. The priestess brushed alongside him, her pearlescent flesh sending tingles through this body of his that had roasted out here only a few short months ago. His weary human muscles, the peeling scalp—all would be forgotten if this experiment worked.

"Blood." Megiste examined the red-stained parchment and purred. "Each scroll has been inscribed with the life force of one of our victims."

"From the Haunt of Jackals?"

"Indeed, it *was* I who started the collage, was it not? Erota has agreed to share from those resources, since my own presence there could be awkward."

"You're saying each scroll carries a human's blood?"

"Each and every person a potential contributor to our cause. Let's put this to the test, shall we?" Megiste eased down the embankment, crouched over the first golem, and slipped the scroll into his mouth. "We'll start here."

"What do you want me to do?"

"Our golems have already been imbued with earth, water, and air, and blood will provide the fire to ignite them. Start marching, my dear—clockwise, slowly, six times around."

While Barabbas complied, he saw her trace long fingernails over the form's forehead as though scribbling words into his mind. If life had power, then death did as well—the power to kill, rob, and destroy—and Barabbas heard the priestess murmuring as she summoned that age-old foe for this strange task.

Undead life.

A slow, subservient death.

Was that Hebrew she was garbling? It sounded . . . backward.

In the pall of the cool morning, flames flickered in the golem's eye sockets—volcanoes coming back from extinction, or coals plucked from Hades' throat. The creature had no vocal chords with which to speak. He stared into the sky.

"Sit up," Megiste said.

He sat up. Even seated, he was taller than his willowy master.

"Touch your head," she said.

The golem's huge red arm made a rubbery half circle that belied skeletal restraints. Subhuman, he was also pliable and strong.

Megiste pointed. "Golem, pick up that boulder and throw it."

The monster rose and covered five meters with one stride. He lifted a rock the shape and size of a kneeling camel, brought it back over his head, and heaved it to the far end of the gulley, where it disappeared in a burst of yellow dust and debris.

Erota nosed forward from the damp fissure in the crater's northern wall. In the basin below, the golem forces were coming to life, ready to serve their sculptors, Megiste and Barabbas.

Fair enough. But hadn't Erota supplied the scrolls? Hadn't she harvested the blood by which these golems would be enlivened? In the event the priestess and henchman were removed, she would be next in line to command them.

And that was her plan.

From the beginning, Erota's Collector had bemoaned the divisions that undermined clusters worldwide. How were they to bring about Final Vengeance when they spent so much time dismantling each others' efforts?

Now, however, she found herself setting a trap of her own.

Well, why not?

She had long been a victim of Megiste's manipulation, sold as a prostitute to hairy, foul-smelling men—men like Barabbas—on the steps of pagan temples. Not that she minded using her wiles to weaken bodies and foster jealousies, but she took exception to being viewed as a source of pleasure and nothing more.

Let Megiste and Barabbas rot.

They would be banished for their waywardness.

Until then, they still needed to fill out the numbers of this battalion. Once that was done, Erota would take charge of the golems herself and offer their services to Lord Natira. She alone deserved his praise, his affection. Under her rule, the golems would assist the Black King as he looted the Tmu Tarakan and squashed the life from the Nistarim.

Megiste showed no fear of the golem, only glee. "Ohhh, isn't this *marvelous*, Barabbas? Go on. You try it."

"Now?"

"Certainly. Be simple and direct, the same as you'd order about a child."

Barabbas had never had offspring of his own. In those years during which the Nazarene walked the earth, Barabbas had led a band of murderous political zealots and nearly been crucified by the Romans for it. Never, though, had he harmed a little one, and he still found the thought repugnant.

Shouldn't he feel the opposite? What human inclination produced this empathy within? If the cluster knew of it, he would suffer their wrath.

"You're his master," Megiste said. "Don't be afraid to exert your authority. Even the most intelligent two-leggers, at their cores, like to be told what to do. Nothing but drones, really. It's *sooo* much less complicated than navigating their measly lives alone."

"What should I make him do?"

"Anything you like."

"Go stand guard," Barabbas told the creature. "Blend into the rock, and don't come back unless you're warning us of trouble."

Eyes aglow, the slave turned. He had no hair, no fingernails. A wall of brick-red mortar, he traversed the crater's floor with ground-shaking steps and took up position at the base of the cliff.

Ruins of Kerioth-Hezron

The first break came on an evening in November.

In the nearly two years that had passed, the cluster had followed leads pertaining to the Knights Templar ring, and each had looped back upon itself or been unmasked as a fraud. During medieval times, the alleged powers of sacred relics had reached a zenith in which Crusaders and clergymen alike took advantage of the superstitious, the uneducated.

Even these days, it was difficult unraveling lies to get at the truth of any such claim. Fear and manipulation were still wielded by those in power.

And more power to them, as far as Natira was concerned.

So long as the Crown of Thorns could be found.

With each failure, he grew more aggravated. His migraines became commonplace, the pounding in his temples a constant reminder of MTPs and the threat of the Nazarene.

The Tent Peg. The Sure Foundation.

Bah.

With Kransberg now in Iraq, still unable to pin down Number Thirty-Four, Natira had this evening to himself in the main cavern. He drew comfort from the cries of victims in the walls, from the sight of gristled stumps and glowing vines.

"My lord, are you free to talk?"

The voice was placid, easing him from bitter thoughts. He turned his attention to the doe-eyed woman before him. "What is it, Mother?"

Helene glided forward. "Have you found the Tmu Tarakan yet?"

He shook his head. Oh, even that hurt.

"I know you've been frustrated, son, and so it's only fitting that I bring to your attention the man I tapped earlier today. An American. A curator visiting Israel from his museum in St. Louis."

"Let me guess. He claims he too has a medieval icon."

"Not quite, I'm afraid."

"A sliver from the One True Cross. Veronica's Veil."

"Nothing quite so ostentatious as that."

"Then what, Mother? Leave me be, if you come with empty words."

Helene wore a sympathetic smile. "You're tired."

"I'm a Collector. I'm cold. I'm thirsty. I want only a moment of reprieve from these infernal headaches. More than anything, I want to crush the Humble Oh-So-Hidden Ones and watch the earth run with rivers of blood."

"This curator specialized in American history."

Natira snorted.

"And, considering his location, he was an expert on all matters related to Capt. Meriwether Lewis, the one from the Lewis and Clark Expedition."

The lord vampire pulled his shoulders back and folded his arms. "You know, their trail ran along the Columbia River, not far from where I found Kransberg. Even so, I'm not sure how this relates to the Tmu Tarakan."

"Lewis was a Mason. In fact, he served as master of Lodge No. 111 in St. Louis at the turn of the eighteenth century. Based on facts from this curator's memory, I discovered Captain Lewis was in possession of a relic or two passed down from the founding fathers—most of them Masons themselves."

"Was one of these relics a signet ring?"

"Would the veins of a curator lie?"

By his own research, Natira knew the Knights Templar had disbanded in the 1500s after internal strife as well as persecution from without. Many of them headed for the British Isles and from there the group's tendrils sprouted up through the Masons, the Scottish Rites, and Mary Queen of Scots, before arching across the Atlantic to the New World.

A ring in the hands of Lewis?

Unlikely, though not beyond reason.

Natira broke a thorn from his throne's arm and sipped, swallowing each diluted drop, enjoying the transitory warmth. He was still unsure about this latest lead—another wild-goose chase?—but it was worth some exploration. "Is your passport in order, Mother? Good. I want you and Dorotheus to go to St. Louis. Search this curator's home, his office, the museum. See what more you can find."

CHAPTER
FORTY-ONE

April 2008—Corvallis

Gina and Jed held hands at the nursery window, gazing upon infants in cozy incubators. This was Good Samaritan Hospital, twenty-five hundred miles from Chattanooga's Erlanger East Medical, and yet all the terrible memories came rushing back through Gina's head.

Twisted metal. Sheet-rock dust. Splintered glass.

And Jacob's pierced skin.

Jed rubbed his thumb along her wrist. "It's okay," he said.

"Weird how the mind works, isn't it? Even knowing he survived, I feel like I'm right back there, like my heart's about to get torn out all over again."

"Not this time. This time we're here to celebrate with our relatives."

A nurse entered the nursery with a swaddled pink bundle in her arms. The newborn was tiny, maybe four or five pounds, a couple of weeks premature. She was set in a bed marked *Esther Addison Turney.*

"That's her," Jed said. "Sarge and Josee's little girl."

"Esther," Gina mouthed.

It felt right being here in this moment, a chance to redeem the awful memories. Not only did they have their birth son back from the dead, they could rejoice with their family over this precious new life. Was it a mistake having a child in this crazy world? Well, who said little Esther couldn't make a difference? Was there a rule against believing she could make it a better place?

"What do you think?" Jed said. "Does Addison work as a middle name?"

"It's beautiful. Look at her, Jed. She's a doll."

"Did you know this is the same hospital where Josee was born?"

"And," said a voice behind them, "the first place she and I really met."

They turned. Though Sergeant Turney was bleary-eyed after a long night on the premises, his smile was incandescent. He bellied up to the glass, his entire countenance softening as he took in the sight of his daughter.

"As petite and pretty as her momma," he said.

Gina and Jed offered congratulations.

Sarge smiled. "Can't take much credit, can I? I had the easy part."

"How's Josee?" Gina asked.

"Snuggled up and sleepin' in her bed. Needed a few stitches, but the doctor says she oughta be just fine."

"That's good to hear."

"Suzette'll be coming by in a bit to read to her and keep her company."

"If you need anything from us," Jed said, "let us know."

"Will do, kiddo."

"Kiddo." Jed rolled his eyes.

Sarge was focused again on his daughter's incubator, oblivious to the world around him. Encased in little pink mittens, Esther's hands grasped at the air. She smacked her tiny lips, turning her head in search of nourishment.

"Daddy's right here," he cooed.

She pawed at the air again.

"Must feel like you're all by your lonesome in there," he said. "But I'm here watchin' after you, Esther. Dontcha doubt it. Your daddy loves you."

Gina touched a hand to her neck and thought of her own childhood, the way her mother had bled away her past, the way her father had been in and out, trying to teach her without endangering her. In many ways she had felt alone, abandoned. She still bore the scars of that fanaticism, and in years past she'd viewed them as evidence of an Almighty Being who remained distant and uninvolved.

Yes, she'd been that baby in the incubator—too small to see the bigger picture, too self-absorbed to recognize the sacrifices made for her.

All along, though, love had been there.

"Someday," Sarge said, still peering through the glass, "you two'll have kids of your own. Tellin' ya right now . . . This feeling? Woo-boy, ain't nothing like it in the whole wide world."

"Guess we'll just have to imagine." Jed turned and gave Gina a wink.

Shores of the Dead Sea, Israel

The second break came from an unexpected source.

Lord Natira was standing on Masada's natural ramparts—ancient site of King Herod's summer stronghold and later a hideout for Jewish Zealots. In AD 73 they'd taken their own lives rather than surrender to the troops of Rome.

Humans and their noble gestures.

Martyrs. Heroes. The pious. The profane.

In the end, did any of them matter? Did any one person alter the tides of time? Frankly, the answer was yes. A fact Collectors were wise to disguise.

Gazing down at the valley that stretched north along the Dead Sea, Natira visualized the ambush to come. Others had died here at this Valley of Bones, and more would follow. First, he needed a hostage. And the Crown of Thorns. Here, at this lowest point on earth, at this spot where saline waters inhibited the survival of living creatures, he planned to inflict maximum misery.

Behind him now, a group clumped around their tour guide as she spoke of *mikvehs*, ceremonial baths, used by the Jews to cleanse their bodies.

Why this preoccupation with cleansing?

Did humans sense the infections running deep in their veins?

The revenant turned his broad back to the tourists, teased by the blood scent that lingered about them. He had supped last night from a woman wandering alone at Ein Bokek, buried her shriveled corpse in a nearby wadi. To avoid further suspicions, he must keep his thirst in check.

"Natira, can we talk?"

"Who are you?" He hovered over a man in khakis and sandals.

"Mr. Monde. I come from the Consortium in America, on liaison from Helene and Dorotheus."

This conversation, Natira decided, should be conducted in private. He led the man across the way, down a stone stairwell that veered deep into a huge water cistern carved out by the Zealots for survival. It was empty now, dusty and quiet. A lone shaft of sunlight speared through a gap above.

"Make it quick, Monde."

"Your mother sends word from St. Louis. She's healthy and safe—"

"Skip to the point. I have no room for such indulgences."

"She's found evidence that the item you seek did belong to Captain Lewis. It disappeared in the early 1800s, along with a cache of gold. She's enlisted me and other locals in the search."

"Anything of substance yet?"

"Lewis left St. Louis in 1809 on a steamer to Memphis, Tennessee. With him was a chest full of personal items—journals, pistols, and what have you. Many of those items vanished around the time of his death a few days later. Suicide, by official accounts. But murder does not seem unlikely."

"You mean to say the ring's been missing nearly two hundred years?"

"One of the men Helene's enlisted is—or should I say *was?*—a professor in Nashville, not far from the trail where Lewis was found shot and stabbed."

"And they called it a suicide?"

"A botched job of it, for a renowned frontiersman. As I said, we suspect Lewis was murdered. Believing he was in danger, he hid his treasure beforehand along the banks of the Mississippi."

"Ha. What help is that? The river's over two thousand miles long."

"This professor also knows of a man, an alleged descendant of Lewis, who might have more detailed information."

"Do what you must to get it."

"The professor's already tried in a number of ways. We won't give up, though."

"Find it."

"Yes, Natira."

"And," the Collector added with a growl, "tell my mother that she's not to show her face till she succeeds at this task. She'll be banished if I see her under any other circumstances."

December—Silverton

Casa de Turney was in business.

As a Christmas gift, Gina and Jed had agreed to watch little Esther while her parents shared a romantic three-night getaway at Heceta Head Lighthouse Bed and Breakfast on the Oregon coast. This was the first time Esther Addison Turney had spent an evening away from Sarge and Josee, and the disruption of her routine had resulted in a barrage of dirty diapers.

"Your turn," Gina said.

Jed moaned from the couch. "Again? I did it last time."

"Nope, that was me."

"You gotta be kidding. What're you feeding this girl?"

"The stuff in those jars Josee gave us. Summer squash, I think."

Another moan.

"Guess we're making up for all the years we missed with Jacob." Gina handed over the tub of baby wipes, arched an eyebrow. "Time to man up."

Sighing, he spread out the changing pad on the living room floor. "So, who changed Jacob when he was just a baby?"

"The Unfallen, mostly."

"Wow. Not the most angelic of assignments."

"My mom did it first, though."

"Nikki? A little hard to believe. No disrespect."

"She was his grandmother, Jed, and she did help save his life. Twice, if you count . . . well, you know." Gina slumped beside the couch in a cross-legged position, sobered by recollections of those last days with her mother.

"Then I guess I shouldn't be whining about one simple little—ohhh!" Jed wrinkled his nose. "That is just *wrong*."

Flashing a lone tooth, Esther kicked her stubby legs.

"She's so adorable."

"Not from right here," Jed said.

Gina leaned forward, meeting Esther's turquoise gaze. "Lucky girl. You got your momma's eyes, don't you?"

Esther squealed.

"Oh yeah. You're going to be trouble."

"Already is," Jed murmured.

He cinched the Velcro-style strips, checked that the new diaper was snug but not too snug, then hurried to the trash can in the garage to dispose of the odiferous bundle. Gina bounced Esther on her knee, letting the little girl hold on to her fingers. When Jed returned, he wore a look of relief.

"Think we can go watch some TV in the bedroom now?"

"If you want," Gina said.

"I want. Smells foul out here."

"Seriously, Jed. Thanks for helping me."

"You've got next, don't forget."

"You make a good daddy. One day you'll get to prove it with Jacob."

"I hope so. Sometimes," he said, "I wonder if this whole charade is a waste of our time, if all this junk about Collectors is an elaborate scheme or scare tactic. I want a good reason for staying away from our only son."

"It's for his good," Gina said, though the words sounded flat to even her own ears. "You think that bomb was a hoax? Or the scars here on my arm?"

"The waiting just wears me out, I guess."

She took his hand. "That makes two of us."

Minutes later, they were side by side with backs against the mahogany headboard and the baby propped up by pillows in between them. Strong winds scraped tree branches against the wood siding of the house. Jed scrolled through the TV menu, complaining about reruns and cheesy Christmas specials.

This felt so right, so domestic.

Except for one thing.

Gina thought of their son on Lummi Island. Was he warm enough this winter? Content? Skipper had promised her these things were so, but until she could hear Jacob's voice and hold him in her arms, it was meager consolation.

From the TV, news reports claimed that seventy- to a hundred-mile-per-hour winds were battering the Pacific coastline, leaving thousands in the dark.

Ironic, really. Here on the eve of *Hanukkah*, the Festival of Lights.

Gina knew that the days of Hanukkah celebrated the Holy Temple's rededication as well as the consecrated olive oil that had replenished itself for eight days to keep the temple flame burning. MENORAHS were lit in memory of that miracle. Her own background, however, had been a mishmash of Judaism, superstition, and *orthodoxy*, making her a reluctant participant in such matters.

Lord, I'm not asking for a miracle. Just keep Jacob safe tonight.

"Hey." She sat up. "Go back. There's that show *The Best of Evil.*"

"All reruns."

"The producers, they're the ones who used to do my mother's show. Turn it up. I like this episode."

According to the write-up, the show's participants were given a chance to bless those who had done them harm in the past. The red-and-gold logo topped a byline that read "When Good Things Happen to Bad People." The narrator's voice rolled from the speakers as the subject of tonight's episode walked onscreen. The man's coloring was Mediterranean, his shoulders wide beneath wavy hair. He seemed to be easy going, not to mention . . .

"Easy on the eyes, isn't he?" Gina said.

"Hey."

"Relax." She gave Jed a peck. "You're the only one for me."

Thus fortified, he turned up the volume and they watched the story of this man traumatized at age six by his mother's murder. It was heart-wrenching stuff, made more powerful by the challenge to "*Get the best of evil by doing good.*"

Wasn't that the crux of life itself? Of this conflict with the Collectors?

In conclusion, the narrator explained that the family's private grief had led to a discovery of riches hidden by their forbear, Capt. Meriwether Lewis. It sounded farfetched and Gina gave a cynical huff. People would say anything to get their faces on TV, but it was probably good for the ratings nonetheless.

"Sweetheart, look . . ." Jed spoke in a low whisper as he pointed down at baby Esther. "Out like a light."

"Happy Hanukkah," Gina said.

CHAPTER
FORTY-TWO

Mid-May 2009—Eilat

Nickel waited for Dov outside Dolphin Reef. Once again he thought of his wife, Dinah, now long gone, and how she would've loved this area of Israel—the beach, the marine life, the bay. Through dusty palm fronds, he watched the setting sun gild saw-toothed mountains while pleasure yachts cut through seas turned choppy by an afternoon breeze. The scent of lemons wafted from the road.

"Nickel?"

"Bet you didn't expect to see me here."

Dov shrugged. Wearing soccer shorts and a red tank top, he pushed a bike with his stout, tan limbs. On his forehead, the Letter was vibrant. "Every day," he said, "I expect the unexpected."

"Atta boy."

"What's happening?" The kid's eyes were dark, his back bent. "I've felt the weight growing these past few months."

"Those Who Hunt, they're getting closer."

"You mean Natira? Does he know I'm here?"

"Not yet. You off work for the night? Perfect." Nickel tossed the bike into the trunk of his rental. "I'll take you back into town."

"The ride's good exercise."

"You'll get plenty of that in days to come."

Without further explanation, Cal Nichols slipped into the front seat and waited for Dov to join him. They headed into Eilat's city center, passing docks and cranes. A cargo vessel reminded him of munitions he'd shipped here for the upcoming battle, and he wondered if his crates were aboard this very one.

Nickel pointed. "See there? Over two years ago, Natira snuck back into the country aboard something just like that. Up at the port of Haifa. Since then, he's been working with an extra set of eyes."

"Extra eyes?"

"A son he calls Kransberg. They've marked three more of the Nistarim."

"Kransberg? That's a German name."

"His mother was the daughter of a Nazi, and she worked with Natira in the days of the Third Reich. I'll let you guess where this half-immortal came from."

"This sounds like trouble."

"That's why I'm here."

"How many of us remain undetected?"

"You, one of the originals—a man I served with in Jerusalem centuries ago—and, of course, the Nazarene."

"They'll never find Him, will they?"

"That's up to Him. He's nowhere, He's everywhere, hidden in plain sight. One day He'll be visible to all, but for now only to those with immortal eyes."

"And me?" Dov said. "You want me to go deeper into cover, is that it?"

Nickel circled a roundabout and parked near the beachfront promenade. With the temperature mellowing and darkness pooling behind the shops, tourists and locals alike strolled beneath bright lights. He led Dov toward the coarse sand, where the Gulf of Aqaba stretched into the Red Sea and the far-off Indian Ocean.

"No," he said, "I actually want them to see us together."

"Who?" Dov glanced at lovers cuddled in the beach's evening shade.

"The local cluster. Once they recognize me with you, they'll suspect you and send word to Natira and Kransberg. Can't be too obvious, of course, but if we're going to set a trap we have only you and my long-time buddy Isaac left as bait."

"Bait?" Dov kicked at the sand, churning the odor of a dead fish. Recoiling, he eyed the portentous thing. "I don't like the sound of that."

"Remember what Tolkien said: 'A man that flies from fear may find that he has only taken a short-cut to meet it . . .'"

"No, Nickel, I'm not afraid. I will do as you say."

"Good. Once we've raised suspicions, I'll take you back to the Shelter. In the morning, go to work as usual. No biggie. Within a few days, few weeks tops, you'll be a marked man, guaranteed."

Elusive Number Thirty-Four . . .

Oh, this particular target was a nuisance. The hunt for him had pulled Natira and Kransberg from Cairo to Beirut to Mosul and numerous villages in between. Everywhere, it seemed, there were accounts of Those Who Resist studying tactics from the Nazarene, finding communion through His Blood.

That elixir. That fragrant drug.

To Collectors cut off from the five senses, the chance to experience such redolence through a host caused an overload, an overdose, and even now it hung thick in the air along this Eilat beach.

"He's here," Natira said in Hebrew. "The local cluster sighted him a few days ago with my old nemesis, Cal Nichols, and they believe he's staying at the Shelter Guest Hostel. The scent around that place can be intoxicating."

The beast's hooded eyes cut toward his father.

"Don't let it distract you, Kransberg. Sear your nasal passages with a match, if you must. It's the Letter you're looking for, nothing else."

"We are Those Who Hunt."

"Today you hunt alone. Claim this one for your own."

"I found one in Syria."

"The teacher? Bah. I practically shoved him into your path."

"In Dubai, I—"

"You?" Natira chuckled. "You did nothing but follow in my footsteps."

Kransberg's lip curled into a sneer.

"It's true, son. This time, though, you'll do it without my help. I'm staying here to enjoy the beach and its bevy of tanned bodies."

With one shoulder dipped and his neck bent, Kransberg was a crippled giant ready to hit the town in black canvas work pants and a gold athletic jersey. Tufts of hair covered his forearms and sprung from the top of the shirt, but otherwise he was clean-shaven and well groomed.

"Go on," Natira said.

The creature jolted off in the direction of the guest hostel.

Truth be told, Lord Natira was an addict in need of a fix. He loved the smell of that Nazarene Blood, and it drew him now toward the shipyards on the south end of town. Why it was emanating from there, he didn't know. Did he care?

No, he only wanted to be near it, to breathe it in.

He recalled tasting that one smear of it on the rock along the Oregon riverbank. Even stale and miniscule, the drop had swelled with richness on his tongue, offering him unsurpassed succulence—before it nearly destroyed him.

Towering hydraulic lifts fronted the docks where ships were loaded and unloaded. Cargo containers lined a huge fenced lot off the road.

The smell was coming from down there.

Natira pressed his tongue stump against the roof of his mouth. Should he follow this scent to its source? He figured his son would take some time completing his task, so there was no reason not to explore. The containers were padlocked, left unattended, and it was only a matter of hopping the fence to move closer. The lack of activity on the docks suggested it was lunch time.

He scanned the road in both directions. To the north lay the main tourist area with its IMAX theater and shopping mall, to the south the

Underwater Observatory and Dolphin Reef. Two cars and a van zipped by.

In a bounding leap, he cleared the fence.

His host's senses were locked in now, and he viewed the aroma as a scarlet vapor. It wavered in the gulf breeze, tickling his nose. He wished—oh, more than anything he wished—he could slurp it down.

The guilty container stood before him.

Natira hooked his thumb into the padlock and snapped it open with a satisfying pop. He worked the levers, swung open the door, and discovered crates packed with outdoor supplies. Hundreds of metal spikes, to be specific.

Who would want all of these? Avid campers? The Israel Defense Forces?

Most telling of all, each MTP had been dipped in Blood.

These were no simple tent pegs, Natira recognized. These were poison-tipped weapons for the destruction of Collectors and their strongholds. Someone was shipping them into the Holy Land, and that would have to stop.

"What are you doing there?" a sturdy dockworker said.

The vampire turned, fangs already elongated and eyes burning with thirst. He watched the man approach. Any closer and Natira would attack.

"Do you have passes? Get off this property, both of you."

Both?

Natira swiveled to find Kransberg only meters away. The brute was zeroed in on the temptation within those crates.

"Where did you come from, son?"

"I found him. He is at Dolphin Reef."

"Number Thirty-Four?"

"Are you two listening?" the dockworker shouted. "This lot is closed for a reason, and you have no business here."

"Name is Dov Amit. He is a teen."

"You found him on your own. Well done."

"That's it, you two. I'm calling the police."

Kransberg took ten strides and intercepted the man. He gripped both of his arms and swung that solid body into a storage hut, where it slumped to the ground in a daze. Kransberg hunched over his prey and tore into the exposed jugular amidst a spray of blood. Natira wanted to reprimand this offspring of his, yet his own desire had been stirred. He needed to quiet these hammers in his head, if only for another few hours.

"We drink in celebration," he said.

In the shade of the hut, they drained the dockworker. The hot flush of liquid stained their lips and teeth, but it was pallid stuff, unable to compare to the lingering aroma from the crates; it was cheap table wine in place of aged, oak-barreled quality.

Once they had finished, they turned their attention to the stockpile of tapered spikes. Applying themselves together, they scraped the cargo container across the pavement to the edge of the loading dock. Men were back on duty, pointing, yelling at them, yet two minutes later Natira and son had dispatched the crates over the edge where they sank from view into the choppy waters.

CHAPTER
FORTY-THREE

Late October—Silverton

Another year was slipping away. Jed now supervised his own crew at Gelfand's Garden Supplies while Gina continued at the Tattered Feather Gallery. On weekends they often hiked and/or camped, using the solitude to hone weaponry skills and study Nazarene strategies. Who better to learn from than He who'd faced down the Master Collector?

Their thinking, as a couple, was mutual. Why be Those Who Slink Away in Terror when they could be part of Those Who Resist?

Not that Gina lived without doubts.

True, each month was a step closer to seeing Jacob—a prospect that thrilled her—yet also a step closer to his unveiling and larger purpose. Things could turn ugly. They had in times past, hadn't they?

Outside, dusk chased shadows across the street and into the back-yards. Dogs were locked up. Trick-or-treaters appeared in groups of two or more, most of them accompanied by adults.

The doorbell rang.

"Got it," Jed called from the entryway.

Gina stood at the curtain, peeking out at the array of ghouls, trolls, Freddys and Jasons and Michaels, and those jaw-stretched Scream masks that made toddlers look like psychopaths. She wondered about the effects of all this on the children. Did it help them face their fears? Or stew in them?

Harmless fun, most of it. And a good haul on the candy.

"Your choice: Starburst or Bottle Caps," Jed was telling their visitors.

Somewhere out there real monsters were at work, clusters of Collectors looking to feed, to breed. They spread infestation, corroding the lucidity of otherwise able minds. They operated through hosts both human and bestial, angling for an advantage. No foothold was too small to ignore, and they clambered up frail psyches in hopes of capturing them for the Collection of Souls.

"The next trick-or-treaters are yours," Jed said to her.

"Huh?"

"You okay, sweetheart?"

"I wish Jacob was with us."

"Me too. You ever wonder what it'd be like to have more kids?"

"Jacob has to be with us before I can even consider that." She moved to the couch. "For now, we have baby Esther to love."

"Definitely. So whaddya think Jacob would dress up as tonight? Does he even know about superheroes and scary movies and all this stuff?"

Gina nodded. "He reads a lot. And Skipper says he gets on the library computer every once in a while. I bet he's not as out of touch as we think."

"Might be more in touch. Less distractions and all."

"Let's hope he doesn't watch the nightly news. Remember how agitated he got during my pregnancy, kicking up a storm every time a tragedy aired? He's a burden bearer. He's ultra sensitive to that sort of thing."

"It's what he was born for, isn't it? He'll be okay."

"By the time we get to talk to him, he'll be done with trick-or-treating and all the kids' stuff. He'll be busy with shouldering the weight of the world."

"Then we better be there for him when that thirteenth birthday hits."

Gina put her hand on her husband's chest. "I love you, Jed Turney."

"Love you back. Now watch the front door while I run to the bathroom."

She stood at the entryway and thought of Halloween five years earlier in Junction City. She had been with her adopted son, Kenny, and her

Romanian childhood friend, Teo. Teo had tried biting her neck and she'd thrown him out of her house.

According to Nickel, Teo succumbed only days later to the ravenous hunger of a vircolac.

So many lost . . .

Why, God? Don't You see what's going on down here?

She thought of Apostle Peter in the Garden of Gethsemane, drawing his weapon to defend his lord. The Nazarene had reprimanded His disciple for it.

For what reason, though? Hadn't the Nazarene also stated that He didn't "come to bring peace but a sword"?

As far as Gina was concerned, she would strike without hesitation if anyone came calling at this address. She had seen her share of Collectors and victims, and she would fight them with all her strength. She'd never allow her own blood flow to betray her son's location.

The doorbell jarred her from her thoughts. Her fingers twitched, ready for action, even as she reminded herself this was only Halloween.

She scooped up the sectioned candy bowl, then peeled back the door to reveal a Grim Reaper with sickle in hand. A frayed black hood concealed the kid's face, and only the shallow breathing indicated anything human underneath.

"Uh, Bottle Caps or . . . or Starburst?" Gina said.

No response.

Breathing. And that intimidating presence.

Dread oozed down her neck and shoulders. She detected something briny—a Collector's sulfuric scent?—and when she tried to peek beneath the hood, the head lowered. She took a step forward, goodie bowl dangling, and the Reaper reached for her with pale-green nails. Images flashed through her head: claws prying at her, fangs grazing her throat in a Romanian cave.

And she reacted. She whipped the dagger from its sheath on her shin and visualized driving it into the Reaper's chest the way she'd once done to Lord Ariston. She would put this enemy down. She would—

"Gina!"

She wavered.

"Hey." Jed's hand lighted on her shoulder. "The kid just wants some candy. Relax, sweetheart. Relax."

She blinked and stepped back, trembling as she sheathed her blade. The hood lifted to reveal a young teen boy. That salty smell? Adolescent sweat.

"Did she scare you?" Jed said to the trick-or-treater, giving an airy laugh. "Yeah, that knife of hers looks real, doesn't it? Here you go." He took the bowl from Gina's hand and shoveled the entire batch of Starbursts into the kid's bag. "Stay safe out there."

Jed closed and locked the door, flipped off the porch light, and swung toward Gina. Though he looked ready to bark out recriminations or demand answers, he softened the moment his eyes met hers.

"Come here." He pulled her to his chest.

"I . . . I don't know what I was—"

"S'okay, Gina. Whaddya say we sit on the couch and eat the Bottle Caps all by ourselves, just you and me?"

She nodded.

"First dibs on all the root beers," he said. "They're the best."

She wrinkled her nose. "In Europe, that's more like a toothpaste flavor."

"Does that mean I don't have to brush before bed tonight?"

She shoved him away. He dropped onto the couch and dug through the bowl while she waited for him to bring up the Reaper incident again. But he had let it go. Sighing, she snuggled beside him, her head on his shoulder. He fed her a candy.

"What flavor?" he said.

"Cola."

"Three cheers for artificial flavoring."

She sucked on the disk till it was the size of a dime on her tongue. "Sorry for . . . you know . . . being on edge lately."

"Listen, sometime soon we'll be facing the real thing. When that day comes, you're the one I want next to me. Nobody else."

"I'll be there."

"Better be."

"Oh really? Or what?"

"Or I'll . . ." He waved a brown Bottle Cap. "I'll make you eat one of these."

She thought of the poor kid waiting for candy on the doorstep, only inches from tasting her blade. Swallowing the last of the cola flakes, she opened her mouth for another round.

Jed dropped the Bottle Cap onto her tongue. "Flavor?"

"Uggh." She coughed it into her hand. "Toothpaste."

"There. Now that we've both brushed, I think it's time for a kiss."

CHAPTER
FORTY-FOUR

February 2010—Ruins of Kerioth-Hezron

Erota chose her moment with care. She lit scented candles, placed a bowl of warm honey beside her bed, and turned back the jackal bedspread checkered with soft fox pelts. With Kransberg now sharing Domna's chamber, Erota had Natira to herself, and by the time she'd satisfied him, the candles were burning low. He fell into a stupor, his broad chest rising and falling, his old battle scars pale pink in the flickering light.

"Natira?" she said.

"Mmmm."

She traced the ligaments of his arm with her finger. "I've been meaning to tell you the truth about Barabbas."

"Mm-hmmm?"

"You've been busy, mostly absent, so I've had no good time to bring it up."

"Bring what up?" he grumbled.

"Well, it's true that I sent him away on an errand, but he never returned. I had heard rumors that Megiste—"

"The priestess?" Natira opened his eyes.

"She was said to be operating in the middle of the Negev, at Ramon Crater. Barabbas was to verify this and report back to me, nothing more.

When I went to check on him, though, I found he had joined her activities there."

"What activities?"

"Maybe it was silly of me to send him alone, knowing she was once his mistress. He's always been so susceptible but I never dreamed he'd take her side."

"Her side?" Natira rolled onto his hip. "What're you talking about?"

"Megiste's a manipulator, always has been. With his help, they're raising up their own army in the crater." Sticky with honey, Erota's lips brushed his neck. "Of course, if you banished them, you and I could take control of their golems, the hundreds hidden along the makhtesh walls."

Early March—Jerusalem

"You are sure of this? This is what Yeshua wants?"

"That's not my place to say, Isaac." Nickel faced the spice merchant in the curtained area of the David Street shop. "I can only tell you what He asks of me."

"Ahh, my old friend, this is a good point you make. He can speak for Himself, yes? Of course He can. Still, we listen and learn from each other."

"You're willing to go along with my plan, then?"

"Have they found me yet?"

"They get closer each day. Keep low a little longer, that's all I ask."

Wearing his ubiquitous smile, Isaac shrugged. Remembrance tassels swayed from the bottom of his wool shirt. "Those Who Hunt . . . it is what they do, no? Before you or I were born, they hunted. Even before the prophet Ezekiel. What is any different now?"

"Final Vengeance is drawing near."

"Why do you say this? You cannot tell me you know the hour for it. Not even Yeshua knows such a thing."

"Hear what I'm telling you," Nickel said. "The day is coming, and Collectors are trying to cut in with their own form of vengeance. Those from the Akeldama, they're particularly active, hoping to take down the

Nistarim in a multipronged attack. Aside from the Nazarene, you're the only one they haven't found."

"Perhaps if they shopped in the Jewish Quarter."

"I bet they've looked here."

"We are Jews. Since when have persecutors been unable to find us?"

"In your case, I'd say the Unfallen have been working overtime."

Isaac patted Nickel's arm. "They watch after you also, my friend."

"Listen, I should keep this visit short. The Collectors have a hard time keeping up with me, but they do know my face when they see it. I don't want to lead them to you."

"Very kind."

"At least not yet. Not till everything's in place."

"You do as you must do, and I will go about my business."

"Always spicing things up, aren't you, Isaac?"

The merchant's eyes twinkled. "Imagine when the Separation is no more. Our fellow humans"—he waved toward the shoppers out on the cobblestones—"will discover flavors the way they were created to be, yes?"

"Talk about out of this world. All of our senses fully alive."

"Doubly alive." Isaac rested his hands on Nickel's shoulders. "Your dear Dinah beat us to it, but we will know this one day for ourselves."

"I'm still waiting."

Nickel felt cocooned here in the Old City, a place some called the navel of the world; he felt safe with his longtime friend, one with whom he had shared the woes of ancient Israel. Safety, though, had never been the goal of Those Who Resist. They found their strength in obedience, in self-denial.

As always, this land was pregnant with possibility and yet the Master Collector's malice threatened to abort it.

"Okay," he said. "I'm outta here. Got stuff to do back in Oregon."

Including updates of the bloodstains on this map for Jacob.

"It will be as you ask," Isaac said. "A few more months I will stay hidden."

Nickel patted powdery streaks of saffron from his clothes, gave his companion a farewell embrace—lingering longer than usual, wondering if this would be their last—then ducked through the curtain and joined those walking the narrow street. He felt as though he were reentering a battle, and it brought to mind the words of Capablanca, former world chess champion: *"Chess is a story in symbols . . . the plans suggested by one, spoiled by the tactics of the other—the lures, the wiles, the fierce onset, the final victory."*

Yep. Time to arrange some tactical maneuvers.

Ramon Crater

From his workplace in the shallow gulch, Barabbas noted a plume of dust as someone drew near. Whereas ibex, toads, and horned vipers avoided detection, this intruder seemed unconcerned about such things. The henchman would've thought it a jeep, except for the silence that enveloped the crater.

"Megiste, we should take cover."

"Oh, don't be foolish," she said, tossing her auburn ringlets. "It's much too late for that."

"What do you mean?"

"It's Natira, I'm quite sure. Come to pry, as lords are prone to do."

"Sodom's salt," Barabbas cursed. "He could banish you where you stand. It's all there in the Principles of Cluster Survival, and you ran off when he—"

"Ran off? Please, you can be *sooo* very dense. Have I ever run from *anything*? I think not. And I certainly won't begin such a nasty habit now. We are here to earn back our lord's favor, are we not? I have plans to pursue and here you are participating in them. Shouldn't you be just as worried, considering that you left your cluster?"

"Left? No, never. Erota told me to—"

"Erota sold you out, don't you see? She's set on one thing: the success of the cluster under *her* rule. She's always despised you, since our days in ancient Jerusalem. Her eyes were on Natira, her beloved warrior, and you were the smelly old thing in her way."

"Is that how you think of me?"

Megiste clutched the white robes about her waist, fingers polishing the gold belt that clung to her hips. "I'm not sure that it matters now."

Lord Natira came into view, mammoth thighs driving up and down, feet tearing through sand beneath slate-gray skies.

"I don't understand." The Adam's apple hopped in Barabbas' throat. "He didn't have to come all the way out here, did he?"

"What is it you're saying?"

"With one command he could send you to the Restless Desert."

"You too. Let's not forget that."

Natira's strides ate up the distance between them, his jaw set, his glare slicing through the ozone, bands of sinew snapping tight with each movement. Beneath obsidian eyes, sweat beads carved his face.

The henchman frowned. "If you knew Erota would turn her back on me, why'd you let me join you, Megiste?"

"Oh, I didn't *know*, not precisely."

"You used me."

"I missed you, dearest. Now look, he's nearly upon us."

The priestess raised an alabaster hand and beckoned her legions. They rose one by one from positions in the dirt, along the walls, and beside stark basalt formations. Unable to speak, the golems advanced on stomping feet, and the intruder slowed at the sight of them.

"Lord Natira, they're here to serve you," Megiste said as he came to a halt. "There's no need to be afraid."

"Afraid?" The revenant threw back his head and laughed.

"These soldiers respond to my voice, and they're sworn to protect me."

"And if tragedy befalls you, who then will they obey? Barabbas? I can banish him as well. My voice is the one they'll turn to when both of you are gone."

"Please, my work has ever been to serve our cluster."

"You abandoned your household."

"I feared your wrath, yes. Weak creature that I am, can you blame me? I suppose I still have my uses, or you would've expelled me years ago."

Barabbas watched Natira's chest heave from his sprint across the crater. Muscles roped through his arms, formed knots along his stomach. Slicing from right shoulder to left hip, the scar from a Roman sword only added to his intimidating presence, and Barabbas knew firsthand the man's formidable strength. Could he hold up against the golems, though?

"Tell me," Natira said to Megiste, "how it is that you will help me?"

"I was derelict in my duties to you years ago, and so I've worked to enter your good graces again. I present to you now my army's services. Oh, I know they can be *burdensome* lunks, but there's no denying their abilities. Put them to the test, if you will."

"A test, you say."

"Try to take hold of me. Come, my lord—no need to be shy."

From a stone's throw away, Natira charged the woman, his pincered hand aimed at the flesh of her porcelain throat. Barabbas had never seen the golems move as one force, hundreds up on their feet. They converged from all sides, cutting off access before the warrior-king could reach the priestess.

Natira halted to consider this obstacle. "Very well." Monstrous fangs punched down from his gums, and he rolled back his shoulders. "Let's see what they're capable of."

The first golem swung a hammer-fist toward the vampire's head.

Natira dodged to the side and parried the blow with his arm. The impact shattered bone, leaving his limb flopping.

He roared, twisted the appendage loose at the elbow, and jabbed the dripping stump into the golem's eyes. The creature staggered back. Wiped at his face. Threw a blind punch. Natira launched forward, colliding into the brick-wall abdomen and managing only to wrench his shoulder from its socket as evidenced by sounds of grinding cartilage.

The golem could see again. He aimed a kick at the Collector's ribs. Curling his body to absorb the blow, Natira caught the leg and was lifted into the air. He clamped incisors into his enemy's outer layer and drew forth an oily substance—the blood of crushed minerals and rock.

Barabbas was transfixed. Could these creatures be defeated? Could their oil be heated and pressurized to make the clearest of earthly diamonds? Or were they tar, clay, and stone, nothing more?

Fire blazed in the golem's eye sockets as he tried to shake the overgrown leech from his thigh. The third attempt sent Natira wheeling into another golem, from which he bounced onto the ground—a ragged, bony stump for one arm, the other out of commission, his mouth smeared with grit and goo.

"You see?" Megiste said. "I offer an army like no other."

Lord Natira chortled through black bubbles.

"Are you not impressed?"

"You should've done this work while under my authority."

"My goal, always my goal, was to present these creatures as gifts to you."

Another chortle. "In German, the word *gift* means 'poison.' "

"Is that so?"

"You're a poison within our cluster, Megiste."

"Please, that is *sooo* unfair. I've meant only the best, and I—"

"You've spread mutiny and you've stolen our henchman away."

"Barabbas? The dear wanted to come. Surely he deserves as much blame as I."

"You're accusing *me*?" said Barabbas.

"You should know," Megiste said, directing her words to Natira, "that the oaf was prodded along by your beloved Erota."

"Enough! I am done with you and your cunning."

"Very well. I've tried to cooperate with you, but you truly leave me no choice."

Stepping back from the lord's rage, Megiste raised both arms in a grandiose gesture. Framed by ringlets, her eyes revealed the knowledge that this would be her final benediction, her last act as a priestess of the damned. Barabbas saw no remorse there, no apology, only sparks of prideful defiance.

"Be *rid* of him," she told her clay soldiers.

Natira wiped his lips, fixed her in his sights.

"Do it *now*," Megiste shrieked. *"Kill him!"*

As one, the golem army moved forward, yet already fateful words were on Natira's tongue. He fixed her in his sights and, by his authority as cluster leader, by the stipulations governing Collectors everywhere, he meted out punishment in accordance with her transgression.

"Wander forevermore," he said, "in the sands of the Restless Desert."

One moment, Megiste's willowy frame was there; the next, her robes lost all form and billowed to the sand beneath rings, bracelets, and a thick gold belt. Barabbas stifled his anger, his sense of loss. Why mourn the woman who had betrayed him moments ago? He'd been used by her all along.

Megiste's cry faded into ghostly silence.

Her army froze.

"Well, look at these brutes now. Impressive, sure," Natira said, "but they have no minds of their own."

Barabbas said, "They'll listen to me, my lord. I'm next in command."

"I should banish you too. You disobeyed Erota in my absence."

"That's not true. She gave me the bus ticket to this place and told me to follow Megiste's orders."

"Erota told you this, hmm? I know she's snubbed you all along. Perhaps you lie to strike back at her."

"I'm not that clever, my lord."

The cluster leader considered the henchman through unblinking eyes.

Barabbas swelled his chest and called out, "Back to your places."

Reanimated by his voice, the supplicants marched off in all directions until the crater floor was vacant, raked clean of footsteps by a cool gust.

"Thank you," Natira said. "How long will they stay hidden?"

"Until their master speaks."

"I'm their master now. Tell them."

"Lord Natira is your master," Barabbas shouted. "Obey his orders alone."

Pleased, Natira fetched his mangled left arm from the dirt and shoved it into place at the elbow. Undead sinew and skin went to work, stitching together the two ends with molecular DNA as their template. Though Barabbas had seen this done before, even utilized the process himself, he was ever amazed at the rejuvenating properties within the Almighty's creation. He doubted the Master Collector would have been so generous.

Natira sighed. "What should I do with you, I wonder?"

Barabbas bowed a knee. "I'm a servant. What can I do but follow orders?"

"Tell me, do you remember that moment standing beside the Nazarene? Watching Him wear that Crown of Thorns? Watching Him bleed? If you hadn't been there, perhaps He would have gone free. But no, you were loosed that day so that He could die instead. I envy you that honor, you know."

"I did not choose it."

"A prisoner? No, you couldn't choose, could you?"

"The crowd called for His Blood, called it upon their own heads."

The vampire smiled, his receding fangs still stained oily black. "Stay by my side, serve me well, and together we'll reenact that moment of triumph. We may no longer have Power of Choice, but soon we'll possess the Crown of Thorns—yes, that very same Crown. Who will wear it next, I wonder?"

CHAPTER
FORTY-FIVE

Mid-June—Ruins of Kerioth-Hezron

The anticipation of an event often overshadowed the event itself. It was a human predilection, this insatiable hope for something greater, something fulfilling, and it was one the Collectors had used against them for millennia.

Lord Natira knew this. Of course, he did.

Yet here he sat upon his throne, awash in disappointment.

Even as Kransberg scoured Jerusalem for Number Thirty-Five, Natira held a battered cell phone between his pincers. It had arrived this morning, shipped from the United States to a post office box in nearby Arad. This was the same box the Akeldama Cluster used for receiving passports, credit cards, and the typical minutiae that cluttered these two-leggers' lives.

At Helene's bidding, a Professor Newmann had sent the object, along with a typed note. This erudite fellow had sunk his talons into the mystery of Captain Lewis' treasure and served a semester at Nashville's Lipscomb University. He'd picked out a shred of truth from the numerous speculations and . . .

"All he can send me is a cheap phone?"

Natira's voice carried across the cavern, blending with the moans of those in the stone walls. He stared down at the accompanying note.

*I followed the clues and found nothing. I made threats—chop, chop. Still nothing.
In resorting to more drastic measures, I confronted the gentleman from the televi-
sion show, the alleged descendant of Mr. Lewis, and managed to pilfer his phone
as well as the information it contained. With pesky detectives still searching for me,
the phone could betray my whereabouts. I leave it to you to take the next step.*

That was it? After months of waiting?

The phone was dead.

Natira refused to let this go that easily and sent Kyria into Arad for a
new battery, which she found at an electronics shop in the city center. At her
age, Kyria was a natural with technology, and he watched her clip the battery
into place, hold the Power button, and bring the cracked screen to life.

"Are you seeking anything in particular?"

"Messages," he said. "Or saved numbers. I'm not certain."

Kyria scanned the menus. From the dial list, she read off locations.
"Bowling Green, Kentucky . . . Nashville, Tennessee . . . Nashville . . .
Nashville . . . Columbus, Ohio . . . Silverton, Oregon . . . Nashville . . ."

"Oregon?"

"Silverton, Oregon," she repeated.

Oh, Master, could it be this obvious? The Northwest once again.

"Write that number down," he said. "Is there a name?"

"Jillanne Brewster."

"Brewster. The family name sounds familiar."

Young Kyria brightened at the chance to flaunt her research. "Many
early American leaders had Masonic roots. From that very first ship, the
Mayflower, a man called Elder William Brewster became one of the leaders
of the colony."

"Quite the little student, aren't you? Well done."

"Thank you, my lord."

Natira mulled the information while rolling the cell phone in his
hand. Had someone contacted this Brewster woman to make arrangements for her share in the spoils? Had she been given the signet ring? Or
was this another in a rash of false leads and misdirection?

Either way, it would give troublesome Erota a task with which to occupy
herself. Or better yet, Natira could assign her a traveling companion.

Erota strolled the underground tunnel alone, travel documents poking from the back pocket of her designer jeans. She'd earned Lord Natira's favor and he was sending her off on a whirlwind mission. Only hours till she boarded a plane in Tel Aviv, destined for Seattle. From there, she would transfer to Portland.

"What is my assignment?" she had inquired.

"You'll both be told at the airport."

"There's someone coming with me?"

"Considering your beauty," Natira said, "it's unwise to leave you alone."

She now fanned long brown hair over her jacket's collar, confident she could turn heads in the matching fur-lined boots that added to her height and tightened her small, round buttocks.

She was anxious to go. She was done with this monotonous peace.

Chilled, she warmed her fingers on the vines running at waist-level along the sandstone, snaking toward recent victims in modern Jerusalem. Each translucent thorn pulsed with the life force of humans who'd left themselves open to infestation, in big ways or small. The new harvest was underway.

A drink, she told herself, would restore her core temperature. She could almost smell, almost taste their rich hemoglobin.

She broke off a thorn. Tossed its contents down her throat. Broke off another. She pounded shots the way some people pounded Jack Daniel's—including her ex-husband, who'd been a fan of that Tennessee whiskey. With papers marking her as a Ukrainian bride, she had gone to him in Atlanta, Georgia, but it had been a short-lived relationship—at least for him.

Now, Erota was headed back. Ah yes, back to American soil.

She tossed down another shot and licked the residue from her lips. Already she felt warmer, emboldened for her looming assignment.

The boldness soured in her mouth, however, when she reentered the main cavern and saw that cretin, Barabbas, standing beside Natira. He had a rolling travel bag at his side, a light coat stretched over his large frame.

What was he doing here? He should've been banished in that crater.

The cluster leader rose from his throne of thorns, a smirk plastered upon his granite face. He was finding pleasure in her displeasure, and Erota had to gulp back the acidic words that burbled onto her tongue.

"Meet your travel companion," Natira said. "For the next few days, you'll work together. Ha. And you thought he'd never come back."

"He betrayed your trust."

"He did as he was told. Meaning it's your loyalty I now question."

Although lies roiled through Erota's thoughts, she knew they would do her no good. She had always been a realist, and this time she knew she was caught. She looked to the wall panels, where victims wriggled like worms on hooks, their cries echoing her own despair.

"You can't do this to me," she said.

"Barabbas cares for you, Erota."

"Please, my lord."

"It's your decision. A trip to Oregon for two? Or a solo trip to the Restless Desert? It took only a few words to be done with Megiste. Ask Barabbas if that wasn't the case."

Erota sulked. Her scheme for both priestess and henchman to be banished had gone awry.

"Ask him!"

"Was that the case?" she said.

Barabbas nodded. "Gone in a moment."

Brief satisfaction flared in Erota's mind. At least Megiste would never bother her again.

"Now," Natira said, "I want you two to kiss and make up."

"My lord?" Erota doubted her own ears. "I don't understand."

"Soldiers must work together, one unit committed to the same objectives. You mustn't let your petty differences compromise this task."

"But, Lord Natira—"

"Kiss him."

Erota felt humiliated as she stepped toward the henchman. She thought Megiste's demise would have signaled the end of such mistreatment, yet Natira was prodding her into those same lascivious behaviors.

Barabbas purred at the touch of her lips.

Men . . . Every last one of them, slaves to their lusts.

"See there," Natira said. "That's what I call camaraderie."

Erota spat onto the cave floor.

Unfazed, he said, "We ought to get moving since you two have a plane to catch. On our way to Tel Aviv, we'll go over your mission's details. I would travel with you, of course, except that Kransberg and I are nearing the end of our own assignment."

Cascade Mountains

Evergreen shadows and the rush of the river cooled the ranch's ten acres. Unwavering and unseen, a dozen Unfallen stood guard along the perimeter, while MTPs stood chiseled, sharpened, and stacked beneath a blue tarp on the left side of the log cabin. Inside, Clay Ryker and family resided with Kenny Preston, who was now nineteen and earning college credits online.

Cal Nichols paused on the broad planks of the front porch.

Had he miscalculated?

For the last few months, he had visited various continents and imparted instructions to the chessboard's real-life figures—the *piese de sah*, as they were called in Romanian. Though his strategy was daring, the Concealed Ones had pledged their cooperation, with all efforts geared toward early September, toward Jacob's thirteenth birthday.

Except the Akeldama Cluster was now on the move. There were even reports Barabbas and Erota had boarded a plane headed this way.

In these situations, a chess player had two options: defensive maneuvers or counterattack. And the game's outcome could hinge on that decision.

To Nickel's left, the mound of MTPs reminded him that he had already shipped such armaments to the port of Eilat, where they should've been picked up and stockpiled. Those Who Resist were few in number in Israel, and their silence on this matter indicated they were under increased surveillance. Regardless, he'd already arranged visas, tickets, and permits, and so he would assume the best. Sarge and Josee were also ready to play their part with a trip to the Holy Land. Okay, then—if his gambit needed to be accelerated, so be it.

"The plans of one, spoiled by the tactics of the other . . ."

He prayed he would be the one doing the spoiling.

Shouldering through the cabin door, he was greeted by Gussy's friendly bark. Clay and Kenny emerged from the weight room in the back.

"Hey, there," Kenny said. "I thought you were coming next month."

"Me too. Some things've changed."

"Doesn't sound good."

"It is what it is." A stalwart white rook upon the board, Clay stepped closer and draped a gym towel around his neck. "Tell us what's going on, Nickel."

"What's going on is we're entering the endgame already."

"Okay. What do you need us to do?"

"I want you to head over to Silverton, pass on a message to Gina for me."

"Covered."

"Thanks. As for you, Kenny . . ."

"I'm all ears."

Nickel hesitated. If this entire thing unraveled, it would bring the world crashing down. These Lettered men were the remnant, yet even they would be unable to bear so catastrophic a weight. It all came down to this. Defensive maneuvers? Or counterattack?

"You and I," Nickel said, "we're about to take a little trip."

"Where to?"

"Tell you on the way."

"Okay."

"And we might not be coming back."

"Is that a joke? It's not, is it?" Pain flashed through Kenny's eyes, a recurring symptom that Nickel recognized from his own stint as one of the Nistarim. The kid blinked it away. "Well, if you say it's time, then I say let's do this. Can I get in a quick good-bye to Gussy and the Rykers?"

"If you do it while you're packing. We leave in an hour."

CHAPTER
FORTY-SIX

Corvallis

Gina was worried about Jacob. She moved to the large front window at the Tattered Feather Gallery. A gale moaned beneath the eaves, rain dotted the street, and leafless branches scraped the belly of a darkening sky.

"Supposed to be getting worse."

Suzette Bishop joined her. "So I've heard."

"We haven't had a customer in two hours."

"Thank you for covering Josee's shift."

"Not to mention me babysitting for her."

From behind the counter, two-year-old Esther babbled in her car seat. Gina had elected to play Mommy for the day while Sarge and Josee took care of official business at the state capitol—applications, birth certificates, and whatnot.

"Say, let's call it a day." Suzette gave a nod toward the toddler.

"Really? I'd appreciate that."

"I don't suppose we'll be seeing many more customers, and I can count down the till. Go on, Gina. Go. You'll be racing this squall back to Silverton."

Gina situated keys in her left hand, car seat in her right, and shambled through the downpour. She strapped Esther into the back, adjusted her pink footed sleeper, and headed home.

Sheer winds rocked the car on Interstate 5, then shoved it eastward along Silverton Highway. Pooled water dragged at the tires, forcing her to slow down. An ambulance zoomed by in the direction of nearby Salem, and she tried calling Jed on her cell to make sure he was okay.

The reception was spotty, and she lost the call. Minutes later, she received a call from their home, but it too was dropped.

He must be safe and dry, at least. Off early for the day.

As Gina rolled into Silverton, she sensed the eerie aftermath of a disaster. The torrential summer storm had already ambushed the small town, shoving down street signs, flinging branches onto lawns and parked cars. Shops were closed, windows dark, streetlights out of commission.

Esther started crying. "Want Mommy."

"You'll see her soon, cutie. You've been a good girl today."

Braking, Gina reached back to offer reassurance. As she did so, movement darted along the edge of her vision. She came to a complete stop and gave her full attention to the tree-canopied street to her right.

A figure moved from behind a panel truck. Were those screams?

Through the drizzle, a large, barefooted woman lumbered into focus wearing shorts and a voluminous T-shirt. Her left hand was twisted and bloody.

The cell rang again.

"Jed?" Gina answered. "I lost you earlier with this storm, and I—"

"Sweetheart, you need to get home right now."

"What? What's wrong?"

"You know your dad's friend, Clay? He's here. Says there could be Collectors headed this way and we need to take cover."

Silverton

Finding this two-bedroom home off the main thoroughfare had been easy. An online search revealed address, directions, and a quaint little map that even marked the closest eateries. True, Erota and Barabbas had entered without permission, but since when had Collectors been hindered by legalities?

"So it's true? You're Jillanne?"

"Yes," the woman said. "I'm sorry. Did . . . did you knock?"

Erota rolled her neck. "No, we did not knock."

"Are you here for help? Did you . . . bring food?"

While Barabbas watched from across the Formica dining table, Erota bared her fangs at this obese two-legger with the shaped brows and light-blue eyelids. How brave she was. Did she not know what she was up against?

Jillanne Brewster . . .

Descendant of Elder William Brewster? The owner of a signet ring? Were her name and location coincidences or clues to something significant?

Erota snarled. What a day this had already been.

Early this morning, she and Barabbas had departed Israel, been rerouted due to a freakish storm, spent three hours in Denver International, then bounced down in Portland. Of course, there'd been no avoiding the close quarters in the Avis rental car, and the Kia sat now at the curb, still rank with the henchman's sweat. Despite these delays, the time change had worked in their favor so that they arrived here by suppertime.

And, yes, they'd found Jillanne eating.

And eating.

And spitting each bite into a separate bowl.

Even though she fed herself while resting one hand politely in her lap, her human self-indulgence was revolting in the extreme.

"What are you doing, woman?" Erota demanded.

"Why are you . . . in my house? What . . . do you want from me?"

"You can't even talk without running short on breath. You disgust me, you knuckle-dragging swine."

"I am . . . working on my weight."

"Sure you are."

Jillanne pointed to her own cotton shorts and an autographed T-shirt that read *Johnny Ray Black* in gray across a black Stetson hat. "I jog every day."

"From the refrigerator to the couch, no doubt."

"I am tasting . . ."

"That much is obvious."

"Tasting others' pain."

Erota looked to Barabbas. "Is she making sense to you?"

"If you bake me . . . cookies . . . or bread . . . or . . ."

"What happens?"

"I can taste your . . . emotional anguish. Your guilt."

"Really?"

"It's a gift," Jillanne said. "I use it to . . . serve Yeshua."

"Oh." Erota rolled her eyes. "Him."

"Is that why you . . . came here? I see that you're in turmoil."

Erota glanced across the table at Barabbas, who seemed intrigued by all this jibber-jabber. "Hey, don't tell me you're gobbling this stuff up."

"My friends," Jillanne went on, "and even strangers . . . They bring me food, and . . . I taste and see what they are going through. Then . . . give them advice, or a verse from the Holy Scriptures."

"Holy. Wholly. Holey. That word can be used so many ways."

"Only God is holy, isn't He? I sense that you're . . . hiding unholiness."

Erota was done with this nonsense. Standing lean and curvy in her designer jeans, she stared at the tubby specimen before her, repulsed by the extra chins and flapping jowls. The scent of the woman's blood wafted about the room, exquisite and tantalizing, yet off limits to any Collector.

Nazarene Blood.

Undiluted, undefiled, and . . . holy.

"Let's try this a different way," Erota growled. "We will take a few bites from your corpulent flesh and tell you what *your* pain is. Oh, don't act so surprised. Did you really think we came to you for advice?"

"Doorbell's broken," Jillanne said. "I don't always hear it. I thought . . ."

"You thought wrong."

"How do you do this?" Barabbas said. "Could you taste my pain?"

"If God shows it to me."

"You're an idiot for believing a word of this, Barabbas." Erota leaned toward the woman in the chair. "Ignore him. All we really want is the ring."

Jillanne's eyes widened, showing fear for the first time.

"A signet ring," Barabbas said. "Show us your left hand."

For her size, Jillanne Brewster moved with surprising agility. She upended the dining table in Erota's direction and sent bits of food flying into her face, then spun from her chair toward the front entryway. Barabbas snagged her hand, crushing fingers, tearing skin, yet she broke free with a yelp and caromed into the night.

"Should I chase her?" Barabbas said.

"Did you get that ring from her finger?"

"Are we sure it's the right one?"

"I'll search the house while you find out. Get going!"

Although a bit slow in the head, he was no slouch when it came to land speed. His explosive movement tore the door from its mooring and left it tilting into the box shrubs.

Erota wiped the mess from her face, then swiveled in the living room, jeans still damp from the rain. Where, she wondered, should she begin her search?

Outside, the passing storm served as a reminder that the Concealed Ones were buckling beneath mankind's agonies. Each time they faltered, the earth shivered. Earthquakes. Tornadoes. Floods. As far as she and the Akeldama Cluster were concerned, all of it was evidence of their successes in the Haunt of Jackals and in the latest harvest fields of Jerusalem. The Oh-So-Ridiculous Ones could only endure so much more.

She rifled through a myrtlewood jewelry box, with its tangle of bracelets and necklaces, then moved next to the bookcase on the wall, where titles ranged from *Gourmet Tuscan Cooking* to *Spiritual Health for Your Physical Body*.

She swept the entire library onto the throw rug.

You want to taste pain, Miss Brewster? Well, let Barabbas oblige you.

Through the windshield, Gina watched the barefooted woman stumble, nearly fall. Wheezing, she cried out for help.

"Please tell me you're on your way, Gina," Jed said through the phone. "I called the gallery, and Suzette said she let you leave work early."

"Coming," Gina said. "See you in a few."

She closed the cell and considered the scenario before her. She'd been

given a warning about Collectors in the area, yet this woman was in obvious need of assistance. How could Gina ignore that? She stepped from the
car, keys in hand, and surveyed the street, where rain still dimpled puddles
and debris littered the pavement. Menacing clouds had drained most of
the color from the sky, leaving a monochromatic setting for some artsy—
or very campy—horror film.

"Please . . . help . . ."

Gina tickled the yellow duckling on the front of Esther's pink sleeper.
"Be right back, cutie pie. This lady's in some sort of trouble."

Though the toddler's lips quivered, she fell silent.

Gina closed the driver's door, thumbed the fob on her keychain to lock
her car, then jogged around the front of the vehicle. Hope fluttered in the
large woman's eyes as she saw Gina coming, but the momentary distraction
sent her reeling over a plastic trash container that blew sideways across the
street.

With the woman's fall clearing the view, Gina noticed a man a half
block away. He was picking up speed, hurdling downed branches. She
leaned next to the woman, whose left hand bore a large gold ring streaked
with blood.

"Are you two in a fight? Is that your husband over there?"

The woman blubbered through her pain. "Get me away . . ."

"Did he do this to you? I'll call the police." Gina weighed one-thirty in
her khaki skirt and black boots, so she had little chance of lifting a woman
two or three times her size. She hooked her hands under thick arms, and
said, "I'm going to need your help here. Can you get up?"

The woman clambered to her knees.

"What's your name?"

"Jillanne."

"I'll take you in my car, Jillanne, but we have to hurry."

To her credit, Jillanne heaved herself to her feet and wobbled toward
the vehicle. Gina disengaged the locks, watched her crawl into the front
seat. Gina then turned toward the approaching threat, determined to give
this jerk a piece of her mind. She knew a confrontation was unwise at this
moment, yet no woman deserved to be beaten. Basic stuff, right? Keys to
Happy Marriage 101.

The man was sixty feet away, giving no indication of slowing.

Against this black and white nightmare-scape, Gina now spotted the emerald sheen of his eyes, the protruding ivory canines. His chest muscles flexed and shifted beneath his shirt, and his pumping fists were armed with tapered green nails capable of gutting a rhino in a single swipe.

A Collector. Just as she'd been warned.

And not just a simple mortal playing host to his demons, but one of Jerusalem's Undead from the soil of the Akeldama.

Gina realized her own foolishness. She had Sarge and Josee's baby in the car, and experience told her these creatures had zero respect for life at any age. Best thing to do was hop behind the wheel and try to hightail it.

The Collector was thirty feet away.

Two or three seconds tops.

She decided there wasn't time to circle to the driver's side and drew the dagger from its sheath beneath her skirt. Thus armed, she crouched low, ready to attack and defend. She wasn't sure why this Collector had gone after the woman now seated in the car or how he had arrived here in sleepy Silverton. She knew, though, she would fight to protect those in her care, and if she lost her life doing so, she would try taking down her attacker in the process.

The ruddy, bearded beast slowed to a halt at the sight of her blade, as though he'd heard stories of its bite. Automobiles passed by on the main thoroughfare behind her, fixated on their own destinations this ugly night.

"All I want is her ring," the Collector hissed.

"Can't have it."

The creature threw a glance over his shoulder and turned back. "I won't hurt any of you, you understand? Hand it over and I will go."

"I know what you are," Gina said. "You're a liar."

"By the sails of Sicily, hand it over before she comes."

"Who?"

"Erota."

That name sounded klaxons in Gina's head. "Let her rot in hell," she said.

"The ring." The revenant gestured with his curved nail.

"Over my dead body."

The Collector bellowed at the storm, at the heavens above. He fixed the car in his sights and leaped forward. She sidestepped his bulk and stabbed upward, but he batted her aside and drove his fist into tempered glass. Skidding on her back over wet pavement, Gina saw the window crack in multiple places and snap from its setting. Her own brain felt dislodged by the brunt of his blow. Even as she rolled onto all fours, the Collector threw an elbow into Jillanne's face and split her eyebrow.

"Leave us alone," the woman shrieked. "God, please . . ."

The toddler wailed.

Esther's still in there! Oh no, you don't.

Gina locked fingers around the dagger's handle, climbed back to her feet. If she advanced to take a stab, she would put herself within the creature's reach. If she threw the dagger and missed, she would be left without viable options.

Trusting her training, trusting the power of this Nehushtan bronze, she cocked back her arm. Took aim. The assailant had one hand shoved against Jillanne's neck, choking off oxygen, the other ripping at her ring finger.

Gina slung the weapon through the rain the way she had practiced with Jed in their backyard and at Silver Falls, the way she'd done in her dreams.

The knife spiraled.

Sunk deep.

Blood geysered from the Collector's back. As he arched in pain, Jillanne used her immense bulk to shove open the door and knock him off balance. He rocked back a step, then two. Collapsed to a knee. He tried stretching an arm over his shoulder to remove the dagger, yet it eluded his grasp, and he seemed to wither under the metal's potency, morphing from fearsome attacker to surprised victim.

Gina planted her boot on his lower spine, yanked the dagger free.

The vampire groaned, curling into a fetal position.

She stabbed him again.

"My ring," Jillanne said. "He . . . took my ring."

Gina knew better than to search him while unnatural life still writhed through his limbs. She checked the backseat, where tears pooled in Esther's round eyes. "I'm getting you out of here, cutie. I promise." She turned to

Jillanne. "We'll let the cops take care of his corpse and sort out the knick-knacks later."

"But it . . . it's an heirloom."

"Small town. Good people. I don't think a cop'll steal it. Now close that door and I'll take you to my place. We'll make the call on our way."

Jillanne's mouth dropped. "There she is."

"Who?"

"The other one. She called herself Erota."

Gina pivoted to see a woman far down the street. "You're sure?"

"They were in my house."

"Erota," she breathed. "The name alone gives me the creeps."

Though the shape on the ground twitched between gasps of agony, his fingers clenched tighter the moment Gina ventured to pry them apart. His nail scraped her palm, drawing blood, and he winced at that Nazarene scent.

"Drink up." Gina slapped her dripping hand across his chapped lips. "You can't survive a drink of this Blood, can you, mister?"

"She's coming this way." Jillanne was conflicted. "But he still has my—"

"We'll get you another ring, okay?" Gina dashed to the driver's side. "Let's scram. I'm not risking this baby's life a second time in one night."

"Thank you . . . for helping me."

"Close the door."

Jillanne was still pulling it shut when Gina stomped on the accelerator.

CHAPTER
FORTY-SEVEN

Jerusalem

Natira entered the Old City in the lavender light of daybreak. The Tower of David guarded Jaffa Gate, with side streets and alleyways spidering in all directions.

Many hours ago he had bid farewell at the airport to his wayward acolytes, Barabbas and Erota. They would be in Silverton by now, and he was confident they'd bring back what he needed within a week or two.

In the meantime, why not help his son find Number Thirty-Five?

Massive walls enclosed the four quarters of this historic area, where civilization built upon civilization, where religions clashed and extremists spilled innocent blood. Yes, regional clusters deserved some credit for fomenting dissent, though ultimately it came down to individuals' choices. With free will at their disposal, some embraced greed and narcissism. Others used it like a weapon, tearing down strongholds erected by the Collectors.

Natira found that unacceptable.

He sniffed the morning air, detecting Kransberg's scent. The brute had canvassed the Armenian, Christian, Jewish, and Muslim Quarters and still came up empty-handed. Was it possible Jerusalem was another false lead?

No. Even now, Natira sensed the claustrophobic presence of Those Who Resist. Number Thirty-Five was very near.

My Master, direct our steps.

"Lord Natira!"

The urgency in that gravelly voice spun him around. "Son?"

Kransberg gestured toward an alley, then hobbled on those big feet of his into the shadows beneath a restaurant awning. Both father and son scraped the canvas with their heads while Kransberg's gaze swept the environs.

"What's got you so excitable this morning?"

"I saw them," Kransberg said in English. "They are close."

"Them?"

"Yes, Number Thirty-Five and—"

"Good. This should've been accomplished long ago."

"And Thirty-Six."

"What?"

Kransberg jabbed a finger. "A spice shop. They sat together."

"On David Street?"

"I saw the Letter. Blue scribbles, both of them."

"Let's go. I want to verify this in person."

Kransberg's eyes narrowed to slits. "Thirty-Six is gone. I will stay here."

"They don't know you. Bleeding hearts that they are, they'd probably give you alms as though you were some pitiable beggar. Now that you've identified them, you need to inform the local clusters so they can keep them in their sights."

"Thirty-Five is a merchant, all the time smiling. Number Thirty-Six? Both of his hands have holes."

"Scars, you mean. That'll help us identify him."

"Holes." Kransberg jabbed at his own wrists. "Straight through."

Natira reeled back at this revelation. The *Nazarene?* He was the pre-eminent leader of the Concealed Ones? Hardly surprising, come to think of it. How poignant that the Meek Ever-So-Mild Lamb still bore those scars, His wartime medals of honor. He probably considered Himself Number One.

"Did you hear any of their discussion, Kransberg?"

"Too much noise on the street."

"That's why I avoid this area. It gives me headaches."

"They laughed," Kransberg said. "Talked. Then Holey Hands was gone."

The bad pun was enough to trigger Natira's rage. To think he had searched this globe for decades, tracking righteous souls, yet restraining himself in hopes of a collective strike . . . And all along, their leader was the most humble of all, the servant of all, the saving grace of these knuckle-draggers.

The Collector turned and kicked at the restaurant window, shattering glass. He snatched the awning and tore its mountings from stone blocks, producing shrieks of metal. Across the way, a taxi driver witnessed the rampage and circled his car back through Jaffa Gate.

Natira removed a shard from his boot. "Take me to this spice shop."

"Now?" Kransberg responded.

"Yes, now. Are you deaf?"

"Too early."

"Don't challenge me. I'll tear your heart out again where we stand."

Kransberg's eyes smoldered. His shoulders widened, spine straightened, and knees popped into position. Father and son faced off in the alley, and Natira wondered what perverse miracle had undone his son's afflictions. Then, as swiftly as the change had occurred, the monstrosity was back in his crooked undead form.

"I will take you." Kransberg averted his gaze. "What is your plan?"

"If this Number Thirty-Five is so special that he shares company with Yeshua, why should we wait any longer? We've pegged all Thirty-Six, have we not? I say it's time we grab the bait for our trap."

"Why not kill him?"

"And watch another rise to take his place? No." Natira and son strode side by side down the steps of narrow David Street. "We will hold him hostage, make threats, and demand that the others come. They'll do it. 'All for one, and one for all.' Honorable ideals, but oh so exploitable."

Kransberg pointed through an archway. "Here. It is this place."

A rolling metal door had been lifted already to waist level, revealing sacks of turmeric and cumin, saffron and za'atar. Legs came into view. A man was whistling. Broom bristles whisked back and forth while blue tassels swayed in rhythm with his work.

"Shalom," Natira called out in greeting.

But there will be no peace this morning, my friend.

He hefted the metal door upward while Kransberg squatted underneath and batted the Jewish merchant off his feet. Even as the older man fell, as his Lettered brow struck the edge of a table, his mouth remained fixed in a smile.

Silverton

Standing on the doorstep, Sarge had one arm over Josee's shoulder. "Heyya, what about that storm? Thought we'd never see the end of it."

"We survived," Jed said. "Just barely."

"Where is she?" Josee edged into the house. "Where's my baby?"

Gina stepped from behind her husband, little Esther clutched to her chest. "I don't want to let her go," she said.

She kissed the toddler's cheek and relinquished her to Josee, heart aching for the touch of her own son's skin, the smell of his hair. The Collector attack two hours ago had served notice that their enemies were still active. Heck, even now Erota could be lurking outside.

Jed ushered his uncle and wife into the living room, where the box lamps cast a gentle glow over metal tent pegs laid out on the table.

"Going camping?" Sarge kidded.

"A Collector steps into this house, things're going to get bloody," Gina said.

"Have at 'em."

Josee rocked Esther against her chest. "We saw the cops just pulling away, so I'm sure you're tired of talking about it, but give us the rundown."

Gina shared the uncensored version, starting with the drive from Corvallis, the sight of the running woman, and the Akeldama Collectors. Clay Ryker had tried delivering a warning and was now headed back to his own family, while Jillanne was spending the night at Suzette's—a safe haven from her ransacked home. As for the vanquished foe, the one called Barabbas, he had vanished by the time haggard police officers reached the scene of the attack.

"But you got him with your dagger, right?" said Josee.

"And gave him a few swigs of the Blood."

"So where'd he go? Shouldn't he be bye-bye once and for all?"

Gina picked up an MTP, rolled it in the light. "We're guessing Erota disposed of his body, along with any other incriminating evidence."

"I'm just glad Esther's okay." Josee smoothed her daughter's fine hair. "Straight up, Gina—thanks for watching her. Sarge and I, we've faced this kinda evil before and even have the scars to prove it." She rubbed the line of pink tissue beneath her eyebrow ring.

"Me?" Sarge inched up his sleeve. "Got these fang marks on my arm. Don't let me start yappin', though, 'cause that's a tale for another day."

Gina touched her forearm, where she had torn through thorns to free herself from Zalmoxis Cave six years ago. Jacob, too, had his scars, from a pipe bomb full of nails. It struck her that Jed had no such markings. While she envied him that, she wondered if battle wounds weren't in fact a necessary part of the process, the price for final victory. Referring to the Nazarene, the Scriptures said: "If we are to share His glory, we must also share His suffering."

Their home phone rang and she scooped up the handheld. "Should take this. It's my dad."

"Gina?"

"Hi. Where are you?"

"On my way back to Israel, to the Valley of Bones."

"Where?"

"Between Masada and En Gedi. By the Dead Sea."

A tremor ran from Gina's neck to the base of her spine, as though seeking refuge beneath her tattooed angel wings. She edged into the hall, phone cupped to her ear. "Tell me what's happening, Dad. We have Sarge and Josee over, and something's gone very wrong. You know what I just saw, not more than two hours ago? I saw Erota and Barabbas here in stinkin' Silverton."

"In Silverton? I knew they were headed that way, but—"

"You might've warned us. I don't think she spotted me, but it was her."

"And what about the henchman?"

"I killed him. Stabbed him twice with my dagger. He disappeared soon after, not a trace that the cops could find."

"Disappeared? You're sure you pierced his skin with that bronze?"

"Not a doubt in my head."

"Hmm."

"What?"

"You're sure he didn't survive?"

"Impossible, Dad. Tell me that's impossible."

"Forget I even asked. So what about Erota? She wasn't after you specifically?"

"She wanted a ring."

"What kinda ring? Gimme details, Gina. This could be important."

"Belonged to this lady, Jillanne Brewster. She says it was passed down through her family for generations but was lost till just recently. Crusaders. Masons. I don't know. My mind's in a blur right now."

"A signet ring?"

"Yeah, maybe."

"You remember the Tmu Tarakan? There've been rumors that Rasputin encoded a map to the place on a ring and . . . Well, anyway, find out if this Jillanne lady has any photos of the thing or could draw it for you. Scan and e-mail it my way, okay?"

"Okay." Gina tried to stay focused. "What were you saying about the Dead Sea? What's going on?"

"They've captured a Concealed One. I knew it'd be either Dov or Isaac."

"What? Oh no. Please tell me it wasn't—"

"Wasn't Dov. They got my pal, Isaac. Boy, he and I go way back."

"I can imagine."

"I've set some bait of my own, though. Listen, we'll stretch this thing out as long as we can, try to buy some time, but you remember the Sovereign Game? The one I showed you between Anderssen and Blackburne? To win, we have to put it all on the line. Plain and simple. Isn't that what I've always taught you?"

"Yeah."

"I want you to get out of town tonight, Gina. Both you and Jed."

"You kidding?"

"No more waiting around. Throw your stuff into a bag, grab your weapons, and go into hiding. Give it a coupla days. Once you know that nobody's followed you, you can head up north."

"Dad, please . . ." Gina's heart wedged in her throat. "Don't mess with me."

"I'm serious. It's time for you to be a family again, the three of you. Don't worry. With the Unfallen keeping watch over you, I'll be able to find and make contact with you whenever necessary."

She closed her eyes. With life and death at stake, it would be vital that she ease Jacob into this new reality. She'd stay cool. Stay calm. This was the moment she had waited for, the chance to be who she was meant to be: Queen of the Resurrected.

"Now," Nickel said, "if you can hand the phone over, Sarge and I need to talk."

CHAPTER
FORTY-EIGHT

Lacey, Washington

It made the national news, one more serial killer confessing sins to his apprehenders. Did he do so to clear his conscience? Gain notoriety? Or simply leverage prosecutors for a plea bargain?

Edwin J. Marstens . . .

Madman, molester, and murderer.

Sick to her stomach, Gina watched the story unfold while Jed thumbed through a Chinese take-out menu from this cheap motel's night stand.

On the TV, Mr. Marstens blinked into the lights, a twitch pulling at one corner of his mouth. He had killed dozens, he claimed. Buried their bodies in the Arizona desert. All of them attractive, middle-aged women, similar in appearance to his mother, who had set herself ablaze in a trailer home bed.

Yes, said Mr. Marstens, he had even taken the life of one celebrity.

N. K. Lazarescu.

News channels lapped it up, airing retrospectives on the Romanian self-help guru's 2004 disappearance. At the time, many assumed she had gone into hiding due to tax evasion, embezzlement, or an affair. However, investigators found no such evidence, and her show's coproducers had defended her innocence. Adding to the intrigue, public records showed she had filed stalking and harassment charges against Mr. Marstens in the summer of '03.

"According to officials," the anchorwoman said, "Nicoleta Lazarescu had no living survivors."

Gina leaned into Jed. And she wept.

When she was done, she went into the bathroom and splashed cold water on her face. She'd been growing out her hair for the past year, letting it return to its chestnut brown as a statement to the purveyors of fear. Concealed, yes—but she would not remain silent.

She picked up the store kit from the sink and read the directions.

"Jed, I'm doing the pink streaks," she said.

"Sure that's what you want? Isn't that just begging for attention?"

"We've done the tranquil American thing, and I am so over that. We are Those Who Resist."

Jed moved into the doorway. "Then rock those pink streaks."

"Plus, I don't want Jacob thinking I'm some boring old woman."

"Boring? No. Old?" He winked and said, "I plead the Fifth."

She pushed the door shut.

"He's gonna love it," Jed added. "Coolest mom ever."

As she worked in the coloring, Gina stared into the mirror and bolstered herself against the harsh consequences of the news. Once the Collectors heard about N. K. Lazarescu, they would send one of their kind to sample blood from the exhumed corpse—whether in police custody or not—and that would lead to the unveiling of Gina's survival, of Jacob's hideaway.

She wanted to fly this very hour to Arizona and demand custody of her mother's remains. She wanted to protect her family from further harm, give her mother a decent burial. She'd been issued orders from her father, though, and any time now she and Jed might be going to Lummi Island. To deviate now from their mission could be disastrous.

Where was Nickel? Had he heard the latest? She had to trust that he had a plan.

From the motel room's front door, a muffled knock shot spurts of adrenaline into Gina's limbs. She braced herself in the bathroom, her dagger out, knees bent, legs slightly apart—ready to go to war.

"Got it," Jed told her. "It's probably the Chinese delivery guy."

Another knock.

"Nope," Jed said. "Hard to tell through this peephole, but I think it's that friend of your dad's again."

"Really?" Gina stepped into the room. "I bet this is our green light."

Bakersfield, California

Barabbas sat in the back section of a Greyhound bus that cut across arid vistas. He pressed his forehead to the tinted window and frowned. Why was he still alive? Why hadn't that Nazarene Blood sizzled through his intestines and left him in a pile of ashes and dust? The dagger—that ancient blade—had also failed to destroy him, despite its effects on others in the cluster.

He was undead, yet still breathing.

He was not banished.

Why?

In the minutes after he faced off with Gina—hadn't she died years ago in a car crash?—he had spasmed on that wet asphalt, expecting the worst, anticipating pain beyond any he'd ever known. And, most definitely, it had hurt. It was Sodom's salt poured into his wounds; it was pools of fire flaring where the knife cleaved his back.

Presuming his death, Erota offered no words of comfort. She stooped beside him and pulled the signet ring from his fist, then, in farewell, threw a foot into his ribs before leaving him for dead.

Barabbas stared out the window, thoughts churning. Oaf that he might be, he was not stupid. And he was not destroyed.

Why?

It was Natira's recent words in the crater that supplied the answer. The cluster leader had recounted that moment when Barabbas stood side by side with Yeshua, when a choice was given to that crowd and they demanded a crucifixion: *"Let His blood be on us and on our children!"*

Had the curse of that Nazarene Blood been removed from Barabbas' hands? Was he free from its wrath, even susceptible to its healing? And if that Blood could not vanquish him, what could?

He replayed the cluster's reanimation from the tombs beneath the Field of Blood. Yes, the animus of the Betrayer and the Master Collector had enervated those bones and made room for the waiting Collectors, but what if this skeleton of his was free to go? Free to do as it pleased?

He thumped his forehead against the glass.

What if he was not a spawn of hell as he had believed, only a vessel invaded by a Collector's presence? He had not chosen this host. This Collector had no right to hold him down. He'd been taken hostage, as it were.

Another thump.

He was still undead, still thirsty for blood to warm him, and yet he was not bound to the cluster's wishes. For too long, he'd suffered rejection, humiliation, and indignities. He realized he had the Power of Choice.

Wearing thorns for a crown, the Nazarene had once fixed Barabbas in his golden-brown gaze. As the crowd shouted, a moment of connection had occurred—and then Barabbas had looked away. Recently, he'd tasted that same Man's Blood and felt it spread through his limbs.

There was power in the Blood.

Was that what he wanted, though? Did he dare accept the repercussions?

Right now, he knew only that he wanted freedom from these chains. He held his breath and steeled his will against his host, demanding release.

I'm done with you! he decided. *Done bowing to your every wish.*

A wheezing sigh pushed from his lungs, and a wisp of darkness smudged the windowpane before dissipating into the ether.

He had made his first choice.

Empowered, Barabbas removed the newspaper from the pocket of his light coat and reread the article on the serial killer's arrest. Barabbas, too, had brought about the destruction of human beings, and the guilt of that came crashing down upon him in the absence of the Collector. He could envision the wounds, the horrible tears and ripping, the broken bones . . . He could taste their life flow on his tongue, feel it coiling in his belly.

What could he ever do to pay for his misdeeds?

Gina, he knew, was still alive, but surely other secrets simmered within her mother's remains. The slavish mentality that had propelled him onto this bus for Arizona now wilted in the heat of his new convictions.

He did not have to hunt, to kill. He felt no need to persuade or possess.

That being the case, what should he do once he arrived?

Tel Aviv

Erota's flight descended toward Ben Gurion International an hour after midnight. From her window aboard Delta Airlines, she watched the surf draw silver shapes on the Mediterranean's black slate, then splash upon the shore where hotels stood sleek and tall.

She shifted in her seat. Despite her host's exhaustion, she was anxious to hail a taxi and get back to Lord Natira. With the henchman off her back and the desired relic upon her finger, she felt renewed enthusiasm in her service.

Natira, of course, would ask about Barabbas and suspect her of foul play, yet what could she have done?

While Erota searched Jillanne Brewster's house, the henchman had chased after their prey. By the time Erota went to find him, it was too late. He was curled on the pavement, barely breathing, a pair of stab wounds in his back. Not that earthly weapons could've bested him. No, it must've been the Nazarene Blood on his mouth that took its toll.

Hadn't he heard Jillanne's yapping about Yeshua? Hadn't he smelled that heady liquid?

Served the idiot right for taking a nibble.

A week had passed since that stormy encounter, during which Erota had tried hunting down Ms. Brewster to keep her from enlightening Those Who Resist with a report. She'd failed, however, to find the woman.

Then, only hours ago, the news about Nikki Lazarescu had surfaced. Of course, her entire family line had been wiped out already so there was little chance of her blood being helpful, but local Collectors had been sent to investigate—with no luck. Nikki's remains had vanished from the morgue.

Never mind. Loose ends were inevitable.

Erota fastened her seatbelt for landing and turned her attention to the coveted gold ring. This was what really mattered. Wiped clean of blood, it gleamed in the cabin lights and revealed a Latin phrase encircling the *B* monogram.

Virescit Vulnere Virtus. "Courage grows strong at a wound."

She knew from their cluster's research this had been a favorite saying of Mary Queen of Scots, the same royal who'd funneled aid to the Knights Templar. As for these other etchings within the ring's signet circle, Erota would leave those for her lord to decipher.

After all, he was the Black King.

Lacey

The chain fell away and the motel door swung open, revealing a tall man with kind eyes and sandy-blond hair.

"Clay Ryker."

"Did I hear someone say 'green light'?" Clay let himself in, threw a glance outside, then locked the bolt. "For you, Gina—yes. Jed, you'll have a few errands to take care of first."

"No. I'm ready to see my son."

"Ah-ah. This is all straight from Nickel, so if you have any complaints you take them up personally with your father-in-law."

Jed clenched his teeth.

Gina took her husband's hand and joined him on the edge of the mattress. "We're not doing any of this till we know more. We're done with secrets, okay? We're a family, so we all need to be on the same page."

"Fair enough."

Clay pulled over an armchair and laid it all out.

If things went well, the Akeldama Cluster would be destroyed forever. Though Collectors would still exist in mortal hosts and dangers would abound, Jerusalem's Undead—the ones stained in unholy blood—would no longer be able to identify and terrify those Nistarim set apart to stand in the gap.

If things fell apart, however, hundreds of thousands would be infested, tapped, and drained. The Collection of Souls would brim over, making way for vengeance on horrific terms. Jerusalem's Undead—those enlivened by Nazarene Blood—would crumble beneath the weight.

Dov and Kenny included.

Jacob too.

"So," Clay concluded, "are we in agreement?"

Gina searched her husband's eyes. According to Nickel, it was not *He* Who Resists or *She* Who Resists . . . It was all of them in this together, right? She blinked as Jed took her face in his hands and kissed her with lips that tasted like spearmint gum. He gave a slight nod. She nodded back.

"Yes," Jed said. "We're in."

THE FIFTH SENSE: HEARING

Here we are, kiddies . . . surrounded by a battalion of bloodsuckers who wish no more than to sip freely of my bonded, 100-proof hemoglobin.

—RICHARD MATHESON, *I AM LEGEND*

Later he destroyed those who did not remain faithful.

—*JUDE 1:5*

Journal Entry

September 6

There's nothing quite like the sunset views over the San Juans. But this? The Gulf of Aqaba shoots up between Egypt and Saudi Arabia to the southernmost tip of Israel, and the water here is clear and alive. As we skittered over the bay toward Eilat, we saw dolphins jumping off to our left. You'd think we were on a vacation—and you would be wrong.

At Port Customs, Mom and Dad told me to stay calm, to simply answer the man's questions. With our American passports, we had little trouble. No need for visas. Despite ocean squalls and a rogue wave off the Horn of Africa, Skipper has guided us here all intact. Feels good to have earth back under my feet.

"Watch after yerself," Skipper told me, scowling through his bushy beard.

"Thought that was your job," I kidded him.

"Aye, not this time 'round. Be waitin' with the boat, if ever ya make it back."

Tonight we checked in at the Shelter Guest Hostel. I like it. Clean, nothing fancy. The owners are among Those Who Resist, and that alone is reassuring. I sat in bed with my map, double-checking the bloodstains for helpful clues, but the contents of each seem to end back in June. From this point forward, I guess we're writing our own story, discovering it as we go.

"Should get some rest," Dad told me a minute ago. "First thing tomorrow, we'll be meeting up at the border with your relatives, Sarge and Josee. The board is set, Jacob. You'll be hidden away for a day or so, till it's your turn to step into battle."

Stomach knotting, I nodded and touched the scars on my forehead. "Game on."

CHAPTER
FORTY-NINE

Early September—En Gedi, Israel

The trap was set.

Natira held Isaac captive and vowed to slaughter the old fool if the rest of the Concealed Ones failed to gather in this valley along the Dead Sea's shores.

For weeks now, Cal Nichols had placated his enemy by summoning the Thirty-Six one at a time. These were the Lamed Vov, the Nistarim. Each week more had been added to their number at En Gedi, and tomorrow—in accordance with Nickel's plan—the last would arrive. Would Yeshua then reveal Himself to them in the flesh, as He had long ago? Would their immortal eyes catch yet one more glimpse of Him?

So this would be the battlefield. Seemed fitting enough.

The terrain here hadn't changed much over the millennia. High above, the plateau stretched from the Judean Desert before plunging four hundred meters toward waters said to have restorative powers while being unable to sustain life. Flood runoff and rain sliced from the heights toward the sea, creating a steep valley where waterfalls plummeted and vegetation thrived. Surefooted ibex plied crags on either side, while hawks wheeled overhead on the lookout for prey.

Situated north of Masada, this oasis was rich with history. In the days of ancient Israel, the victories of young David, slayer of the giant Goliath, had stirred reigning King Saul's jealousy. Hunted like a dog, David had fled to En Gedi with his band of faithful men and awaited his chance to step up as rightful king.

Today, Nickel realized, his band of faithful men also waited, hunted by their most lethal of enemies, the Akeldama Collectors.

Two thousand years earlier, the Master Collector had personally inhabited a mortal host—the Man from Kerioth, known also as Judas Iscariot. Upon his death, the Betrayer's polluted blood had seeped into bones beneath the Field of Blood, and the vampiric creatures that arose were impervious to typical man-made implements.

Well then, why not fight bone with bone?

Nickel had known this day would come, and made arrangements with that in mind. Certain variations on a chessboard involved a "poisoned pawn," one that could be trouble if captured, and Nickel had offered Dov and Isaac as such. And Isaac had been taken.

It was only after the fact that Nickel discovered his shipment of MTPs had been intercepted. For the past weeks, sequestered in the caves above this oasis, the gathering Nistarim had been forced to arm themselves by hammering out spikes for the coming confrontation.

"How much longer?" Kenny asked.

"One more day, maybe two." Nickel adjusted the JanSport daypack on his shoulder. "'Course, we can't launch a counterattack till the pieces are in place."

"You think they're on their way?"

"Last thing I heard."

Gina and Jed. Sarge and Josee. Jacob Lazarescu Turney.

Nickel prayed that even now they were moving into position.

Israeli/Jordanian Border

Jacob's parents returned from the Arava Border Control with passports in hand. His mom, the experienced traveler, dealt them out like playing cards, and Jacob opened his to see a round exit stamp in English and Hebrew.

"Thanks," Sarge said, sliding his own into his shirt pocket.

Despite crew-cut hair salted with gray at an early age and an extra bit of weight around the midsection, Sarge seemed unworried about his appearance and Jacob liked him right off.

"Josee and me," the sergeant added, "we had a few minutes to get in our introductions with Jacob. Guess he'll have to wait to meet Esther, since she's with Grandpa and Grandma Addison at the vineyard. Sure as rain, though—you two got yerselves a good kid here."

Josee winked. "And a good-looking one."

Jacob wasn't sure what to think of that, considering his facial markings.

As though reading his thoughts with her turquoise eyes, she said, "You know, those scars of yours are kinda cute. Like freckles in reverse."

The way she said it, Jacob believed her. His great aunt was prettier than he'd expected from his exploration of the scenes within the droplets on his map, and he turned away to hide his reddened face.

Jed put his arm over his son's shoulders. "We should get moving. Onward to the next building."

They passed Israeli guards, male and female, armed with semi-automatic weapons as big as anything Jacob had seen in a movie. Gina was stopped at the metal detector, and her sheathed bronze dagger was removed from her pack.

"A souvenir," she said.

The male guard drew it halfway, touched the blade, gave a disdainful sniff. "It is not so old. Maybe you buy a fake." He shoved it back into her belongings.

"Guess you just never know."

Go in Peace, a sign told them as they headed toward a whitewashed structure and a billboard featuring the King of Jordan and his son. After visas and money exchange, they zigzagged through concrete restraining blocks and found taxis and tour buses in a line. To Jacob, their destination was still a mystery.

A driver strode forward. "You need ride to Aqaba?"

"To Petra," Gina said.

Jacob's eyes widened at the thought of visiting one of the Seven

Wonders of the World. In seclusion on Lummi Island, he'd never imagined going there.

"Petra, yes," the driver said. "No problem. I take."

"Five people in one taxi."

"Two taxis. It is law. Police want dinars if we break."

"Two taxis, one special price," Gina haggled.

"Very special," he said. "I give bounteous price for you."

Ruins of Kerioth-Hezron

Cluster after cluster reported that the last of the Nistarim were emerging from hiding and converging on the Holy Land. What else could they do? One of their own was held hostage, and a ransom would have to be paid.

"How predictable they are," said Lord Natira.

Before him, in this deepest chamber of the Haunt of Jackals, Isaac lay facedown and blindfolded on a slab of stone. Thorns were knotted about his naked body, securing his neck, wrists, and ankles to bolts in the floor. Only two candelabra provided illumination, both set on the opposite end of this room.

Helene entered through the lone gap in the limestone wall and eased up beside Natira. "Son, it seems almost too easy, does it not? We should never underestimate the Almighty's schemes to rescue these knuckle-draggers."

"The Almighty? He sleeps. He pays them no mind."

"You know better than that."

"I know our Master will not lie down in defeat, not with Final Vengeance still to carry out—on our own terms, of course."

"I've long admired your warrior spirit, but don't let it blind you." Helene cast an eye toward the entryway. "With Megiste banished, our numbers are dwindled."

He wrenched her close with a handful of hair. "I will not be spoken down to by a woman. As Akeldama Collectors we're imbued with unparalleled destiny."

She lowered her chin.

"Don't doubt me, Mother. I have the ring that points to Rasputin's cache, and in the next day Kransberg and I will decipher its meaning. We'll unlock that treasure and use it to great effect. In the meantime," he continued, "Erota will call forth our golem army, indestructible and hundreds strong. A few dozen old men and little boys will be no match. By this time tomorrow, the Thirty-Six will be lying in bits and pieces."

"I have no doubt, my son."

"The prophecy must be fulfilled. As the Black King, I'll wage war and take dominion. I'll unlock the Tmu Tarakan and strike at the Concealed Ones already huddled like lambs on the northern fringe of the Valley of Bones. My one concern? This talk of the Lazarescu woman killed and buried in the desert. Why could none of the Collectors find her body? The U.S. Consortium is inept, it seems. I wonder what secrets might've been hiding in Nikki's blood?"

"I know you'd hoped to kill her yourself, but you must let it go."

Natira nudged his foot at one of the thorn bindings and listened to the little man groan as thorns split his skin. Crimson beads spilled down Isaac's hand, each one a perfumed crystal emitting rich aromas, turning this chamber into a spa of titillating promise. That Blood was off limits, yet so warm, so inviting.

Why not strangle the hostage now? It would be easy, very easy.

If even one should fall . . .

Would it be enough, though? Would another rise in his place? This was the reason for calling them all to a central location. Why crush one when the entire lot could be stomped underfoot? And, once discovered, the Crown of Thorns would guarantee success. A secret weapon of sorts.

Natira crouched beside the merchant's ear. "Has your hunger weakened you, your nakedness left you ashamed? If the last of your companions does not arrive soon, I'll keep you here till the end of days, undying, immortal, and in never-ending pain. Is that what you wish?"

"My wish is to be like Yeshua."

"Then you can wear His Crown."

"If that is His will," Isaac said. "We are called for this, to fill up the cup of His sufferings, yes?"

"Fill it you shall."

Natira tugged again at the thorns and watched them slice deeper.

Ancient City of Petra

Jacob's first exposure to Petra had been at the end of *Indiana Jones and the Last Crusade*, where the wizened, robed Crusader sat in one of Petra's caves surrounded by jewel-encrusted chalices, only one of which was the Holy Grail.

According to legend, that grail had once held the Blood of Christ—Nazarene Blood—and it was rumored to offer eternal life.

More truth there than most people realized.

When, however, a Nazi collaborator drank from the wrong cup, he paid the price. His skin twitched, hair snaked from his scalp, and his lips peeled back as wrinkles knifed his face. He began aging rapidly, his skin splitting, shedding, melting away until all that remained was a gaping skeleton. And then that deteriorated as well, leaving nothing but rubble.

The Crusader uttered the classic understatement: "He chose . . . poorly."

In the next day or so, Jacob knew his own purposes would be put to the test. As in the film, eternal life—and mankind's future—would be on the line.

"So, Mom, we're really going to the place from the movie?"

"Yep," Gina said. "Should be there soon."

After a ninety-minute drive along the King's Highway, they wound through sparse terrain to the famed city as the driver dealt out factoids in broken English.

This was one of the best hidden spots in the world—and, being nestled not far from the Dead Sea, a perfect place for them to wait. Two thousand years earlier, spice traders called Nabataeans had happened upon this fortress of gorges and ridges. With one main way in and out, it was easy to defend. They whittled homes from the cliffs, as well as temples, treasuries, theaters, and tombs; yet political rivalries and territorial disputes exacted their toll, and the entire city was lost from public knowledge. In 1812, a Swiss explorer rediscovered the site.

Jacob had seen pics online but was ready to experience the real thing. After paying entrance fees at the booth, he and his parents made the long walk through the Djinn Tombs to the canyon called the *Siq*, the Snake. With the sun climbing, the walls turned to gold, then caramel, then rust.

Great Uncle Sarge waddled ahead of them, his weight carrying him down the incline. Great Aunt Josee jogged along, gesturing to water channels cut from the cliffs.

"How long're we supposed to hide here?" Jacob asked.

"Till tomorrow night. Till you turn thirteen." Gina ran fingers through his hair. "We need to be careful, because Collectors'll be hunting for you."

"Where are we going to sleep?"

"Don't worry. Tourists keep to the main paths, but there are miles of other passages and caves. We'll buy some food from a vendor, a few blankets from the Bedouins, and we'll be good."

"Will anyone else be able to see it?"

"The Letter? Nope, I'm the only one from our group."

"Which isn't exactly fair," Jed said with a grin. "But I can live with it."

Jacob wondered whether they had this all wrong. Maybe the mark would never materialize on his brow. Maybe there was nothing different about him, and they'd all slink back to their regular lives. What if it did appear, though? Would he choose . . . wisely?

Lord, help my unbelief.

The narrow Siq opened before them, unveiling the spectacular pillars and chiseled cornices of Petra's Treasury. Gina and Jed joined Jacob on either side, arms linked across his shoulders, and for the first time in ages it seemed that the weight of the world lifted.

"If the Letter does show up, what then, Mom? Where do we go?"

"Sarge and Josee'll head to Jerusalem to find the Tmu Tarakan."

"They have a way to open it?"

"Sarge has the black chess king, remember? The one Lenin stole from Rasputin. And Josee's Fabergé egg will be their compass. With the photos Jillanne Brewster took of her ring for insurance purposes, your grandpa has an idea of the general area where they should start looking."

"My grandpa. As in Nickel."

"Youngest looking grandpa ever," Jed chimed in.

"And what about us? Where will we go?"

"For a late-night swim," Gina said. "Now stop with the questions."

After hours of sightseeing, they took a forty-minute trek beyond the trail's end into the honeycombed hills. A Nabataean had carved a simple abode in the wall of a ravine, replete with entryway and open square window. Though whiffs of animal urine hung in the air, they were not likely to be disturbed here.

"Looks good to me," Jed said.

They snacked. Sang a few songs. Josee led Sarge in a set of fifty jumping jacks while mosquitoes buzzed in the twilight. Before bed, Josee doused each person in repellent, then sprayed around the stone openings.

"Doesn't hurt to be prepared," she said.

Throughout the night, those bloodsucking squadrons hovered just outside.

CHAPTER
FIFTY

When Jacob woke, the sun was cresting the hills, spilling down into the ravine. He lifted his head from his wadded jacket and sat up. Buckets of lead seemed strapped to his shoulders, causing him to stagger as he stood. Though aches and pains were commonplace for him, today's seemed more aggravated.

"You get some shut-eye?" Sarge asked from the corner.

"Slept pretty good."

"Ya look a little wobbly there."

Jacob didn't want to gripe. "Not much of a morning person, I guess."

"I hear you, kiddo."

His gaze moved to his parents, curled in each others' arms near the doorway where they'd vowed to ward off attackers. Right now they were snoring.

Another invisible weight crushed down upon Jacob's shoulders. He doubled over, wincing. Gina had warned him about this, but how much heavier could it get? Maybe he was the wrong guy for the job.

In the early afternoon, their group of five threaded back in amongst the Petra tourists, bought food at the outdoor café, and ordered Turkish coffee served in small cups. Once, on the island, Jacob had tried instant coffee and spit it out. This stuff, though, was thick, rich, and potent.

Gina elbowed him. "You like it?"

"Love it."

"'Course you do," his dad said. "By the time this day's over, you'll be a man—hair on your chest and everything."

"C'mon, Jed, what're you talking about?" Gina flicked his earlobe. "You have a chest patch about the size of a postage stamp."

"That's right. One hundred percent U.S. Male."

"Hardy-har-har."

Grinning, Jacob knew this was the banter he'd missed over the years.

"Well," Sarge said, waggling an ebony chess king, "looks like Josee and I oughta get moving. We got ourselves some treasure huntin' to do in Jerusalem."

"See you on the other side," Gina said.

"Whoa." Josee clutched the vial at her throat. "That sounds too doom-and-gloomy for me. It's already hard enough being away from our daughter."

"Sorry, Josee. I was referring to the Dead Sea."

"Right. Like that sounds any better."

Gina hugged her. "If all goes as planned, Nickel should be rendez-vousing with you guys around dusk, so you'll be in good hands. Meanwhile, Jed, you better make our travel arrangements. It's going to cost us extra, but haggle anyway."

Jacob tried to disguise another stab of pain.

Ruins of Kerioth-Hezron

At sunset, Rosh Hashanah would begin. Lord Natira knew the Almighty's beloved Jews marked their new year at this time and examined their souls in view of coming Final Vengeance. On that day, they believed, the Messiah would stand with one foot on either side of the Kidron Valley—known to some as the Valley of Jehosophat—and dispense judgment according to each person's deeds.

"'Vengeance is mine,' says the Lord . . ."

How preposterous. The sheer conceit of their Oh-So-Just Deity.

Natira was staring off over the ruins, tan and dusty in the midday sun, and charting his strategies for the next twelve hours when his mother joined him on the slope and informed him his son was missing.

"He told no one he was leaving?"

"Kransberg is not one to share such things," Helene pointed out. "He has always carried out his activities in private."

"His activities? Is this a pattern you're only now reporting to me?"

"He's made a habit of wandering the tunnels at night, or so says Domna. He does seem fascinated, my lord, with the vintage now aging in Jerusalem."

"Fresh infections, ripe souls—they're our cluster's nourishment."

"He appreciates a good drink, yes."

"I'll find him," Natira said. "Today we have a task to fulfill."

The cluster leader did find his son within the hour, trekking through the flood-hewn tunnels that burrowed north.

"Son, where do think you're going?"

With his back turned, Kransberg hesitated. Untrimmed growth bristled on his neck, and his spine was locked at an awkward angle. In his gnarled fingers, a glint of gold revealed the beast's purpose.

"You mean to find Rasputin's hoard without me, is that it? You think you can access the treasure and bend it to your own desires?"

Kransberg did not move.

"Give me the ring."

Nothing.

"Hand it over and we'll go hunting together. I understand your desire, but don't think you can do this without me. I am your king, your father, your lord."

Kransberg shuffled around and offered up the signet ring with its etchings and inscriptions. From a string about his neck, that old cinched pouch of his now dangled in plain view, its leathery surface marred by an unidentified bulge.

"And what's this, son?"

Kransberg offered no information.

Recalling the images of Trudi Ubelhaar wandering through the woods, Natira stepped closer and loosened the pouch's opening. He lifted an onyx chessman into view, the six points of its odd crown visible in the light. "Hmm. A gift from your mother, I take it?"

Kransberg seethed.

Natira caressed the black monarch and recalled those moments in

Trudi's cell, siphoning memories from the bloodflow in her foot. She had met with a Russian fellow. A man familiar with Engine 418. Had he discovered the duplicate key that was rumored to exist? Had he surrendered it to her?

This was that key. It had to be.

Wearing a greedy smile, Natira said, "Well, how propitious. My old, feckless lover serves a purpose after all. Did she tell you what this was for, hmm?"

Protruding brows shaded Kransberg's eyes from the glow of the wall sconces, and the flare of his nostrils revealed indignation.

"Here. No need to be miffed, my son." Natira slid the figurine back into the pouch, then slapped an arm over his son's shoulder, digging deep with his pincers. "I'll allow you to hold on to it for us, since we are in fact partners in this. You're my likeness, and you've been delivered to me according to the prophecy. Bah. We've narrowed the options over the past weeks, made a few missteps, but today the Tmu Tarakan shall be ours."

En Gedi

In this cave cooled by the nearby waterfall's spray, Cal Nichols slid chisel and hammer into his daypack beside his cherished shofar. How much longer till he blew that battle horn? When would their Thirty-Fourth member arrive, and would the Nazarene be close behind? Throughout the previous night, the Concealed Ones had toiled in the Valley of Bones, and Nickel was pleased with their work—ambushes, obstacles, stashed munitions—yet couldn't shake his worries.

Would Gina and Jed follow his instructions? Would Jacob make the journey unscathed? Even now, Sarge and Josee should be headed this way.

"You okay?"

Closing his pack, he turned toward Dov and Kenny. "I'm fine."

The two were young men now, one still somber and focused, the other carefree. They seemed to get along despite the decade spent apart, and Nickel recalled the bond that existed between those with the Letter. The Nistarim bore no pride in their calling, only a sense of purpose and unshakable unity.

"Are you worried about Isaac?" Dov said. "I wish they had taken me instead."

"No." Nickel shook his head. "No, don't even say that."

"Or me," Kenny said.

"Stop. Both of you. We knew this time would come, and we knew it could be any of you. You two are healthy, strong, ready to fight. Isaac would want it this way. Don't get weighed down with thoughts of his . . . his situation. That's one of our enemy's tactics."

"We attack and defend, with no fear and no regrets."

"That's right, Dov. I bet Gina taught you that while playing chess."

The dolphin trainer from Eilat nodded.

"Anyway," Nickel said, "it's too late to turn back now."

"We'll never turn back," Kenny stated. "Isn't that right, Dov? Never."

A commotion stirred at the mouth of the cave, and the three of them moved forward to find their counterpart from Nigeria had arrived intact. He was short and lean, his skin the color of coffee. The others cheered at the sight of him, and his wide smile seemed to brighten the cave.

This left only the Nazarene.

Nickel, considering his own failures, wondered how that would go.

The Concealed Ones' joy was stifled by the Nigerian's announcement that hundreds of golems were creeping in this direction. Though lumbering and massive, their shape and color camouflaged them in the desert terrain as they tried to avoid the detection of civilians and Israeli forces. At the present rate, he guessed, they would reach the cliffs of Masada by nightfall.

So the monsters had been unleashed.

For the next hour, Nickel evaluated this latest intel and their best response. Through the millennia, the Thirty-Six had encountered Collectors in bestial forms and demon-ravaged hosts, yet none had faced a foe quite like this. Formed from earth and sand, brought to life by water and blood, golems had traditionally been servants of rabbis, whereas these were foot soldiers of the Akeldama.

His ruminations were interrupted by a tug at his arm.

"Nickel?" Dov said. "He's here. He wants to talk to you."

"Yeah, I saw him arrive."

"I mean Yeshua. I can't see Him but I can hear His voice. He came in on the Nigerian's heels, and I'm told He's outside now beneath the trees."

"Me? You're sure He asked for me?"

"By name."

Heart racing, Nickel moved between the Concealed Ones. They had not all been in one place since that fateful flight from Portland to Seattle in late 1971, and the energy was palpable as men bowed, shook hands, and exchanged stories.

He slipped from the cave and cut beneath the large, green fronds that overarched the dirt path. With immortal eyes adjusting to dappled shadows, he found himself face-to-face with the Nazarene, Firstborn of the Undead.

"Yeshua, you came."

"I'm never far away. I thought the men should be reminded of that as they go into battle—with the Blood I've already shed, of course."

Nickel swallowed. "Of course."

A silence ensued, during which Yeshua's eyes seared into Cal Nichols' soul. Only small-minded, religious sycophants portrayed Him as doe-eyed and impotent. Doe-eyed? Hardly the case. His irises, a dark honey color, roiled with intensity for seconds that seemed like hours, then softened at last. This man with rugged features lifted His pierced hands and pulled Nickel into an embrace.

"You've done well, Cal."

"Most of these guys call me Nickel."

"You're worth more than that."

Cal wanted to believe it, wanted to make those words true. Secure in the Nazarene's arms, he felt a deep calm envelope him—peace beyond understanding, love without restraint. His eyes swam with moisture, and he touched his forehead to the Nazarene's chest as droplets spilled down his cheeks. How had he ever doubted, ever strayed?

"I wish I could guarantee your success," Yeshua said, "but the Power of Choice can be nerve wracking at times, letting my children grow and make mistakes."

"I . . . I've made mine." Nickel blinked and took a step back. Through the branches of a balsam tree, the Dead Sea appeared placid and cobalt blue this evening, while the lights of a Jordanian town flickered on the opposite shore. "Don't You ever get upset thinking of all that's been done to You? The betrayal. Your arrest. The way people demanded Barabbas' release so You could be nailed up instead."

"Romans, Gentiles, rich and poor, the Jewish high priests . . . The guilt was certainly spread around, wasn't it?" Mischief glimmered in the Nazarene's honey eyes. "Well, don't forget I was born a Jew. True, all sorts played a part in my sacrifice, but I chose to accept that role. It's all behind us now, though, isn't it?"

"We still have enemies to face."

"Fight bravely, my friend. This particular battle will be over by morning. If that first miracle of mine—water into wine—was any indication, you can imagine the celebration on that day we gather as one to drink the New Wine."

Shifting his pack, Nickel blew air from his lips. "I can't wait."

"Me either. You'll be there soon, which I know will make Dinah glad, and I'll have a new name waiting for you—worth more than a nickel, I promise."

"Thank You." Man, his throat felt dry.

"I need you to do something for Me."

"Anything."

"As we speak, Natira and son are in the Holy City, closing in on their coveted relic." Yeshua combed back His hair, revealing dotted scars along His brow. "In the wrong hands, that Crown could be calamitous."

"Your Crown of Thorns."

"Don't believe for a moment I didn't feel those barbs. Each one was a fang stabbing into my thoughts, my skin, injecting venom from that Serpent of Old."

"The Master Collector."

"None other."

"Listen," Nickel said, "Sarge and Josee crossed over the border into Eilat this afternoon, and I'm supposed to meet them on their way to Jerusalem. They have the key and the compass so that we can be first to grab that Crown. After studying pictures of the Templar ring, I believe Rasputin hid it near the Mount of Olives."

"Gethsemane, to be exact."

"Okay, I wish I'd known that a lot earlier. Now it could be too late."

"Answers come when you need them, no sooner." Yeshua leveled His gaze in response to Nickel's dour expression. "Don't worry, my friend—if you leave in the next few moments, you may yet beat Natira to the site."

"It's over an hour's drive, and I—"

"You're no slave to the Separation, are you? Bridge the gap."

"It's too far. I've never—"

"Cast fear aside, Cal. A few final instructions, so listen carefully, and then I want you to bridge like you've never bridged before."

Jerusalem

"See here?" said Lord Natira. "It's no wonder we failed to recognize it before."

From the Mount of Olives, he and Kransberg compared the ring to the convergence of the Kidron and Hinnom Valleys outside the Old City walls. These famed ramparts had once extended farther south, thus influencing the engraving's details, and the signet circle—the X on the map, as it were—indicated a spot just down this slope.

Below the hillside graveyard, stone walls and pitted trees partitioned various religious sites—Mary's Tomb, the Church of St. Mary Magdalene, the Basilica of Agony—and many tourists professed they felt something special here.

Nauseating, all of it.

Or so Natira had thought up to this juncture.

This evening, for the first time, he felt something too, as he surveyed the domes of St. Mary Magdalene's, bulging black against the sky. "Of course," he said. "Where else would Rasputin hide his relics but near a structure built by the tsars?"

Beckoned by riches, the revenant and his offspring picked their way between the tombs while Kyria hovered in their wake, using a blackbird as a host.

Ahead, the Garden of Gethsemane waited.

Ancient City of Petra

As the skies turned tangerine, Jacob, Gina, and Jed hiked back to their hideout in the ravine. Rosh Hashanah would start once the land grew dark, and Jacob knew he would cross the line into his thirteenth year.

A child no more. A man of the law.

And a man of the Letter?

He huddled with his parents around a fire in the cave, letting the smoke ward off mosquitoes as they went over the plans for this evening. Back on Skipper's yacht, they'd spent time catching up on the lost years between them, and he would never forget those days at sea together, fishing, reading, singing, even diving overboard in the Atlantic Ocean on a serene windless morn.

Relaxation was now over. Time for war.

"Be sure to seal your stuff in the bag I gave you," his mom said. "We could be going for a long swim."

"For my birthday?"

"The three of us." His dad tussled his hair. "A family excursion."

"Let me guess: the Dead Sea."

"Jacob, Collectors are watching for you at the borders, even the airport. Nickel says this is the best way to sneak into Israel undetected. There's no marine life to worry about nibbling on your toes, and the water's so buoyant you couldn't sink if you tried."

"Sounds easy enough."

"You'll be dehydrated from all that salt, though."

"And, since we won't be able to dive for cover, we'll be fully exposed. For now," Gina said, "try to get some rest. We could have a long night ahead."

"Yes, Mom."

It was dark when Gina shook Jacob from sleep. She was beaming as she gazed at his forehead. "Just as we thought," she whispered.

He sat up. "Does this mean I should grab my towel?"

CHAPTER
FIFTY-ONE

Jerusalem

Woozy and depleted, Cal Nichols settled among the olive groves. An evening breeze fanned his hair, while the scent of candles wafted from a nearby shrine. He had never bridged more than a kilometer—off those cliffs into Ramon Crater—and this journey had lasted many times that.

Exhilarating, yes. And exhausting.

With his last reserves of strength, he propped himself against a tree trunk. Crenellated walls hovered golden and stalwart along the Kidron valley, yet he knew Jerusalem was under siege. Pain was written into these stones, scrawled into the hearts of these inhabitants. This was the epicenter of a battle for souls, and the city's wounds rippled across the globe.

Christian, Muslim, Jew . . .

They had all suffered here, caused suffering here.

The City of Peace knew little peace, her citizens choked by the tendrils that snaked up from the Betrayer's birthplace. Nickel had seen the recent proliferation of vines at bus stops, kebab stands, markets, and places of piety. They curled from the soil, sapping creativity, feeding addictions, inciting violence. To cut these victims loose, he needed to chop the thorns at their roots.

Footsteps . . . coming near.

Nickel's ears picked out two sets of them—one, even and quiet; the other, heavy and dragging. Could it be Sarge and Josee? Had they found their way?

"Here, this should be it," a gravelly voice was saying. "Help me push aside these rocks."

Lord Natira examined the incline behind the Church of St. Mary Magdalene. Though trees, caves, and grottos clogged the area, the signet ring zeroed in on a set of grave mounds butted against the hill.

"That way," he said.

Kransberg started forward.

"No." Natira jerked him back a step. "I will lead. Yes, we hold the old spice merchant hostage, and yes, our troops are on the march, but Cal Nichols is a sly one. To ensure success we need to 'unlock riches to strengthen this campaign.' I am that Black King, so don't you forget your place or I'll tear out your heart and eat it whole this time."

Kransberg hunched low, his form matching the pitted olive trunks.

"Here, this should be it," Natira said. "Help me push aside these rocks."

Kransberg applied his shoulder to the pile. It teetered, then fell away to reveal weeds and a flat grave marker.

"Very well," he said. "Let's try this next one."

His son threw a large foot into limestone bricks, disrupting pebbles and ants. When another kick crumbled the right side of the mound, blackness yawned from the opening, and Natira saw that it was a thick iron door set into the slope.

Nothing to draw attention. It appeared undisturbed.

"Nice work," he said, slapping his son's chest.

Kransberg nodded toward the church, where a Russian Orthodox monk walked the path, head down in meditation. Did he have nowhere else to go? His mumbling grated on Natira's nerves, that ceaseless praying to the Almighty.

Best to stay patient, he reminded himself. No reason to rush.

Master, I'm at your service. I know my labor is not in vain.

Cape Costigan, Jordan

The sea was brooding and ominous. Jed, Gina, and Jacob gathered in the lee of a salt-rimmed bank while the lights of Israeli hotels on the opposite side streaked the surface like oils on black canvas.

"There's not much of a current, so we'll make good time. Just stay close and stay quiet," Jed whispered. "Sound carries over the water."

"And don't cut yourself on these rocks. The salt'll sting like crazy."

"Okay, Mom. Okay, Dad."

"Oh." Gina waggled her water bottle. "And make sure to keep hydrated."

Despite the gravity of this moment—or because of it—Jacob couldn't hide his grin. "Thanks for all the advice," he said. "Remember, I'm a man now."

"That you are," his dad said. "Let's go."

The Turney family excursion had started with a westward trek through the gorges of Petra to a taxi waiting, as prearranged, off a remote road. Only Gina and Jacob could see the Unfallen that hovered outside, blocking the car from view as it raced north along the salt flats. Together in the backseat, they partook of the Nazarene Blood before being dropped at this tongue of land that jutted from the Dead Sea's Jordanian side. The driver accepted his large tip with a larger smile—"So long as it keeps him quiet for one night," Gina had commented.

Jacob stepped into the sea, his foot stirring the surface viscosity. The temperature was mild. With no fish to be caught, there were no fishing boats about. He waded to his waist, then eased onto his back, where he bobbed without doing a thing.

"We all good?" Jed checked.

"All good," Jacob and Gina said in a hush.

Shores of the Dead Sea, Israel

Erota's scheming had come to fruition. No Megiste to stand in her way.

No Barabbas to gawk at her. True, she'd been embarrassed many weeks earlier by her shared assignment with Barabbas, by food flung into her face, and by the henchman's convulsing body on the Silverton pavement. With the signet ring, however, she'd earned back her favor.

As evidenced by Lord Natira's summons this morning.

"I want you and the cluster to gather the golem army," he had told her. "Guide them quietly from Ramon Crater to the shores of the Dead Sea. There, in that valley between Masada and En Gedi, we will crush the Concealed Ones."

"And these golems will obey my commands?"

"I'm told they owe you allegiance, since you supplied them life via scrolls stained with blood."

She bowed. "Only to assist you, my lord. I meant no disloyalty."

"I've issued the order that your word is now second only to mine."

She bowed again, silken hair draping his sandals.

"By nightfall, Erota, have them in position along Masada's base. Do not attack until I appear with my prophesied gift from Rasputin. A month or two ago, Collectors in the Pacific Northwest claimed they saw Gina parading about with that young husband of hers, so we—"

"She's dead, though. You confirmed it yourself."

"I may have been fooled once, but this time we'll put an end to it."

It was nightfall now, and, as instructed, Erota's troops encompassed the monolith where Zealots and the dagger men known as *Sacarii* had made their stand against oppressors. Hadn't Judas been one of the Sacarri?

How serendipitous. All the betrayals leading her to this point.

She bounded over the rocks, rechecking the placement of her clay monsters. They were tireless statues, prepared to stand silent for centuries or go on the attack in mere seconds. Crouched nearby in the mouth of Wadi Mishmar, Domna, Dorotheus, Hermione, Shelamzion, and Matrona waited. Farther back and out of view, Helene stood guard over their prisoner, prepared to dice Isaac's frail form with a few tugs on his razor-edged snares.

Before Erota, the Valley of Bones lay barren in the starlight, except for scattered boulders, acacia trees, and dry streambeds. Cliffs towered along the western perimeter, while the Dead Sea hemmed in the eastern fringe. So this would be the site of their final showdown, the plains upon which the Akeldama Cluster established their superiority.

A few kilometers to the north, En Gedi sheltered the Nistarim. Erota's superior vision detected movement. Shapes of men cut back and forth from the lush oasis to a small rise, where mounds began to form. Defensive barriers? Stacked armaments? If her foes launched a preemptive strike, she had no instructions as to what to do.

Where was Natira anyway? Lost or banished? How long should she wait before ordering an attack?

In the gloom, the Nistarim kept working.

Jerusalem

The moment the monk disappeared around the corner, Natira turned back to the small door in the slope. He swept away rubble and kneeled before the obstacle, but doubts flitted through his thoughts. Bah. Why question his place here?

He was the Black King.

Prophecy incarnate.

Examining the keyhole in the iron, his hopes surged once more. The opening was oddly shaped, and he knew it would require an unusual key.

"Come, my likeness," he said, gesturing to his son. "Give me what's there in your pouch and let's open this door."

Kransberg gave no response.

"Here. Do it now. We don't have all night."

An inky rebellion bloomed in the beast's black eyes, and his bent form rose to full height. He said, "You are not the Black King."

"What?" Natira glowered. "Stop your muttering."

"I am the prophecy."

"Yes, you're my key to this door, and—"

"I am the King."

With that statement, Kransberg joined both hands and swung them clublike into his father's face. The blow caught Natira while still on his knees. His lip tore back along the left side of his nose, and a broken tooth shot into the back of his throat. Kransberg's backswing rocked his father's head into the slope, smearing his cheek and ear against the rock.

Natira coughed out the tooth. Dove for his son's legs. With wood stumps for thighs, Kransberg paid no attention and hammered his fists into the top of Natira's cranium. The creature's fury burst forth with each shot. A primal scream spewed from his lungs in a shower of spittle.

Despite red-black spirals in his head, Natira understood that Kransberg meant to destroy him. He could banish the boy, could he not? Send him packing?

Yet that seemed so cowardly. No, this was father to son, man to man. Ever since the Master Collector's mutiny, since the defiance of King David's own son, Absalom, this streak had run deep through the male race, and the one way to suppress it was through brute force—a method Natira knew well.

He shook off the pain that his host insisted was life threatening, marshaled his strength, and encircled his son's knees with his arms. In a single Herculean effort, he yelled, lifted, and drove the body backward. They landed hard in the dirt in the shadows of this garden, where ultimate betrayal had been born.

Kransberg tried to roll his hips, to thrust Natira away, but his father used his left hand to pin down that squirming abdomen while his right slammed up into that hairy throat. With pincers wrenching at Kransberg's Adam's apple, he pulled himself face-to-face with his son.

"You are my likeness," he hissed. "Nothing more."

"I am the Black—"

Natira stifled that sentence with a kiss on the mouth. His fangs raked his offspring's lower lip as he pulled away, producing twin crimson spurts.

"How do you like it, this taste of betrayal? Only I fit the stipulations of the prophecy. Only I am 'from the holy ground,' the one who takes dominion 'from the Haunt of Jackals.'"

"Angel's Rest is my . . . holy ground," Kransberg sputtered.

"What? No, don't be a fool. I found you at Devil's Rest."

"I have the key. I will take dominion."

"Are you challenging me, son?"

With a howl, Kransberg plowed his fist into his father's torn ear.

Oh yes, yes, yes, Natira had to admit that hurt. Hurt so good. What was pain but a diversion from one's goals? It removed the weak, honed the strong.

He lifted his head, stared into black eyes that mirrored his own, then slammed his forehead into Kransberg's broad frontal lobe. The impact was bone shuddering, brain rattling, and he did it again even harder.

The sheer agony. Ah, what joyous torment.

He gave a third head butt, then stumbled to his feet, hooked his son by his hairy pate, and dragged him to the base of the iron door. Cackling like the blackbird in the branches, he yanked the pouch from that gnarled neck and fished inside for the onyx chess piece that would give him access to long-hidden riches.

Why, thank you, dear Trudi. I always knew you were good for something more than a romp in a Nazi fortress.

CHAPTER
FIFTY-TWO

Nickel's plan had succeeded. While the monk passed by, he had released his grasp on the one realm and stretched toward the other, bridging beneath the garden's canopy of branches and thus sneaking behind the distracted Collectors' backs.

His aim was true. He passed through black iron.

Found himself in the darkness of the Tmu Tarakan.

He felt slightly ridiculous. Objects dug into his buttocks and lower back, while the cool touch of metal greeted his hand. Those were coins, weren't they? And was that a crucifix? His fingers found a jeweled box that he knew must be a reliquary. What sort of holy treasures had the Knights Templar stored here?

A stench pervaded the small cave, a combination of mustiness and mildewed cloth and—

Were these bones beneath him?

He shoved himself away from the skeleton that seemed large enough to be human. How had *that* ended up in here? He was wondering if he had even bridged into the right spot, when his fingers lighted upon the cold barrel of a revolver—more bizarre by the moment.

He took calming breaths. He was spent. Twice in one night he had bridged, and the drain from his physical form was immense.

From without he heard arguing, clambering, and a hard thud against the door. He inched forward for a peek through the keyhole, but the darkness outside nearly matched that within.

Someone was cackling.

Nickel knew that sound all too well. It stirred memories of his fight with this Akeldama Collector decades ago, while his own son, Reggie, lay trapped beneath water and river debris. Here they were again, only an arm's length apart.

He squinted at the keyhole, where a key of some sort poked through and fought with the mechanism. In this cramped space, the scrape of metal was amplified, and he knew his nemesis was trying to get in. He felt about for his pack—his trusty JanSport with its hammer, MTPs, and shofar—then realized he'd left it at the base of the olive tree.

Should Natira open this door, Nickel would be easy prey.

Nah, not so quick. Where's the Crown of Thorns?

He searched through coinage, heirlooms, and icons—the significance of which tended to be exaggerated. The power was not in the symbols themselves so much as in the hearts of those who believed. Of course, Collectors believed, and even trembled, at the symbolism of metal tent pegs and Nehushtan bronze.

Except for Barabbas. He alone had survived that revered blade, according to Unfallen reports from the night of his disappearance in Silverton.

It was news Nickel had dealt with himself.

Now, as his fingers skimmed the cave floor, something scraped his wrist.

The Crown . . . This, of all relics, signified something potent. Each thorn, each infection, the stings of pain and death—all had been woven together and shoved down upon the Nazarene's scalp. The power of His Blood had confronted, had counteracted, each one of the thorns, while assimilating the worst of their venom.

What better weapon for the evil now crouched on the doorstep?

More rattling. More grating in the long-undisturbed lock.

Nickel ran his hand along the desired object, careful to avoid the briars with their iniquity-laden stains, and his fingers encountered something spindly-legged and alive.

A spider?

Panic shot through him as the thing scampered up his forearm, and

he reminded himself it was only a freak occurrence that Dinah had succumbed to a creature such as this, an aging woman susceptible to the
venom.

How he missed her.

He flailed his arm, knocking over something heavy with a dull clang.
Had the Collector heard that? Would he assume it was nothing but a rat?

At the door, Natira was snickering. "Ah, here we go."

The iron screeched open from its granite frame and ushered in the
dim light of the stars. Nickel blinked, noted Natira's astonished gaze, then
grabbed for the nearby tangle of thorns and shoved it toward his enemy's
face. In a lightning-fast reaction, the revenant pushed back from the opening and tripped over Kransberg, who lay groaning in the dirt.

Kransberg . . . the one who had attacked Isaac in his shop.

Nickel stamped the Crown of Thorns into the beast's thick skull.
Kransberg's entire body jolted as remnants of that Blood sizzled into his
skin. He tried to lift himself. He frothed. Vomited. On hands and knees
he plucked himself loose from the Crown he had no right to wear.

Behind him, Natira stood. He glared at Nickel in the doorway and
growled—a throaty, feral sound.

"Is this your revenge?" he said. "Cal, the Oh-So-Forlorn? You think I
care for this boy? Ha. I'm a king, and all I want is that Crown."

"I'll slam this door shut, and you'll need hours to dig around it."

"We shall see." The vampire closed his hand over the black chessman
in the lock and tore it away. Lofting the knobby implement, he said, "You
can take my son from me, but you can't deny me my destiny."

At his feet, Kransberg shriveled into a ball of coarse hair and dust.

Too weak to flee, Nickel shrank back into the Tmu Tarakan. He was
trapped, with these Blood-dipped thorns alone to hold off his enemy, and
he could only hope Sarge and Josee had lost their way.

Groaning, his arm flopped into the nearby bones.

The revolver . . .

His hand located the weapon, took hold of the wooden grip. He
edged to the opening and cocked back the hammer.

Natira was ten meters away, seated on a limestone block, twiddling
the black king in his fingers as he leered in Nickel's direction. His eyes

widened. He seemed perplexed by the appearance of a firearm, yet the scowl on his lips revealed an utter lack of fear. He was undead, right? What damage could a bullet inflict?

Nickel fired twice before the gun jammed. The thunderous noise and recoil caused his first shot to go wide, but the second found its mark and obliterated Natira's lone key to this treasure in a shower of splintered black onyx.

The vampire shrieked. Emerald flames roared through his black pupils as he charged the opening of the Tmu Tarakan.

Cal Nichols dropped the weapon, hooked the door with his thumb.

And pulled it shut.

Shores of the Dead Sea

Erota observed a solitary truck winding north along the shore. Though it passed the En Gedi turnoff, headed perhaps for Qumran or Jericho, the swath of its headlights brushed over the items stacked by the Nistarim. She saw sparkles in that instant, like the fireflies from her days in Atlanta, and she recognized the objects for what they were.

Those cursed MTPs!

One had split her father's temple.

In days of yore, another had nailed mighty Sisera to the earth.

She was confused, though. Hadn't her lord intercepted such items at the docks in Eilat? It seemed the Concealed Ones had been working overtime these past few days, and she wondered how much longer she should let them replenish their stock.

Where was Natira?

His absence was no real surprise. He'd always been self-seeking, leaving their cluster while he served his own purposes. Even with Erota's discovery of the lost prophecy, and of Natira's part in it, he had abandoned her to go hunting in the Pacific Northwest. Always on his own terms, his own timetable.

Erota brought olive-skinned hands to her lips, done waiting on the vows of a fickle male. If she failed to act, their cluster would be ambushed. She raised her voice from the foot of Masada's bulwarks and gave the command:

"Crush the Concealed Ones!"

Her clay statues came to life on either side, their huge red feet shaking the earth as they rumbled forward.

Jacob had never been so scared. With night skies stretched high across this rift, he felt small and vulnerable as he kicked his legs and fanned his arms through the waters. He imagined creatures of the deep coming up for him or falcons spearing him from above with sharp beaks and talons. He tasted salt on his lips. His breathing filled his ears.

Lord, I'm weak on my own . . .

But this sea was lifeless, wasn't it? Nothing to fear. The ripples from his and his parents' bodies lapped at the nearing shoreline—En Gedi, according to Jed, on the north end of the Valley of Bones.

Why the scary name? Please, give me boldness.

Each kilometer across the sea's surface had increased the weight of his sorrows, his pain, until he was certain the saltwater's buoyancy would fail him. He would sink. He'd drop into the belly of this ancient sea and lie salt encrusted, immobile, with a portion of immortal blood somehow keeping him alive in a murky grave.

He unscrewed his water bottle, drank, then swam on. How did the others do it? Only two or three hours bearing the Tav on his brow, and already he felt overwhelmed.

"Watch the rocks," his dad said in muted tones. "Some are pretty rough."

"We made it, Jacob. You okay?"

He found his footing on the pebbled shore and rose alongside his parents, unable to see over the gradual incline. He nodded, trying to hide his discomfort.

"Here," Gina said. "We need to clean off this residue."

They took turns rinsing with fresh bottles from the sealed bags tied to their waists. After they toweled off, Jacob pulled on jeans and a black long-sleeved shirt. Gina strapped her dagger in place. Jed slung a pouch of MTPs over his shoulder.

"Mom? Dad?" The ground seemed to be quavering, and he hoped it was only the recent exertion throwing off his equilibrium. "Do you feel that?"

CHAPTER
FIFTY-THREE

Jerusalem

Natira was clawing at the Tmu Tarakan's door when he felt the soil tremble beneath him. He would have figured it for a seismic tremor except that he knew of a more logical explanation encamped thirty or forty kilometers from here.

What was going on? Why had Erota defied his orders?

"I told you to wait," he yelled.

Or maybe she was responding to an offensive by the Concealed Ones.

He bellowed, kicking the iron with both feet and pounding the rock with his hands in a last-ditch effort to break into Rasputin's cache. It refused to budge. This limestone and granite slope had been here since the days of Abraham, and it would require tools, machinery, or explosives to compromise it.

"I want that Crown!"

Golem forces were on the move at the Dead Sea while he rampaged like a madman against metal and stone. There was no time to wait on excavation crews, not while his cluster members were entering combat. He was their king. He should be there to lead them on the fields of battle.

Give me direction, my Master. How best do I redeem this situation?

As always, he heard no reply. Redemption seemed absent from the Master Collector's vocabulary.

Lord Natira stared at that square iron door. It was still unfathomable that Cal Nichols had accessed the treasure and armed himself. The sneaky runt. Well, let him rot here while the warrior joined his battalion, while he let old Isaac swing from a thorny noose. If the death of one was not enough to do the trick, Natira knew where the rest resided. They were the Not-So-Concealed Ones now.

Countermanding his thoughts, Cal spoke through that blasted key-hole: "You can't win, you hear me out there? You may be the Black King, but in this Sovereign Game you'll get checkmated."

"Shut your mouth, two-legger."

"Always happens that way when you attack too soon."

"Oh, and who's the one hiding now? The valiant knight runs for cover as soon as the conflict begins, is that it?"

"You're still a king without a crown."

Natira growled and rammed the door with his foot again, then turned to the black-beaked host in the nearby branches. "Kyria," he said, "fly to my mother at Wadi Mishmar and give the signal."

The hostage had served his purpose. Time now for Isaac to hang.

Shores of the Dead Sea

Jacob, Gina, and Jed sprinted to the small rise outside En Gedi, where they were welcomed by men arming themselves from stacks of MTPs. Dov Amit and Kenny Preston took turns hugging Gina, and her eyes clouded.

To Jacob, their Letters shone like electric-blue beacons, thrilling him even as he faced the reality of their predicament. He'd studied maps and books of the area, yet nothing prepared him for the monsters now marching from Masada's battlements.

No wonder the ground shook. No wonder his adrenaline surged.

"How long till they get here?" he said.

"Three minutes, maybe four. Glad you made it," Kenny said, handing over an allotment of seven spikes. "Jacob, meet your fellow Nistarim."

A chorus of acceptance greeted him.

Followed by a human wail.

Moving at the speed of sound, the prolonged cry spilled from a wadi to the south and rolled ahead of the advancing golems. It spoke of torture, of personal affliction, and this remote landscape seemed to amplify the gasp that signaled the end.

"Isaac?" Dov froze. *"Noooo."*

As one, the entire group of Nistarim buckled. They pulled Jacob into their midst and linked arms, seeking strength in unity as their muscles weakened and their backs bowed. Many shed tears without shame.

"Jacob, it is good you came," said a sinewy black man. "You are the last one chosen to stand in the gap. This is what the Nazarene told us earlier."

"He was here?" Jacob could only imagine.

"He was. He still is. You do not see Him, but He reveals Himself in His time."

"Use this." Dov nudged forward and tapped the vial around Jacob's neck. "If you see our immortals fall, revive them. As for the mortals—me, Kenny, and a few others—we are the most vulnerable, so we have to take precautions."

"What about my dad?"

From his pouch, Jed withdrew two metal pegs and fitted one in each fist. "Ready to go," he said. His hands were shaking.

"I'll keep an eye on him," Gina said with a half grin.

Golem troops approached through the dun-colored valley, with its cliffs to the west and seas to the east. The ground rumbled beneath them—the sensation of thunder, of chariots, tanks, and mechanisms of war. The vibrations dislodged a boulder from a high outcropping, from whence it fell, bounced, flattened a tree, and rolled over three of the golems.

Seconds later, the trio rose and marched onward.

"Wait." Jacob scanned the Nistarim around him. "Where's Nickel?"

"He left for Jerusalem and hasn't gotten back," Dov said.

"We need him here, though. We need him to fight with us."

"He would want us to fight regardless."

"But I . . . he's my grandpa."

"He'll be here, Jacob," Gina said. "I know he wants to meet you too."

Dov paid no mind to their sentiments. His jaw was set, his eyes steeled, as he turned toward this assembly of men from all corners of the globe. Jacob sensed no apparent hierarchy or age considerations, only shared purpose.

"We are Concealed Ones," Dov spoke out. "Servants and nothing more. In moments we'll each choose whom we will serve—our courage or our fears, our faith or our doubts. Mankind has always wrestled with Collectors, but right now we have a chance to destroy these ones from the Akeldama. The Master Collector's own hatred seeped into them through Judas' blood, and if we let them survive this night, humans will be infected like never before. Already, Jerusalem is under siege. Are you with me? Are we ready to end what started in the Field of Blood and carried over into the Haunt of Jackals?"

"We fight for the Nazarene," Kenny said.

"'All for one, and one for all,'" Gina and Jed agreed.

The rest stepped forward as a single unit—the Nigerian, the Brazilian, the Americans, the Chinese, and so on—and mouthed their solemn vow.

"We are ready to serve."

Could this be it? Could it be over as easy as that?

Erota had whipped her head toward that strangled cry from the wadi, half expecting this mortal sphere to grind to a halt beneath the strain of a fallen Concealed One. She'd felt similar anticipation before, specifically at the medical clinic in Chattanooga when Gina's son took those nails through the skull.

So, Helene had done her dirty work.

So, the spice merchant had been hanged, sliced, and eviscerated.

At the foot of Masada, Erota felt her heart give a celebratory leap . . . before realizing nothing had changed. The globe still spun. Stars still glittered. And the golems still lumbered across the dark plains. All of which meant that another soul had filled the gap.

Who this time?

Was there no end to this supply of humble fools?

Tonight, however, the entire affair would be decided once and for all. Akeldama Collectors would become the laughingstock of clusters everywhere if they fumbled this opportunity, and Erota was determined to set things right.

With that in mind, she climbed a bit higher on this vantage point and watched the progress of her battalions. Moonlight oozed over the ridge and revealed the huge forms spreading across the wasteland. Their round red feet tromped over camel bones and molted snakeskin. She imagined their flaming red-yellow eyes as they closed the final hundred meters or so to En Gedi.

The Nistarim sent forth a volley of sharpened stakes, followed by another. The MTPs caught golems in chests, foreheads, and thighs. Each strike caused a momentary lurch yet failed to stop the advance.

The humans fanned out across the sands to meet their foes, launching more tent pegs, still failing to inflict any permanent damage. The monsters absorbed a third volley and marched closer.

A purr rose in Erota's throat.

Poor boys, you've never seen soldiers quite like mine, have you?

At a small crest, the original Nistarim prepared to meet the enemy head on. She could see their smudged blue markings from here. She suspected that the mortals among them, such as Dov and Kenny, would be farther back, but even the immortals could be torn to shreds. Of course, they did have three days to hope for revival—assuming any survived to administer their sacrament.

Concealed Ones and golems collided again.

Handheld MTPs strafed clay arms and abdomens, whipping ropes of oily fluid into the night. From the rise, Gina and her husband threw four spikes simultaneously, one from each of their hands, drilling the eye sockets of a golem who staggered about unable to see. Some golems paused when struck, as though intrigued by their own invulnerability, while others pressed forward to fill the ranks.

A gargantuan fist snatched up two immortals, hammered them head first into the ground. Another golem swatted a Syrian man into a withered tree, where his leftovers blotted the trunk like bits of peach and pomegranate.

Ahh. See, now, you're making me hungry.

To Erota's left, activity stirred at the mouth of Wadi Mishmar, and her eyes darted to the Collectors clustered there. Where would Natira be without her oversight of these various groups? While he chased after relics, she put feminine guile to use.

The Black Queen fighting for her Black King.

A Collector's scream gave notice that all was not well in her kingdom.

Jerusalem

Lord Natira had watched Kyria take wing, then spent thirty minutes pacing the garden, surveying the slope for an alternate entry to the Tmu Tarakan. How could he leave now, after striving so long for this prophesied prize? On the other hand, how could he stand on the chessboard's perimeter while the battle raged?

He was deciding to race to the Dead Sea when a pair of knuckle-draggers entered the grove's shadows. Led by a penlight's beam, they headed his direction—a male, large and rotund; a female, shapely and lean. Their American English was audible over the still shuddering earth.

"Sarge, this is it," the female said. "I think we've actually found it. Look, the compass is aiming right through those trees."

"Woo-boy, and after all these years."

"Doesn't seem right without Nickel here, though."

"He's a big boy. Betcha he got caught up with somethin' or other."

The Collector rose to his full height. "Nickel, you say? As in Cal Nichols?"

"Who are you?"

"He's locked in here, if you must know." Natira banged against the iron door. "Are you his noble rescuers?"

The woman clutched a jeweled object to her stomach. The male's penlight swung up and shone on Natira's face. Considering his protruding fangs, he was sure to give this couple a fright.

As expected, they gasped and stepped back.

"Sarge, Josee—is that you?" From the cave came a muffled voice.

"Nickel?" the two-leggers exclaimed.

"Get away from here," he called. *"Run."*

Although Natira chuckled at their wide-eyed expressions, he saw no signs of them hastening a retreat. The lady, Josee, reached for a vial around her neck. The corpulent fellow, Sarge, balled his right hand, while his other clung to a stone chess piece topped by a cross and a knobby crown.

Hmm. A black king . . .

"Where'd you get that?" Natira gestured. "Mind if I have a look?"

"Heyya," Sarge said. "Aren't you Natira? Your ol' girlfriend, Trudi Ubelhaar, we faced off with her a coupla years back, so I guess it's your turn now."

The Collector had no interest in frivolous banter. He was fixated on that chess figurine, sure that it must be the one stolen by Lenin and left on Engine 418. As foreseen, Natira's own "likeness" had provided a key to the Tmu Tarakan—a duplicate—yet here was the original that'd been fashioned by Rasputin.

"You don't scare us," Josee said. "We've run into your kind be—"

Natira backhanded the mouthy female. No sooner had she sprawled across the dirt than her companion came storming forward.

Though Sarge was smaller than Barabbas or Kransberg, there was strength in his solid jaw and burly arms. Natira sidestepped the initial attack and hooked the man's wrist in his pincers. He wrenched it around, hoping to loosen the chess piece, but Sarge spun with surprising agility, thus relieving the torque on his arm, and popped free. In the same motion, he drove an uppercut into Natira's chin and rattled his jawbone. Natira lashed back, curved nails slashing Sarge's chest with parallel red lines.

Dense with Nazarene purity, the scent of that blood taunted the vampire. He was after the king, he reminded himself. With it, he could open the door, finish off Cal Nichols, and head for the battleground with the Crown of Thorns in hand.

"Give me that chessman," he said. "That's all I ask."

"Say please," Sarge insisted.

The Josee woman was up on her knees, eyes flat and fearless. Had the first blow addled her brains? Did she not realize the world could be over in the time it took to kill Isaac? In fact, shouldn't that old man be dead by now?

During Natira's split-second distraction, Sarge feinted a left jab, then put his full weight into an overhand right that landed like a hammer on the Collector's temple. Sparks shot through his vision. A migraine swelled from the impact, as hard as anything he'd suffered from his son or henchman.

Oh, to be sure, Sarge was becoming a nuisance.

Snarling, the vampire crisscrossed the male's belly with deep claw swipes, then reached for the chess piece while reveling in the groans.

CHAPTER
FIFTY-FOUR

Hazy moonlight dribbled through the keyhole. Though Nickel knew Sarge and Josee were out there, he was convinced that if he bridged to them in this feeble condition he'd get stuck halfway through the iron, a prisoner to his self-doubts and earthly frailty. That would do none of them any good.

He heard voices, thuds, and scuffling.

Still wobbly, still clutching the Crown of Thorns, he pulled himself through jewels and icons to see what was going on. That same spider scuttled across his fingertips and he smashed it with the heel of his palm. A second later, his torso contracted and bolts of pain skewered his head.

What was this? There was no way that nasty arachnid could deliver such a fast-acting poison.

Another bolt.

"Arrggh." He clenched his fists, screwed his eyes shut.

Images of Isaac filled his mind, and he thought of Natira's words to the blackbird—something about "giving the signal." He knew in his gut that his old friend was gone. The thousands of years shared . . . the days of Ezekiel . . . the meals with their wives . . . the vigil kept from a shop on David Street . . . the waft of those spices . . .

It was all over.

A part of Nickel wanted to rest his head forever. He had travailed for so long, left behind a spouse, his best of friends, and the mother of his twins. One good thing, though: the earth was still spinning, which meant his grandson must have received the Letter. In fact, by now Jacob should've gone through the waters of a Dead Sea baptism to take his place among the Nistarim.

I'm going to see him, Nickel told himself, *if it's the last thing I do*.

He gathered his strength and put his eye to the keyhole, from where he viewed Josee rising to her knees with dust and leaves in her spiky hair.

Farther on, Natira was fighting Sergeant Turney. Sarge, a former boxer, was no slouch, but how long could he compete with the undead? Hadn't Nickel tried to warn them? Told them to run?

Sarge rocketed a fist into Natira's temple, and the creature's snarl proved some damage had been done. In that moment while his enemy was distracted, Sarge tossed something to his wife—too hard to tell what it was in the darkness.

Scrambling, Josee found her footing and sprinted for the iron door.

Behind her, the Collector tore at Sarge's stomach with elongated nails, then pried apart his clenched fingers and ransacked his pockets. Searching . . .

For the key!

Josee was clutching that black monarch. She reached the Tmu Tarakan and shoved the Rasputin chess piece into the lock. Tumblers gave way, the door swung open, and Nickel fell forward, the Crown still cradled in his hand.

Natira roared as he saw what had happened. Dropping Sarge, he drove forward with powerful strides.

"Go!" Josee pushed the black king into Nickel's hand. As he stood on weak legs, she shoved the iron door back into place. "They need you."

"I can't leave you two. What about—"

"Go!"

With that, Josee tore loose her vial and waved it in the face of their foe. Natira's eyes widened, yet he kept coming. He leaped into the air, completed a roundhouse kick, and sent her tumbling over a pile of limestone and detritus.

Nickel knew there was only one way to keep this creature from doing further harm to his friends here in Gethsemane. He had to draw Natira away to that valley where their forces now clashed.

Time to leave this place, yes. But did he have the energy to survive?

He closed his eyes and let go, sensing the *l o o s e n i n g* of neurons and molecules, the *ssssttrrrretchhhinggg* of time's fabric. Natira was upon him, grasping at his form. Those claws found nothing to grab hold of as Nickel made a final foray into the gap between spirit and flesh. The Akeldama Collectors had never seen such a demonstration from Yeshua, and Nickel knew they lacked the creativity to even think of bridging the Separation.

Too bad for them.

Shrieks of rage faded as Cal Nichols headed for the Valley of Bones.

Shores of the Dead Sea

Aware that the golem troops could take care of themselves, Erota had run the dirt path to Wadi Mishmar. It was one thing to hear the dying sounds of the cluster's hostage, another altogether to hear screams from her cluster members.

At the dry streambed, she found that both Dorotheus and Hermione had been hooked by metal stakes. A quick scan of the rutted ground showed it was seeded with the infernal things, disguised by weeds and dry grass.

Cal, the knight . . .

The trickiest piece on the checkered board.

He had been here, that much was obvious. Most likely, he and his beloved Concealed Ones had crept through in the past week to set ambushes.

"I'm stuck," Hermione cried. She tried to tear her foot from one spike and fell backward onto another. The tip thrust through her cranium, shooting brain matter and clumps of hair onto the sand.

Horrified, Dorotheus stared down at her own impaled shin. Domna and Matrona watched from the bank.

"Don't panic," Erota told the older Collector. "Let me come to you."

"Hurry."

Erota was still a step away, hand extended, when Dorotheus tried to close the gap by lurching forward. She did break free, but plummeted into a pit full of spikes hidden beneath a scattering of reeds.

Her pain was short-lived. A few gasps, puffs of air, then nothing.

Erota swiveled back toward the valley and gave a scream of her own. Even as her troops north of this position ripped through the Nistarim, she spotted a few—the mortals, perhaps?—sneaking off toward the vegetation of En Gedi. She sneered, her fury honing in on a new target.

Jerusalem

What had happened? How had his nemesis slipped from his fingers into the ether? Some magic had been conjured, some immortal disappearing act.

In a rage, Lord Natira honed in on the whimpers of those he'd already injured in this olive grove. Worthless conquests though they be, they would receive the brunt of his frustration.

He aimed for the most vulnerable one first. The one called Sarge was still on the dirt, his belly clawed open and innards glistening dark in the starlight. The revenant stomped a foot down on the man's chest, causing the wound to burble and widen, to send up the stench of viscera and filleted flesh. Sarge emitted a groan, his eyes rolling back in pain.

With pincers ready, Natira eyed an exposed section of his prey's liver. Mmm, yes. Always tasty.

As he reached down to scoop out that prized tidbit, Sarge took hold of his ankle and tried to push him away. A pathetic attempt at self-preservation. These humans were so easily—

From behind, Josee slammed into Natira's broad back and rocked him forward. With his foot pinned by Sarge's grasp, he seesawed over his victim's torn stomach and rolled onto the ground, his shirt sticky and damp with Sarge's fluids. Josee was still there, a small hand prying at Natira's lips, trying to insert a vial of that Nazarene Blood.

"Drink it," she said. "See how you like it!"

He scrambled to his feet, clamped her wrist between pinkie and thumb, and swung her over his head into the bole of an ancient tree. She crumpled at its roots, her nose misshapen by the impact, her arms folded over ribs that were assuredly cracked or broken.

"Try tasting your own blood," he shouted at her.

The reappearance of the blackbird shook Natira from his fit of blind fury. She pecked at his head, fluttered about his ears.

"What is it, Kyria? What? What do you want?"

She landed on his forearm, a high-pitched shrill letting him know something had gone wrong.

"Was Isaac executed, as ordered?"

The bird's head bobbed an affirmative before she screeched again, and he made the connection that a new Concealed One must've made an appearance. Were the rumors about Gina and Jed true? Were they alive? Had their long-lost son, Nickel's grandson, survived by way of deception?

"Go, Kyria." Natira shook her loose. "Survey the field of battle, so that if Gina's son does exist you can lead me straight to him. I'll be right behind you."

On feathered pinions, Kyria's Collector took flight.

Natira shot a last glance at dying Sarge and huddled Josee. Their pain gave him pleasure, gave him fuel for his greater mission, and true to his word he took off after the blackbird. He ran like he'd never run before, pumping his arms and legs in unison, hurdling the stone walls along this slope, weaving between the pitted trees. He followed the Kidron Valley beyond the city's outskirts into barren ravines and wadis.

Forget the complaints of his host's lungs and muscles. Forget the momentary aches. The earth funneled him down, down, down, toward the Valley of Bones.

Shores of the Dead Sea

One day, Jacob knew, Final Vengeance would come, during which the dead would rise and give an account before the Almighty.

Collectors, on the other hand, hoped for vengeance of their own, and that same craving activated these golems to new atrocities. Jacob darted between the swarming armies as they grasped at him and the other Concealed Ones. He lost sight of his mother, yet knew she was close. His father was atop the rise with the other mortals, still spearing MTPs into the melee.

Jacob dove clear of a swinging arm, rolled back up onto his feet.

Beside him, a cavernous mouth with red lumps for teeth chomped onto the leg of the Brazilian and tore it away in a gushing torrent.

The clamor of war was deafening. Another of Jacob's companions cried out as chunks of flesh were gouged from his back and thigh.

"Jacob!" A female voice. "Where are you?"

"Over here."

Gina shot between two golems, causing them to collide in a burst of brick and dust as they reached for her. She came face-to-face with Jacob. "These things aren't dying," she said. "My dagger, the stakes—nothing hurts them."

"Let's at least lead them away from Dad."

"No, we need to stick close."

Two more Nistarim went down—the Jordanian and an American. Another fled the raking arms of a golem.

From the hillside, Kenny Preston came rushing at the thing and plucked the MTP that already protruded from its thick calf. Black sludge dripped from the tip, but Kenny clamped the object between his jaws like a pirate's blade and vaulted onto the monster's thigh.

"What're you doing?" Dov yelled at him.

"Helping."

"No, Kenny!" Gina stiffened beside Jacob. "Get back here! Get *back*!"

Undeterred, Kenny climbed the golem's wide ribs as though playing on school-ground monkey bars. When a stone hand swatted at him, he swung to another rib and pulled himself higher. Incensed, the creature swatted harder, clawing furrows from its own chest in a billow of clay-colored dust. A third swat broke through the entire left side of its abdomen.

As the huge head stared down at the damage, Kenny windmilled his MTP into the open mouth. The spike lodged in the back of the throat, and the golem gagged on the encumbrance while its attacker made the long drop to the sand.

And the forces kept coming.

Beneath fiery eyes, golem faces were bathed in their victims' blood.

Jacob hopped into a shallow depression to escape the descending foot of one of the giants. Dirt cascaded over his head, and he lay flat till the thing had moved on. He rose and saw the man from Beijing darting off in an attempt to divert another of these marauders.

How could they defeat this army? The odds seemed insurmountable.

"Nothing is impossible," Jacob yelled. *"Nothing."*

The battlefield was a kaleidoscope of fluorescent blue Letters, splashes of blood, spiraling silver stakes, and clay-red limbs. Weaving amongst the golems' shadows, the sinewy Nigerian man used his dark skin tones to his advantage to gather up the misfired armaments and cart them back up the rise for Jed, Kenny, Dov, and the others.

Jacob and Gina lifted a long tree root, set out earlier by the Nistarim, and stretched it between them. A stone soldier bumbled over the obstacle, landing facedown on a boulder. Rubble rained down, paring Jacob's ear, yet what did he care? His face was marred already, his forehead dotted with scar tissue. He was here to fight, not to stress over minor abrasions.

The monster tried to stand. Its cracked eye sockets leaked flame like lava, and its neck was snapped sideways. With vision and limbs no longer working in conjunction, the golem shot them a look as though ready to advance, but its legs carried it at full speed in the opposite direction.

"That's right," Jacob cheered. "You better run."

CHAPTER
FIFTY-FIVE

As proud as Gina was of her son, she could not tame the fear rampaging through her veins. Her dagger had always served her well. MTPs had always done the trick. Now, however, none of it was working.

Where was her dad? Where were her in-laws, Josee and Sarge?

At least she had her husband and son with her.

"Fall back," the Nistarim called out. "Fall *back*."

With nine of their number mowed down, they retreated, encircling their most vulnerable members on En Gedi's fringe. From here, Gina watched some of the golems teeter and crash headlong into one another, over and over, like short-circuiting automatons. Behind them, though, a hundred more soldiers moved up the valley, too many for this group to handle.

"We need to get the mortals out of harm's way," someone said.

"No," Jed said. "I'm not leaving my wife and son. I can—"

"You can't," Dov admitted. "We can't. It's too risky. Why don't you and I lead the way to the cave by the falls? We'll wait there until Nickel gets back."

"Is he coming back? How long has it been? An hour? Two?"

Gina hated to consider the possibilities. She hugged Kenny and Dov, gave Jed a farewell kiss, then pushed him and their group toward the oasis. It was for the best. She turned and wrapped her arm around Jacob's waist, convinced that if they backed down tonight it would lead to irreversible, cataclysmic defeat.

She raised her voice over the tumult of a hundred stomping feet. "We are the doubly alive," she said. "The doubly dead have to go."

"We all agree," someone said. "But how?"

"That I don't know. Why don't two or three of us get down to our fallen friends and revive them. You know, we do still have the Nazarene Blood."

"Some of them are in . . . pieces."

"Then we gather the pieces and get them back here. It's not impossible."

"That's right." Jacob met the others' eyes. "Nothing's impossible."

From the white rotem bush a few meters away, a familiar voice rang out: "You can say that again. The fact I made it back is proof of that."

Nickel spoke with a bravado he did not feel. He called from the shrubbery simply because he could not move his limbs. Good thing he'd made it across the desert plateau, down into this heralded valley.

The Crown of Thorns had made the trip, too, and he held on to the sharp-pointed object by the braided vines that tied it together. The briars, stained red-black, were evidence that this Crown had once been worn by Yeshua, King of the Jews. What had that King said to Nickel earlier?

"A few final instructions, so listen carefully . . ."

"I need your help," Nickel told the astonished gathering.

A pair of Concealed Ones hooked hands beneath his arms and brought him into the center of their circle. Others, facing outward on the perimeter, gave updates regarding the plains below.

"The golems are regrouping . . ."

"They're fanning out, coming up here from both sides . . ."

"They just . . . they're taking our fallen comrades and . . . and stomping them into shallow graves . . ."

Hunched above Nickel, the gathering groaned and bent lower as vertebrae crackled and drops of sweat mingled with tears and the blood from their battle wounds. If their defeated members were not enlivened once more, the end would be upon them. During Nickel's days with them, he'd experienced their typical burdens, yet nothing to compare with the

devastating weight they now bore. His own bones rattled with the vibrations of the earth beneath him.

Was it the undoing of this planet, the end of all that was holy and
good? The splitting of foundations, the crumbling of pillars?

Or was it stampeding golems about to overrun their position?

"Sit me up," he said. *"Hurry."*

On the small rise, between two meager mounds of MTPs, Gina took a
knee beside the man with gold-flecked green eyes. He had mentored her,
returned her son to her, and she now trusted his words like few others'.
"We're listening, Dad. What should we do?"

His gaze moved from her to Jacob. "You made it."

"Hi, Grandpa."

Nickel grinned.

"You make him sound so old," Gina said.

"I am old," Nickel retorted. "Too old for all of this. Are the mortals
safe?"

"They're back at the waterfall, Jed included."

"Good." Propped on both arms, he let his eyelids close.

"Stay with us, Dad. How can we help?"

"The Valley of Bones," he said. "It will rise."

"What?"

"I need the Nistarim to hold off the golems, to keep them from
reaching me. This Crown . . ." Eyes open again, he sat up taller and lofted
the relic. Deep red splatters stained the thorn tips. "This Blood must have
time to act."

"There's no time left," said the Concealed One from Mexico. "The
righteous are being crushed while the wicked prosper."

"Watch out!"

The warning came too late from the perimeter guard. Hurled by a
golem, a stone slab plowed down two of their group and left wide smears
in the sand. A moment later, columns of the monsters appeared on both
sides of the rise.

"Over there!" Gina told Jacob. "Get your grandpa over *there*."

Amidst the chaos, she darted off to create a diversion while her thirteen-year-old son moved Nickel beneath a large spur of the thrown slab. In this land of her heritage, her Jewish pessimism was rising anew, and she wondered if any of them would survive this night. She bit back on that fear. No, she had to trust that this murky moonlight would hide the two of them long enough for . . .

For what?

She was not certain.

Erota's evening had not gone as planned. Chilled by a lack of fresh sustenance, she was determined to prove herself to Natira by catching the mortal Nistarim in their cozy hideaway.

She would sup from Kenny's neck.

Feed from Dov's femoral artery.

And, to spite Gina once and for all, sever all evidence of Jed Turney's manhood so that this family would remain childless forever. It still brought her some warmth to think of Jacob's infantile body pierced in his incubator.

"How much farther?" Matrona whined. "I feel shaky up here."

"Shut up, child," said Domna.

The three of them and Shelamzion were navigating the narrow ledge cut into the western cliffs, while Helene stayed back in the wadi to mutilate and disperse Isaac's limbs—no need for his corpse to be recovered or revived. About eighty meters below them, the clang and clamor of battle rose from the valley floor.

It was precarious here, no doubt about it.

With sideways glances, Erota counted at least twenty of the Concealed Ones already stamped into shallow graves. What would it take to end this? Where was Final Vengeance? And who said these immortals should get three days to rise again?

Well, the mortals could not be brought back, so they were her target.

Far across the flats, she spotted the familiar figure of Cal Nichols as he was rushed along a dirt rise and given cover beneath a slab of rock. He was here? And still no sign of her lord?

Despite the ledge's narrowing width, Erota quickened her pace to beat whatever enchantment was underfoot. Matrona whined again, Domna wore a sallow face, and even stolid Shelamzion expressed concern. Erota reminded them this was the best way of circumventing the combat zone and sneaking into En Gedi.

Matrona, still whining, steadied herself by taking hold of roots that poked from the cliff. They jerked in her hand, like the chain on a lever-operated shower, and MTPs came down in a silver flurry. Three split her skull into dangling, ripe sections, and she tumbled end over end onto the rocks below.

"They target even our little ones," Erota said.

Shelamzion looked up at the protuberance from which they'd been ambushed and caught a fourth MTP between the eyes. Howling, Domna teetered, but was kept from toppling by a spike that pinned her foot to the ledge.

Erota hurried back to pluck and discard the object. "Hear me now, sis—we don't have time for your petty human's weaknesses. We had better destroy the mortals soon, since Natira, apparently, has left us to fight on our own."

She paused. Come to think of it, where was the Master Collector in all of this? If these were his territories, why did he never show his face?

"I will follow you," Domna said.

"You should. These days, it seems I'm the only one worth trusting."

Huddled beside his grandpa beneath the jagged spur, Jacob heard bodies collide, heard cries of pain rend the air. Screams were cut short by the snapping and popping of human bones. Only meters away, golems stomped back and forth on huge club feet, but Jacob tuned his ears to his grandfather's labored breathing and the Crown in his hand.

"What's wrong, Grandpa?"

"I . . . I'm okay. But I need you to carry out a task for me."

Jacob nodded. "I'm listening. Just tell me what to do."

Gina was low on strength. Mustering her energy, she dashed up the arm of her attacker, found a perch upon its wide cranium, and stabbed her dagger into its right eye. She turned away from the burst of hot sparks.

Only to discover a tableau of continued destruction.

The valley was a blur of clay monsters tearing into outmatched Nistarim. Limbs were pulled from sockets. Bodies were tossed and tumbled like pebbles. A soggy mist hung over the terrain, shrouding the battlefield in its tattered, burgundy fabric.

CHAPTER
FIFTY-SIX

The Crown of Thorns glimmered in the dim moonlight and Jacob marveled at the aroma emanating from the stains.

Nickel whispered a prayer. "Breathe life into these bones."

"What does that mean, Grandpa? What's supposed to happen?"

"I need you to . . ." The flecks in Nickel's eyes seemed to lose their luster, and Jacob felt the man's muscles slacken. "I don't . . . don't have much longer."

"Till what? What's wrong?"

"Wrong?" Nickel closed his eyes and smiled. "Nothing at all. I've done my job, and you're here, aren't you? The Nistarim are here. I . . . I'm tired, that's all. Now it's up to you."

"Why me?"

Grimacing, Nickel lifted himself on an elbow beneath the stone overhang. "It's there in the hundred and thirty-fifth psalm: 'The Lord has chosen Jacob for Himself.' It's referring to this nation, to these people, but you . . . today you get to stand in that gap for them."

Jacob flashed back to talks with his mother, discussing the need to play his part, to attack and defend, to evaluate and act. He felt inadequate, barely a man, yet there was nothing to be gained by shrinking back. Not now. Not while Concealed Ones battled in this darkness.

An arm's length away, a head rolled past the slab and came to a stop, with an Asian man's eyes staring over the rise as though appalled by such brutality.

Jacob stifled his own gasps. He said, "What am I supposed to do?"

"I need you to remember these words," Nickel said, "from the Bible. 'We prayed beneath the burden of your discipline . . . But those who die in the Lord will live; their bodies will rise again . . . For your life-giving light will fall like dew on your people in the place of the dead!'"

"I don't understand."

"This Blood . . . it'll bring them to life."

"Our Concealed Ones, you mean? The ones who have been struck down?"

Nickel nodded. "But not *only* them—if I understood Yeshua's earlier instructions."

"Who else?"

"Be patient." Wincing, Nickel gripped his hand. "Give it time, Jacob, and you'll find hundreds on your side, more Concealed Ones than you ever imagined. Yeshua carried the ultimate burden and it's all here in these stains, in these droplets. His sufferings will raise up an army like you've never seen."

"Ezekiel's army?"

"There ya go. Sounds like you know your stuff, kid."

"You're saying this is the valley that he saw in his vision?"

"The Valley of Bones." Nickel winced again. "Now try to keep your voice down."

One clean kill. Was that really so hard?

Erota and Domna had reached the end of the cliff ledge and crept past darkened buildings into the wadi where the mortals were hiding. The conflict's din gave way to trickles of a stream and the whisper of green fronds and tall reeds. The incline carried the sisters past smaller cataracts to the roar of a plunging waterfall. She knew somewhere nearby they would find a cave.

"There," Domna said. "In that gap behind the falls."

"I see it. Ah, these Concealed Ones—did they think they'd be hard to find?"

"You looking for us?" said a male voice behind them.

Erota admitted to herself that the sound and scent of the falls had numbed her to the presence of others so close. When she turned, a man she recognized as Kenny Preston was backed by ones close to his age. She knew Dov Amit's face, but the set of look-alike brothers was unfamiliar. Their clothing was American. Regardless of nationality, all of them bore the iridescent symbol on their brows.

She smirked, confident in her ability to sweet-talk young men. "Well, boys, look at you. I thought we'd find you cowering in a cave."

"I've hidden for years," Kenny said, hands fisted at his sides. "I came to fight."

"Quite the bold specimen, huh? Impressive."

"You tried killing my mom's baby. Well, now you get to face me."

"Tried? Oh, you're wrong there. That dear baby got *nailed.*"

Kenny smiled. "Today he turned thirteen. Guess you haven't heard, but you've got a mess on your hands." His hand whipped forward, releasing an MTP.

She dodged the projectile with a low spin and came up scything the air with serrated nails. The first slash tore through the meat in one of the American boys' forearm, the second through his brother's shoulder. Domna rushed in beside her, fangs glinting, saliva dripping. To take a bite would be deadly for either of them, yet the temptation was strong. Both were thirsty. Both were used to drinking from men like flasks of cheap wine.

"She's coming at you, Dov!" Kenny shouted.

Turning sideways, Dov used the torque of his pivoting body to slice through Domna's elbow with his crude metal stake. She screamed and clamped anesthetizing fangs into the raw stump.

Any familial concern on Erota's part was secondary to their goals. She jabbed at Dov's thigh with her foot, knocking him back, then took another swipe at the American boys, grazing tufts of hair as they dropped to their knees in positions of supplication.

Oh, that was precious. Did they think the Almighty would listen?

A battering ram exploded into her ribcage. The force of a body heavier than her own carried her into the pool at the base of the falls. The cold liquid snatched her breath away, and she came up sputtering, hissing. She found herself in the grasp of Jed Turney. Had he been hiding among the rocks, desiring retribution? Or could it be true, this idea that Jacob was alive?

Either way, there was something delicious about being in the arms of Gina's husband. Erota writhed her legs around his waist and pulled him close. "You like it wet and wild, is that it, Jed?" Her nails raked his lower back.

He moaned and arched against her, his deep blue eyes widening as he struggled to break free.

"Just one kiss?" Erota teased.

"Bite me."

"Ohhh, don't you *wish*."

"Actually?" he said over the rushing water. "No."

Erota watched Domna land hard on the shore, skewered through both temples by Kenny and Dov. She wondered again if Kenny's assertions were true. Had Gina and Jed managed to rescue their infant somehow? Would he step into the gap even if she destroyed one of these mortals, or had he already done so in the place of Isaac?

Where was Natira?

Lost in despair, she felt Jed's body tense even as his MTP came down in a high-arching blow. She threw her head to the side in an effort to dodge the inevitable. She meant to unlock her legs and push away, but that silver tip had her hypnotized as it rammed through her skull and banished her forever to a cruel and restless place.

Cal Nichols could barely keep his eyelids open. He had given the last drops of his resources to bridge to and fro, to carry out the Nazarene's orders. One task was left to be completed, and that would be up to his grandson now. Beside him, Jacob was describing the battle that had fanned out from the rise into the valley.

"Here," Nickel said. "Help me from under this rock so that I can see."

"I should go fight. My mom's out there somewhere."

"Sit with me for a sec, Jacob. She can handle herself just fine."

"But she's . . ."

"Just a girl? I'd take her over ten men any day. Watch after her, you hear me?"

Jacob plopped down alongside. "Yes, sir."

Nickel saw Gina break away from the fiercest fighting to administer healing to a downed Concealed One. Even as she delivered that elixir from her vial, she was batted away by a golem and did two somersaults across the dirt. She came up with the left side of her face bruised, her left eye blackened.

Nickel tried to get to his feet—his daughter, his precious little girl— but he had nothing left, and he spilled onto his shoulder.

Gina glanced up the slope and gave a curt wave of reassurance.

"Grandpa," Jacob said, propping him up. "Are you okay?"

Nickel stared off, uncertain himself of the answer.

Lord Natira followed the blackbird to the Valley of Bones' northern access. Kyria's Collector moved wraithlike through the night, skirting En Gedi's buildings, pools, and balsam trees, guiding him past outcroppings toward the battlefield.

As he crested a hill, he was ready to bark out orders to the golems when his heart quickened at the sight before him. Only fifty meters away, on the lip of a small rise, his most hated foe was seated with his back turned.

"There you are, Cal," Natira mouthed. "No escaping this time."

He snuck down the slope, keeping to the shadows and using sandstone slabs to disguise his approach. A small-boned boy was leaned against the right flank of his nemesis. Gina's half-immortal child? Jacob Lazarescu? The boy lifted his gaze toward Cal Nichols, and even at this distance his scar-dotted forehead shone beneath his Letter.

So it's true, then. You did survive.

Now that he'd been led to his quarry, Natira flicked away the blackbird. Dark wings carried Kyria's Collector southward toward a wadi where she could reenter her original host. Meanwhile, Natira needed the assistance of guards a good deal larger, and he issued a silent summons to a half-dozen nearby golems.

Nickel had done his duty, mentoring and preparing young men for battle. Tonight, he had received forgiveness from the Nazarene while under the scrutiny of those dark-honey eyes. And now, at last, he'd seen his grandson.

Is it time yet, Lord? I'm ready.

How could he leave now, though?

In the valley, the numbers of the Concealed Ones had been cut in two. Some of them crawled on hands and knees. Others had given way to the overpowering golems, flattened by their fists and feet, broken over trees and boulders. Bloodied stumps hung from limping bodies, and the ground was strewn with metal spikes that had missed their marks or been batted away like so much windblown grass. The survivors averted blows and dove for shelter, reduced to defensive maneuvers against insurmountable forces.

And I can barely lift my own eyelids.

Though Nickel had done everything asked of him, it was time now to pass the responsibilities to one who bore the distinguishing mark. Beside him, his grandson trembled at the anguish on display.

"Jacob."

"I have to get down there. I have to fight with them."

"No, I need you here." Nickel relinquished the Crown of Thorns. "Take this."

"The Crown?"

"And this."

"Isn't this the key to—"

"Rasputin's riches, yes. Tuck it away." He watched the chessman go deep into his grandson's jeans pocket. "Someday you'll get to choose what to do with that, but keep it quiet for now. The thing's caused enough trouble already, and I can't take it with me."

"Where're you going?"

"I'm tired. Not sure I . . . can stick around."

"You can't leave." Jacob leaned into him, gripping his arm. "No."

"We all leave at some point, but listen . . . we'll be together again."

Nickel's thoughts became jumbled as his physical being clung to this mortal realm. His spiritual nature, however, was slipping free from these

bonds, awash in warmth and a peace beyond his own understanding. He
was letting go. Letting go. He saw Gina approaching—or was it his imagination? He felt himself coming apart, as though bridging in slow motion.
A soothing flood ran over, through, and around him.

Oh, I'm ready . . .

The view of the valley started fading into white.

Ready to be at rest, to see Dinah . . .

The heaviness in his body dissipated into buttery warmth.

To hear You call me by my new name . . .

The sounds of the skirmish gave way to his daughter's soft tones.
"Dad, don't close your eyes. Are you crying? I'm right here." She took a
knee beside him. "We can still win this thing."

"I've fought the good fight, or . . . tried to, anyway."

"You have. Definitely."

"I love you, Gina. You've . . . got a great kid here."

"I love you too."

Nickel grinned, then let his eyelids fall shut. Sure, the Nazarene Blood
could revive him, but he had done all that was required and it was time for
release. As an immortal, he'd known his departure would come in sweeping fashion, the same as for the original Thirty-Six, and he now awaited
that moment of exultation.

"You can't leave," Jacob said. "We need you, Grandpa."

"Use that Crown the way we talked about. Victory is there in your
hands."

"But I—"

"No more arguing, okay? Just do it."

Jacob set down the circular brambles and gave him a hug. "Yes, sir."

Now, Nickel thought. *I'm as ready as I'll ever be . . .*

Letting go.

A burst of heat enveloped him, soothing his pain, drying his tears. A
voice called to him, to him alone: "Good and faithful servant, come enter
into the joy . . ." And then a rush of wind swept beneath him like a chariot
and caught him up into the sky, bridging him from darkness into the flare
of a dark-honey light.

CHAPTER
FIFTY-SEVEN

Natira was mere meters behind the family trio when a swirl of wind and shimmering radiance snatched Cal Nichols from his place on the dirt. It was the second time this evening the man had evaporated into the ether and eluded captivity, and fury sizzled down through Natira's fangs, out through his arms and legs.

Gina and Jacob were still staring into the night sky.

Well, let them gawk.

He shot forward, intending to gather a head in each hand and smash them together. He would revel in the sound of crushed skulls and shattered bone. He would—

The Crown of Thorns?

It was there, on the soil behind Jacob.

Alerted by his movement, mother and son turned as the lord vampire scooped up that ancient relic with pincers that were careful to keep clear of its Blood-dipped points.

"Mine at last!" Natira roared.

Even as Gina's dagger whipped into view, he hooked Jacob's neck in the crook of his arm and shoved the thorns down upon his scalp.

"Come any closer and I'll snap his little twig neck."

Gina hesitated. Already, Jacob was going limp beneath the press of those thorns, but his body could still serve as a shield against a well-aimed dagger throw—and that was something Natira knew she would never risk.

"What do you want?" she said.

"Final Vengeance."

"Why him? Take me if you want, please. But let him go."

"I can do more damage to you this way, don't you think? You can enjoy a close up of his demise."

Marching up the slope, six clay creatures formed a wide circle around them. Gina's arm twisted in the grasp of one of the golems, and the dagger clattered to the ground. The creature pounded it into the earth with his granite fist, burying it deep. In Natira's arms, Jacob cried out as the thorns pressed farther into his scalp, drawing forth dark liquid trails that snaked down through his hair.

Gina seethed.

"If only," Natira pointed out, "Cal's activities hadn't diverted your attention, you might have noticed my approach. Then again, if he hadn't abandoned you both, I would have no need to subject your son to the fate his grandfather deserved."

"He never abandoned us."

"Ohh? Then where is he, this hero of yours?"

From the battlefield, Concealed Ones arrived to fight for their newest member, yet the phalanx of golems edged them back.

"He taught me to resist," Gina said. "He spent thousands of years fighting you and your kind, and he saved Jacob's life."

"Yes, well, the fact that Jacob's still alive is the last deception you'll ever get by me. Putting him to death, it's my way of countering you and your father's charades." Natira wriggled the briars. "And you, Gina, get to watch."

Cheeks streaked with tears, she darted forward. Valiant little thing. She stopped, of course, the moment Natira's arm drew tighter about Jacob's neck, producing a raspy cough and bulging the man-child's eyes from their sockets.

"Let him go, you monster! Let him *go.*"

Natira chortled. "You dare make demands of the Black King? Perhaps if you abase yourself, Gina, perhaps then I will show you mercy."

Gina knelt. "Please, Natira—"

"Lord Natira."

"I'm begging you to let my son go. Jacob, I love you. Don't let him—"

"Let me what?" Natira said. "How long do you think he can endure this weight, when the Nazarene Himself could not handle it?"

"Yeshua conquered every one of those infections."

"Bah. They conquered Him."

"Not true."

"Well, every bit of it—every evil, sickness, and vice—is locked within these stains. When He took it all upon Himself on that cross, it was soaked up by His Blood. Imagine your worst days, worst addictions, darkest secrets, then multiply that by a thousand and you'll begin to have an idea of what this Crown can do."

Multiplying by a thousand seemed like an understatement. Jacob's legs wobbled from the immense pressure bearing down upon his skull. From the start, Nickel had believed in his destiny, and his mother had given him life instructions through games of chess.

Is this my purpose? A sacrifice in the game?

The massive Collector had him in a stranglehold. Jacob was only thirteen, no physical match. He had no MTPs on hand. Caught up in his grandfather's departure, he had been foolish to leave this Crown sitting on the ground. Where had Natira come from anyway?

The thorns dug farther into his skin. All of his questions sank beneath this miasmic sludge of disease and hatred, cancer and envy, arrogance and wrath. Every sick, twisted thought imaginable, every siren call of seduction—it all piled upon his head. Each thorn was a nail driven into him, pumping venom.

And this was only the residue, the two-thousand-year-old stains, of the Nazarene's torment.

"Arrrghhhh!"

Jacob knew it was the sound of his own voice, yet it seemed distant and disconnected from the horde of spikes jabbed into his skull.

"Beginning to feel the weight of it, aren't you?" Natira said.

Jacob's spine was caught in clamps on either end while being wrung out like a damp towel. Warm drops squeezed from its fabric, and he realized he was urinating down his legs. He pressed his eyelids shut and told himself that there was no shame, no humiliation, that he was a man.

But there *was* shame.

He felt less than a man, less than a human. Here he was on display, wilting before the golems and Collectors, the Concealed Ones and his own mother. Where was the Almighty in all this?

"Look at me, Jacob."

His mother's voice.

Muted.

Far away.

"I'm right here, sweetheart. You are not alone."

"Alone? No. But helpless, nevertheless. Go ahead," Natira urged, "and let it break you, Jacob. I'll hold these thorns here for another year, if I must. It's been seven minutes, so far. Only seven. You were never made to carry this burden."

The Collector was right. His body was deteriorating by the second.

Natira chortled as his small hostage wept. He couldn't blame the kid, since he or any of his own cohorts would be banished in less than a minute by a single droplet of this Nazarene Blood. Nevertheless, it was glorious to watch the undoing of a two-legger.

And not just any two-legger, but the murdered firstborn of Gina and Jed Turney . . . the resurrected grandson of Cal Nichols and Nikki Lazarescu . . .

Cautious of the woven briars, the revenant tapped them another millimeter or two into that fine, dark-haired little skull. Blood dribbled down Jacob's face, a delightfully torturous demonstration for nearby Gina and the bystanders.

"'It is finished,'" Natira told his hostage. "Weren't those the Nazarene's words before giving up the ghost? Why, I wonder, should you consider yourself any better? 'It is finished.' Say them, Jacob. Just three little words."

Despair tore at Gina's thoughts. This had never been the plan, for her to lose her father and son in the same hour.

The lord vampire was enjoying his game.

He had his head down, taunting his captive.

How could she save Jacob? With Natira's attention diverted, should she dig for her dagger and go on the attack? The thing was mashed down too far, though. By the time she found it, her son would be dead. What if, instead, she dug a nail into her own palm and produced a bead of her own blood, enough to forcefeed the vampire before he swatted her aside? Surely, though, one of the golems would step in to protect him.

Clumped outside the circle of golems, a handful of Concealed Ones formed a circle of their own, travailing for their besieged companion. While others ran diversionary tactics and tried to hold their ground against the stone troops below, these few were here to let Jacob know he was not alone.

Even so, Gina understood that no one could fully appreciate the horrors he now suffered. The burdens were enough to topple not only one but all of them, a domino effect with global repercussions.

His head was down, his eyes half open. He was moaning.

"You are a Concealed One!" she cried out to her son.

The others echoed her sentiment.

She said, "You are one of Those Who Resist!"

Another echo.

In retaliation, Natira screwed the Crown of Thorns farther down over Jacob's head until the spikes seemed ready to puncture his eyeballs.

Beyond the golem perimeter, a movement caught Natira's attention, and he detected the figure of Jed Turney, now running this way from En Gedi. Even in the starlight, the smears on his face and neck indicated he had come through some toe-to-toe combat.

Well, well, let the man mourn with the others as his son withers.

"Gina, is this your husband I see? Why, how very noble. How brave." Natira gave a loud guffaw. "A mighty warrior, by the looks of him."

Spotting his spouse, Jed tested the golem perimeter, unable to access the Black King's makeshift court. Natira mocked his attempts, pointing with elbows toward potential weak spots in the barricade, then laughing at the fellow's blundering. Jed had one metal spike in hand, a shabby resource under the circumstances.

"Please," Gina said. "He can't hurt you. Why don't you let him come to me?"

Natira sneered. "You, my dear, are an untrustworthy queen."

"But Jacob is his son too."

"Not for much longer, I'm afraid."

Rather than eliciting terror, his words fell on deaf ears. Gina was transfixed by her son, her countenance brightening as she basked in the details of his anguish. It was the glow of an art lover, enraptured by beauty; the flush of a wine connoisseur, transported by a sublime sip.

Had she gone mad?

Huffing, Natira used a nod to catch one of his guards' attention. He'd had enough of Gina's beatific smile. Let her join her husband as a distant observer, at best. In response to his lord's gesture, the clay monster caught Gina in a fist, lifted her from the rise, and rolled her across rough earth to Jed's feet.

Much better. The king could now hold court uninterrupted.

"Isn't it clear by this point, Jacob? It truly is finished."

Beneath his thumb, Lord Natira ground the tangled thorns into the man-child's head and watched flesh curl in ragged strips. His revelry was cut short, however, by the urgent yet strong voice of a mother.

"Jacob, listen to me. Hear my words, not his . . ."

"Jacob, listen . . ." His mother's voice cut through his veil of pain. "I saw it myself. Your wounds and your scars, their patterns match up with the thorns on that Crown."

He blinked against the rivulets that ran down over his brow.

His own blood mixing with the Nazarene's.

Drippp, drippp . . .

"None of it's been in vain," she continued. "Be who you were called to be!"

Who *was* he called to be? What did she mean about the scars matching up?

His shoulders sagged, his head bowed, beneath the weight of iniquity. Like sponges, the thorns had absorbed every detail of mankind's woe, and those atrocities oozed through his entire being. He was no savior, no messiah. He was barely a man. He could barely stand, and the stink of his own bodily fluids served as proof that there was nothing special about him.

"Three little words," Natira hissed.

Am I finished?

In this moment, Jacob almost believed it.

Then again, there was no greater love than to give one's life for his friends. Each day was about dying to one's self, wasn't that what he had been taught? Wasn't that what Nickel had tried to explain over the years?

"For the Lord has chosen Jacob for Himself . . ."

A globule of spit landed on his cheek.

"You're nothing," the Collector said. "Nothing at all."

"Be who you were meant to be," Gina's voice called out again.

Jacob thought of the Nazarene—spat upon, mocked, and scorned. No, he could never match up to that example, and even his own scars were mere shadows of wounds that had gone much deeper. This Collector was right: he was nothing, nothing at all. And yet, by the Nazarene's sacrifice, his life had been bought back, hadn't it?

An orphan no more.

No longer an exile on a forgotten island.

He was a child of the Almighty, ransomed by Blood.

Head still bowed, Jacob stood a little taller. He could barely think, barely speak, but he remembered his grandfather's final wishes and steeled himself with fresh resolve.

This Crown was not his to wear. That had never been its purpose.

It was to be shared.

Drippp . . .

"No, Jacob." Natira breathed into his ear. " 'It is finished,' do you hear me?"

"Not yet," he gasped. "I am one of Those Who Resist."

CHAPTER
FIFTY-EIGHT

Gina read the confusion and disgust on her husband's face. His cheeks were speckled with gore, his back torn open in multiple places, yet a seasoned look resided in his eyes.

"We have to destroy Natira," he said, "before he destroys Jacob."

"Agreed."

"I have an idea."

"Let's hear it, buddy boy."

"You'll need this. It's the last of my MTPs, and if we lose it we'll be sunk."

His suggestion that followed was no less insane than anything else that had gone on this evening, and thirty seconds later—before they could second guess themselves—Gina and Jed were sprinting full-speed at the closest golem. The creature stood on alert, flaming red-yellow eyes tracking their approach, his voiceless mouth gnawing at the air. Beyond the mammoth guard, Natira remained in the circle, fangs dripping with saliva over their son's long-spiked crown.

Jed was a step ahead of Gina, his MTP flashing silver with each thrust of his arm. For the moment, he was the man with the weapon.

The primary threat.

Bait.

The golem swiped at him, his hand coming down like the counterweight of some medieval catapult. In the moment before impact, Gina took the handoff from Jed and tucked the spike against her stomach. Her husband, her precious mortal husband, spun left, leaped to avoid the golem's blow, and darted out of reach. The golem maintained his position on the perimeter, but kicked at the fleeing man and scraped his entire back with the edge of a club foot.

Shirt in tatters, Jed sprawled face-first in the sand. Then scrambled out of reach.

Stick with the plan, Gina told herself. *This is your only chance.*

Bulling ahead, she released her hold on the material world and felt herself come apart bit by bit.

> Elements and molecules—
>> *S–h–r–e–d–d–i–n–g* . . .
> The bands of time—
>> *Ssssttretccccchhinngggg* . . .

The night darkness gave way as she floated free of mortal restraints into a place of luminosity and—dare she say it?—joy. This weightlessness, this carefree existence, coaxed her onward between spherical and angular shapes that seemed to represent oxygen, hydrogen, sodium . . . She could only guess at the salty content of this air from the Dead Sea, at the briny components wafting over the Valley of Bones.

None of that mattered.

She would be weakened in the bridging process, which meant she needed to regain form and strike without delay. Was there a way to end the bridging process abruptly, to brake to an emergency stop?

Jacob . . . My little man is dying!

That image jarred her back into the realm of concrete facts.

Time shifted back into gear.

She was still running, still churning her legs, and her body lurched as her feet made contact with the earth. Metal tent peg in hand, she fought off the initial wave of fatigue and locked her fist around her weapon, lifting, aiming . . .

Where was he? Where was her enemy?

There, to her left.

For our son, she told herself. *No hesitation.*

Still moving forward, Gina planted her foot, switched the MTP to her left hand, and spun hard to her weak side, swiveling so that her entire weight and momentum would drive the stake backhanded over Jacob's head into the vampire's temple. The maneuver was flawless, but Natira sneered as he sidestepped and let her sprawl off balance.

"You are *finished,*" he spat at her. "Both of you!"

In that moment of his hubris, she rolled into a kneeling position, aimed her finger along the chiseled metal, and torpedoed it through the space between them. Jacob's eyes—those blue irises like Jed's, flecked with gold like Nickel's—peered up from beneath sweat- and blood-drenched hair and understood what must be done.

Now, Gina thought. *Do it now!*

Her son dropped his head forward, then reared back with all the force his small frame could muster, threatening to ram those stained briars into his captor's chest.

Recognizing the danger, Natira craned away from the sharp implements.

And left himself exposed.

Gina's crude, tapered MTP spiraled forward—the way she'd practiced in the woods at Silver Falls, the way she'd seen her father do on past occasions—and pierced Natira's skull. Wedged deep into undead bone.

The Akeldama Collector, this warrior who had taken her twin brother's life and now tried to take her son's, lost hold of his hostage and careened backward, dropped to both knees. As Natira made one feeble swat at Gina's leg, she stepped out of reach. He tottered forward, facedown into the dirt. His entire body jerked. Twitched. From the split section of his cranium, blood and brain matter bubbled, then began to crystallize, expanding like some malignant reef of fluids and organs as it consumed his body from the inside out.

"Like you said," Gina told him. "'It is finished.'"

Jacob collapsed beside her, then cried out as he plucked the Crown of Thorns from his own head. She crouched over him, enveloping her son in an embrace.

"Look," she said.

Jacob followed her pointing hand. On the dirt, two meters away, Natira's desiccated body collapsed in on itself, pebbles and sand rolling down into that huge ribcage before the entire mass crumbled into granules.

No time for celebration. The battle was not over.

Jacob clung to his mom, his legs unable to hold him any longer. The pain was excruciating, yet there was still a task to be carried out.

Across these plains between Masada and En Gedi, he could see enemy forces on a rampage now that their commander was down. Fixated on their final orders, they tore up vegetation and desecrated the ground of this Holy Land in their search for the Concealed Ones amidst the moon-washed flats and dry streambeds. Here on the rise, the half-dozen golems crashed into one another in their attempts to grab hold of their prey.

Not much time, Jacob realized.

For ages, this country's dead had bled down from the Kidron and Hinnom Valleys, down through the numerous wadis, into this sea. Others had been tossed from Masada's heights, or slain by invaders, and all this time the remnants of their DNA had waited in this burial place at the lowest point on earth.

"Let me take this," Gina said, reaching for the Crown.

He met her eyes. "I need it, Mom. It's part of my purpose."

She let go.

"Sit me up," he said, echoing his grandfather's earlier pleas. *"Hurry."*

Gina responded to his strident tone.

From a sitting position, Jacob studied the nest of spikes in his grasp. He hesitated. Would this really work? He then pressed the Crown into the ground and watched crimson pools begin to bubble up from dry earth. The scent of his own wounds, his own suffering, mingled with the intoxicating richness of redeeming Blood and reactivated that sacred flow.

Drippp, drippp . . .

He continued pressing down. Close by, combatants tore at one another, but he remained intent.

Drippp, drippp, drippp . . .

He blurted Scripture from memory: "'Suddenly as I spoke, there was a rattling noise all across the valley. The bones of each body came together and attached themselves as complete skeletons . . . muscles and flesh formed over the bones. The skin formed to cover their bodies . . . They all came to life and stood up on their feet—a great army.'"

Although golems stomped back and forth on huge feet, he listened only to the droplets that had now become a stream. The flow was fast and steady, pouring from each briar in that twisted wreath, feeding over the parched ground, pooling in the cracks, racing down the slope through earthen veins toward the valley's heart.

Nickel's prayer: *"Breathe life into these bones . . ."*

"What's happening?" Gina asked.

"This is what Grandpa wanted. Time to raise up an army."

Drip-drip-drip-drip-drip . . .

Gina saw the spectacle unfold. Despite silhouettes of mayhem that blotched the plains, the dark gray tableau was being overrun by rivulets of red—thick, glowing blood that coursed across the soil. Jacob was pressing the Crown into the dirt, calling forth an army, and yet her rational mind bucked at the audacity.

Who but the Firstborn of the Undead had the right to beckon souls from their rest? Who but the Nazarene had crawled into hell and spoken freedom to the captives there?

Freedom from infestation.

From death itself.

Across the valley floor, bleached white bones began to appear. They shook to the surface the way oxygen bubbles rise from the ocean deep. Between the golem hordes, skeletons took shape at an accelerated pace—femurs and pelvises, spines and ribcages, all knitted together by invisible hands.

The Valley of Bones was coming to life.

"Jacob!" Gina said. "I think it's working."

He remained fixed on his task.

With red veins still marbling the valley floor, the dance of death and life took on aspects both macabre and promising. The Dead Sea reflected stars and faraway lights, while the crags to the west remained shrouded in shadow.

She lifted her eyes. *Dad, I hope you're seeing this.*

The appearance of these bodies was disquieting, even to the golems—maybe more so, since they too had been called forth from the earth. For every clay monster, two skeletons emerged. As the army of bones rattled into place, tendons and muscles stretched alongside and produced soft tissue. Arteries threaded beneath layers of skin, and hair follicles generated fresh growth. Each flesh-and-blood soldier stiffened, awaiting the last moments of rejuvenation—and the iridescent blue mark upon their foreheads.

The final touch. The letter Tav.

An entire new generation of Nistarim, called forth by Nazarene Blood.

The golems gazed around, unsure. Without specific orders, they were mindless, unable to fathom this new foe or the best response.

The flesh-and-bloods lurched into action. Hundreds upon hundreds, they cheered as one, a swell of sound that blew dust from the ridges and leaves from the trees. They were men, women, and children—all colors, races, and sizes.

In various groups, the reborn humans swarmed golems and pried at their legs, at their fingers, their clay-red ribs and fiery eyes. The unholy creatures, enlivened by drops from the veins of human victims, found themselves unable to resist a holy army called from the grave by the Blood of the Nazarene.

Columns of golems lumbered about, attempting to escape. Limb by limb, stone by stone, pebble by pebble, they were dismantled and disintegrated. The flesh-and-bones teemed over their foes, chasing them into the wadis, along the cliffs, and toward the shores of the sea. Although some fought back, catching and pulverizing the reborn in their fists, they failed to stem the tide.

Gina felt tears spill down her cheeks—relief and joy, pathos and pain.

She felt her husband come alongside, still panting from exertion. He hugged her with one arm and pulled their son close with the other.

So much sorrow along the way, she thought, *but so much to be thankful for.*

Jacob had done his part, finding victory in simple obedience. Together, he and his parents surveyed the battle below. All around, flesh-and-bones were tearing down clay and stone. The entire expanse churned with the desperate actions of combat. Dozens on both sides fell, then dozens more. The number of fallen golems surpassed that of the humans, their corpses crumbling into dust.

Jed gathered his wife and son into his arms while deafening shouts of conquest rang across the plains. Jacob felt something wet and sticky as he reached a hand around his father's midsection.

"What happened, Dad? You have gouges in your back."

"Oh, those? Guess I'm gonna have me some battle scars, huh?"

Gina flashed a weary grin.

Together, the Turney family faced the Valley of Bones as the golems fragmented, returning to the elements from which they'd been formed. The flesh-and-bones harnessed their forces and converged on the last of their foes, overrunning them, pulling them down in a simultaneous assault, so that they fell with an earth-rumbling impact.

The time had come for the original Nistarim and their mortal members to step forward. They were wounded. Dismembered. Some slain. One by one, they took turns administering healing drops and restoring life and vitality.

At last, the newly risen army joined them. Meeting for the first time, they caught each other up in warm embraces and celebrated their victory. Each of their brows glowed with the Letter, distinguishing them as those who would walk on, who would bear the world's burdens as their own. The assembly stretched south toward Masada and to the edges of the Dead Sea; they lined the cliffs and spilled into the wadis; in groups of two or three, they mounted the piles of pebble and stone, putting enemies underfoot as they prepared for their deployment.

New assignments would be given, new locations chosen. The Concealed Ones no longer carried their load on the backs of only three dozen, but on the shoulders of a multitude—and, as always, their head was the Nazarene.

"Where are Sarge and Josee?" Jacob said.

His father stood again. "I need to find them. My uncle said they were headed for Jerusalem, somewhere near the Garden of Gethsemane."

"We should all go together."

"Actually, Jacob," his mom said, touching his hand, "you and I have one thing left to do."

CHAPTER FIFTY-NINE

Ruins of Kerioth-Hezron

Cal Nichols' original strategy had been to recover the Crown of Thorns and use it to attack the root system at the Betrayer's birthplace. With the relic now in hand, Jacob stumbled alongside Gina through pockmarked hills and ravines. From the map he'd studied the last few months, he knew the way and directed her at each turn in the terrain.

Jacob would do this in his grandfather's memory.

While they made this trek, his dad sped toward Jerusalem to locate Sarge and Josee. Though the Concealed Ones and their swelled ranks had already found and banished Helene and Kyria, Isaac's remains had been too scattered to trace.

The old spice merchant was better off with Nickel anyway.

The two longest of friends.

In Jacob's pocket, the chess piece given to him in Nickel's last moments hinted at riches and possibilities. No one else knew. No one needed to know, did they? Maybe one day there'd be a moment for exploration, though for now life and family would remain purer if he left that door unopened.

By the time they reached the Haunt of Jackals, the blood odor was so strong Jacob thought he would lose his breakfast—if he had eaten any.

From the volume of the wails, it seemed they were entering a medieval torture chamber.

Only this was worse.

His back was still bent, his arms limp. Breaths raked his lungs. He wondered how the original Thirty-Six, his grandfather among them, had managed to stand almost two thousand years. How did anyone with half a heart endure the things witnessed on the news and in their own homes?

All of that and more was on display in these Six, No Seven panels—everything the Almighty despised. A maze of glowing red tendrils fed to and from this monstrous collage, where bodies and limbs poked at perverse angles.

Jacob tried not to look . . .

Eyeballs. Hands. Noses. Tongues. Ears.

The very worst uses of the five senses, all on graphic display.

Gina bent and unhitched the Crown. "Don't wait around," she told him. "Do what you came to do."

He accepted the braided circle and heaved his legs across the stone floor. The stench was overpowering, the shrieks enough to drive a man insane.

I am a man.

He came within arm's length of the first panel.

Please, God—I need a man's strength.

His hands pulled back and, with all that was within him, he stamped the Crown of Thorns into the panel the way a magistrate might stamp a letter with the king's private seal. This Crown was the ultimate proof of the Almighty's love, a seal dipped in Blood.

The entire conglomeration of flesh and bone cried out, then exhaled the last of their torments. Body parts broke free from their snares, spilling onto the floor.

He moved to the second panel. And the third.

Stamppp . . . Stamppp . . .

His back straightened.

Stamppp!

His shoulders broadened.

Along the cave wall, bodies began reassembling piece by piece, energized by the power stirring along this Crown's prickles.

"Jacob."

Stamppp!

"Jacob!"

He jolted, aware that he had left himself vulnerable. Turning toward his mom's voice, toward the cavern's outer wall, he saw an imposing figure at the narrow gap. If Jacob was supposed to feel concern, it was too late. With all he'd been through, one more obstacle seemed trivial.

"Barabbas?" Jacob said. "Why are you here?"

"I thought I . . . I killed you in Silverton," Gina said.

The bearded man gave her a shrug and headed toward them.

Gina wielded the dagger she had retrieved from the dirt. "Don't you touch my son! Don't you dare."

"I survived that thing once before."

"I must've . . . missed. Or not cut you all the way through."

"Go ahead," Barabbas said. "I'm ready to die."

"What?"

"It's my price to pay. It's what I deserve."

Something was rattling in the back of Jacob's mind, something heard more than once while plying the droplets on his map. He thought back to Barabbas on a Greyhound bus.

How had those memories ended up on the map?

Who had gathered them?

As Jacob mulled that over, the former henchman paused to take in the remaining panels with their spooling tendrils. Thirst welled in his eyes and he licked his parched lips, the epitome of a man dying for a drink. "I deserve to die," he choked out. "I didn't want this, any of it. They gave me orders and I obeyed."

Something clicked in Jacob's thoughts.

Barabbas continued. "I killed. Maimed. Collected. So many people, so many."

"Because you thought you had no choice, right?"

"I didn't know, not till recently." The man's voice cracked. "But how am I supposed to live after this?"

"Who says you're alive?" Gina challenged. "You're a walking corpse."

He offered no rebuttal.

"You're trash from the Akeldama."

Eyes down, he gave a submissive nod.

"Where have you been since Silverton, huh? You know, I should've finished the job there." Gina lifted her weapon, ready to strike.

Jacob touched his mother's arm. "Don't you see? He's not under the curse. When the crowds chose the Nazarene to take his place, he was pardoned from all of that."

"Pardoned? I find that hard to believe."

"Am I wrong, Barabbas? The Collectors hijacked your body while you were dead, never guessing you still had the Power of Choice."

The barrel-chested man dropped to his knees.

"What's wrong?" Jacob said. "I'm not pointing fingers here."

"Put me out of my misery. I beg of you."

"I'm confused," Gina said.

Barabbas pulled at his beard. "It's true, all of it. When your dagger didn't kill me, I began to understand. I even cleared out the Collector within, but this . . . this undead body still thirsts for . . ." He waved a hand at the wall panels. "For *this*. For *blood*. I killed again, less than a week ago."

Jacob stepped toward him. "You're not a slave to your desires."

"I hate this flesh of mine."

"Nazarene Blood, Barabbas—it's the only type that satisfies."

"No." He shook his head. "No, it's . . . it's too much. I've done my good deed, and now I just want this to be over. Please, it's what I deserve."

"If any of this is true," Gina said, voice still laden with doubt, "then I can only assume you've been spared for a reason, Barabbas. Don't waste that."

"I don't want to be spared."

"Well, that would be the easy way out, wouldn't it? Instead, you can be like the rest of us, choosing day by day by day between good and evil."

"So," Jacob added, "choose wisely."

Barabbas lifted his eyes. "After Silverton, I did make a choice."

"Okay."

"I decided to hide Ms. Lazarescu's remains before the cluster could find out you two were still alive. If they knew, they would've told me to destroy you."

"You . . . you did what?" Gina gasped. "What did you do with my mother?"

"I did as Cal Nichols instructed."

"What?"

"He was there guarding her when my bus arrived in Phoenix. After hearing from you that I'd disappeared from Silverton, he said he figured things out and decided to give me one chance at righting my wrongs."

"My father did this? Why you? Start talking some sense here."

"He saw my knife wounds, heard my story. He'd made mistakes of his own, he said, and told me I could 'get the best of evil by doing good,' by giving Ms. Lazarescu a proper burial in her homeland."

Jacob's mom was blinking in disbelief.

"My map," Jacob said. "The Romanian postmark. You sent it to me, didn't you, Barabbas? Nickel had been gathering the droplets for me, but then he handed that assignment to you when he got stuck dealing with this stuff in Israel."

Barabbas nodded.

"Where is my mom?" Gina demanded. "Where'd you bury her?"

"In the town of Cuvin." His Adam's apple lurched as he swallowed, and then he angled his eyes up at Gina. "Beneath a white marble gravestone."

She slipped her hand into Jacob's and looked away.

"Your father told me to let you know. He made me promise."

"Thank you," she mouthed.

Jacob squeezed her hand. "We'll go there someday, as a family."

"Now, please," Barabbas said, "return the favor and end my life for me. If you don't, I'll be left to wander in misery, don't you see that? I can't fight it any longer, and this blood thirst won't leave. Help me."

"We can't. At least, not that way," Jacob said.

"I beg of you."

"Day by day," Gina reminded him. "Join the human race."

The man growled and rose to his feet, red eyes gleaming as they panned the cavern walls. "Good-bye, then. I can't stay, not in this . . . this place."

"If you wait, we can—"

"No, Jacob. Don't. I have to go."

"Thanks for what you did to protect us."

A haunted look filled Barabbas' eyes. "I've done too many things." With ruddy hair draping his hard features, he aimed for the cleft in the rock and vanished.

Jacob started in the same direction.

"No, you can't save everyone," his mom said. "Now c'mon, sweetheart—don't you have a job to finish?"

He nodded. Rallying his strength once more, he faced the sixth panel and lifted the Crown of Thorns above his head: *Stamppp!*

The seventh: *Stamppp!*

From the cold stone floor, the bodies regained shape and grew flush with color. They weren't pretty. They bore scars and deformities. But they were alive. Jacob and Gina led them from the cavern into the warmth of a Negev dawn.

Journal Entry

September 10

We met this morning at the Mount of Olives, wounded and worn. Mom and Dad stood beside me as we gazed across the above-ground tombs that cover these slopes, waiting for the Day of Judgment, the Final Vengeance—or, as the Jews call it, Rosh Hashanah. The holiday started two nights ago, on my birthday, and ends tonight at sunset. It marks the Jewish New Year, and at points throughout, the shofar is blown to alert people to coming judgment.

I thought of my grandpa and his trusty instrument, and my eyes grew misty. Mom pulled me close, probably sensing my thoughts. Sure, I only got to spend a few minutes with him, yet, from the drops of blood he gathered for me, I feel like I really knew the man they called Cal Nichols.

As for my great aunt Josee, she's still in a room at Hadassah Hospital, with three broken ribs. Sarge is there, too, recovering from emergency surgery that probably saved his life.

So much has happened. Things I'll never forget. Back on Lummi Island, I began putting it all down on paper—thoughts and ideas, concepts to remember—and hid it in a family-sized Ziploc bag in the church cemetery. Didn't want the Collectors stealing it away. Later, I'll add all the rest of it, the stories compiled from this final battle.

Who knows? Maybe one day it'll encourage others—the honorary Nistarim, Those Who Resist, not to mention anybody who's ever dealt with the thorns. Sometimes it just gets so lonely. Nice to know you're not the only one.

"Shana tova," my mom said to us. A good year.

"Where'd you learn that?" Dad asked her.

"Your wifey, I'll have you know, is no slouch in the foreign languages."

"Shana tova umetukah," I said back. A good and sweet year.

Mom tilted her head. "There you go, Jed. Looks like I'm not the only one who's been doing my homework."

In the distance, the distinctive blast of the ram's horn signaled the start of this new day and it roused something ancient and deep in me. My arms felt heavy, my scalp was still healing, but hope surged through me.

"Okay, Dad," I said. "I think I'm ready for it now."

"Thought you'd never ask."

He hefted the JanSport daypack, the one he had found still sitting in the grove at Gethsemane, and handed me my grandpa's favored horn. Though this particular one is small, it produces a sound like no other—a call to remembrance and to repentance.

"Okay," Mom prodded me. "Let's hear what you've got."

I, Jacob Lazarescu Turney, placed the shofar to my lips and I blew.

ACKNOWLEDGMENTS

Amanda Bostic, Leslie Peterson, Becky Monds, and Allen Arnold (editors and publisher)—for joining me on this fictional journey between realms seen and unseen . . . I hate to see it end.

Jennifer Deshler, Katie Bond, Micah Walker (marketing team)—for being tireless, reliable, and always ready to crack a joke.

Kristen Vasgaard (cover art and design)—for hitting another one out of the ballpark with this cover. Well done!

Dave Robie and BigScore Productions (literary agent)—for walking with me this far and cheering for me even as I continue on a different path.

Carolyn Rose Wilson (wife)—for almost twenty years of marriage, friendship, and romance . . . You still make me hot-blooded!

Cassie and Jackie Wilson (daughters)—for believing in my work, even though you've never read my books . . . You are bright spots in my days.

Linda Wilson (mother, now deceased)—for your love, your life, and for the Isaiah passages featured in this story . . . I know you are singing for joy.

Mark and DeeDee Wilson (father and wife)—for being living examples of new life and new horizons, even in out-of-the-way places.

Shaun and Jade Wilson, Heidi and Matt Messner (brother, sister, and spouses)—for hospitality, humor, and honesty. We've visited Lummi Island together, met up in Jerusalem, and shared memories in Tennessee . . . Oh, and thank you, Matt, for performing a "two for the price of one" wedding.

Tim and Shelly Johnson (friends and pastors)—for serving so faithfully even when it seems like you've been forgotten, and for letting me change your children's ages so I could sneak them into the story. Who else could I trust as parents of two Concealed Ones?

Silvia Krapiwko (Israel Antiquities Authority)—for hosting my family at your museum during my latest visit to Jerusalem . . . We're still wearing the T-shirts.

Rachel Cohen-Kennedy and Cindy at TheEdge.com (correspondents)—for so enthusiastically embracing this trilogy and its ideas.

Anne Rice (author)—for taking a stand for your faith, sending a personal e-mail, and writing about the Nazarene in the profoundly beautiful *Christ the Lord: The Road to Cana.*

Tracey Bateman and John B. Olson (authors)—for your part in exploring both godly good and bloodsucking evil in imaginative ways.

Jake Chism, Cory Clubb, Karri Compton, Randy Singer, CJ Darlington, Mindy Starns Clark, Mike Duran, Michele Hauf, Tom and Kari Hilpert, Mara McGuffey, Jeremy McNabb, Calvin Moore, James Nichols, Josh Olds, Michelle Pendergrass, Julie Porter, Frank Redman, RelzReviewz, Susan Sleeman, Nora St. Laurent, Brandon Vazquez, Meli Willis, and many more (bloggers/reviewers)—for listening, sharing, and cheering me along when I thought nobody cared.

The others in the Council of Four (Matt Bronleewe, Kevin Kaiser, and Chris Well), Tosca Lee, Claudia Mair Burney, Mike Dellosso, Rick Acker, and Ann Severance (novelists and editors)—for doing what you do so well with humility and great skill.

Sean "The Scandalizer" Savacool (friend and author)—for walking with me through death and life, darkness and light . . . You're a faithful friend.

Rodney and Lori Marett (organizers), Ray Blackston (author), and the Gideon Film Festival—for including me in the company of artistic souls.

Debbie Whitaker, WordFest '09, and the Tennessee Writers' Alliance—for allowing me the honor of challenging another generation of storytellers.

Steve and Patty Guynn and all the staff at Sherlock's Book Emporium (Lebanon, TN)—for the great events together . . . You're my favorite independent bookseller in the South!

As Cities Burn, August Burns Red, Bloodgood, Bryan Duncan, Coldplay, Eastern Block, Flyleaf, Modern Mosaic, P.O.D., Project 86, Radiohead, Red, Switchfoot, Steve Taylor, Theocracy, They Came with Sirens, and U2 (rock bands, young and old)—for keeping me alert while stirring my creativity.

Readers everywhere (young and old)—for following me along this path through blood, jackals, and bones . . . Though this trilogy is over, there are more stories to come. The Nazarene Blood will prevail!

AUTHOR'S NOTE

If you'd like to delve deeper into stories related to the Jerusalem's Undead Trilogy, read some of my other books: *Dark to Mortal Eyes, Expiration Date, The Best of Evil,* and *A Shred of Truth.* Although they are not Undead novels, many elements do overlap, with certain characters and settings trading places. To read all seven of the books is to better understand each one individually. Have fun discovering the hidden things between the pages.

I welcome your feedback online:

www.JerusalemsUndead.com * JerusalemsUndead@hotmail.com
www.myspace.com/JerusalemsUndead
www.erics-undead-fans.webs.com

ABOUT THE AUTHOR

 Eric Wilson is the author of suspense novels that explore Earth's tension between heaven and hell. He lives in Nashville, Tennessee, with his wife and two daughters.